# REMIND ME

# AGAIN

# WHY

# I MARRIED

# YOU

ALSO BY RITA CIRESI

SOMETIMES I DREAM IN ITALIAN

PINK SLIP

BLUE ITALIAN

MOTHER ROCKET

# REMIND ME
# AGAIN
# WHY
# I MARRIED
# YOU

## RITA CIRESI

DELACORTE PRESS

REMIND ME **AGAIN** WHY I MARRIED YOU
A Delacorte Book / June 2003

Published by Bantam Dell
A Division of Random House, Inc.
New York, New York

BOOK DESIGN BY LYNN NEWMARK

Delacorte Press is a registered trademark of
Random House, Inc., and the colophon is a
trademark of Random House, Inc.

Library of Congress Cataloging in Publication Data
Ciresi, Rita.
Remind me again why I married you / Rita Ciresi.
p.   cm.
ISBN 0-385-33584-9
1. Married women—Fiction.   I. Title.
PS3553.I7 R46 2003
813'.54—dc21                    2002035097

Manufactured in the United States of America
Published simultaneously in Canada

BVG   10  9  8  7  6  5  4  3  2  1

*for Jeff, with love*

## ACKNOWLEDGMENTS

I am grateful to the Ragdale Foundation for providing me with the solitude to write the first draft of this novel. My thanks to my agent, Geri Thoma, and my editor, Jackie Cantor, for their support and their many useful suggestions on the manuscript. I am indebted to Kathy Lord for her meticulous copyediting and to the staff of the New Tampa Regional Library for proving to me that a library card is a writer's best friend.

As always, my deepest thanks go to my husband, Jeff Lipkes, for reading multiple drafts of this novel and helping me to shape the story from beginning to end. I also am grateful to our daughter, Celeste, for her faith and encouragement.

REMIND ME

AGAIN

WHY

I MARRIED

YOU

FRIDAY, FEBRUARY 14, 1992

# SAINT VALENTINE'S DAY

## CHAPTER ONE

# LISA

**My married name is Lisa Strauss.** From the outside, I resemble a respectable woman. A photographer seeking to capture the essence of the American female might stroll into my local supermarket and take a snapshot of me unloading a cart full of milk, maxipads, Cheerios, Boston butt, Idaho Spuds, onion bagels, and a king-size box of Junior Mints. Later the photographer would develop the picture and say: *Voilà. Yet another ten-pound-overweight wife and mother who wears a stained jogging suit, drives a Toyota Camry, and pigs out on Smarties or Dum-Dums when she gets pissed at herself. Or her husband. Or her kid.*

Okay. So maybe that's an accurate portrait of me from the outside. But on the inside, I'm anything but an ordinary wife who purchases California prunes for her sometimes-constipated husband at the Price Chopper market (her eyes firmly turned away from those *Cosmo* and *Redbook* headlines that read TEN WAYS TO FIRE HIM UP 2-NITE! and TURN YOUR MARITAL ANGST INTO MARITAL BLISS). And my true self is miles away from the regular mom who mock-threatens her son squirming in the front seat of the shopping cart, "Put a stop to that whining right now—or I'll put you on the grocery belt and refuse to pay for you when the cashier says, 'And your grand total is ...' "

I loathe admitting this to anyone, but I'm an (aspiring) writer. Which means I'm a professional liar. Or maybe it just means I lead one lusty-slut of a fantasy life and that I neglect myself and my family—never mind my broom and my mop and my toilet brush— to nurture the odd assortment of characters who keep moving their cumbersome furniture around in my head.

My husband, Eben, on the other hand, is so grounded in reality—so normal, so disgustingly logical—that people often remark on what an "unusual couple" we make (translation: *Whoa! Are you two ever mismatched!*). If I were seeking a shorthand method of characterizing Ebb, it might run like this: For the past ten years, he has worked for the same pharmaceutical corporation, whose hottest-selling drug is an over-the-counter medicine meant to promote regularity. Plus he wears a lot of gray. Plus—I mean—the guy has never ridden a bike in his life!

But I love him anyway. And even though Ebb always tells me *'love you* instead of *I love you* (as if to disavow any responsibility for harboring such a foolish and uncontrollable emotion), I know he loves me just as much back. He, after all, was the one who proposed we honor Valentine's Day by cocooning at home. I didn't put up an argument. Although I know that a truly sexy woman (i.e., a single woman) would expect to be wined and dined at some romantic candlelit restaurant, the moment I got married I morphed into the world's cheapest date. Nothing makes me—or Ebb—happier than sitting cross-legged in front of the coffee table eating take-out Chinese, watching our son, Danny, crack open the fortune cookies and phonetically sound out our fates. ("Daddy, your cookie says: Hap-pee is he who is CON-tent with his lot. Mommy, your cookie says: Life is a tray-juh-dee for those who feel, and a co-muh-dee for those who think.")

But this year fate wouldn't let Ebb and me stay at home—and thus stay out of trouble—on Valentine's Day. At the eleventh hour, Ebb's CEO and his wife found out we had "no plans to speak of" for the evening, so they asked us to substitute for them at a benefit cocktail hour and dinner for the American Heart Association. Ebb—ever the good company man—said yes, which meant I had to do everything short of calling a dog kennel to find a last-minute place to park Danny (who kept repeating, "But I don't want a baby-sitter. I want chop suey").

Ebb was the designated driver that evening—not because I planned on boozing it up, but because his car (a silver Audi with a meticulously vacuumed gray leather interior) was much more presentable than my car (a baby-blue Toyota with Froot Loops pulverized into the floor mats and sticky grape Juicy Juice splattered on the red plastic booster seat).

Ebb had picked me up straight from the office, so he had to heave his heavy briefcase into the back before I could climb into the passenger side. I was too aware of the date—a holiday meant to celebrate *amour*—and so the kiss I first gave Ebb felt obligatory. My lips hit his cheek, and my nose bumped his glasses. But then Ebb drew me closer—or at least as close as we could get with the stick shift between us—and said, "Again?"

"Yes," I said. "Definitely. Again."

The second time we kissed was a lot more *wowsa*. Ebb sneaked his hand underneath my unbuttoned winter coat and I slipped my hand beneath his gray wool jacket. My mistake—because when I pulled away, Ebb's jacket fell open, revealing that he carried one of the worst masculine genetic deficiencies nature ever invented. The specifics pain me, but they must be admitted: My husband is severely color-blind. And he wore a turd-brown necktie that made me want to shudder!

I might have strongly suggested that Ebb change his tie (with these loving words: *Lose the tie!*) if he hadn't told me, "You look nice tonight."

I glanced down at my white silk blouse and black velvet skirt. "I look like I should be standing on a riser, belting out the 'Hallelujah Chorus' with five hundred other amateur singers."

Ebb peeled back my coat placket and gave my blouse a closer look. "I think I can see your bra—"

"That's because you are *looking* to see my bra."

"Do you want to change?"

"If *I* change," I said, "will *you* change?" I pointed to his tie.

Ebb immediately put the car in reverse. "We're running late," he said. "Do me a favor and look out your side window."

"What for?"

"This morning—when I backed down the driveway—I almost crushed a cat."

Once we made it out on the main road (without flattening a single feline), I looked down at my wrinkled skirt and sighed. I couldn't believe I had married a man who thought that brown went together with gray. And I just *knew* I should have put on a better outfit. But I'd been in a rush to feed Danny a consolation meal of La Choy chow mein before I dropped him off at the home of one of his Montessori schoolteachers. I hadn't had time to fix myself up. And I guess by not paying much attention to what I wore, I was making a silent statement (which, of course, Ebb completely failed to get). I was telling Ebb that even though he was a loving, faithful husband who just that afternoon had sent me the standard overpriced dozen red roses, I still didn't like the way he forced me to call around for baby-sitters at the last moment. I didn't like the way he always put the office before home. And I especially didn't like attending these work-related parties where, whenever I got separated from him, I was forced to introduce myself as "Eben Strauss's wife."

Just for the record, "I Gotta Be Me" was *not* playing on oldies radio as we sat in traffic on Route 9. But the lyrics to that obnoxious song were running through my head as Ebb idly drummed his fingers on the steering wheel, then glanced over at me when I reached beneath my skirt to fix my twisted slip.

"I know you don't like to go to these ... *doo-rahs,* as you call them," he said.

"Whatever gave you that impression?" I asked.

"You keep fidgeting."

"I'm wearing control-top panty hose," I said.

"Decode, please."

"They're squishing my ovaries." I stuck my thumb under the too-tight waistband of my stockings and gave the elastic a dissatisfied snap. "And speaking of fashion—"

"Let's not. Since I know exactly what's coming."

"But, Ebb. Really. I just have to say. That tie of yours—"

"This is a perfectly respectable tie."

"—is the color of diarrhea."

Ebb cleared his throat. "I prefer to think of it as burgundy."

He pushed up his glasses. I bit my tongue. Someone really needed to inform Ebb that gold-rimmed glasses never should be worn by men whose jet-black hair is getting shot through with glistening silver. But it wasn't going to be me. I had compassion (never mind a few gray hairs coming in myself).

I pulled down the mirrored visor, fished my lipstick out of my clutch purse, and applied a sloppy coat of Winter Frost to my chapped lips.

"You know," I told Ebb, "we hardly ever spend any time together anymore."

"But we're together right now."

"Together *alone*." I tossed my lipstick back into my purse and closed the gold jaws with a decisive click. "Why do I have to accompany you to every social shebang?"

Ebb kept his eyes on the road. "Because."

" 'Cuz why?"

" *'Cuz* if you don't, then people will think—"

"What?" I asked.

"—that we have marital problems."

"Imagine!" I said.

"I don't *have* to imagine."

I laughed. Ebb didn't. At first. But after I puckered up my Winter Frost lips and blew him a kiss, he finally smiled. "This tie is burgundy."

"No, it's *turds*."

He shook his head. "You're impossible to live with."

I nudged him on the arm. "And yet you do it."

"I take my vows seriously," he said.

"So do I," I said. "I love. And I cherish. But I never promised to choke down smoked oysters and bacon-wrapped scallops at cocktail parties. Nor did I pledge to act like I'm fascinated while your colleagues drone on about the virtues of this or that junk bond or hedge fund. Although I have to say, even after all these years—"

"All these years," Ebb said. "*Five* years we've been married."

"—that I still get a kick out of watching people's faces when you introduce me and fail to pronounce my name right."

Ebb flicked me a warning look before he glanced over his shoulder and changed lanes. I didn't heed the warning. I put my hand up to the base of my neck as if I were adjusting my own imaginary turd-like necktie, made several manly-man throat-clearing sounds, and said (with just the right touch of Ebb's Brooklynese), " 'This is my wife, *Lisar.*' "

It took a second. But the corner of Ebb's eyes finally crinkled up with pleasure, the way they always did whenever I displayed my talent for mimicry.

"I give you an A for accuracy, Lisar," he said.

"Not an A plus?" I asked.

"Now, *that* I might give to your imitation of Nixon."

"I'm most fond of my Liberace," I said. "But unusual voices like that are easy to get down."

"Mine wasn't?"

I shook my head. Ebb's voice—at least initially—had eluded me. Maybe I had trouble capturing it because my own voice is loud and raucous (like a donkey braying or a shore bird cawing), whereas Ebb's voice is low and level, like the sad, smooth notes that come out of the dark, black bell of a clarinet.

"I really have to listen to you," I said. "And watch you. At these thrilling social pageants we have to attend."

"And what have you observed?" Ebb asked.

"That you like to keep me by your side."

"Most women wouldn't complain about that, Lisar."

"I'm not *most women*. And so I've been wondering why—lately—you get this totally hemorrhoidal expression on your face every time I head for the ladies'."

Ebb tucked his tongue into his cheek. "I just know you're getting yourself into trouble in there."

"How so?"

"Everybody knows," Ebb said, "that the ladies' room is where women go to complain about their husbands."

"I never complain about you," I said, "to anyone *but* you.

Besides, you know I can't take the women at these parties." I shuddered. "Those wives ... are such *wives*!"

"What is so wrong with being a—"

"They own punch bowls," I said. "And belong to the Soroptimist Club. And have three children each."

"Any other—more-relevant—objections?"

"They make chitchat so boring I want to yawn until my molar fillings fall out."

Ebb considered this for a moment before he said, "Well, Lisar. I guess that explains why—at these parties—you take such a clear interest in the men."

"Me?" I asked. "The men?"

"Yes. You. The men."

I shrugged. "I'm scouting."

"For what—my understudy?"

"Material," I said. "For my novel."

"Which happens to be about?"

I bit my lip, and the waxy taste of Winter Frost lipstick filled my mouth. I knew that sooner or later I was going to have to confess to Ebb the subject matter of my novel. So I said, "If you insist on knowing. Infi—"

"Infertility?"

"In*fidelity*," I said.

The silence in the car wasn't deafening. But it certainly was palpable. I watched the green digital clock on the dashboard click from 6:26 to 6:27.

"Whose infidelity?" Ebb finally asked.

"The main character's."

Ebb kept his hands on the steering wheel in the position that his driver's ed teacher had taught him was safest: ten and two o'clock. "I see. So the main character in your novel is unfaithful to her husband."

"No, he—"

"He?"

"Yes," I said. "The main character in my novel is in possession of a penis."

"What do you know about possessing—"

"I've tried on your pants," I said.

Ebb blinked.

"Just to swagger around the bedroom a bit," I added.

"And you seriously think strutting around in my chinos," Ebb asked, "gives you permission to write from the male point of view?"

"I don't need permission," I said. "I'm a writer. Or at least I want to be."

Ebb gave me a level look. As we pulled into the horseshoe-shaped driveway of the Hilton, he said, "This seems a wise time to end this conversation."

He pulled the Audi over to the valet stand and flipped the power locks. The passenger door opened, and a disembodied valet-hand reached in. I gratefully grasped the hand and swung my feet onto the curb. Unfortunately, the rest of my body stayed firmly ensconced in the passenger seat—until Ebb reached down and snapped the release of my safety belt, practically catapulting me into the arms of the red-vested valet.

"Welcome to the Hilton, madam," he said.

*Madam?* I yanked down my skirt, gave him a tight smile, and prayed that later Ebb would forget to tip him.

"And how are you this evening, sir?" the valet asked as Ebb came around the back of the car.

"Fine," Ebb said before I could answer, *Constipated as ever.*

Ebb surrendered his car key to the valet. He took my elbow in his hand and escorted me into the marble lobby, where a huge floral arrangement on a massive stone pedestal overpowered us with the pungent smell of gardenias. A sign on an easel directed us to the Starlight Ballroom. Ebb looked over his shoulder to make sure no one was following us down the red carpet before he said, "I hope I don't pick up this novel of yours and find that your main character—who possesses a penis—wears size-thirty-five-waist chinos."

"He used to," I said, "before he got a gut and graduated to thirty-six."

I felt Ebb's stomach pull in as I gave him a loving mock-punch in the belly. "Relax," I said. "I'm not writing about you."

"Then who—pray tell—is your masculine subject?"

I stretched onto my tippy-toes and breathily whispered in Ebb's ear, "He's a combination of Moshe Dayan. And Fu Manchu. And Lawrence Welk. And Marcus Aurelius. And Richard Nixon, Winston Churchill, and Liberace—"

Ebb put his hand on my back and steered me—like some runaway train engine—through the double wooden doors, where a reception line longer than an Italian wedding party awaited us. I held out my hand and immediately started shaking hand after paunchy American-Heart-Association hand, as Ebb repeated, "This is my wife, Lisar. I'd like you to meet my wife, Lisar."

Also known as She Who Passed Herself Off at Parties as a Housewife/Stay-at-Home Mommy/Lady Who Occasionally Lunched. Because she didn't want anyone to know she harbored the ludicrous dream of becoming an Authoress.

Although it made me feel like an impostor, I never admitted my literary aspirations to anyone at these parties who asked, "And what do you do, Lisa?" I didn't dare announce, "I am a novelist!" because I knew people would reply, "Published?" or "What's your novel about?" or "Hey, I've got a great story for you—let me tell you about my great-uncle Max, who was *such* a character. . . ." Ebb called my secrecy unnecessary, but I suspected he was inwardly pleased he didn't have to admit he was married to a woman who heard voices (other than his own) in her head.

Once upon a time, I'd had a career that I could speak of. I was an editor at Boorman Pharmaceuticals—until Ebb, who used to be my supervisor (and now only *thinks* he is) got me *in the family way* and proved himself to be a total control freak by firing me and asking me to marry him in the same breath. Obviously, I said yes. But I had said a whole lot more to Ebb—not all of it loving—before we became an uneasy version of Mr. and Mrs., and then two of the most disgustingly doting mommies and daddies to ever push a Graco stroller on the face of this earth.

Being a wife and mother, I soon found, was kind of nice. When it wasn't kind of . . . stifling. And stultifying. And so utterly unfulfilling that I had to retreat to the kitchen and stuff my face full of Chicken in a Biskit crackers. Occasionally the drudgery of my domestic life seemed so hopeless that, after I scarfed all the crackers, I thought to myself, *Well, what's to stop me from chowing down on the cardboard box?*

You know the old story: *She wanted something more.* Something that would last long after her nagging voice ("Why am I the only person living in this house who picks up after herself?") had gone silent, forever, in the grave. So after Ebb and I got married—in between burping Danny and rocking Danny and diapering Danny—I had penned an overblown, overly punctuated autobiographical opus about my previous relationships with guys before I met Ebb. When I finally had screwed up the courage to show my oeuvre to Ebb, we got into the most plug-ugly argument of our marriage. (Me: "So you're saying *Real Men!* sucks the big banana?" Ebb: "I'm saying—if you would listen for half a second without interrupting, Lisar—that you are too concerned with your characters' genitals, instead of their hearts and their heads.")

I begrudgingly admit it now. The only good thing that Ebb could have said about *Real Men!* was that it was a quick read—made even quicker by his concerted effort to keep his red pen off every page. Every paragraph. Every sentence! The plot—

- girl meets boy
- meets boy
- meets boy

—probably had a few amusing moments. But when I dared to go back and look at the manuscript, I saw that the prose was purpler than a prune, the sloppy chronology zigzagged from past to present like a clock on cocaine, and the characters spouted off at one another with a regularity that rivaled Old Faithful's. My own mercurial heroine, in particular, threatened to burst the bulb on the emotional thermometer. Her name was *Deedee.* She had an *equine face* and a *long brassy mane* that kept getting so *whipped in the winter wind* that any editor worth her salt would have written in the margin, *Is this a woman or Man O' War at the starting gate?* The real men Deedee dated all had some salient repulsive characteristic—cabbage breath, brown belly-button fuzz, hirsute ears. Hope flourished. Expectations were dashed. Cocks rose and fell. Hearts got broken.

All in all, *Real Men!* was a most dubious debut. But because I was all puffed up with authorial pride, I didn't realize what a bum job I'd done until I surrendered the book to Ebb to get his constructive feedback. Ebb was a swift reader. He devoured my novel one Saturday afternoon while I took Danny to the playground and pushed him, for hours, on the baby swings. When I brought Danny home asleep in his stroller, Ebb glanced up from the last page of my manuscript and cleared his throat. Several times.

"Well, Lisar," he finally said. "This novel of yours ... has a lot of ... um, *heart.*"

I sat down at the dining-room table next to Ebb. "Oh, I was praying you'd like it."

"But maybe *too* much heart."

I bit my lip. "How can you have too much heart? That's like saying cake has too much frosting."

"Too much frosting," Ebb said, "sometimes can get messy."

I gave Ebb nothing but icy silence, then said, "I get it. You think *Real Men!* is a mess."

"Not at all," Ebb said. "But these characters always find themselves in such trouble."

"No trouble, no story," I said.

"But can't your female character get a grip on her emotions? Act in a more orderly fashion? Put a stop to this ..."

"What? Unseemly behavior?"

"*Contradictory* behavior. For example—"

"Yes?" I said, pulling the manuscript from Ebb's hands.

"Here, halfway through the first chapter—"

I turned the pages so quickly, so violently that static seemed to fly off the paper.

"Stop there," Ebb said. "First Deedee says—"

"Wait," I said. "Where are you on the page?"

"A third of the way down." Ebb pointed. "After the phrase *his eyes were darker than a Tootsie Pop.*"

I looked at Ebb's pointing finger with distaste. "You don't like that phrase?"

"I'd change it to Tootsie *Roll*. Otherwise, his eyes have the potential to be orange or purple."

"All right. So *Roll*. Get to the larger issue."

Ebb cleared his throat. "First Deedee claims she's madly in love with this guy with the Tootsie Pop eyes, and then in the very next sentence she refers to him as a quote—*big swinging dick*—unquote."

"So?"

"Well, how did she get from point A to point Z?"

"Astute readers," I said, "will make the connection."

"I have to tell you frankly, Lisar, that I did not."

I pushed Ebb's finger off the word *dick*. "Maybe you just don't identify. The characters are young. And confused!"

"Yes, but you don't want readers to say the author is too."

Silence. Then I said, "All right. Keep going. What else sucks?"

"Does this guy who's . . . so amply *endowed* . . . have to be called Magnus?"

"That's a legitimate Latin name. Given to many Scandinavians!"

"But earlier you claimed he was German."

"Oh," I said.

"And not to be a prude," Ebb said, "but in the episodes featuring Magnus, there's entirely too much emphasis on bodily functions."

I clenched my fist. "People sweat! And burp! And fart! And fuck!"

"But do they have to do all four things simultaneously, so the bedroom sounds like a one-man band? Lisar, these sex scenes—"

"What about them?"

Ebb lifted—not so gently—the manuscript from my hands. "Take page two—no, here, page three, don't you think this is a bit much for page three? The phrase beginning *His tongue tucked into her pulsing cunt*—"

"I spent a lot of time on that sentence," I said. "It has some very good vowel sounds."

"But you've failed to explain the significance of this cunnilingus."

"What significance," I asked, "can be found in a guy eating a girl out?"

"For starters," Ebb said, "why does this Deedee want it?"

"Because it feels good."

"What is she thinking about while he does it?"

"That's answered in the next sentence: *She wondered how long she could last before blowing an aorta—*"

"Does Deedee have to time him after this—what's the wording here?—*swift penetration* occurs?"

"It's integral to the pacing of the scene!" I said.

"But—not to get too nitpicky—on page one you clearly stated her Timex was digital. And yet here you refer to the second hand of her watch."

The way Ebb pointed out these minor—and yet so major—flaws in my writing deeply offended me. I began to gather up the pages of my manuscript, as if his touch had contaminated it. "I just knew you'd do this," I said. "Read my novel like a *male*."

"How did you want me to read it," Ebb asked, "like a poodle?"

"You side with the guys in the book."

"I most certainly do not. These aren't *real men,* Lisar. These are two-dimensional specimens of the male sex, which makes your novel sound like a feminist diatribe."

"How can it be feminist if the heroine paints her nails?"

"Green?"

"Green nail polish was all the fashion in 1986, when my novel takes place!"

A more mature couple (or at least one seasoned by a marriage counselor to engage in so-called *fair-fighting* techniques) probably would have backed off right there. Ebb and I argued to the point of tears (mine), and then I thanked Ebb for his time and told him I planned to solicit other, *more-informed* opinions. This consisted of shipping *Real Men!* off to a dozen literary agents, bearing a cover letter that described the novel as a *hip city picaresque.* I didn't know whether to laugh or cry when I remembered how I had written, *I hope* Real Men! *appeals to all adult readers who still think Dr. Seuss is a hoot but who also find truth in the darker vision of life espoused by Chekhov and Dostoevsky....*

After *Real Men!* had garnered a full dozen rejections—which I could only compare to repeatedly *not* being asked to the high-school prom—I melodramatically ran the entire manuscript through our paper shredder, stuffed the curlicued papers beneath a cheater log in our fireplace, and tossed a match. (The gesture was merely symbolic, as I had several copies backed up on computer disks.) Once *Real Men!* went up in flames, I stopped writing—for all of twenty-four hours. I dusted the furniture and vacuumed the carpet and scrubbed the toilet so pristine that I hesitated to defile it with my own urine.

Then the house grew messier and messier. I had begun my second novel. In my latest untitled opus (referred to by Ebb as *Number Two*), I vowed to keep myself out of the realms of autobiography and pornography. So I gave myself a little distance. I wrote about not me but Ebb.

Now, you may ask: Why did I make my husband into a character when I had to live with the real thing? Good question. To which I had a sad answer: I wrote about him because I felt lonely. Ebb used to travel for his job so much that I prayed every night his plane would never crash. But then when he *was* in town, he was so preoccupied with all the mess at the office that he might as well have been a million miles away. I knew that saying this made me sound like one of those whiny wives reporting her side of the story in that magazine column "Can This Marriage Be Saved?" But I had to say it: Ebb was there, but not really *there* for me. Because he never really talked to me. About the *F* word. His *feelings*.

So when I started writing *Number Two,* I made up a man who had very deep feelings and who didn't mind confessing them. I thought it would be a snap to write about my Ebbish hero—a mildly Jewish man in a gray flannel suit. Yet the more I wrote, the more I realized my own husband was a stranger. What *was* going on inside Ebb all day? I didn't know. So I had to imagine. I had to give my main character, Simon Stern, some tragic flaw that I myself could understand. Which meant I made Simon the kind of man who sometimes wanted to be married—and other times did not.

In my heart I believed that Ebb wasn't really Simon (after all, Ebb was happily married! to me!) and I knew for certain that Simon truly was not Ebb. Simon was more like me (in male drag) when he wasn't a composite of every creature on earth who got up in the morning and pulled on a pair of trousers and knotted a tie over his starched white shirt. So I hadn't been lying to Ebb when I told him that the man who figured so prominently in *Number Two* was many men indeed.

Too bad there was only one author—She Who Was Me—to catch all the flak.

As Ebb and I moved through the reception line and got our respective nonalcoholic drinks, I tried not to get too down-in-the-dumps about my situation. But there I stood in the Starlight Ballroom, fantasizing about the thunderous applause that would follow my Nobel prize acceptance speech *(I owe it all to Chicken in a Biskit . . .)*, when in reality everyone was crowding around to congratulate not me—but Ebb.

"Great job." "Way to go." "Nice work." Don't get me wrong—I was happy that Ebb had just gotten promoted. But I also was jealous that Ebb was a Somebody whose name had appeared just that morning in the "Who's News" section of *The Wall Street Journal (Eben Strauss, 41, formerly vice president for new-product development at Boorman Pharmaceuticals, was named executive vice president for internal relations at the newly merged Scheer–Boorman LifeSciences)*. Ebb was a winner. I was a loser! And it made me feel like all of two *pfennigs* that Ebb's professional star just kept on rising, while mine had sunk below the horizon, probably never to be seen again.

Ebb gave my hand a squeeze. "I'd like you to meet my wife, Lisar. Lisar, this is . . . I'd like you to meet . . ."

I instantly forgot the name of the beefy Husband who Ebb introduced me to. I also failed to catch the name of his Wife—who was so monstrously pregnant that I almost blurted out, *Shouldn't you go home and rest in bed? Or, better yet, whip out a metric ruler and measure your dilation?*

Mr. Husband congratulated Ebb on his promotion, then asked me, "So how does it feel to be married to Mr. Who's News?"

"Like a million bucks," I said.

"And what about you—Lisa, was it?" asked Mrs. Wife. "Do you work too?"

"Lisar's home right now," Ebb said.

*I am not!* I felt like saying. *I'm standing right next to you.*

Mrs. Wife, of course, automatically assumed I was "home with the children," because she asked, "Oh, how many children do you have?"

I didn't look at Mrs. Wife (or her big belly). I didn't look at Mr. Husband. I didn't even look at Ebb. But I *felt* Ebb. He didn't touch my arm, he didn't re-squeeze my hand, and yet I sensed something quintessentially Ebbish leaning into me to show his solidarity.

"One boy," we said in unison.

"How old?" asked Mrs. Wife.

"Almost five," we both said.

Mr. Hub gave Ebb a playful punch on the arm. "Time for another?"

I pressed my clutch purse against my inexplicably aching stomach, then smiled too politely—which only made my stomach hurt even more. After I had endured my requisite three minutes of small talk with Wife and Hub, I finally whispered to Ebb, "I'm heading for the ladies'."

Ebb nodded.

The ballroom was festooned with pink and white streamers dotted with red foil hearts. The band was playing some medley of cardiac-related songs—"Heart and Soul!" and "My Heart Beats for You Alone"—as I managed to make my way across the carpet without stepping onto the heels of any of these punch-bowl-owning women or pressing up too tightly against their well-suited men.

I reached the end of the red-carpeted hallway and entered the door marked LADIES. I was the sole woman in the rest room. Still, as Ebb had predicted, I managed to find trouble there. The last stall bore a plaque that seemed to suit me: HANDICAPPED. I looked over my shoulder to make sure I wasn't being followed by a woman in a wheelchair before I clicked my heels into the handicapped stall and locked the door. I yanked up my skirt and slip and peeled down my control-top panty hose, then practically cracked my tailbone as I sat down—too hard—on the unnaturally high toilet.

It was then that I discovered my stomach had been hurting for the past quarter of an hour with good reason. A glob of blood, gross and bulbous as a brown toad, sat in the crotch of my underpants. I let out a sigh. Then I blinked back tears. This would make the subject of a great novel, I thought, if it didn't hurt my heart so much to write melodramatic lines like *Each month the blood that stained her underwear seemed to come from an inner wound no medicine could ever heal....*

Like most other would-be writers, I had followed the advice doled out by authors of books such as *Start Your Novel Right Now (And Try Not to Strangle Your Spouse Before You Finish It)*. I had *made my life my material*. But even I had a limit. I already had vowed to myself that I never would write about the problem that now had come to dominate my marriage. It was just too humiliating, too ridiculous, to admit that Ebb and I had conceived our sweet little son, Danny, by accident, but now that we wanted another child, I couldn't get knocked up if my life depended on it.

And it was all my fault (or at least all signs pointed to me as the guilty party). Before I got involved with Ebb, I had messed around with more than my fair share of guys, and somewhere along the line I had picked up a disease that sounded like a root vegetable—chlamydia—which had sat silent inside me, undiscovered, until my gynecologist finally asked, "You've been trying to get pregnant for *how long?*" How I broke the bad news to Ebb that I had a venereal disease that scarred my tubes is a story too long to go into. Suffice it to say that misfortune does not always draw a couple closer together. Although Ebb had done the gentlemanly thing and told me, "I could have given the chlamydia to you, Lisar," his subsequent silence on the topic seemed to state with most Aesopian overtones: *For every bad action there is a corresponding bad consequence. No good can ever come of recklessness.*

I now had only one functioning fallopian tube. And Ebb and I were failures as lovers. At least *I* felt like a failure, sitting there in the handicapped stall with my head in my hands, when I remembered how hard Ebb and I had tried to conceive that month: six sweaty, desperate shots in a span of forty-eight hours, until Ebb—who must have known I needed a good laugh—finally whispered in my ear, "I won't even ask if that last time was good for you, Lisar." I had laughed—what else could I do?—but inside I'd been thinking, *God, this is so tiresome! I swear I would pay you! never to touch me! ever again!*

So another month had passed, and nothing whatsoever had come of all that effort. I swabbed the blood off my underwear with toilet paper and reached into my clutch purse for the sole super plus I always carried (the way some guys carried an umbrella—to ward off rain on a cloudy day). I stuck the tampon into my uncooperative body. Then I flushed the toilet and went over to the brown marble sink to wash my hands.

As I held my wrinkled fingers beneath the gold faucet, I made the mistake of looking into the mirror—and what I saw made me want to crawl inside myself and disappear. No matter how hard I tried to present myself as a woman who was smooth and polished and put together, I always looked like a woman who was *trying* to present herself as smooth and polished and put together. There was always something *off* about me. My very eyebrows—never mind my sallow skin—seemed tired. My chapped lips hadn't held the Winter Frost. A halo of frizz puffed up the top of my hair. I leaned closer to the mirror. Yes! That was an eye snot—why hadn't Ebb told me I had an eye snot squatting in the corner of my lashes? And my body. Even though I gave birth to Danny almost five years ago, gaining fifty pounds with my pregnancy (only thirty-three of which eventually came off) had done such a number on my once-muscular frame that for a while I'd been ashamed to undress even in front of Ebb.

*Infidelity.* How could Ebb even begin to think that I would … with this body, this face, this pathetically tight black velvet skirt, which once had belonged to a crazy, wild, promiscuous girl— but now belonged to a one-hundred-and-twenty-nine-pound chubette whose fashion motto ought to have been *Give me an elastic waist—or give me instant death.* The mere thought of shedding this skirt or any other article of clothing in front of another man made me want to howl with laughter—or toss myself off a very high cliff.

I finished washing my hands, shook the water off my fingers, and punched the silver button on the automatic dryer. I rubbed my palms beneath the blast of tepid air until the dryer came to an abrupt halt. Even though my hands were still damp, I grabbed my purse off the counter and pushed open the ladies' room door, which thudded behind me. At the entrance of the ballroom, I looked out on the sea of strangers, knowing that any minute now someone would come up to me and say "Lisa, darling, how are you?" and I'd actually answer "Fine," when what I really wanted to say was *Can't you see I'm dying of grief?*

I wanted to go home and cry wet, weepy, hormonal tears as I tossed my ovulation chart and basal body thermometer right into the trash basket. Failing that, I wanted to go stand by the only man in the room who understood what I was going through—because, after all, Ebb and I were going through this torture together.

I scanned the room. Since Ebb was on the shorter side for a guy—five ten—I only had to skim over the heads of most of the high-heeled women in the room to spot him by the windows, holding a glass of designated-driver's club soda in his hand. With a pang of pleasure, I thought, *Ebb still looks sort of sexy to me, at a distance, after all these years.* My next thought was: *Hey, who's that gorgeous blonde standing right by his side?* In her Easter-egg-blue suit, she seemed so soft and pale and pretty. Clearly I'd been writing from the male point of view for too long, because I instantly fell in love with her—or, at least, I saw how easy it would be for a man to collapse like a ton of bricks at her trim size-six feet. Something about her posture (confident and assured, as if no one ever interrupted her) told me she wasn't married. And something in her unwrinkled appearance (as if no one ever pulled on her hem or yanked her sleeve) signaled to me that she didn't have kids.

Immediately I set out to close the distance between me and Ebb. Usually Ebb kept a vigilant eye on me at these parties (as if he felt compelled to illustrate this statement found in my infertility manual: *Humans are the only species in which there is no visible way of determining if the female is in estrus; therefore, the man must be very attentive to the woman at all times*). But now he didn't even notice me by his elbow until the woman finally smiled and told him, "I think someone wants your attention."

Ebb turned. For a second he looked at me as if I were a stranger. Then he told the other woman—with no audible period or comma or dash—"I'm sorry this is my wife."

## CHAPTER TWO

## EBEN

**You know what they say:** Husbands—the kind who don't fool around on their wives—are always the last to know that something is going wrong with their marriage. *It came right out of the blue,* these shell-shocked guys tell their lawyers. (Or their rabbis. Or their mothers. Or their buddies in a bar, or their child-custody mediation specialists.) *I had no idea she felt that way.... I didn't have a clue she wanted...*

I had an idea—I had a clue—about what was going awry between Lisa and me. I wasn't blind. I wasn't deaf. And yet I remained dumb—that is, *silent*—about the whole thing, until February 14, when another woman stepped into the picture.

Ordinarily I had a good head for names. Yet that night at the party I was still brooding about the subject matter of Lisa's novel— adultery—and so I was distracted when a woman in a pale blue suit came up to me and lightly touched my forearm.

"Eben Strauss?" she asked.

I nodded.

"I'm ..." she said in such a soft, seductive murmur that I could hardly hear her. "And I've been told that you're the one man at this party I most need to meet."

She was far too attractive to be giving me a line. Nevertheless, I smiled and said, "Tell me why."

"I've heard you're contemplating moving."

"Yes," I said. Then added as an afterthought, "With my wife."

"Is she here?"

"Somewhere." I gestured with my glass of club soda toward the door and said, "Actually, she went off to the ladies'."

"I'd love to meet her."

"I'd be happy," I said, "to introduce you."

"You see," she said, "I think I'm in a very good position to help you. If you don't mind hearing me out for a moment—"

I ought to have minded. Ever since word had gotten out that Lisa and I wanted to make a move, real-estate agents had started circling us the way family-law attorneys surrounded a husband and wife who were on the edge of divorce. But the voice of this woman in the pale blue suit was so much more pleasant to listen to than the squawking of those sharp but pushy women who Lisa called "The Location-Location-Location Ladies." I was still listening to her soft sales pitch—and actually enjoying the tone—when she pointed to my elbow.

"I think someone wants your attention," she said.

I turned. Lisa had sneaked up behind me, waiting to be introduced. I gave her a blank, helpless stare. *How awkward,* I thought. *Any second now I'm going to have to say "Lisa, this is ... this is ... this is ..."*

"I'm sorry," I told the other woman. "This is my wife."

Right away I could tell that I had said something wrong. But what? Lisa blinked as if to hold back sudden tears, then swallowed— as if she needed to get an icky taste out of her mouth.

"Hi, I'm Lisa Strauss," she said.

"Cynthia Farquhar. Pleased to meet you."

Lisa and Cynthia Farquhar clasped hands. Lisa then took a sneak peek at Cynthia Farquhar's left hand, which—I noted along with her—was bare of diamonds or even just a plain gold wedding band. Lisa clearly was sizing up this Cynthia. This *Farquhar.* So I stepped forward and pointed out Cynthia's major flaw.

"Cynthia is in real estate," I said.

Lisa smiled.

"Your husband told me you're looking for a house," Cynthia said.

Lisa nodded. "But did he tell you—you told her, didn't you, Ebb?—that we've already arranged for someone to sell our condo?"

"Oh, I don't list property," Cynthia said.

"She's a buyer's agent," I told Lisa.

"Actually, I'm a little bit like a matchmaker," Cynthia said. She leaned forward to make herself heard over the band, which was playing "Piece of My Heart." "You tell me what you want in a home, and I find it."

Lisa glanced at me. "Ebb and I definitely need more space."

I clinked the ice cubes in my glass.

"Whoa," Lisa said. "That sounded—"

"Pretty dire?" I suggested.

"Oh, Ebb. You know I didn't mean ..." Lisa reached over and squeezed my forearm—but I could tell she made the comforting gesture more for Cynthia's benefit (*Look at what a loving couple we are!*) than for my sake. "I meant, Cynthia, that one of the reasons we have to move is because Ebb just got promoted—"

"Congratulations," Cynthia told me.

"Thank you," I said.

"—and we're going to have to start giving ..." Lisa looked around the ballroom at the vast sea of dark suits and sequined dresses. "Well, *parties.*"

"You sound a little hesitant," Cynthia said. "About being a hostess."

Lisa shrugged. "The only things I'm good at entertaining are my own problems."

"Oh, I'm totally with you," Cynthia said.

Lisa suddenly perked up. "You mean you don't like to cook either?"

"I'm hopeless in the kitchen," Cynthia said.

"I'm hopeless all over the house," Lisa said. "I swear, our place looks like pandemonium."

"Mine used to," Cynthia said. "But not anymore."

"Did you hire a cleaning service?" Lisa asked.

"No, actually ..." Cynthia gave me an apologetic look. "I got divorced."

"Oh," Lisa said. "I'm so sorry."

"Oh," Cynthia said. "I'm so *not.*"

Lisa let off a wicked laugh. "So you're here on your own?"

Cynthia nodded. "I knew it would be awkward on Valentine's Day—"

"Then be our date!" Lisa said. "Sit with us during dinner. It's open seating, isn't it, Ebb?"

I nodded. When the band stopped playing—and the president of the AHA gave the requisite speech of thanks and announced that our heart-healthy dinner was about to be served—all three of us made our way to the back of the ballroom to one of the circular tables that seated eight. To my left sat Lisa, and to her left sat Cynthia and two other couples. To my right sat an empty seat. Most guests had come in pairs, and so Cynthia's presence at our table threw off the balance. I wouldn't have felt the emptiness on my right so keenly if Lisa and Cynthia had made a better effort to include me in their conversation. But they clearly were smitten with each other— or, rather, with the topics they were discussing, about which I had not a whit of interest. Shoes were shoes. Moisturizer was moisturizer. And one shampoo, as far as I was concerned, was just as effective as the next.

Lisa and Cynthia were so keen on bonding with each other that neither seemed to notice when the waiter approached the table and filled Cynthia's glass with dark red wine. I was just about to reach out and cover Lisa's glass with my hand when the waiter asked Lisa, "Wine, madam?" and Lisa simply answered, "Sure thing."

I watched as the liquid gurgled into the goblet and sparkled in the candlelight. I was going to gently nudge Lisa's foot under the table to remind her that she wasn't supposed to be drinking—at least during the last two weeks of her menstrual cycle—when I suddenly realized: *Oh.* Oh. Of course Lisa had looked upset, if not teary-eyed, when I introduced her to Cynthia. She had just come back from the ladies' room. And I wasn't certain, but I just had a feeling that when she was in the bathroom, she discovered that she had gotten her period.

If I had been a better man—a less disappointed man—I would have reached out with my left hand to squeeze Lisa's hand, in consolation, under the table. Instead, when Cynthia said, "Cheers," I used my left hand—not my dominant hand—to raise my glass. Then I took a big swallow of wine.

Lisa took one bigger.


Usually I tried not to dwell on the reason that Lisa and I couldn't conceive another child. Yet all during dinner, as the centerpiece of red roses quivered whenever any of us sawed too vigorously at our dry chicken piccata, our underbaked potatoes, or our stringy asparagus, I kept turning around in my head that uncomfortable conversation I'd had with Lisa last autumn. Lisa had called me at the office to tell me that her fallopian tubes probably were clogged—and that the doctor wanted to flush them out with radioactive dye—and that the dye was *lime green*.

"The color makes a difference?" I asked.

"I can't take the thought of my tubes," Lisa told me, "looking like those gurgling pipes on the Liquid-Plumr commercials. Plus it's supposed to hurt. Will you go with me?"

"When's the appointment?"

"I don't have one. Yet. That's what I really called you about." I could hear Lisa swallow. "First I have to take antibiotics. And you do too."

"What for?"

"Please don't get . . . just don't get—"

"*Say,*" I said.

"I have this silent infection. Called chlamydia."

I looked down at my phone. Lisa had called me on my private line. But my office door was open. "Hold on," I told her.

I took my time—and a few deep breaths—as I crossed the carpet and gently closed my office door against the too-sharp ears of my secretary. Then I sat down and reluctantly picked up the phone again.

"Are you there?" Lisa asked.

"I'm here."

"Then please say something."

"What do you want me to say?" I asked. "And why did you have to tell me this on the phone? At the office? When I'm on my way to a meeting?"

"Because I can't stand the way you look at me—"

"But, Lisa, I hardly look at you at all."

"—and lecture me, like I'm totally out of control—"

I opened my mouth—to lecture that I would not need to lecture Lisa if only her behavior did not beg for lectures—yet I thought better of it when I heard the unmistakable rip of a Kleenex being yanked from a tissue box. The sound reminded me of my father's funeral, the awful way my mother had sat on the folding chair, pulling one tissue after another from the box parked on her lap.

Life was short. I wanted to do the right thing. So I told Lisa, "I could have given this to you."

"That's not likely. I was the one who—you know, went all wild with guys before we got married. Unless—"

"There hasn't been any *unless*," I said. "On my part. You know how I feel about that."

"I feel the same way, Ebb. I swear. I've never been unfaithful to you, not once."

I turned to my credenza to pick up my *Physicians' Desk Reference*. So I was caught completely off guard when Lisa blew her nose—into her Kleenex, but also right into the phone receiver—and blurted out, "I haven't! I don't have time to fuck other men! I have laundry to do! And a novel to write!"

"How heartening," I said, "that you have your priorities in order." Then I set the *PDR* down on my desk with a thump. "What's the name of the antibiotic?"

"What does it matter?"

"I want to look up the side effects."

"Erythromycin," she said.

"Then it's diarrhea. When you're at the drugstore, pick up some acidophilus."

There was a long silence. Finally, Lisa said, "Ebb, I just told you that I might not be able to have more children—"

"You don't know that for certain, Lisa."

"—and you're concerned about the friendly bacteria in my intestinal tract?"

Something childish inside of me wanted to holler, *My intestinal tract will be affected too!* But someone had to be mature in this relationship.

"I'm late for a meeting," I told Lisa. "We'll have to talk when I get home."

But we didn't talk when I got home. Lisa left the antibiotics and the acidophilus on the bathroom counter—far back against the mirror, where Danny couldn't reach—and stocked the refrigerator with yogurt containing live active cultures. For ten days we took the pills and ate the yogurt, and I only stopped to think about how odd and sad and confusing our silence was after I took my last dose of erythromycin and tossed the empty brown vial into the metal wastebasket in our bathroom, where it landed with a clang instead of a thunk. I remember looking down at the vial—marked EBEN STRAUSS—in the wastebasket. Lisa's vial—marked ELIZABETH D. STRAUSS—still sat on the counter, and when I picked it up I noticed she had three pills left.

Those three forgotten doses in the vial depressed me more than I could say. I lowered the lid on the toilet and sat down. Danny was snoring in the next room, and as I listened to him whistle and rasp, I had to take off my glasses and press my fingers against my eyes. Lisa is so irresponsible, I thought. And reckless. And unmindful of the rules that ought to govern daily life. And yet if she had not been who she was—and I had not been who I was—we never would have gotten married and then there never would be a boy named Danny. At least, not our Danny.

I had to be honest with myself. Lisa and I fought. A lot. And sometimes our marriage didn't feel completely *right*. Yet surely it was mostly right, because now it felt partly wrong. But what exactly needed to be fixed between us? I knew I was, as Lisa sometimes called me, an emotional groundhog. I did prefer to burrow underground and pop my head up only once a year to check out the situation. Whenever a problem arose at home that needed to be addressed, I tended to stay half an hour longer at the office, while Lisa tended to *not* go into the kitchen. And *not* bake a cake. Lisa's way of dealing with conflict consisted of pouring her guts onto the page. Sometimes I thought that if only I talked to her more, she might not feel so compelled to manipulate the things that went on between us—things that ought to be kept private—into a story that was about the way things really were and yet also about the way things really were *not*.

The *not* was what bothered me about this novel she was writing. On our drive over to the hotel, Lisa had sworn that she wasn't writing about infertility. But the longer I sat at that dinner listening to Lisa and Cynthia gaily chatter away, the more I was convinced that Lisa had seized upon the reasons why we couldn't conceive another child—her own adulterous impulses and her own promiscuous behavior—and transferred them onto her male character. He whom every reader would think was me! Unless, of course, Lisa had gone heavy on the Fu Manchu. Or the Liberace.

The red wine served that evening felt rough on my tongue, but Lisa obviously had no objections to the taste. I forgot which glass she was on—her second or her third—when she told Cynthia, "Even though we have only one kid, we want four or five. Bedrooms, that is. Not that we plan on having quadruplets or anything. I mean, one bedroom for us, one bedroom for our son, Danny, and then Ebb really should have a place to park his fax machine—which right now is squatting at the bottom of our bed—plus I really, really need a room of my own to work in."

"Eben told me you didn't work," Cynthia said. "Outside the home, that is."

Lisa stabbed a piece of chicken on the edge of her fork. "I work," she said. "But I tell people—and I make *Ebb* tell people—that I don't, because I'm totally embarrassed by what I do."

"Now I'm dying of curiosity," Cynthia said. She looked at me mischievously. "What does she do, Eben?"

"I never speak for Lisa," I said.

"Tell me what you do, Lisa."

Lisa took another generous swallow of wine. "Well," she told

Cynthia, "you know how some little girls dream about getting married and having two-point-five kiddos who puke all over the white picket fence?"

Cynthia nodded.

I nudged Lisa's foot under the table.

So Lisa said, "Ebb is nudging my foot under the table. He doesn't want me to tell you that my girlhood dream was to be on *The Ed Sullivan Show*. I swear I wanted nothing more out of life than to hear Ed announce—"

I tried not to wince as Lisa hunched her shoulders, gripped her elbows, and said à la Sullivan, " 'And now—ladies and gentlemen, boys and girls—I give you Lisa Diodetto, that most marvelous of female ventriloquists!' "

The two other couples sitting at our table looked over at Lisa as if she belonged in a loony bin. But Cynthia seemed delighted by Lisa's killer imitation. "You make a marvelous Ed," she said.

"Oh, that's nothing," Lisa said modestly. "You should hear my Louis Armstrong."

"Cynthia does not," I said, "want to hear your Louis Armstrong."

"Maybe later," Cynthia said.

"Don't encourage her," I said. "Or we'll be here all night, listening to Robert Goulet and Daffy Duck and Friedrich the boy soprano from *The Sound of Music*."

"But I still don't understand exactly what she does, Eben." Cynthia looked deep into Lisa's eyes. "Are you a stand-up comic?"

"Not intentionally," Lisa said.

"Then are you an impersonator?"

"Yes," Lisa said. "I'm a novelist."

"A novelist!" Cynthia said. "How fascinating! Where can I find your books?"

"In my too-tight-lingerie drawer," Lisa said.

"I don't understand," Cynthia said.

Lisa shrugged. "I haven't published any novels yet."

"Do you have an agent?" Cynthia asked.

"Well, I—"

"Take it from an agent," Cynthia said. "You *must* get an agent.

An agent can make all sorts of wonderful things happen for you. But may I ask? What's your novel about?"

"The plot," Lisa said, "is too complicated to explain."

"Is it autobiographical?"

"Maybe halfway."

"Is it a romance?" Cynthia asked.

"I guess you could call it a love story of sorts." Lisa stared down in disgust at the remains of her baked potato. "But lately—the more I look at it—the more I want to call it a complete piece of excrement."

"You should be proud of your work," Cynthia said. "Don't you think, Eben?"

"Absolutely," I said.

"Well ..." Lisa hesitated. "Part of me *is* kind of proud that I write. But then there's this other part of me that says to myself: *God in heaven, girl, compared to every other woman on the planet, you are Chief Weirdette.*"

"Chieftess," I corrected her.

"Huh?" Lisa asked.

"Chieftess," I said. "Weirdette. Both should be feminine."

Lisa cocked a thumb in my direction. "Meet my editor."

Cynthia smiled at me. "Are you one of those supportive spouses who reads every draft? And cheers the author on until the final *i* has been dotted?"

To my surprise—but, really, why should I have been surprised by anything that came out of Lisa's mouth that evening?—Lisa told a whopper lie. "Ebb goes over every word I write. Until—I swear— his voice is on the page as much as mine."

The evening finally was over. After Lisa told the valet who helped her into the car, "I *greatly* admire your manners, young man," I was thankful I was the one sitting behind the steering wheel. Lisa leaned back in the passenger seat with a grin on her face that seemed to say, *Wheeeeeee!* I suspected that in the morning, when Danny jumped into bed between us and hollered, "Mommy! Daddy! Wake up and be my parents!" Lisa would crack open her eyes and groan, "Where did this child come from? And how can I fulfill my maternal duties when the room is spinning?"

I knew Lisa was truly pizzled when I turned on the front-windshield defroster—which blasted us both with stale, hot air—and she did not complain. But at least she had enough wits left to register the change in temperature. She threw her coat off her knees and kicked off her shoes. She rubbed some of the condensation off the side window with her gloved hand and said, "For once, going to a party wasn't so bad."

I kept silent for a few moments. Then I said, "You forgot to ask Cynthia if she owned a punch bowl."

"I am *positive* she does not own a punch bowl."

"And you forgot to comment on the color of the wine."

"The wine? What color"—Lisa hiccuped—"was the wine?"

"The same color as my tie."

"Oh, bullshit," Lisa said. "It was burgundy. Could you turn off that defroster now?"

The windshield wasn't totally clear, but I snapped off the defroster.

"Did you like Cynthia?" Lisa asked.

"In what way?"

"Enough to *work* with her, you ... you ... you lovable dunder-heart."

"Kindly refrain," I said, "from such malicious name-calling."

"Okay," Lisa said. "You ... you ... you lovable dunder*head*. Tell me what you think."

What did I think? I thought Cynthia had all the qualifications of a successful real-estate agent. She was a member of Century 21's Million-Dollar Club. She had given me satisfactory answers to all of my questions about her credentials, how many closings she had presided over last year, and how far under the asking prices of the properties her clients had paid. And yet she was distracting. In a way that disconcerted me.

"You'll be doing most of the house-hunting," I said. "So you tell me what *you* think."

"I definitely want to work with a woman agent," Lisa said. "I just think it would be weird, marching in and out of strangers' bedrooms with some guy I don't even know."

"You're right," I said. "That might be dangerous."

"Dangerous! For who? Whom? Who-the-whom-ever?"

"You. Never mind him."

"Him! How him?"

"Because you'd roast the poor guy—on a spit—in your book."

Lisa hooted, then pounded her chest with her fist. "He Big Man—With Turdish Tie—Hath Spoken!"

I shook my head. "You have drunk," I said, "entirely too much of that lousy wine."

"Yeah. Well. *In vino*"—Lisa hiccuped again—"*veritas*. So I vote for Cynthia. I *really* like her hair."

"What does her hair have to do with it?"

"Everything. If I like Cynthia's taste in hair and clothes and jewelry—which I do—that means I probably like her taste in homes and her taste in—" Lisa looked so dreamy-eyed that I thought she would say *men*. But then she said, "*Meaningful* things. Like novels."

"I can't believe you told her that you were writing a novel," I said. "You never tell anyone that you're writing a novel."

"So maybe I'm tired of being undercover," Lisa said. "Tired of being Little Miss Incogito."

"*Nito*."

"Whatever. I'm just tired of being a nobody."

"You're not a nobody, Lisa," I said. "You are a wife and a mother—"

"Like I want that written on my grave? *She Fetched Slippers*—"

"I don't own slippers."

"—*and Sold Overpriced Gift Wrap for the PTA*. Like I *like* keeping my real self secret?"

"Your real self," I said, "is anything but secret. Your real self is—"

"Pissed," Lisa said. "You're pissed, aren't you, Ebb—"

"I think that word more adequately describes your frame of mind."

"—that I told Cynthia I wanted a room of my own?"

"It might have been prudent," I said, "to withhold that information. It might have been prudent—"

"I don't want to be prudent!" Lisa said.

"Obviously," I said. "Or you wouldn't have told her that we have a fax machine at the bottom of our bed."

"But we do have a fax machine."

"That doesn't mean you have to *tell* people."

"Oh, phooey," Lisa said. "You told your friend Josh about the fax."

"Josh is our accountant. He needs to know these things so we can take the home-office deduction."

"Well, Cynthia needs to know these things so she can find us the kind of home that reduces our chances of getting audited by the feds."

"Tell Cynthia . . . what you want. But my point is—"

"Well, *my* point is," Lisa said. "*My* point . . . Shit. I don't know what my point is. I just feel like I can really talk to Cynthia."

"I hope you don't," I said. "*Really talk.* Too much. With Cynthia."

"What are you driving at?" Lisa asked.

"I'm trying to tell you—if we decide to work with Cynthia—that I hope you'll remember that this is a business relationship, not a friendship."

"Sure," Lisa said.

"Involving large sums of money."

"All *right*. I know how much a house costs, Ebb." Lisa leaned over and switched down the heat. The car suddenly felt much quieter, which made Lisa's announcement seem all the more surprising. "I'm thinking about getting a job."

"What for?"

"To make some moola."

"But we don't need the moola."

"Well," Lisa said, "at the risk of sounding like Betty Friedan— which, of course, is only slightly better than *looking* like Betty Friedan—I need some self-respect! Besides, you're always telling me that I should get out of the house more. Make more friends, be more social—"

"But you have *Number Two.*"

"I wish you'd stop calling my novel that," Lisa said.

"I would," I said, "if you'd just tell me the title."

*"I'm Sorry This Is My Life."*

I blinked. "Catchy."

"I thought so."

"Where did you come up with that line?"

"Never mind," Lisa said.

"When can I read it?" I asked.

"When I'm on the absolute last draft."

"What's your deadline?"

"I don't have a deadline," Lisa said in a crabby voice. "And I don't have a publisher and I'll probably never even have any readers besides you. So I'm thinking of going back to work—"

"But then we'll run into all sorts of problems," I said. "Face it, I can't ever come home to help you out with Danny. And pretty soon you'll get pregnant again—"

"*That* doesn't seem to be in the cards."

I glanced over at Lisa. She was staring resolutely out the window at the darkness of the pine trees on the side of the road. For the second time that evening, I wanted to reach out and touch her hand— but didn't. Of course, I was driving. And somebody had to keep a hand on the gearshift. Somebody had to steer, and somebody had to brake, just in case ... well, just in case a rabbit scurried out in front of the car, or a deer suddenly leaped from behind the trees, or a woman who happened to be my wife said something that made my heart thud harder than any animal hitting the fender. . . .

"Oh, Ebb! Stop! Where are you going?"

"Home," I said.

"But you just passed the turnoff. We have to pick up Danny!"

"Oh," I said. "I forgot about him." I looked at Lisa out of the corner of my eye. "Some father, huh?"

Lisa looked down at her hands. "Actually, you're a pretty good father, Ebb."

"And you're a ..." I cleared my throat. "You're a pretty good mother, Lisa."

As I pulled into the left lane to make a quick U-turn, Lisa craned her neck and gazed into the empty back of the car. "If we're such whopping-good parents," she said, "then how come neither one of us remembered to bring the booster seat?"

I shook my head, then laughed. "Does the man in your novel have children?"

"One."

"Boy or—"

*"Girl,"* Lisa said.

"And what wise words have you written about parenthood?" I asked.

"That it is marvelous. When it isn't ghastly." Lisa looked at me slyly. "Care to hear my thoughts on marriage?"

I sighed. "I think I just did."

"I might have more to say on the topic."

"No doubt I'll get to read all about it," I said. "But when?"

Lisa didn't answer until we pulled into the baby-sitter's driveway. As we walked up to the lit house to pick up our only (and cranky) child, she sadly said, "Maybe next month."

"Next month you'll let me read your book?" I asked.

"I meant . . . oh God, never mind what I meant."

I held out my arm and drew her against me, then awkwardly kissed the top of her head. I didn't want to repeat it—because by now it was beginning to sound more like a threat than a promise. But nevertheless I told her, "Okay, next month. Next month we'll try again."

FRIDAY, MARCH 20, 1992

SPRING BEGINS

## CHAPTER THREE

# LISA

**On the first day of spring,** I woke up with a start. Ebb grabbed the blankets I must have thrown off in the heat of the night and turned his back to me, emitting a single grunt of unmistakable sexual pleasure. I bit my chapped bottom lip. Of course, I had my own nocturnal fantasies. When Ebb used to travel a lot—and the only man I could actually get my hands on during the day was the squiggly, giggly Danny—my dreams had been populated with commando soldiers, tae kwon do masters, surgeons in full scrub, and once even a matador who held me tightly in the clutches of his red cape. Still, it didn't seem possible—it didn't seem fair—it didn't seem right!—that Ebb could be making it in his sleep with some tigress when I was lying right by his side.

I reached out and touched Ebb's arm. "Wake up," I whispered. "You were having a nightmare."

"I was?"

"Yes, you were having sex with another woman."

Ebb let out a sleepy sigh.

"And it snowed," I said.

Ebb rolled over onto his back. "How do you know?"

"Look at the skylight."

The skylight above our bed resembled the bottom of a thick

block of ice. I raised my head and peered at the lit face of the clock on Ebb's side of the bed. It was 4:47 A.M.—thirteen minutes before Ebb usually woke—when a snowplow pushed down our dead-end street and a pair of yellow-white high beams swept over the walls like searchlights. Ebb and I lay there, watching the lights of the lumbering plow play upon our walls, until the plow finally cleared the street and receded. Then the rumble of the plow was replaced by a fearsome noise coming from across the hall: a series of snores more suited to a sumo wrestler than to a five-year-old boy with bad adenoids.

I groaned. Danny always had been a mouth-breather—and prone to one ear infection after another—but lately he had been snoring with such ripping vigor that he woke us both during the night as often as a newborn baby.

"Do me a favor," Ebb asked.

I pulled the blankets over my face. "No. No favors. Not at the crack of dawn."

"Just call the otolaryngologist sometime today."

My voice sounded muffled beneath the blankets. "But, Ebb, I don't want Danny to have surgery. What if they cut out his vocal cords instead of his adenoids?"

"Adenoids are behind the *nose,* Lisar."

"What if they give him too much anesthesia?"

"It's just like twilight sleep," Ebb said.

"But what if he never wakes up?" I asked.

I waited for Ebb to say something typical, like *Please put a brake on your imagination, Lisar.* But in the silence that followed I could almost hear Ebb thinking along with me, *What if his heart stops on the operating table and we can't have any more children and we spend the rest of our lives blaming ourselves for making this one dumb decision?*

Ebb took my hand and brought it quickly up to his lips. I shivered, and Ebb pulled me closer. I put my head down on his bare chest and Ebb tucked the sheet and the heavy wool blankets around my shoulders. We used to sleep under an electric blanket—with dual controls—until the doctor told us that the currents were linked to higher miscarriage rates. Now I slept in flannel pajamas, while Ebb (Mr. Stoic) continued to sleep in just his Jockeys.

"I just don't want anything bad to happen to Danny," I said.

"I know," Ebb said.

"On the other hand—"

Ebb sighed. "I know."

"He's really been a pain in the ass lately," I said. "I think he's afraid to move."

Ebb smoothed his hand over my hair. "I forgot to ask: How did the house-hunting go yesterday?"

"Fine," I said. "Cynthia and I looked at two places."

"You didn't have time for three?"

"Well, then we wouldn't have had time to stop at the Coffee Clatch," I said.

"The Coffee Clatch?"

"We always go to the Coffee Clatch after we look at houses."

"What for?"

"To talk. And drink cappuccinos."

Ebb was the master of silent disapproval (when, of course, he wasn't the master of not-so-silent disapproval). He kept quiet for a few moments, then said, "I know it's five o'clock in the morning."

"Not quite."

"Which is not the optimum time for this discussion. But I was hoping that you and Cynthia could have come up with a short list of houses by now."

"I'm looking for the perfect house," I said.

"No house is ever perfect."

"I want mine to be." I stretched out my legs and touched my cold big toe against Ebb's even colder ankle. "Besides, you were the one who warned me that we should proceed with caution. At that Valentine's Day party, you practically stood up and applauded when Cynthia said, 'Choose your house the way you choose your spouse.' "

"I don't recall Cynthia saying that."

"Well, I recall you replying"—I lowered my voice to imitate Ebb—" 'Yes, this is a decision that should be made with the utmost prudence.' "

Ebb gave me a mild swat on the butt. "I did not say *utmost*."

When I laughed, I heard my voice echo inside Ebb's chest. "I insist—*most vociferously*—that you did."

My imitation must have annoyed Ebb, because he said, "I don't want to be critical, Lisar—"

"Then don't be."

"—but I wish that you and Cynthia would spend more time on the task at hand and less time on telling each other your life stories at the Coffee Clatch."

I rolled off Ebb and lifted myself up on my elbows. "I am not telling Cynthia my life story at the Coffee Clatch."

"Then are you showing her your novel? At the Coffee Clatch?"

"Of course not. She might spill her cappuccino all over my only hard copy."

"Didn't your doctor tell you not to drink coffee?"

I flopped on my back and stared up at the skylight. "I drink decaf."

"Decaf still has three percent caffeine."

"Well, that's the three percent I need to keep myself from strangling Danny." I listened to Danny snoring. "Oh, I swear, if you don't get home early tonight—"

"I always come home early on Fridays."

"—then I'm going to end up a headline in the *Daily News*. MOTHER STUFFS SON IN TRASH CAN. Sub-headline: THANK GOD DAD FORGOT TO TAKE OUT THE GARBAGE."

"Twice I forgot," Ebb said.

"Three times," I said. "And you keep telling me that you're going to fix that stubborn front-door lock."

"This weekend," Ebb said. "I promise."

As Ebb plucked his glasses off the nightstand, the alarm clock kicked into action. I brought my hands up to my ears. Ebb hastily put on his glasses and reached over to turn off this obnoxious clock—a gag gift that I had purchased for him in Chinatown—which was shaped like a crowing bantam rooster. At the designated hour, Mr. Chanticleer opened his beak and squawked in an Asian voice, "WISE AND SHINE! WISE AND SHINE! WISE AND SHINE!" Usually Ebb woke up between 4:55 and 4:59, before Mr.

Chanticleer even had a chance to crow. Now he turned the alarm forward—as he always did—to wake me at seven A.M.

I tapped him on the back. "Who *were* you dreaming about before you woke up?"

Ebb hesitated, then put Mr. Chanticleer back on the nightstand. "Stay out of my dreams, Lisar, and I'll stay out of yours."

"Fine," I said. "You weren't in mine, anyway. *I* was dreaming about—"

"Spare me the explicit details."

"—a deep, dark fjord."

"A fjord? A fjord!"

"Oh, stop saying *fjord*." I wrinkled up my forehead. "How do you spell *fjord*, anyhow?"

Ebb sighed. "I'm getting out of this bed now, Lisar."

"You could stay."

"I also could be late for work. Besides, someone has to shovel out the driveway, since you're not supposed to lift."

I clucked my tongue. Not that I was exactly eager to strain my ripening ovaries by heaving great shovelfuls of snow out of the driveway. But I was getting just a bit sick of the way my useless eggs and clogged fallopian tube dictated every aspect of my behavior. And I confess my feelings got hurt when Ebb squeezed my hand and told me to go back to sleep. I didn't need sleep. I needed—or at least wanted—some hot, screaming sex (the kind that would wake up not only Danny but our neighbors).

I watched Ebb stand up and pluck his bathrobe from the top of the monstrous pile of clothes he had discarded on the armchair. He put on his robe and then padded—bare feet on cold carpet—into the bathroom that separated our room from Danny's room. I grabbed his pillow and hugged it against my body. After that, I held my breath. And listened. To the awful sound of a forty-one-year-old man valiantly attempting to complete his mandatory morning push-ups on the bathroom tile. Oh, the huffing. The puffing! That last desperate grunt before Ebb hit the floor with a final thud.

I pulled the covers over my head and wondered why Ebb thought I had no pride or shame or sense of decency. I would never admit to Cynthia that I was married to a man who couldn't even complete two dozen push-ups. I would never reveal that whenever Ebb took off his socks at night, he merely tossed them in the general direction of the laundry basket (rarely scoring two points)—or that once Ebb (whose head had been buried between my thighs) had mistaken a paper jam in our fax machine for my admittedly loud moans of pleasure. I would never confess that Ebb's marriage proposal had made ample reference to that ludicrous study issued in 1986 that claimed a woman over the age of thirty had more chances of getting blown up by a terrorist bomb than of getting hitched with Mr. Right. And I never, ever would admit that after we had conceived Danny accidentally, Ebb and I had been so puzzled, and repeatedly disappointed, to find we couldn't get pregnant a second time that I had begun to think: *Maybe Ebb and I should get divorced— but keep on fucking each other like crazed weasels in heat—and that way we might just get pregnant and have to get married all over again.*

I knew Ebb thought that Cynthia and I had gone straight from "Hello, how are you?" to "Is your gynecologist, like mine, a real prick?" But I hadn't gone *straight*. It had taken me all the way until the end of February before I obtained the name of Cynthia's gynecologist (and why shouldn't I ask, since a good physician is so hard to find?) and all the way up to Saint Patrick's Day before I wheedled out of her the name of her hairdresser. Although I bitched about myself to Cynthia, I never once complained to her about Ebb. And why should I? Cynthia had everything under the sun that I wanted—a well-paying job, great clothes, good looks, a swell house. The only thing she didn't have was a husband. A good husband. I wanted her to envy me for *something*.

So I kept all my stories about Ebb inside. Instead, it was Cynthia who opened up to me during our little tête-à-têtes at the Coffee Clatch, Cynthia who (over the obscene gurgle of the espresso machine) complained about men, Cynthia who told me the sad tale of her relationship with her ex-husband, Angus Farquhar. I listened. Perhaps too closely. As any would-be novelist would. *Oh, please don't tell me this,* I silently begged, when Cynthia revealed that Angus had hairy shoulder blades, that Angus had a crooked cock, that Angus routinely threw his orange peels into the side of the double sink without the garbage disposal. *Oh, please don't give me a single slice of information that I would be tempted to swipe and stick in my fiction!* But Cynthia kept on delivering. And so I kept on listening—noting a detail here, a detail there—about Angus Farquhar's rakish behavior.

"He leched after my friends," Cynthia said.

"Gross," I said. Then I looked down at my wrinkled khakis and scuffed loafers and said, "Do you think he would have leched after me?"

"Lisa, he went after anything in a skirt! And then he even carried on a shamefully indiscreet affair. With his trashy-assed little secretary."

"Uh-oh," I said. "I wish you hadn't told me that."

"Why not?"

"Because that's what happens in the novel I wrote. The guy in my book gets the hots for his secretary—"

Cynthia sniffed. "That's so typical."

I blushed. "I guess it is kind of an overused plot."

"But a realistic one," Cynthia said. "Men just love their secretaries."

I licked the last of the foam off my coffee mug. "Ebb hates his. He's always complaining about her."

"She does sound odd on the phone."

For a second, I felt hot jealousy flame up inside me. "You call Ebb?"

"Just to check in with him once or twice a week," Cynthia said. "But I hardly ever get through to him."

*You and me both,* I thought, then said, "His secretary is kind of overly protective of him."

"So was she the inspiration for the secretary in your novel?"

"Oh, hell no," I said. "Vicki's totally undesirable. She must be around the same age as Ebb, but she's one of those churchy old ladies who ... well, have you ever driven by those huge craft stores on Route 9? And wondered who shops there? Vicki knits and crochets. She does needlepoint and crewel. She makes *samplers.*"

Cynthia shuddered.

"For all I know," I said, "she even gets weird with pipe cleaners."

"That must be wonderful."

"What, the pipe cleaners?"

Cynthia shook her head. "Being married to a man you actually can trust—to go to work and not wander."

I wanted to tell Cynthia that Ebb *had* wandered—so far away from me that when he was in Boston or Cincinnati or even just downstairs while I was upstairs, I sometimes needed to remember why I still loved him, and so I buried my face in his shirts and jackets and breathed in his cool, clean smell: a combination of Edge and Sure and Zest. I wanted to tell Cynthia that even though I felt lonely when Ebb wasn't home, sometimes when he *was* home I felt even lonelier.

But I simply said, "Oh, Ebb ... Ebb ... Ebb works too hard to think about wandering."

"In the fifties," Cynthia said, "women would have called him a good provider."

"What do you suppose they'd call him now?"

Cynthia smiled. "You call him, Lisa."

"No, you."

"A keeper?"

My face flushed with pleasure. "I'll tell him you said so. The next time he forgets to throw out the garbage."

"If that's his worst fault—"

"It isn't."

"Then what is?"

I thought about it for a moment, then laughed. "There's so much to choose from! But if I can fault Ebb for just one thing, it's this: He's just so busy being Mr. Successful that he never takes the time to consider that I really want to make it too. I really want my book to sell."

"It'll sell, Lisa. But I wish you'd listen to me. I wish you'd get an agent."

I must have felt the caffeine kicking in, because I blurted out, "I already have one."

"You do?"

Cynthia looked so impressed that I couldn't resist piling it on. "A Norwegian one."

"Norwegian!"

"Well, sort of faux-Norwegian. Manufactured in Minnesota, not Oslo. I think Ifor's parents or grandparents came over to till the wheat on the Great Plains."

I knew I had piqued Cynthia's interest when she sighed and said, "He sounds very . . . sturdy."

"Sturdy is not the word," I said. "Ifor looks like a big bad bo-hunky sailor. No, I take that back. He looks like a Norse god. Plus he's single. Not that I'm on the market." I glanced around the Coffee Clatch—caught the eye of a too-cute college boy at the counter who was ordering an espresso—and then sighed. "Cynthia, my agent is so hot—so totally on fire—that he already got me—"

Cynthia's blue eyes shone. "Published?"

I waited until the espresso machine stopped gurgling before I nodded, leaned across the table, and whispered, "Swear you won't tell Ebb. But I'm in *Playboy*. This month. My words, if not my breasts."

Keeping secrets from your spouse was supposed to spell disaster for your marriage. But in my case, secrecy kept my marriage on track. Ebb would have had a cow—no, he would have given birth to a whole herd of Holsteins—if he knew what I really was hiding from him.

Last year—determined to make it as a Lady Author—I had sent off a query letter, synopsis, and the first fifty pages of what was then *Number Two* to a young hotshot literary agent whose photograph I had spotted—and swooned over—in *Publishers Weekly*. I don't know why Ifor "I. I." Iforson (whom I secretly had rechristened "Aye-Aye") had fished my hopeful envelope from the vast ocean of manuscripts that flooded his desk. I only knew my lungs felt punc-tured of air when I picked up the phone and this deep, bullish voice growled, "Lisa D. Strauss. I. I. Iforson. Tell me about this novel of yours."

My throat suddenly felt dry. The entrepreneurial skills I'd learned in Girl Scout Troop 482 ("How about a box of Trefoils—which freeze really well—to go with your Thin Mints?") failed me, and I stuttered out to Aye-Aye the most retarded sales pitch of the century. "My novel is about . . . a man."

"More specific."

"A man," I said, "in midlife crisis."

"So an Everyman," Aye-Aye said.

"Not every man—"

"Yes, *every* man goes through that tiresome midlife shit."

"Oh," I said. "Do you think my plot is . . . um, tired?"

"It's definitely been written before. These pages you sent me are intriguing—"

"Oh, thank you, thank you!"

"—but the whole opening moves slower than a turd from a tortoise."

I hesitated. "I guess I can step up the pace a bit."

"A lot. Not a bit. I want you to boil these fifty pages down to five—"

"Five!" Some little voice inside me—which sounded suspiciously Ebbish—said, *Temper, temper, Lisar.* But I didn't heed the warning. "I spent hours writing those first fifty pages."

"Well, spend another minute chucking them into the wastebasket," Aye-Aye said. "And get on with the story. Now, give me your plot in two sentences or less."

I swallowed. "Simon Stern—who up until this point in his life has been decent, dependable, and dull as pie—wakes up one morning and realizes he no longer loves his job—or child—or wife."

I heard the scritch of Aye-Aye's pencil on paper. "And then?"

Shit! I only had one sentence left! I swallowed. "Well, after Simon attempts to . . . um . . . break free from his life by . . . um . . . getting it on with his secretary . . . um . . . he realizes he can't escape his destiny—" I cringed. "No, scratch that."

"Scratch what?"

"Aren't you taking notes?"

"No, I'm scribbling down my lunch order for my assistant. Hold on." The phone clattered. A chair squeaked, and then Aye-Aye's muffled voice said, "No seeds on the kaiser. Light on the oil and vinegar. And absolutely no banana peppers." The phone clattered again. "You were saying?"

"I forget." I paused. "Didn't you get the synopsis I sent you?"

"It's sitting right in front of me. On my desk." I heard Aye-Aye shuffle through some papers. "Or at least it was a moment ago."

I wanted to throw the phone across the room. How insulting! demeaning! humiliating! Aye-Aye had used my synopsis as scratch paper. He had written, *Bring me a turkey sandwich, slave!* and dispatched it in the hands of his lackey to the corner deli. And I had devoted hours to crafting that summary—until I had memorized the damn thing and could have (and should have) repeated it word for word to Aye-Aye:

*This is a modern morality tale about an ordinary man who wakes up one spring morning dissatisfied with his life and who dreams of ditching it all and starting over. But the more he fantasizes about getting rid of his job, his house, and his family, the more he becomes consumed with guilt. Simon Stern wants to prove that he is a good son, a good husband, a good father, and a good company man—but by almost succumbing to the charms of his secretary he finds himself on the brink of becoming the type of guy he most despises: a man without a moral compass.*

"Didn't you get a chance to read my synopsis?" I asked Aye-Aye.

"Of course I skimmed it. But tell me: Is Simon based on someone you know?"

I scrunched up my face. "Sort of."

"Are you married?"

"I'm hoping to stay that way. But maybe I'm just a dreamer."

"Have you shown this novel to your husband?"

"Of course not. He's so hypercritical."

"Ah. Just like—"

"No. Not just like, *sort of* like—"

"—this fussy Simon Stern." Aye-Aye laughed. "God, I just *love* the stuff you have here about his constipation."

"Ebb isn't constipated," I said. "I mean, maybe he could stand to eat an extra prune every now and then—"

"And the way he wears those lousy-looking ties. And refuses to cheat on his morning push-ups. But does your husband really lie to the IRS?"

"Well, we do have this fax machine—at the bottom of our bed—so we can claim a home office—"

"So would we need a legal vetting?" Aye-Aye asked.

"Huh?"

"For instance, would your husband's lover sue if she saw herself in this book?"

"Wait a second," I said. "My husband doesn't have a lover."

"Oh yes, he does," Aye-Aye said.

"Oh no, he doesn't."

"Honey, he's nailing—or at least *thinking* about nailing—this Take-A-Letter-Maria in your novel, and for most people that's good as gold he's porking his secretary in real life."

"But *I'm* his Maria," I said. "In real life."

"Wait. I'm confusing the dramatis personae here."

"In real life, *I* used to work for Ebb," I said.

"But how can you be your husband's lover—if you're his wife?"

I bit my lip. Raw. "I've been known to ask myself that same question."

"I mean," Aye-Aye said, "this wife in your novel is such a nag and a half! I just can't wait until Simon dumps her for Take-A-Letter-Maria."

"But he doesn't dump her for Take-A-Letter-Maria."

"He doesn't?"

*Read my synopsis!* I silently commanded Aye-Aye. "To leave would be completely out of Simon's character."

"Yes, but that's your story. Make that your story and I'd fall for it in a heartbeat."

"Oh. So. Do you like ... uh ... want me? I mean, want my novel?"

"My dear girl. I'm on the *phone* with you. I'm *talking*. Probably more than your husband—if he's as emotionally constipated as this Simon Stern in your novel—has talked to you all week."

I nodded. Joyfully. Until Aye-Aye said something that made me gulp: "How quickly can you deliver the rest of this manuscript?"

Years ago—while Ebb stood by the side of my birthing-room bed, methodically cracking his knuckles to release his nervous energy—I had grabbed thc arm of the head nurse. After panting through a paralyzing contraction, I had asked her the very same question: "How quickly can you—the general you—I mean *I*—deliver?" The nurse had disengaged her arm from my death grip and resumed swabbing cold mustardy stuff all over my rotund belly. "Some women push their babies right out," she said. "Others take anywhere between twenty-four to thirty-six hours." I had turned toward Ebb. "Stop cracking your fucking knuckles!" I had bitched at him before begging the nurse, "Oh please, please, time has never felt so long, just put me under. . . ."

"I think I can send you the whole manuscript around the start of next year," I said.

"And in the meantime—remind me—what else have you published?"

"Well. Like. Um. Nothing."

"You need exposure."

I didn't dare tell Aye-Aye that for ycars I'd been trying to expose my heart and soul to the slick pages of *Cosmo* and *Vogue* and *Vanity Fair,* only to sink into deeper and deeper funks when their editorial assistants (who undoubtedly were named Ashley, Tiffany, and Brittany) mailed my proposals back with form rejection cards attached. I'd come to translate *We regret to inform you that your proposal isn't suitable for our publication* into this piece of catty advice: *WE tweeze OUR eyebrows right, even if YOU haven't got the knack!*

"What do you suggest?" I asked Aye-Aye. "I mean, I've tried sending off one or two proposals to the women's magazines."

"Forget the women," Aye-Aye said. "There's more money in the men. Cut off all the fat from this first chapter and I'll try to get you into one of the men's."

I didn't want to cut a single word from my chapter. But I really wanted my byline in *Esquire* or *GQ,* and so I went back to my desk and trimmed my prose as mean and lean and manly as I could get. I must have gotten too heavy on the testosterone, though, because six weeks later Aye-Aye called me back and told me, "Lisa D. Strauss. You are no longer a nobody."

"I'm not?"

"You have been accepted. By *Playboy*."

I gulped. "I can't publish in *Playboy*."

"Why not?"

"What'll my husband say?"

"Whew," Aye-Aye said. "What a relief. I thought you were going to say: 'What will the *feminists* say?' "

My head immediately began to hurt. I didn't have to live with the feminists. I had to live with Ebb. But I also had to live with myself. And *my* self, quite honestly, had no quarrels with skin magazines. I knew for certain that if I were a man, I wouldn't mind gawking at pictures of naked women—since I (as a woman) often sighed over the photos of buff, muscled men in much tamer publications (like the underwear pages of the Sears catalog, not to mention the already-mentioned *Publishers Weekly*).

So I told Aye-Aye, "Okay, let *Playboy* have it, under one condition: that they don't use my real name."

"Your *name* is what we're trying to get *out* there," Aye-Aye said.

"Then let me use my maiden name."

"Then no one will know who you really are."

"But no one knows who I really am when I use my married name."

Aye-Aye clucked his tongue. "I don't have *time* for these *Ms.*-magazine-like discussions. Call me back when you decide who you really want to be."

"I wanna be—me!" I said. "I wanna be—Elizabeth Diodetto."

Aye-Aye paused. "Could you spell that for me?"

Well, that explained why I had taken Ebb's last name in the first place. It really was tiresome having a last name that always prompted clerks or bank tellers to say "That's a mouthful!" or "Repeat that again?" (Never mind that my real first name—Elisabetta—was impossible for most people to pronounce.) Five years ago I had convinced myself that my life would be easier if I just became Lisa Strauss.

But who had I been fooling? I'd had second thoughts about taking Ebb's name. Yet I'd had third (and fourth and fifth) thoughts about reverting back to my maiden name for *Playboy*—until I got the acceptance letter. And eventually, the check. I *kissed* the check. My heart bobbed with the same girlish joy I had felt when I held the first five dollars I ever earned—from an all-day baby-sitting job—in my hand. Then I had a thought: *Oh shit. Now I'll have to report this income on our taxes—and how in the world can I bribe our accountant to keep it a secret from Ebb?*

## CHAPTER FOUR

# EBEN

**Every morning I tried** to do twenty push-ups on the bathroom floor. And every morning I made it to nineteen and then fell to the tile, thinking, *One more and Lisa will have to call an ambulance.* When I grasped the counter and hauled myself upright, I took a glance at my bleary-eyed face in the mirror. I never used to look so wiped out in the morning, I thought. Or have so much gray—that didn't even sparkle—clawing its way through my black hair. And my stomach. Much could be said about that stomach. But why waste the breath? I got down on the floor and forced myself to do that final push-up before I got into the shower. As I lathered up with soap, I tried to remember the dream I'd been having just before Lisa woke me. I *had* been on top of a woman. Who wasn't Lisa. But who was she?

She was ... she was ... Cynthia Farquhar. Sans that fetching pale blue suit. Sans pager!

I reached over and absentmindedly turned the shower knob from HOT to COLD—then yelped and hit the knob with the palm of my hand. The blast of freezing water stopped abruptly. I slid back the frosted-glass doors, stepped onto the bath mat, and rubbed myself down with a towel. Then I wrapped the wet towel around my waist and reached into the medicine cabinet for my shaving cream and razor.

As I shaved, I wondered where this fantasy about Cynthia had come from. I hardly ever saw Cynthia. She called me—perhaps once or twice a week—just to "keep me in the loop," but I saw her only on Saturdays, when we visited the houses she and Lisa already had screened during the week. I always looked forward to these outings—after all, it was exciting to think of making a fresh start in a new home—but sometimes I found it draining to be in the same room with Cynthia (who wanted to conduct a reasonable conversation about mortgage rates) and Lisa (who wanted to hoot about a deer head hanging on the wall or a cactus-shaped lamp). Now my dream complicated this situation even more. I knew the next time I stood in the presence of both Cynthia and Lisa, I would remember this shameless fantasy and go walleyed trying not to look at both women in the same glance.

Not that either one of them would have noticed. I guess it was inevitable that I would feel like the odd man out in this triangle. But Lisa and Cynthia had become so close that sometimes when all three of us were together I had to remind myself: *Yes, you are a man whose thoughts and feelings (never mind money to pay the mortgage) really do exist.* Lisa spent all of her free time with Cynthia, touring Tudor homes, Cape Cod homes, Italianate homes, and homes in dozens of other architectural styles I had remained blissfully ignorant of until all this house-hunting began. And then the two of them went to that blasted Coffee Clatch, where they no doubt huddled over their cappuccinos, confiding their darkest secrets.

Deep inside, I believed, Lisa was fiercely loyal to me. But when I tried to figure out if she would relate to Cynthia some of the lowlights of our marriage—*You know, Ebb gets impossibly irritable when he can't take a good poop.... You know, Ebb is such a slob that I have to leave little messages around the house commanding him to pick up after himself.... You know, there's a reason why Ebb and I only have one child*—I only ping-ponged back and forth between: She *wouldn't.* She *would.* She *wouldn't.* She ...

Well, whatever. I couldn't control what Lisa told the whole world. Which only made me more determined to keep a strong grip on what I said myself.

I finished shaving, set my razor down on the counter, then threw several handfuls of icy-cold water on my tingling face. Since Lisa slept later than I did, I always set the clothes I was going to wear in the bathroom the night before. When I pulled my clean underwear off the hamper, a pee-yellow pellet, shaped like a heart, fell to the bathroom tile. I leaned over and picked the heart off the floor. The shaky red letters stamped on the candy Valentine said:

BAD BOY

I laughed. At first. Lisa loved giving gag gifts, and ever since Valentine's Day, she had been demonstrating her affection for me by planting these "contemporary" conversation hearts stamped with messages radically different from those on the Sweet Hearts of my childhood, such as LUV YA, NICE TIME, and KISS ME. Yet she planted the hearts in strategic places, so the messages often had a double meaning—rude as well as loving. After I made the mistake of telling Lisa that I had a constipation-induced headache, Lisa taped onto a California prune a yellow heart that said EAT ME. After I had abandoned my coat on the couch for the third time in a week, Lisa left a pink heart on the sofa cushion that announced HANG IT UP. After I failed to spray our stubborn front-door lock with WD-40 for the fourth weekend in a row, a puke-green heart taped to the doorknob commanded me JUST DO IT.

Ordinarily I didn't mind being henpecked by these hearts. However, this BAD BOY—which initially amused me—now confused me. What was the real message here?

YOU'RE TOO GOOD?
YOU'RE NOT BAD ENOUGH?
GET RIGHT BACK INTO BED RIGHT NOW, YOU DUMB
DUNDERING DUNCE, AND LET SOMEBODY ELSE WORRY
ABOUT SHOVELING OUT THE DRIVEWAY?

This last interpretation struck me as the most appealing. I held the BAD BOY heart between my fingers. Then I crept back into our dark bedroom. If Lisa were narrating the scene, she would have written, *He advanced upon the marital bed, naked and ready for action.*

And then he/I bumped into the fax machine. And then he/I saw his wife had gone back to sleep and was deep in dreamland. Lisa stirred slightly beneath the sheets. Her hips came forward as she murmured, "Aye-Aye. Oh, Aye-Aye."

I frowned. Why should I feel guilty about having sex with Cynthia Farquhar in my dreams, when Lisa was having sex with a *sailor*? I left the BAD BOY heart on my pillow. Then, by the dim light seeping through the curtains, I reset Mr. Chanticleer to give Lisa a wise-and-shine wake-up call at six, instead of seven, A.M.

*That* should send her fantasy man packing, I thought. Although another mythical man soon would step in to take his place. Sometimes I just felt like Lisa may as well have been conducting some hot, steamy daytime affair with the main character in her novel for all the energy she had left over for me. And thinking about it made me so crazy that I wanted to shake her out of her slumber and ask, *What's this fictional jerk's name, anyway? And how can you love him more than me, when I'm the one who shovels out your driveway?*

After I downed two cups of coffee, I stuffed a sheaf of papers in my briefcase, put on my coat and rubber boots, and opened the front door. In the dark blue light before dawn, I could just make out a valiant daffodil peeking through the thin blanket of snow and a robin swooping down from the white-coated maple tree. *The New York Times* lay on the welcome mat; a headline visible through the blue plastic bag read WARMEST WINTER SLIPS (ON ICE) INTO HISTORY.

I tossed the paper inside and crunched down the walk. Lisa's Camry was in the garage, which meant that my Audi was parked at the end of the driveway next to our condo's for-sale sign. That sign suddenly irked the fuck out of me. I lowered my briefcase between my feet and scooped up a handful of snow, which I packed with satisfying smacks between my leather gloves. Then I hurled the snowball at the sign, causing the sheet of snow covering it to instantly fall to the ground. When the sign finally stopped swinging back and forth, I saw that the snowball had dented the tony-toothed photograph of our seller's agent, crinkling the words below:

FOR SALE

CALL MRS. JOAN ORDER

EVERYTHING SHE TOUCHES TURNS TO SOLD!

Our condo had been on the market for six weeks and Mrs. Joan Order had yet to prove she had the Midas touch. Yesterday, however, she had proven that she could set off more than a few fireworks between Lisa and me.

"Mr. Strauss," Mrs. O. told me when she called my office, "I need to be very frank with you: We are not getting a good response to your condo from prospective buyers. So I wonder if you can talk to your wife. About her housekeeping. I specifically asked Lisa to keep each and every room extremely neat."

"Lisa's very busy," I said. "She's very involved with ... our son."

"I don't doubt she's a devoted mother," Mrs. O. said. "But maybe she could bring in a maid? I really don't say this to be judgmental. But your property is not showing well. I need you to declutter!"

"Declutter?"

"Tell your wife: declutter."

I wasn't quite sure what decluttering involved. But I was positive Lisa would go right through the roof if I directly passed on Mrs. Order's suggestion. So I waited until after Lisa and I had tucked Danny into bed and then retired to the living room before I said in my most noncommittal voice, "Hmm, it's getting kind of messy in here."

"Kind of?" Lisa asked.

"Maybe we need to bring in a cleaning service."

"And maybe," Lisa said, "I've already told you—all of a million times—that I can't tolerate another woman in this house. It breaks my concentration when I'm writing. Besides, I refuse to clean before the cleaning lady gets here."

"What are you talking about?" I asked.

"I can't let another woman see that I put up with this masculine mess. I mean, just look around this living room, Ebb."

"I'm looking."

"And what do you see?"

I shrugged. "Looks fine to me."

"Then why did you say it looked messy?"

"I just think we need to . . . um, declutter."

Lisa slit her eyes at me. "You've been talking to Law and Order."

"Law and Order?"

"Don't deny it! She's the only person I know who uses that word. Oh! Doesn't that woman realize that if I really wanted to declutter, the first thing I'd have to throw out the door would be Danny—"

I laughed. Until Lisa said, "—followed by *you*, Ebb."

I was more than willing to move on to another topic. But Lisa wouldn't let this one go without a fight. She pointed out that Danny tossed enough G.I. Joes and other combat action figures around the living room to wage World War III. She also claimed I never hung up my coat. Or recycled the *Times* or *The Wall Street Journal*. Or tossed my junk mail.

"Which means I have to hang!" she said. "And I have to recycle! And I have to toss! All for love. Or personal sanity. If you can mention the two together and still make sense."

I—prudently—reserved judgment on that one.

"Listen, Lisa," I said. "I know you don't want to be a hausfrau—"

"Most observant of you."

"—but we have to face facts: You are the *frau* and you are in the *haus* all day."

"But I'm not in this house. Why don't you get it? I'm in *another,* imaginary house all day, the same as you're in your office."

This, I thought, was a stretch. But since the last thing I wanted was to find myself sitting on some couch in a marriage counselor's office, staring down at my loafers while Lisa cried, "He does not support my professional goals!" I tried to let off the appropriate *mm-hmm* and *ah-ha* and *I see* kind of noises as Lisa went on and on about how important her writing was to her, etc., etc., etc.

I guess I overdid it, because Lisa said, "Do you have something stuck in your throat?"

"I was trying to demonstrate that my concerns were your concerns."

"Well, do you have to sound like Foghorn Leghorn while you're doing it?" Lisa asked. She stared up at the ceiling. "God! What do you care? You love your work."

"I don't always love my work," I said. "Lately."

"You don't?" Lisa said.

I didn't answer.

"Oh," Lisa said. "Well, I know you have a weird thing going on with your secretary—"

"I do not have a *weird thing* going on with anyone but you, Lisa."

"—but you don't really complain about other stuff." Lisa paused. "Do you want to talk about it?"

"Do I look like I want to talk about it?"

"If you don't talk about it," Lisa warned, "you're going to get an ulcer. Or a heart attack. Or, I don't know, maybe you'll just spontaneously combust."

"Should combustion occur," I said, "which I think is *not likely,* you'll find my life-insurance policy in the bottom left-hand drawer of the brown file cabinet."

"Which brown file cabinet?" Lisa asked.

"The one in the bedroom with the gray handles."

Lisa opened her mouth so wide I could see the fillings in her molars. "Hello? That cabinet is *putty*? And the handles are, like— *silver*?"


Lisa thought I loved my job more than her. But if only she could have seen how wearily I brushed the powder from the windshield and roof of my Audi. If only she could have seen how slowly I drove the quiet back roads into work and felt how far my heart dropped when I pulled into my reserved parking space, stomped my snow-ridden boots on the black rubber mat, and stepped into Scheer-Boorman LifeSciences by the back door—as if I were entering a prison.

I didn't want to tell Lisa any of this, because I was afraid she'd write about it. But lately when I signed in with the security guard, I looked down at my own name as if it weren't really my name. And I felt old—and stuck in a rut—when I looked down at the hallway carpet and realized it had been replaced—three times—during the ten years I'd worked there, in the same tired shade that I would call *tan* (and that Lisa probably would call *clay* or *ochre*).

As I passed through the crescent-shaped lobby, I averted my eyes from our new CEO's idea of artwork: an overblown photograph of a freshly lit match blazing with a red flame. ATTITUDE IS CONTAGIOUS. IS YOURS CATCHING? asked this motivational image. I hoped not. Maybe it was just Friday—and my constipation was talking—but I had arrived at the office with enough bad attitude to burn down a barn and then some.

I took out my keys and unlocked the door to the office suite marked EBEN STRAUSS, EXECUTIVE VICE PRESIDENT FOR INTERNAL RELATIONS. How could I tell Lisa—without making her feel guilty—that I had accepted this position not because I wanted to be Mr. Big Shot but because I wanted to do the right thing by my family? Formerly I'd been in new-product development—a fine job (as my mother once said) for a bachelor. But the moment I got married—or, rather, the moment I became a father—I started to realize what a toll it was going to take on my home life to be away for days at a time visiting labs and university research centers. Danny had spiked fevers and developed ear infections while I was nowhere near home to relieve Lisa from the round-the-clock job of comforting a peevish baby. He had said his first word (*baba* for bottle) when I was scurrying through an underground tunnel in the cold of Toronto, and he had sprouted his first tooth when I was sweating through my wool coat waiting for a cab back to the airport in the blistering heat of Phoenix. Meanwhile, Lisa kept ovulating while I was in Raleigh or Seattle or San Diego.

I knew I couldn't keep up the traveling much longer. And so last year, when Scheer LifeSciences swallowed Boorman Pharmaceuticals in a hostile takeover (and emptied three quarters of the executive suites), I had considered myself lucky that the new CEO tapped me for the demanding job of making B blend together more successfully with S. I now did what a chief administrative officer did (at half of his pay): managed home base.

I actually enjoyed most of the responsibilities of corporate reorganization—the reconfiguration of sales territories, the consolidation of our accounting operations—but there was one part of my new job that I had come to hate: handling the so-called *sticky issues* formerly within the realm of the Human Resources Director (whose position had been collapsed, right after the merger, into my own). Over the past month, I had brought in psychologists and fashion consultants to expound upon how casual-dress codes affected employee productivity and morale. In response to demands for more vegetarian and heart-healthy entrees in the employee cafeteria, I had hired registered dietitians to revise the lunch menu (then took serious flak when Funny Bones and Ding Dongs disappeared from the dessert section). During final planning for the new wing of our headquarters, I had supervised a lengthy survey on employee workplace satisfaction (discovering the following fascinating fact: forty-nine percent of those at SB thought the building temperature was too hot and forty-nine percent thought it was too cold, with two percent expressing this precise or similar opinion: *Why do you jerkoffs even ask what we want, when you're not going to give it to us anyway?*) I had fingered Sherwin-Williams paint chips as I listened to interior decorators talk about the psychology of color (blue soothed, red stimulated) and even suffered through a presentation—complete with transparency overlays—from a La Leche League representative called in to advise the architects on the proposed lactation station in the day-care center. For nights after that discussion, my dreams were populated by clogged nipples and mastitis-blue breasts.

A Yiddish blessing bestowed upon the bride on her wedding day said, *May you be mother of millions.* As EVPIR, I now personified Mama to an enormous family of disgruntled employees who expected me to settle every petty squabble they had with the organization. Instead of wearing a suit and tie to work, I should have donned an apron whose front placket read: FOR THIS I WENT TO COLLEGE?

I entered the outer office of the EVPIR's suite, turned on the lights, put down my briefcase, and took off my trench coat, hesitating a moment before the brass coat rack. I didn't like sharing this coat rack with my new secretary. It made me feel married to her. No doubt she felt similarly hitched, because (claiming the brass pegs were extremely harsh on our outerwear) she had decorated the rack with two hand-knitted hangers, one pink and the other blue. When I failed to use my blue hanger—resorting back to the brass peg or simply tossing my coat over a chair—Ms. Victoria Wright took the liberty of rehanging my coat, going so far as to button the entire placket and tie the belt, as if she were a department-store window dresser doting over a mannequin. Just the thought of her presumptuous fussiness made me want to stuff either the pink or the blue hanger—or better yet, the happy couple!—into her electric pencil sharpener and grind them to bits.

Some guys dreamed about having torrid affairs with their secretaries. I fantasized about giving mine the ax.

"I don't get it, Ebb," Lisa said when I complained—probably ad nauseam—about my secretary. "You *chose* Victoria. You could have had any of the senior secretaries. You could have slapped your hands on some hot little number right out of the Empire State Secretarial School, and yet you ended up choosing the one woman in the corporation who would drive you *nucking futs!*"

Actually, Victoria drove me *futs nucking*—not because she was too loyal or too organized or too efficient, but because I had come to know all too well her most annoying personal habits. Which were, as follows:

- Victoria drank Postum.
- Victoria sucked too loudly on Jolly Rancher candies.
- Victoria stabbed with a white plastic *spork* at her fat-free yogurt in weird flavors like boysenberry.
- Victoria spent the rest of her lunch hour stationed at her desk, whipping up cross-stitched pillows emblazoned with folksy mottoes like SEWING AIDS THE DIGESTION!
- Victoria eavesdropped on every verbal tussle I had with every

whiner in the corporation and every low-level quarrel I had with Lisa on the phone.

◆ Victoria knew whenever I stepped out of the office to use the men's room (and how long I spent in there).

It was bad enough that Lisa knew me like a book—but to have Victoria on my case made me feel like I had absolutely no privacy whatsoever. So the more Victoria wanted to micromanage me ("You can't go *there,* Mr. Strauss, because you need to be *here!*" "You can't call *him,* Mr. Strauss, because you need to call *her!*"), the more I started feebly lying to her, the way a guy committing adultery told transparent lies to his wife. "I'm getting some coffee," I told Victoria, when really I was headed for the john again. "My real-estate agent is taking me out to look at another house," I said whenever I had an appointment with the fertility doctor.

I was sure Victoria—with her censorious looks and comments such as "I'm having difficulty keeping track of your comings and goings"—suspected I was up to no good with some wanton woman I'd met at the last Kiwanis luncheon. As if a guy in my position—who had an in-box so full it strained my back to lift it!—had the time to chase skirts. *Get real,* I wanted to tell her. *I barely have a moment to make it with my own wife!*

Lately I'd fantasized about ... well, *doing away* with Victoria. Relocating her. Deporting her back to Information Systems, where for five years she had worked side by side with those rumpled, bearded, B.O.-derous gnomes in ponytails who maintained our computers. Yet I could not. Victoria was just as indispensable to me as she was annoying. In the miles of files archived in the basement, she could locate a memo dating back to 1963. 1954. 1945! When the pointer froze on my PC, she freed it herself or immediately commanded one of the aforementioned ponytails to stop whatever he was doing to come and fix it. She never bitched about the heavy amount of work—or the short notice—I often gave her. Unlike Lisa, she never, ever said, "You want it *when?*"

Yet she was always there! always suspicious! always smelling of Postum's main ingredient: molasses! Thus I wanted—needed—

these first solitary morning hours at work, where I could cruise through the contents of my in-box without having to listen to Victoria uncrinkle yet another watermelon Jolly Rancher wrapper or chide me (just like Lisa) to remember appointments and responsibilities, which I inevitably disremembered, with these stern words: *Don't forget ... don't forget.*

I flicked off the lights in the outer office and stood there in the dark, trying to imagine the bliss of having Victoria call in sick. Then I sighed. Back in October, Victoria—proclaiming herself a "very hearty soul"—had passed on her free flu shot. She hadn't missed a day of work in years. Short of spiking her Postum with arsenic, there was no getting rid of her—or the cross-stitch behind her desk that greeted me every morning.

> GOD GRANT ME THE SERENITY
> TO ACCEPT THE THINGS
> I CANNOT CHANGE

I entered my office and sat down at my desk. As always, the framed photo I kept next to my in-box made me smile. It showed Danny and Lisa on the banks of the Croton Reservoir: Lisa squatting and pointing at some geese, Danny with his hand in the paper bag, ready to draw out a handful of stale Italian bread to feed these ravenous hordes. I loved this picture less for the actual moment I had captured and more for the one I had missed. Had I snapped the shutter a moment later, I would have caught Lisa scolding the entire flock of geese as Danny fled in fear from a particularly aggressive gander.

The silver Tiffany clock on my credenza—a gift from Lisa, for our first wedding anniversary—chimed a subtle six A.M. A moment later, my private line lit up.

I picked up the phone on the first ring.

"Bad Boy?" Lisa asked, in a peeved voice.

I cleared my throat. "Speaking."

"Remind me *again* why I married you."

Maybe I just had tinnitus. But the moment Lisa posed that question (so rhetorical it didn't even require a question mark), a faint ringing similar to the high-pitched whine of the Emergency Broadcast System began to hum in my ear so I could not hear, even within myself, the wild Babel of answers that came from my heart and head.

Finally the ringing stopped—only to be replaced with another odd sound. "What's that weird gnawing?" I asked.

"I'm eating your BAD BOY heart," Lisa reported. "And grinding it to bits."

## CHAPTER FIVE

# LISA

**Ebb scolded me so hard,** I thought he'd have a coronary. "Take that heart out of your mouth, Lisar," he said. "The sugar will throw off your body temperature."

I drew the blankets up to my chin, swallowed the last bits of the BAD BOY heart, and glanced at the nightstand, where the pastel pink case holding my basal body thermometer seemed to glow beneath the lamplight. "You already threw off my body temperature," I said, "by setting the alarm for six instead of seven. Besides, it doesn't matter if my temperature spikes today."

"Why not?"

"It's Friday."

"I don't follow."

My forehead grew hot. "Friday nights we *always*."

Ebb paused. "We do?" He paused again. "I guess I hadn't noticed."

I held the cordless phone away from my ear and looked at it as if it were an evil invention. Even Alexander Graham Bell's first words to his same-sex assistant—"Mr. Watson, come here! I want you!" (or was that: "I **need** you"?)—seemed more romantic than Ebb's.

When Ebb's voice finally came back on the line, it sounded like he was talking to me long-distance from Fargo or Grand Forks or some other cold, forsaken place. "I meant to say—"

I brought the phone back to my ear.

"—I didn't notice we had such a distinct pattern." Ebb cleared his throat. "You think this constitutes a problem?"

"*Constitutes?*" I asked.

"That's a legitimate verb."

"We're talking about *fucking,*" I said, "not *We the people of the United States, in order to form a more perfect union.*"

"Just answer the question, Lisar."

"It's not a problem," I said.

I stated—in part—the truth. Sex on an unspoken but regular schedule had its advantages. Ebb and I both knew when to thoroughly brush our teeth (and scrape our tongues). We knew when to shut the bedroom door to guard against any interruptions from Danny. And I knew I should wait until Saturday morning to change the sheets (although years ago, if someone had warned me that after I got married I would think about laundry and sex in the same breath, I probably would have elected to stop breathing altogether).

What I didn't want to admit to Ebb was the downside of our Friday-night trysts: they seemed as predictable as the calls that came from telemarketers just as we sat down to dinner. It was fine to inform these folks from AT&T and Chase Manhattan Mortgage, "I'm just not interested," but how could I say the same to Ebb? I *was* interested. Yet I felt like it would bruise his feelings if I said, *Could you get back to me on Monday . . . or Wednesday . . . or Thursday . . . at three o'clock or four o'clock or any other unpredictable o'clock?* That I loved Ebb but didn't know how to tell him that I wanted to make love to him at crazy, unexpected times and in even crazier, unexpected ways made me sad. Only once had I broached the subject by asking Ebb, "Do you ever want something different in bed?" Ebb had hesitated as if he had come to a four-way stop in the road before he said, "I want . . . the same." (Not even *more* of the same: That was quintessential Ebb.)

"About Fridays," Ebb said. "I guess I'm just tired. During the week."

"I know," I said. "Really. I'm tired too."

"I have a lot on my mind."

I nodded. "I have a lot of laundry."

"I know I need to leave the office at the office."

I looked across our sloppy, cluttered room at the PowerBook sitting on my desk. "I sleep, dream, write, and make love in what's supposed to be your home office," I said. "But don't tell the IRS."

Ebb laughed. "We should make some time," he said. "To be with each other."

I bit my lip. I didn't want to *make time.* And I didn't like forcing Ebb to rearrange his busy schedule so he could come home on his lunch hour on that fateful day, once a month, when my stubborn, impenetrable egg began its sluggish journey. I was tired of schedules. I wanted to be taken by surprise! I wanted Ebb—or some other unknown, muscular hunk—to burst through the front door, stride purposefully into the kitchen where I stood preparing dinner, click off the stove burners, yank off my apron, and growl something manly like "You know you want it!" while he ... well, *did me* ... on the kitchen counter ... in the sink ... no, up against the refrigerator (so hard that my lusty butt bumped up against the automatic ice dispenser and a flood of cold cubes clattered to the tile floor).

I sighed. I stretched out my still-sleepy bones first on my side of the bed (warm) and then on Ebb's (where the sheets felt decidedly cooler). I cradled the phone between my shoulder and ear, as if cuddling with the cordless brought me closer to Ebb.

"Sure," I told him. "We could make time."

I knew Ebb was smiling—kind of sadly—when he said, "So remind me."

There were plenty of other things I wasn't exactly pleased to keep nagging Ebb about—like taking out the garbage and oiling the front-door lock. So I told him, "I'll be *happy* to remind you."

"I want you to be happy, Lisar."

I hesitated a long time before I said, "I want ... the same. For you."

◆　　◆　　◆

After Ebb bid me his customary good-bye (*Have a good one, Lisar*—as if I were a business associate instead of his wife), I put the cordless phone down on the nightstand and reached for my basal body thermometer, thankful I couldn't cry my usual whopper hormonal sobs with a thin glass tube stuck in my mouth.

I was supposed to record my temperature—before I got up to urinate, brush my teeth, or eat breakfast—at exactly the same time every morning: seven A.M. But I'd been cheating mightily with the BBT method ever since I began. On weekends I always slept later than seven. On weekdays I dreamed really hot dreams and kept hitting the snooze bar on the rooster alarm clock to prolong my pleasure. Sometimes, regardless of the day of the week, I awoke and thought, *I just can't face that thermometer—even if I'm not using it rectally!—until I get some forbidden caffeine coursing through my system.* Other times Danny burst into the bedroom and forced me to take the thermometer from beneath my tongue to explain, "No, I'm not sick—but I feel miserable, anyway."

As I lay there with my lips pursed around the thermometer, I stared at the ceiling and wished I were the kind of wife who gave her husband Old Spice aftershave for his birthday instead of a venereal disease that rendered them both infertile. I wished I were the kind of wife who could keep a tidy house—instead of always resorting to this lame excuse: "You simply cannot write a good novel and maintain a clean toilet." I wished I were the kind of wife who vented about her marriage to her girlfriends—instead of writing a three-hundred-page opus devoted to that same dangerous topic. Most of all, I wished I wasn't the kind of wife who was always waiting for another man—a Norwegian man—to call her.

The rooster alarm read 6:08. I wrinkled up my nose and looked down, cross-eyed, at the thermometer sticking out of my mouth. *I am tired of mooning around this house,* I thought, *like a lovesick woman in the midst of a dangerous extramarital affair—leaping to answer the phone, pining to hear Aye-Aye's voice, drooling (no, absolutely slobbering like a slavering hound!) over his photograph in* Publishers Weekly. *Aye-Aye has had the complete manuscript of* I'm Sorry This Is My Life *for weeks now, and if he doesn't call me to-*

*day with good news—bad news—any news—then I am going to call—*

"Mommy?" Danny's tiny voice came from across the hall.

I was a rotten mother. I didn't answer.

The voice grew closer. "Mommy? Mommy?" Danny's tiny shadow appeared in the dark doorway. "Mommmmmmmmmy!" he hollered, as he kamikazed himself onto the mattress and took over Ebb's side of the bed. Danny placed his hot, smooth face next to mine on the pillow. Adorable as he was—with his dark brown cowlick, his big cheeks and snub nose and loose front tooth that was threatening to fall out at any minute—Danny had one tragic flaw: he was a mouth breather. I turned my head away from his foul morning breath as he announced, "It snowed outside."

I took the thermometer out from between my lips. "I know. Daddy woke me up early so I could thoroughly enjoy the experience." I gestured at the window. "Open the blinds so I can see."

Danny kneed me in the bladder as he climbed over me, then rolled off the mattress and yanked open the blinds. The bedroom instantly was flooded with the silvery color I associated more with Christmas morning than the first day of spring. The dark branches of the maple tree just outside our window hung heavy with snow, and a few flakes still were falling beneath the streetlight.

"Gorgeous," I said, before I thought, *Damn, now I have to spend the rest of the morning shoveling.*

Danny continued staring out the window. "I hope I don't have school."

And I hoped he did. It wasn't that I didn't love Danny. But just being in the same room with him was work—which, of course, kept me away from my real work. *If I didn't have you,* I sometimes sourly thought when he bothered me, *I could have written six killingly good novels by now.* Then I looked into his cutie-pie face and thought: *Well, maybe one and a half.*

"Come here, sweetiekins," I said, throwing back the blankets.

Danny snuggled up next to me. I gave him a wild, impulsive kiss on his plump cheek before I stuck the thermometer back in my mouth.

Like all new parents, Ebb and I had sworn we'd never let a baby rule our sleeping patterns. Except when he was nursing, Danny hadn't been allowed into our bed. But then Danny grew into a toddler, Ebb was still traveling three or four nights out of seven, and I'd been too lazy—and maybe too lonely—to bar anyone from lying by my side. By letting Danny clamber in beside me every weekday morning (and warning him, "Don't tell Daddy I let you do this!"), I had created a weekend problem. "I don't understand why," Ebb told me, "every Saturday—like clockwork—Danny has to get between us in bed."

I definitely was asking for trouble by cuddling with Danny every morning. But I figured he wasn't going to be this cute forever—and if I couldn't have another baby, then I wanted to make the most out of the one I already had. So I squeezed Danny in my arms. "Mmm!" I said. My tongue buzzed against the glass of the thermometer, which distorted my words. "I love you so much, I can't say how much!"

Then I pushed Danny's head off my chest, sat up, and held the BBT thermometer beneath the lamplight. I squinted at the tiny black lines that marked the higher nineties. I never had mastered the knack of tilting the thermometer so I could read the mercury right (and I had even more trouble comparing the two purple lines on those pee-on ovulation-predictor sticks). My temperature this morning seemed level with yesterday's—but I wasn't one hundred percent sure.

Danny stared at me as I marked my temperature on the graph I kept on the nightstand. "Why do you keep taking your temperature?"

"I told you," I said. "Daddy and I are trying to—but why can't you remember what I told you?"

Danny rolled over and punched Ebb's pillow. "Why do you have to have another baby?"

"Because we *want* one."

"What's wrong with me?"

"Nothing. You're perfect. But—stop punching Daddy's pillow!"

Danny instantly stopped. "Why are you and Daddy so mean to me lately?"

Instantly I felt ashamed of my peevishness. "I'm sorry. I just have a lot of things on my mind."

"Like what?"

*Like selling my novel,* I wanted to say. But then Danny might say, *Oh, who cares about your crummy novel?* and I'd be forced to sob, *Nobody, apparently, beyond me, myself, and crummy I!*

"Like," I said, "like ... well, finding us a new house to live in."

"Why do we have to move?"

"Because Daddy got promoted and now we have to"—my stomach turned, just thinking about it—*"entertain."*

"Entertain who?"

"The big cheeses Daddy works with."

"Do you like those cheeses?"

"I have to be nice to them. But just between you and me? I think most of them are doody-heads."

Danny giggled, then repeated, "Doody-heads! Doody-heads!" nine times before I told him to can it.

"Why do you hate parties?" Danny asked. "I love parties. I can't *wait* until my party tomorrow."

I lay back on my pillow and groaned. I had completely forgotten that Danny was invited to yet another birthday party—which meant I had to crawl through Toys "Я" Us this afternoon to buy yet another overpriced present.

"And I can't *wait* until Daddy's birthday," Danny said. "What'd you get Daddy this year?"

"Nothing. Yet." I plumped up my pillows and flopped back down upon them, staring at the ceiling. Lovers were supposed to know—and deliver—exactly what their loved ones wanted and needed. And yet I didn't have the vaguest idea of what to get for Ebb. "I guess the best present I can get for him is to find a new house."

"Why does Daddy care so much about the house?" Danny asked. "He's hardly ever home."

"That's not true. He's home more now than when he was traveling."

Danny shrugged. "I used to *like* it when Daddy wasn't here."

"Danny," I scolded him. "That's not very nice."

"But it's true! You thought so too. After Daddy left for the airport, you used to make popcorn and say, 'Let's have a party!' "

I heaved a lonesome sigh. True, when Ebb left town on business, I had turned to Orville Redenbacher for consolation. Free from Ebb's sometimes-ponderous presence, Danny and I had refrained from eating our cruciferous vegetables and scavenged in the refrigerator for slumber-party meals (cold pizza, salami sandwiches, vinegar chips and sour-cream-and-onion dip). We had put on our pjs at six P.M. and spent the night sitting on the couch, giggling at Bugs Bunny cartoons and sucking on the salty old maids left at the bottom of the popcorn bowl. But surely we missed Ebb more than we let on, because after I tucked Danny into bed, he always begged me, "Tell me a funny story about Daddy!" Oh, it was all Danny's fault—wasn't it?—that more than one of those stories had worked its way into *I'm Sorry This Is My Life.*

"I think that on Daddy's birthday," I told Danny, "I'll show him this novel I've been writing."

"Why didnja show him before?" Danny asked.

"Because he made fun of my first novel and it really hurt my feelings."

"That wasn't nice," Danny said.

"I totally agree."

"He should have said what my teachers always say: 'This is good, but it can be better.' "

"He did—sort of—say that."

"Well, why didn't you listen?"

*Because I didn't want to!* I felt like blurting out. Because it was more convenient to turn a deaf ear. Because I had felt—at least at the time—that if what Ebb said about my writing was true (that it was too glib, too on the surface, too unwilling to go down deep into the characters' hearts), then I may as well just give up my dream of being a novelist altogether and take up some other ridiculous hobby, like carving decoy ducks or joining a fife-and-drum corps.

"I did listen," I told Danny. "He said I wrote it too quickly, without thinking of how it could be more meaningful. So now I've spent three whole years on this other book—"

"Three years," Danny said. "Why did it take you so long?"

I wrinkled my brow, tempted to say: *Because I had your heavy diapers to change, your bananas to mash, your lunches to pack, and your birthday cupcakes to make.* But that was only one side of the story. The other was this:

"Because," I said. "I was so busy. Loving you. To pieces!"

## CHAPTER SIX

## EBEN

*Have a good one, Lisa.* I hung up the phone, knowing Lisa would have a thrilling day whipping up wacky problems for her even wackier characters. Meanwhile, I was stuck dealing with the real thing. I pulled my in-box toward me. As I riffled through the stack of memos, letters, reports, and spreadsheets, I couldn't find a single document I wanted to read. My secretary's ranking of each manuscript—URGENT! HIGH PRIORITY! ASAP!—made me want to dump the entire contents into File 13. Victoria never rated any task WHENEVER.

Reluctantly, I pulled out the final draft of SB's annual report and read: *These forward-looking statements—not historical facts but only our plans and assumptions about future performance—shall be identified by words such as* may, will, could, should, expects, *and* believes. . . .

Long ago, I could find sense in such a sentence. Long ago, I could do my job without thinking, *I need to spend more time with my wife and less with my secretary. I need a break from all this paperwork. God, I need to go to the bathroom. God, I need a new life!*

◆    ◆    ◆

As my clock chimed half-past eight, the first stirrings—like the rustling of a rodent—came from the outer office. I looked up from the annual report and blinked. The long, dour body of Victoria Wright, hearselike in her black winter coat, was parked in my doorway. On top of her head sat a gray fur hat more suited to the Siberian tundra than to the fertile soils of the Hudson Valley. Suddenly I felt as if I were on the set of *Doctor Zhivago*. Any moment now, Victoria would announce, "Comrade Doctor: We are taking you to the front."

The hat begged to be acknowledged. I cleared my throat. "That's a marvelous ... chapeau ... you're wearing this morning."

Victoria took the thick gray nest off her head. "This is an astrakhan cap, Mr. Strauss. Commonly worn in Russia."

"I was going to say, it seemed suggestive of ... colder climes."

Victoria fluffed the fur with her gloved fingers. "It was a gift," she said. "From a man."

I maintained a heroic silence.

"Well!" said Victoria, and the rosy blush that spread across her thin, pelicanlike face momentarily made her look coy and fresh— someone, I thought, with whom a man might conceivably fall in love, or at least address as *Vicki*. "It's not what you're thinking. You know I'm on my church's interfaith council."

I nodded. "I think you've mentioned that before."

"Did I tell you we were sponsoring a family of Russian refugees? The father gave me this astrakhan hat after I sewed some outfits for his children." She lowered her voice. "Five children—and another on the way."

I tried not to say anything Lisa-like (such as, *la-dee-fucking-dah for them*). For some reason, Victoria—who had never been married nor had children of her own—always commented (with copious references to the Good Book) upon other people's fertility. "Well," she once murmured to me as she sat at her desk during lunch hour, knitting up yet another pair of gender-nonspecific white booties for the next SB baby shower, "the Bible does tell us to go forth and multiply!" Then she gave a loving glance at that too-precious family she had sewn up for herself: a sextuplet of floppy-eared bunnies in frilled gingham skirts who sat huddled, like young unable to leave their nest, in a braided-rug basket next to her Rolodex.

"Your refugees are probably Orthodox," I said. "They tend to have a lot of children."

Victoria plucked at a fuzzball on the point of her hat. "Our pastor refers to them as *refuseniks*. He said that if we asked our refuseniks for dinner—which I plan on doing very soon—we shouldn't serve them meat and milk products together."

"I'd lay off the vodka too," I said.

Whenever I made a joke (however lame), Victoria chided me with a single syllable that called blubbery arctic mammals into my mind. "*Tusk!* You're joking. I'm a Baptist. Our pastor recommends fish."

"A sensible choice," I said.

"My first thought was: halibut. But now I'm leaning toward flounder." She gave me a level look. "How are you with a hammer, Mr. Strauss?"

"Worse than with a golf club. Why?"

"We're building our refuseniks a home through Habitat for Humanity. If you were more skilled, I'd ask for your hand."

I took a deep breath, counted to ten, then tapped my pencil on my Filofax. "I'm ready to go over our calendar."

Victoria pointed a thin, bony finger at me. "I see you already forgot the day, Mr. Strauss."

"The date is March twentieth," I said.

"The *day*. What's different about today?"

"First day of spring?"

She nodded. "And?"

I plunged the depths of my memory, all too shallow these days. When I continued to draw a blank, Victoria said, "I don't mean to get fresh, but—" She blushed. "Stand up and take a good hard look at yourself."

Her command so astounded me, I actually followed it. When I was three quarters of the way off my chair, I realized my dilemma. On the first Casual Friday in Scheer–Boorman's history, I was wearing my very best suit—or as Victoria cheekily told me, "Exactly the wrong dress for the party, Mr. Strauss."

I felt like telling Victoria, *The clothes we wear at the office should differ from the clothes we wear at home.* But why reiterate arguments I'd already made? Our CEO, Rudolf Furlong, had told me to "get with the times" when I claimed Casual Fridays led to a lax working environment, and now every well-pressed chambray shirt I'd see that day—every pair of chinos ordered from Freeport, Maine, and Dodgeville, Wisconsin—would remind me that I was a cultural dinosaur (or at least a man who preferred to see the human race dressed in accordance with SB's outdated rest-room signs, which showed a male form in trousers and a female form in a skirt).

When the new Dress-Down-Friday policy was put in place, Victoria had made it clear that she would remain a skirt-only secretary; she considered herself too high up on the ladder to get away with wearing pants. Now, as I watched her strip off her gloves in the outer office, I found myself wondering what she wore beneath her thick black coat. There were no surprises. She wore a nubby gray cardigan sweater over a gray tweed skirt.

I felt my molars lock together as Victoria placed her funereal coat on her pink hanger, then straightened the shoulders of my trench coat as she hung it on the blue hanger. She turned and tended to her basketful of cotton bunnies—bending an ear down, fluffing a skirt—before she fetched her shorthand pad and a sharp number-two from her needlepoint pencil holder. As she marched into my office wielding her Day-Timer, I counterattacked by placing my Filofax on my desk. Since day one of becoming an uneasy team, Victoria and I had power-struggled over my calendar (where next to SB meetings I penciled in private information such as my appointments with the fertility clinic and that narrow, forty-eight-hour window in which Lisa and I were forced to fornicate like there was no tomorrow). My refusal to give Victoria access to my Filofax led her to believe I was living a double (and immoral) life. Worse, it had resulted in scheduling chaos: conflicting (and even duplicate) meetings, until Victoria snippily announced, "I can't work for a man who needs to be in two places at once."

Thus was born this morning ritual: a comparison of her Day-Timer to my Filofax. Victoria took the padded leather chair on the other side of my desk. The way she primly pressed her knees together annoyed me. *We know all about you,* said those knees. *We have been apprised, Mr. Strauss, of certain negative aspects of your work history—i.e., your prior relationship with a female subordinate!* Although I had long since legitimized my relationship with Lisa, Victoria seemed to regard our marriage as the equivalent of a sustained Satanic rite. Only after Lisa had purchased a piece of Victoria's fancywork at the silent auction—a crewel sign that read SO IT'S NOT HOME SWEET HOME — ADJUST!—did Victoria admit to me, "Why, I like your wife very much. When she explained to me why she bought that sign, she had me in *stitches*."

Victoria perched her silver reading glasses—which she wore around her neck on a mother-of-pearl chain—on her nose. She spread her Day-Timer on her lap. "Before we begin," she said, "I have some good news and some bad news."

"Good first, please," I said.

Victoria modestly lowered her head. "My good relationship with the men in Information Systems has paid off. I've been voted secretary of our new Virus-Free Environment Task Force."

"Congratulations," I told Victoria. "That's a real honor. And the bad news?"

Victoria poked her pencil into the wire coil of her shorthand pad. "The task force has weekly meetings. One-thirty to three-thirty every Monday."

I tried—hard—to keep a straight face. But the thought of two hours of freedom from Victoria caused my heart to swell to the size of Oklahoma.

From the outer office, the phone began to peal, then the automatic messaging system picked it up. "I can do without you," I said. "I mean, manage for myself."

"I'll ask Marjorie or Sharon or one of the other girls to cover for me."

"That won't be necessary."

"Then I'll mark that as prime time to arrange your meetings."

But I already had my pen poised above Monday; I scribbled in from 1:30 to 3:30 P.M.: *bliss.* "Keep it clear, please. I need time to catch up on paperwork."

"You're sure?"

"Completely."

Victoria sniffed, as if she doubted I could survive one second on my own. "I hope that while I'm gone," she said, "I can trust you not to touch my Xerox machine."

I admit I had jammed the machine once or twice beyond Victoria's ability to fix it. Victoria then resented me for the way the repair guy—whom she called *that dirty man*—invaded her office and littered her clean rug with his greasy tools. On the afternoons when this cheerful, whistling serviceman came and went, Victoria always fetched her chicken-yellow feather duster and gave a severe beating to her blotter, her phone, and the black lateral file cabinets. At such moments I lay low, fearing she'd charge into my office to sweep the dandruff off my shoulders.

I knew it was childish of me. And even mean and spiteful. But Victoria got on my nerves so much that the more she complained about her copy machine, the more I stubbornly cited SB's spending freeze and refused to let her order another.

"*That dirty man,*" Victoria said, "is scheduled to service the machine this afternoon. Fortunately he'll be coming during our three o'clock meeting."

I turned back to Friday in my Filofax and saw my afternoon stood remarkably empty. "Which?"

"On the bathroom situation. In the new corporate wing." Victoria seemed pleased to remind me of this toilet crisis. "I don't see how you could have failed to mark this down. You yourself called the town meeting."

"When did I call it?"

"On one of those days … about a month ago…" Victoria pressed her prim lips together. "That … that *woman* called you."

"What woman?" I asked.

"She identifies herself," said Victoria, "only as Cynthia."

I took a deep breath. "Cynthia Farquhar," I said, "is our real-estate agent."

"But I'm confused, Mr. Strauss. I thought your real-estate agent was a Mrs. Joan Order."

"Mrs. Order is selling our condominium," I said. "Mrs. Farquhar is helping us buy a new house. Are her calls bothering you?"

"I'm here to take all your calls."

"Because I can always give her the number of my private line."

"You don't have to do that. I just mean to say that you had me set up the bathroom meeting while you were on the phone with this Mrs. Farquhar. I'm sure I told you about it afterward."

I shrugged. "I must have been distracted."

A more plausible explanation was that I wanted to forget about the whole bathroom brouhaha altogether. Last month, when the architect's plans for the new wing were displayed in the front lobby, the male population of the corporation had examined the square footage of each new office and found it wanting. But their silent dissatisfaction had seemed preferable to the outcry that came from the women, who counted the number of projected stalls in the cafeteria ladies' room—and went into an uproar. Within twenty-four hours, I was presented with a petition (consisting of close to eighty signatures *and growing*) demanding what SB women called *potty equity*. The cover memo stated: *We realize that equity, in this case, consists of giving the women more than the men. However, we insist upon acknowledgment that male and female needs in the lavatory radically differ and respectfully request that you call a public forum in which our grievances might be aired.*

Next to 3:00 P.M. I penned in: *John Whine-a-thon*. "At this meeting?" I told Victoria. "You're sitting next to me. At the podium."

"But, Mr. Strauss—couldn't I take my notes from the audience? Just to give the impression that I'm on the right side?"

"You are on the right side," I said, "if you're sitting next to me."

She looked so glum that I feared she might just rise and put on her hearse coat and astrakhan hat. I sighed. "I didn't see your signature on that petition, did I?"

"I only declined out of loyalty to—well, *you*."

I managed to muster an appreciative grunt. "You can take notes from the audience, if it makes you feel better."

Victoria was so pleased she loosened her knees—and crossed her legs. "Sometimes I'm so happy I work for you, Mr. Strauss."

"Not always?" I asked.

*"Tusk!"*

Victoria grasped her Day-Timer firmly in hand, then ran through the day in proper chronological order. Did I have down the meeting with the external auditors at ten o'clock? The early-bird luncheon with the AARP representatives at eleven-thirty?

I nodded yes to both.

Victoria then marched through four more afternoon meetings. "Now, for Sunday." She flipped forward in her Day-Timer. "I can't get you out of Westchester; you'll have to leave from LaGuardia."

"Leave for where?" I asked.

"Cleveland. Late yesterday, when you were ... wherever you were—"

I'd been holed up in the men's room. With no success.

"—Mr. Furlong called to say he needs you to substitute for him on Monday afternoon—at the ribbon-cutting at the new Scheer plant."

"But I can't do that."

"He said he simply can't go."

I flipped my Filofax forward and stared down at Sunday, Monday, and Tuesday, all marked—by Lisa—with the most revolting of smiley faces to indicate the possibility of her ovulatory surge. "Neither can I."

"You might want to let Mr. Furlong know that."

I reached for the phone. "I'll call Rudy right now. But if I don't get to him before my ten o'clock meeting, you need to call him and tell him I can't make this trip because of"—I searched for a valid excuse and only came up with a lame phrase—"a family commitment."

My phone buzzed on the line that bypassed Victoria's desk.

"Rudy's in now," I said.

"That could be Lisa."

I didn't appreciate this reminder that this phone line kept me on a leash to my wife as well as my boss. As I picked up the receiver, I shooed away Victoria with my hand. Clearly miffed, she exited my office and pointedly closed the door behind her. It was only a matter of seconds, I knew, before the entire outer office reeked of Postum.

◆　　◆　　◆

The CEO of Scheer–Boorman LifeSciences, Rudolf Furlong, was Teutonic in name alone. Although he had been born in Frankfurt and educated in Switzerland and England, the thirty-odd years he had spent stateside had thoroughly Americanized him. The brusque voice on the phone—"Strauss: Get down here right now. I need to talk to a man in a tie"—could have come from the throat of a man who had grown up not in the most select European boarding schools but in the shadow of a five hundred–acre shopping mall in Teaneck, New Jersey.

Rudy was a decent enough guy. But sometimes he was fickle, and it was just like him to get all gung ho on Casual Fridays—and then do a 180. I pushed back my chair and walked through a fog of Postum into the outer hall, taking the long way to Rudy's suite to check out the Friday fashion scene. The glass-fronted reception areas of most offices stood empty at this precious hour of the morning known as Dunkin' Donuts Time. The only woman I passed in the hall—one of our graphic designers—sported black stirrup pants and a tweed jacket buttoned over a T-shirt printed with a bright yellow, bulbous image. I whipped my head around as she hurried by. *Yes! I tawt I taw a ...* But how was I supposed to handle it? If I called out, *Excuse me, but is that Tweety Bird I see on your T-shirt?* I'd only give her opportunity to march down to the sexual-harassment officer and file the following complaint: *The EVPIR wouldn't have seen my Tweety if he hadn't been staring at my breasts.*

I didn't understand why everyone at SB—beginning with Victoria—always took me for a womanizer. I had only *womanized* with Lisa years ago (which, in my book, didn't even count—since I married her). Ever since then I had done everything possible to conform to our unspoken policy: A good company man is a good family man—except, of course, when he's on a junket to Las Vegas.

Rudy's head secretary—now, *he* had an extremely attractive head secretary—waved me in. Rudy's office, which had just been recarpeted and repainted, smelled of rug glue and turpentine. The new color scheme—too brown and burgundy for my taste—made me feel like I was locked inside a humidor. I reluctantly closed the door.

Clutching a tortoiseshell pen in his right hand, Rudy leaned way back in his desk chair; I suspected he practiced this trick after hours to gauge how far he could go without tipping over. As if he were heading straight from the office to the yacht club, he wore a white polo shirt emblazoned with a navy blue anchor.

"*You* don't have on a tie," I told him.

He grimaced. "My image consultant—that is, my wife—told me I needed to look more like a man of the people. But I don't like the way the people look today."

"I warned you two months ago," I said. "Dress-Down Fridays are a slippery slope. In the hall, I just passed a woman wearing a Tweety Bird T-shirt."

"There isn't a woman in this office who's showing any leg today," Rudy said. "They're all in trousers, even my secretary."

"Mine isn't."

"Who looks at *her*?"

"I sure don't," I said—then immediately felt guilty. "But I couldn't do without her. Victoria is a very dedicated worker."

"Her knitting needles make me nervous," said Rudy. "And you do, too, just standing there. Siddown."

I *saddown* on the chair opposite Rudy's expansive cherry desk, which (unlike mine) was completely clear of paperwork. "About this Cleveland trip."

"Right," said Rudy. "Sorry. Short notice. I need someone to—"

"I don't like to say no."

"So say yes."

"I just can't."

Rudy gazed out the window at the white-coated bushes and skeletal trees. "Somebody has to cut that ribbon for me. My wife has to have surgery."

I'd been called—by others—a sympathetic ear. But I knew one reason why I was perceived to be a good listener was because, at awkward moments, words failed me. I only knew how to state the stock phrases: *I'm sorry. I hope it isn't serious. If there's anything I can do,* etc.

Rudy rocked his pen back and forth onto its gold clip. "Dorothy's had these fibroids, you know?"

Of course I didn't know—and quite truly, I wasn't sure I *wanted* to know the specifics. But Rudy, obviously concerned about his wife, kept talking to distract himself. Dorothy's fibroids had bothered her for months, but now the situation was more than just suspicious. She was going into Sloan-Kettering on Monday; the surgeon had told her point-blank that *everything had to come out.*

"I need to be there for the surgery," Rudy said. "And after that, I've been ordered to stay home and function as moral support. So that's why *I* can't go to Cleveland."

I kept silent.

Rudy looked at me closely. "It seems to me that lately you've had a lot of scheduling problems. Give me the truth: Are you one of these guys who all of a sudden develops a fear of flying?"

"No, no, not at all." I didn't know what else to say. I had promised Lisa—and Lisa had promised me—that we wouldn't tell anyone about what we were going through at the fertility clinic. But telling lies (even small ones) bothered me, so for a second I actually considered breaking that promise—until I remembered how insensitive it would be to tell a man whose own wife was about to have a hysterectomy: *I need to stay home and mess around with my wife.*

I hesitated, then found a plausible excuse. "It's the house-hunting. I think we're closing in on a deal. I need to be here. Lisa'll kill me if I duck out now."

"I can't believe," Rudy said, "that you're still living in that condo."

"I know. It's far too small."

"Far too small! It's a rabbit hutch! Your wife even said so, that night you had us over for dinner."

"Lisa doesn't mince words," I said.

"I like that in a woman."

"It has its advantages," I said. "When it doesn't have its dis–"

"You're never home anyway, so why don't you just buy Lisa the house she wants? Unless she wants something different than you?"

"I'm sure we want the same thing," I said. "But we're just having trouble finding it."

Rudy pondered that for a second, then said, "Sounds like a definition of marriage."

I laughed. "No kidding."

He waved his hand. "Stay home. And buy your house. I'll find someone else to go."

"You're sure?" I asked.

"Positive."

I pushed back my chair.

"Wait," Rudy said. "Don't go anywhere. I have a little present for you." Rudy opened the top drawer of his desk and pulled out a thick sheaf of letters and memos (printed on half-sheets in accordance with SB's new save-the-trees policy). "Put out a few fires for me while I'm gone."

I reluctantly reached forward and took the pile of papers from Rudy. Then I remembered the call schedule. Like three doctors in one practice, Rudy and I and the CFO rotated on call to handle emergency situations at SB. Catastrophes always seemed to happen whenever I took over for Rudy on the pager. So far I'd dealt with two major plumbing problems, a surprise picket from People for the Ethical Treatment of Animals, and even an outbreak of food poisoning in the company cafeteria.

"What about call next week?" I asked.

"Substitute for me on Monday and Tuesday. And if anybody wants to know my whereabouts, tell them . . . the Bahamas."

I nodded.

"Remember, not a word to anyone. About Dorothy."

"I won't mention it to anyone," I said, knowing that—in spite of my promise—I'd tell Lisa. "I hope Dorothy's all right."

"Sure," Rudy said. "She's a good sport. A real trouper."

Clutching that messy pile of papers, I left Rudy sitting in his leather chair, looking dejected as a king about to be deposed from his throne. Who could blame him for feeling so low, so powerless? How scary it would feel, I thought, to kiss Lisa good-bye before they wheeled her off to surgery. *Wait!* I'd probably holler after the orderlies. *Don't take her away. I love her—even if I hardly ever tell her so!*

I retreated back to my office—feeling sorry for Rudy but relieved I hadn't confessed why I couldn't go to Cleveland. Let Rudy think I couldn't board a jumbo jet without the aid of Valium. Let Victoria conjecture I was conducting some torrid extramarital affair (with my real-estate agent, no less). Outside of my own home and the doctor's office, I refused to admit why I was so bound to the calendar. Although it was hardly shameful to want another child, I still could not form the words: *We are trying.* The phrase made it sound as if Lisa and I were testing a new recipe for low-fat macaroni and cheese, or fixing a worn-out washer on a faucet—without much passion and even less success.

*We are trying.* I didn't owe this information to anyone. Yet all of the following people seemed to demand I 'fess it up right now:

- The hostess at the local T.G.I. Friday's, who greeted my family (obviously a threesome and no more) with an armful of catsup-stained laminated menus and the cheerful question, "How many will you be this evening?"
- Danny, who claimed he needed a dog—yes, he really really REALLY needed a collie dog—because he did not have a brother or sister to play with.
- Victoria, who—in spite of all my consideration and kindness, my *pleases* and *thank-yous* and the ostentatious basket (big as a laundry hamper) of flowers she knew I would order for her on Secretaries' Day—gave me a sour, disapproving look when I returned from lunch, for the second day in a row, with the back of my collar damp from the postcoital shower I had taken ten minutes before.
- Finally, Cynthia Farquhar—whose lips curled coyly upward when she asked me to tell her the absolute minimum number of bedrooms I would consider in a home. "I need to pin you down," she said in her velvety voice. "To do my job well, I have to understand the needs of you and your family."

I'd rather die than publicly broadcast the specifics of my personal life. Yet lately, the more I clammed up about myself, the more others kept opening themselves up to me. I was beginning to suspect I had some sign attached to my back that said TELL ME YOUR

GYNECOLOGICAL CONCERNS. Since becoming EVPIR, I had to approve all requests for extended leaves of absence; thus, half a dozen women had grown teary-eyed in my office as they reported they had lumps in their breasts, incapacitating hot flashes, nicked bladders, and unfaithful spouses. At home, Lisa regaled me with gruesome tales about her fertility doctor ("He keeps rolling my ovaries beneath his fingers as if they're a couple of vintage grapes he's considering squishing." "He shot that lime-green dye through my fallopian tubes—and callously reported, as if my reproductive system were the equivalent of the seven A.M. traffic report, 'Only one lane seems to be open here.' "). My sister confessed her antidepressants were interfering with her sex drive. Even my own mother had asked for advice on estrogen replacement therapy.

At any moment now, I feared Victoria would consult me about some intimate problem, like vaginal dryness. But when I returned to her Postum-odorous office, I found her sitting with her back paddle-stiff to the door, her eyes resolutely turned toward her computer screen. When I announced, "I'm back," she simply pressed her lips together so tightly they turned silver as sardines.

I had enough problems, I thought, without having to dig for the source of *hers.* I passed by her desk and went straight to mine without comment. And that's when I saw I had left my Filofax—open to next Monday—on my desk. Right next to my joyous reminder that Victoria would be out of my life for two sweet hours—my handwritten *bliss*—lay the itinerary to Cleveland with this yellow Post-it note attached: *Canceled 3/20. Make sure you don't get charged for this on your AmEx.*

I gulped. Victoria had seen that *bliss,* which meant I had committed the most unchivalric of sins: hurt a woman's feelings! Worse, a *lonely* woman's feelings. How could I have been so thoughtless? Even a guy with dirt for brains could see that Victoria fussed and clucked over me (and her basketful of bunnies) because she longed to play wife and mother. Even the dumbest of dolts could tell she regarded the steady stream of men who visited the office (from the ponytailed technical-support team to *that dirty man* who spotted her carpet with Xerox toner) with romantic interest. But now I'd made it clear to her that bliss—for those men and me—wasn't being with Victoria. Bliss was being without her.

Apologies weren't my forte, but I thought I knew a way to weasel myself back into Victoria's good graces. I closed my Filofax and opened my bottom desk drawer, where I pulled from a manila folder an Acquisition Request form.

I took the form into the outer office and looked at her stiff, flat back. "I know you don't want me to touch your machine," I said—and then, because that statement seemed to border on the pornographic, I quickly added, "so I wonder if you could make a copy of this form?"

"*If* my machine is working this morning." Without looking directly at me, Victoria turned, plucked the form from my hand, rose from her desk, and slipped the form into the copier. "It jammed twice yesterday."

"I know," I said.

"How? You had your door closed."

"I heard you say 'fiddlesticks.' "

Victoria lowered her head. "I'm only human."

"We all have that problem," I stupidly said. "Well. What I really came out here to say is maybe it's time we got a new machine."

Victoria gave me a tight smile, then triumphantly pressed her thumb down on the green COPY button.

## CHAPTER SEVEN

# LISA

**School got canceled,** so after Danny and I trooped through Toys "Я" Us to pick out some pirate Legos for his Saturday birthday party, we went back home and spent the rest of the morning rolling the white powder in the front yard into two cold, silent characters: Snow Man (whom I gleefully dressed in Ebb's turd-colored tie) and Snow Lady (whom I posed holding both a broom and a squeegee mop).

Then I suggested to Danny that we give Snow Lady a few more hands.

"How many?" he asked.

I undulated my arms up and down. "As many as a Hindu goddess!"

"What for?"

"So she can multitask—with a vacuum cleaner! And a sponge! And a toilet brush!"

Danny put his hands on his hips and regarded me solemnly. "Mommy, Daddy is right. You're not a normal woman."

My jaw dropped open—and big white furry breaths came out of my mouth. I balled my fist inside my mittens and almost knocked Snow Man's head right off his block.

"Daddy said that? To you? About me?"

"He said that to *you* last night—don't you remember? After he came home and asked 'How did your day go?' and you said, 'You really want to know?' and went into the bathroom and flushed the toilet?"

I laughed. Then I walked over to Snow Man and affectionately straightened his turdish tie before I knotted it tighter around his neck.

"Hey," I called to Danny, "what happened to the for-sale sign? It's dented." I tried to look appropriately stern. "Did you throw a snowball at that picture of Mrs. Order?"

"I didn't, Mommy. Really."

"Well, I didn't do it. And Daddy didn't do it. And now her face looks like a crumpet."

"Crumpet!" Danny said. "What's a crumpet?"

I didn't answer. Because I was busy packing another snowball. After I made sure that none of the neighbors was watching, I winged the iceball at the sign and yelled, "Gotcha!" when I caught Law and Order right in the puss.

"You're dead meat," I told Danny, "if you tell Daddy I did that. Now let's go pig out on some lunch."

I fixed us tomato soup and four grilled-cheese sandwiches. Danny ate one-half of a single sandwich. I did the rest of the math and calculated that tomorrow I'd have to start a starvation diet.

Then I piled the dirty dishes in the sink and told Danny, "Now Mommy needs some time to herself."

Danny immediately started to mope. "What is there for me to do? There's nothing to—"

"Play with your toys," I said. "Color your coloring book. Read a book or two."

"But I'm bored with my toys and I don't want to color and I like when you read to me better than when I read to myself."

I ended up shoving *National Geographic: Life and Death on the Veldt* into the VCR. As the narrator calmly stated, "Violence during mating is not unusual in the animal kingdom," I trudged upstairs and sat down at my desk. I was hard at work trying to block out a new novel (main character: me; minor characters: also, regrettably, me) when the phone rang. I threw down my pen. Ordinarily I never answered the phone while in the throes of artistic vision, but even I could see that my plot was a pile of shit.

"Is this the great Elizabeth Diodetto?" a voice asked.

I sat down on the edge of the bed with the cordless phone in my hand. "Aye-Aye?"

"*Loved* your novel."

"Oh, I'm so happy," I said. "I was worried about the ending—"

"I confess I haven't quite finished it yet—but listen, can't talk long, I have this editor in mind—a forty-something guy smack-dab in the middle of his own midlife crisis—to whom this manuscript will really *speak*. But I want to suggest a few changes—"

"Sure. Totally. Anything you want."

"—so my assistant—" Aye-Aye put down the phone. "Bruce! Bruce!" He picked up the phone again. "Bruce just told me that my Monday lunch has canceled, so let's you and I meet face-to-face."

Other authors might have leapt at the chance to gaze upon Aye-Aye's handsome visage. I, however, thought, *Uh-oh. Aye-Aye wants to gauge if he can pass me off to New York—or Hollywood—or failing that, Sioux City, Iowa—as this year's hot young novelist.*

It was far too late to schedule plastic surgery. "Sounds great," I said.

"Bruce!" Aye-Aye called out. "Tell me where I was supposed to be for lunch on Monday. Ms. Diodetto? Are you there? I hope you like Japanese."

"Love it," I lied—and immediately wanted to belch on the brackish taste of seaweed, miso, and rice vinegar that filled my mouth.

"Ichikawa, then," Aye-Aye said (as if I was supposed to know where this restaurant was located and how many stars it rated in Zagat's).

"Itchy what?" I asked.

"Kawa. At one. See you there and then."

I put the phone back onto the nightstand. Right next to my ovulation chart. And saw, with dismay, that my temperature probably was due to spike within the next three days.

I bit my lip and considered calling Aye-Aye back to cancel lunch—then decided to chance it. I could end up ovulating on Sunday or Tuesday just as easily as on Monday, I told myself. Besides, half the time I couldn't tell if I was dropping an egg or not, since I couldn't read that blasted thermometer right anyway. And I couldn't very well tell Aye-Aye, *Oh, so sorry, can't make it that day, as I must stay home to achieve sexual congress with my husband!* Besides, what was more important to me in the long run, anyway— having a kid or having a novel? As Mommy, I had spent the entire morning packing together two snow people who would melt as soon as the sun came out. As Elizabeth Diodetto, I would spend the afternoon fashioning stupid characters that deserved just as cruel a fate.

Motherhood sometimes stunk, I thought. But then, too, so did authordom. I gazed down at my wrinkly hands. I was sick of being home all by myself, talking to no one but people who didn't even exist, tired of having nothing on my calendar but dates with my fer- tility doctor (whose too-smooth bald head and face—like that of a garden grub—I had grown to hate because he reminded me of my repeated failures). The way Aye-Aye had commanded "one" had made this lunch date sound so important—so glamorous—so ut- terly cosmopolitan!—that I just couldn't say no (even if I didn't know how to eat with chopsticks).

I stood up, went into the bathroom, and gazed at myself in the mirror. God in heaven, I thought. I look like a *mother!* I couldn't decide what was duller—my skin or my hair. And that line on my forehead—marked deep with the worry and aggravation that came with keeping a house—seemed more like a gulch than the prover- bial furrow. My lips were shrinking back into my face. Even my ears looked old! And wouldn't it be a better world if I could just take all those wiry hairs I had to pluck from my chin and replant them on Ebb's thinning head?

If only I didn't look like myself, I thought. If only I looked like: Cynthia Farquhar.

I went back into the bedroom, threw myself onto the unmade bed, and speed-dialed Cynthia at her real-estate office. Amazingly,

Cynthia—who spent the better part of her day schlepping clients around in her black Lexus—was sitting at her desk.

"Cynthia," I said. "I absolutely *have* to get my hair cut—with your hair man—this weekend."

Cynthia gasped. "Lisa, an appointment with Ricardo takes *weeks*."

"But I have a very important engagement," I said. "This coming Monday."

Cynthia made soft, clucking sounds of sympathy. She probably thought I had yet another cocktail party to attend with Ebb. "I'm scheduled with Ricardo at four tomorrow," she said. "Take my appointment."

"But I couldn't do that to you."

"It'll be a swap. I'll give you Ricardo, but you have to give me Eben. At two o'clock tomorrow. I just got wind of a magnificent house that both of you need to see."

"It's a deal," I said. "But how can I ever repay you?"

"I'm really not making much of a sacrifice." Cynthia's soft voice turned breathless. "I've been wanting to tell you—but you know how it is, when you're not sure that everything is going to work out all right?"

"Don't tell me," I said. "You're about to close on another million-dollar property."

"No, much better. I've met a man. I've been seeing him now for three weeks. We're driving up to Bear Mountain after he gets off work tomorrow, and I'd just as soon get an early start."

My good news about *I'm Sorry* suddenly paled in comparison. I leaned my head over the edge of the mattress and stared at a peapod-shaped stain on the carpet. "You must really be in love," I said, "if you're willing to put this guy before your hairdresser."

Cynthia laughed.

I didn't. "Isn't Sunday one of your busiest working days?"

"Lisa, I can't live for work forever. So I'm going to do something very naughty. When we leave for Bear Mountain, I'm leaving my pager behind."

Out of my mouth came a squawk that I hoped Cynthia took as an expression of happiness instead of peevish jealousy. Imagine, I thought, making love without a pager or phone in the room, without a fax machine beeping at the bottom of the bed, without Danny snoring like a warthog across the hall, without trying to conceive ... well, whatever it was that Ebb and I were trying to conceive— another shot at waking up every hour on the hour with a feverish, teething infant, another chance at standing outside the barrier of an amusement-park kiddie ride and hollering at the crying child inside, "Pull the bar toward you and the plane will fly!"

"So who's the lucky guy?" I asked.

"His name is Rob Amore."

"You're dating an *Italian*?"

"Lisa," Cynthia chided. "You're Italian."

"Yes, but I don't have a hairy back."

"But I told you before." Cynthia lowered her voice, so she wouldn't be overheard by others in her office. "My ex-husband was the one with the hairy shoulder blades."

Cynthia didn't need to remind me—since I planned on slipping Angus Farquhar's hairy shoulder blades into my final revision of *I'm Sorry This Is My Life*.

"Where'd you meet this Rob?" I asked.

"At a Rotary luncheon."

"What does he do for a living?" I asked.

"Well. Promise you won't laugh. His company is called Have A Heart Critter Control. They capture and relocate wildlife that has invaded homes." Cynthia hesitated. "I know it sounds rather beastly—"

Actually, I thought it sounded most *manly*.

"—but Rob does very well for himself."

*You do pretty well too,* I felt like saying. But there was no need for me to point this out. Cynthia did fantastic—she made money beyond my wildest dreams, and that she looked so beautiful while doing it only added to my feelings of non-success.

I poked at a ragged cuticle on my dry, dishwater hands. "Listen," I said. "I've been meaning to tell *you* something. But don't tell anyone else—least of all Ebb—just yet." My throat clotted with a wad of conflicting emotions. "I'm meeting with my agent on Monday. He says he thinks he has just the right editor for my book."

"Lisa, this is so exciting!"

"Isn't it?" I said—even though I suddenly felt like I was about to throw up.

"But you don't sound excited."

"I guess I'm just nervous that the editor won't like it."

"The editor will love it. And then your book will get published and get great reviews—"

"Reviews," I said queasily. "Don't mention reviews."

"—and then the media will call you up to do interviews—"

"Interviews," I said. "Oy-yoi-yoi! What'll I tell the interviewers when they ask me where I get my ideas?"

"Tell them the truth."

"The truth!" I said. I couldn't tell the truth. I couldn't tell the whole world that I drew inspiration from Ebb, and Cynthia, and even inanimate objects, like a Sara Lee pound cake. People would think I was a kook if I admitted that even rocks and trees and stop signs seemed to sing to me. And they would find me pathetic if I said, *Sometimes I feel so lonely at night that when I stand over the sink to wash dishes, I make the fork talk to the spoon, who then turns around and gives hell to the knife, and before I know it, my eardrums hurt from the conversation.*

"The truth," I told Cynthia, "is that my life is so damn dull I have to live three quarters of it in my imagination. So whenever I go anywhere—especially parties—I'm there, but I'm not really there. I'm outside of myself, watching myself . . . and watching other people . . . listening to them . . . and then I duck into the bathroom so I can write down the memorable things that people say on little bits of toilet paper." I hesitated, afraid I had weirded Cynthia out. Now she would never tell me anything interesting about her—or Angus Farquhar—or this Rob Amore—ever again!

"Of course," I assured her, "you're my friend—so I never write down anything that comes out of your mouth."

"You definitely could steal some of my life and put it in your novel."

"Well," I said, "now that you mention it, some of the Angus material did interest me—"

"Angus! Am I in there?"

"Oh God, no. Not at all."

"How disappointing," Cynthia said. "I think it would be the greatest compliment to find myself in the pages of a novel."

I laughed nervously. "Maybe you could suggest that to Ebb."

"Oh! Lisa!" Cynthia's voice turned mischievous. "Is your book really about Eben? But how could it be? From what you've told me, Eben just seems too good to be true. I mean, he sounds like the kind of man a woman could actually stand to live with."

I stared, in horror, at the moldy mound of laundry Ebb had been compiling—for weeks!—on the armchair. Then I told Cynthia, "That's right. Ebb is so perfect that sometimes women ask me to clone him."

Cynthia laughed—but she didn't say, *I'll take two!*

"You know, Lisa," she said, "you and Eben make such a cute couple."

"We do?"

"I've always thought that. It's just so darling the way you're complete opposites, and yet so happy—"

"We are? I mean, I am. He is. Both of us together are ..." I repressed the urge to make a big fart noise with my lips and said, "Well, words defy me. But you're confusing me, Cynthia. I didn't think you were interested in getting married again. I thought your job made you really happy."

"Of course. I love my job. But how can I say it? Something's missing here." She lowered her voice again. "Sometimes I think I'd just like to stay home and, you know, really *keep* a home—"

I clucked my tongue. "What did you eat for lunch?"

"Nothing. You know I'm trying to watch my weight."

"That's your problem, then," I said. "You're light-headed."

"No, I think I'm in love."

"Well, in either case," I said, "I recommend that you eat three-and-a-half grilled-cheese sandwiches."

"Three-and-a-half sandwiches! I'd have to sign up with Weight Watchers."

I pinched a slab of fat on my belly and watched, in horror, as it hung there—without snapping back!—for half a second. In the background, I heard voices, and then Cynthia called out in a breathless voice, "Tell him to hold! I'll be off in a minute."

"Is that the Man Himself on the other line?" I asked.

"It is. So—should I pick up you and Eben just before two tomorrow?"

"Sure. No—wait—I have to drive Danny to a birthday party, so fax me directions to this house."

"I just know you'll love this house, Lisa. But I'm a little less sure about Eben. So—if you don't mind—would you let me pick him up tomorrow, so I can sweet-talk him a little?"

"He's all yours," I told Cynthia, then thought, *Whether you want two of him or not.*

Making dinner always depressed me. Somebody, of course, had to do it—but why did it have to be me, the only *Italiana* in the Western hemisphere who couldn't even fix a decent bowl of spaghetti? I grimaced as I brushed too much butter—and way too much garlic— onto six slabs of staleish bread. The dollop of red wine I poured into the Classico sauce to give it flavor slopped on the stove. I cut my finger chopping tomatoes and made the mistake of dragging my hand across my eyes after I cut the onions, which only increased my inevitable tears.

Then I took a head of Bibb lettuce out of the refrigerator crisper and, after maniacally swirling the leaves around in the salad spinner, I started shredding each leaf—no, worrying it!—into confetti-size bits. Now that Aye-Aye actually wanted to meet me, the publication of *I'm Sorry* was starting to look like a real possibility. I should have been overjoyed, but I felt creepily uneasy. I tried to reassure myself that there really wasn't that much overlap between the fictional life of Simon Stern and the real life of Ebb. I reminded myself, too, that my fear that I wouldn't nail down certain essential masculine details had kept my pornographic imagination under wraps. At no time did Simon ever take a leak or a crap or penetrate his wife, Robin, or even his secretary, Take-A-Letter-Maria. The plot, if anything, had been overly sanitized by my insistence that everything lewd or naughty take place solely in Simon's head.

Inside my heart—where the story had originated and where each successive draft had lodged deeper and deeper—I felt the troublesome opening lines of my novel pounding insistently. I'd written and rewritten that opening so many times for *Playboy* that I had the entire first chapter memorized, and now it was all too easy to recall the passages that might cause Ebb grief or offense:

*Every evening Simon Stern took the same route home, on a once-country road full of blind curves. When he first moved to Westchester County—solo—this part of Dobbs Ferry had been heavily wooded and studded with yellow leaping-deer road signs. But gradually, behind the thinned trees, cluster upon cluster of condominiums had sprouted like mushrooms after a hard rain. Sometimes, as Simon drove home, he felt a strong solidarity with the hundreds of men heading back to these double-locked doors and lit windows that shone gold in the dark night. Other times—like tonight—he wondered what he possibly could have in common with these ordinary mortals. As Simon turned onto his own street, easing his foot off the gas pedal and letting the car slowly coast past the DEAD END sign, he wondered: Am I the only guy on earth who, whenever he's at work, longs to be home—but whenever he approaches home, feels like fleeing back to the office?*

*Simon pulled into his driveway. The car headlights illuminated the dining-room window, where his wife, Robin, had posted a picture of a friendly brown dog in a trench coat (THIS IS A MCGRUFF HOUSE!) in response to their daughter's Montessori-school lesson on Stranger Danger. The porch lights shone with a soft, pearly glow; the car-door slam seemed to vibrate in the cold. Robin, as usual, hadn't done a stellar job of shoveling the new-fallen snow from the walkway. The plain black mat before the front door, hastily swept, did not announce WELCOME. Bits of crumpled, long-dead autumn leaves and cobwebs clung to the doorjamb. Just as an observant Jew always touches his fingers to his front-door mezuzah, Simon had gotten into the habit of leaning his forehead against the doorjamb—to steel himself for the evening ahead—*

*before he fit his key into the stubborn bottom front-door lock. On
each of the past three Fridays he had vowed to give the lock a
squirt of WD-40, and on each successive Monday it became clear
that he hadn't kept his word over the weekend.*

*When Simon opened the front door, the warm aroma of toma-
toes, basil, and garlic flooded toward him. A crewel sign (hung by
Robin on the wall) reminded him* SO IT ISN'T HOME SWEET HOME—
ADJUST! *Simon put down his briefcase, stepped out of his boots,
and locked the door, depositing his keys on the hall table next to
the neat stack of mail. He walked into the kitchen. Robin stood at
the counter, madly chopping a large Spanish onion on her beat-up
wooden cutting board. Even from behind, Robin was as easy to
read as a Dick and Jane text—her very butt could give off bad
body language. Simon scrutinized the bow at the back of her
striped apron as if its jaunty loops or frazzled, untied state would
give a clue to her mood. Tonight the bow was neither perky nor
drooping. Her brown hair—the usual wild, static mess—just grazed
her thin shoulders, which were hunched in concentration. When
she turned—her long, wrinkly fingers clasped around a wicked-
looking Wüsthof knife—she broke into a smile wide with pleas-
antly crooked teeth. She put down the knife and gave Simon a
welcome-home kiss, which she instantly wiped away from his cheek
with her thumb.*

*When Simon first met Robin, her lips had been clean and pale
as orchids. Now Robin always seemed to be dabbing away traces
of her lipstick from Simon's rough cheek. She wore the color of
flesh upon her lips, a shade that did not appeal to Simon half as
much as the pale pink found on his secretary, Maria....*

As I shredded the last leaf of Bibb lettuce into oblivion, my
abdomen started to feel raw, as if I had swallowed art and real
life in one big gulp and now they were waging war inside my
stomach. Simon's route home from the office was ... *Ebb's*
route home from the office. Our main drag bore leaping-deer
signs. Our street, a DEAD END sign. Our condo, a MCGRUFF
HOUSE sign. Our front hall, an ADJUST! sign.

*Wait,* I thought. *Please let me revise all that.* But it was too late now. Or was it? Aye-Aye had said he wanted to suggest a few changes. I poured myself a big glass of forbidden wine. As I took a gulp huge enough to make me cough, I thought, I'm Sorry *sucks so badly that I ought to throw the whole manuscript down the sewer for the rats to consume. No, it's so perfect that I wouldn't change a word—in fact, I'm going to retitle it* STET.

Headlights faintly lit the darkened dining room as Ebb's Audi crunched through the thin layer of snow left in the driveway. In spite of the forecast (which called for more snow), Ebb would leave his car parked outside, because neither of us had called a handyman to fix our fickle automatic garage-door opener. Our condominium was supposed to be maintenance-free. Yet our last Mr. Fix It had been dismissed by the homeowners' board for being "too forward" with women. I wondered which of the attractive women on our street he had tried to seduce. Then I wondered why he had never shown the slightest interest in dropping his tools in our front hall and overpowering . . . well, *me.*

Ebb cut the engine. The car door slammed. I hastily jettisoned the rest of my wine into the sink and rinsed out the glass. It would have been wifely to greet Ebb at the front door *(Let me take your coat, let me pour you a drink, let me be your sexual slave, etc.),* but I wanted Ebb to have the interesting experience of trying to insert his key in the front-door lock. I listened. Ebb's key scraped. The tumbler of the lock refused to turn. Ebb muttered, "Fuck." He tried again, and on the third attempt the lock gave way and Ebb burst into the front hall accompanied by a blast of cold air.

He set down his briefcase. I listened, with trepidation, as he riffled through the mail I had left on the front-hall table. Along with a couple of women's magazines whose headlines expressed these sentiments: LET HIM KNOW YOU LONG FOR HIM! GIVE YOUR MAN THE SEX HE WANTS! the mailman had brought me the latest issue of *Publishers Weekly* (which I knew I'd plow through tonight, growing sick with envy as I read about every other author's six-figure advance). Ebb had received a stack of stiff white bills, half a dozen charitable appeals, and a thick crimson periodical that I called *The B School Brag Rag*. I had glanced at Ebb's alumni notes and noticed that he had failed to report his promotion. Maybe he didn't want the development office hitting on him for a bigger contribution. Or maybe he was just so successful that he had ceased to care if anyone else thought he was or not.

Still in his gloves and coat, Ebb entered the kitchen. I knew he was constipated again when he held up the tie that Danny and I had knotted around Snow Man's neck and said, "This *was* one of my better neckties."

"Really?" I kept on chopping with my knife. "I ranked it among your ugliest."

"We have a small difference of opinion, then." Ebb tossed the tie onto the microwave cart and pointed to my cutting board. "Aren't you slicing that cucumber too thin?"

I pressed my lips together. "Last time I made a salad, you said the slices were too thick."

"Did I?"

"Indeed you did."

"Oh. Well. Wait here—I'll get a ruler."

I waved Ebb away. He retreated to the dining room. Because I knew he was going to drape his trench coat over a chair, I called out, "At the risk of sounding rude—"

"I know," Ebb said. "There's a wonderful invention. Called the hanger."

"You stole the words," I said. "Right out of my mouth."

Ebb took a long time hanging his coat in the hall closet. He probably was gazing with longing at the front door—and maybe even considering going back out again. But then he returned to the kitchen and leaned against the opposite counter. I sneaked a peek at him out of the corner of my eye. He wore a gray suit that I had helped him select at Jos. A. Bank (sexy) and an impeccably starched white shirt (also *ooo-la* in my book). But to his immense discredit, he also wore a tie the color of *cow's liver*. God! I couldn't believe he had gone out in public wearing such a shiny, slimy thing. *Undress!* I wanted to command him. *Immediately! Or there shall be dire consequences tonight!*

Ebb cocked his head toward the tomato sauce bubbling in the pot. "Smells good," he said.

I kept whacking away with my Wüsthof.

"All right," Ebb said. "I'm sorry I offended you ... and your cucumber."

"Forgiven," I said, and handed him a cucumber slice wide as an Oreo cookie. Ebb bit into it, and I smiled, knowing it would haunt him five minutes later in the form of an irrepressible burp.

"Where's Danny?" Ebb asked.

"Fell asleep upstairs," I said. "When he wakes up, ask him to smile."

"His tooth finally came out?"

I nodded and fetched what looked like a worn pebble from the back of the counter. The tooth cupped in my hand probably had been the very first white stump to appear in Danny's bubbly, saliva-ridden mouth—yet it seemed like just yesterday that I had gently rubbed the rice cereal off its surface with a washcloth.

"This tooth made me weep," I said.

Ebb blinked, then cleared his throat. He pointed to the winking light on the answering machine. "I don't understand why you can't pick up the phone while you're writing."

"I've told you a million times. It breaks my concentration."

"Did you listen to these messages?"

"The first is from Law and Order," I said. "When I heard her voice, I thought she was calling to find out how our for-sale sign got dented. Did you see? It looks like somebody lobbed an iceball at her picture."

Ebb shrugged. "Danny, probably."

"I had my eye on Danny all day long."

"Maybe the paperboy did it."

"The paperboy is an *old man*," I said—although, as far as I could tell, the guy who tossed the *Times* onto our front porch from his Chevrolet station wagon was all of fifty. "Law and Order wanted to know—again—if we'd be willing to put our front door on a lock-box so other realtors can get in."

"We've already discussed that," Ebb said. "A lockbox makes you a prime target for intruders."

"But, Ebb, I want our place to sell—"

"Case closed. It just isn't safe."

Ebb's voice sounded far too bossy to please me. So I was pleased to report, "The next call is Victoria, leaving us the name and number of a good Christian handyman."

"What for?" Ebb asked.

"To fix our front-door lock."

"*I'm* fixing the front-door lock."

"*Are* you?" I asked.

"Yes. This weekend. With two squirts of WD-40."

"Well, I need some guy—Christian, Jewish, or voodoo—to fix the garage-door opener too."

Ebb winced. "Why do you have to tell Victoria about all our household problems?"

"I didn't," I said. "She noticed the front-door latch wasn't working right when she came by to pick up some old clothes for some refugees."

"Victoria came here? And you let her in?"

"What was I supposed to do? Chase her off the premises with a shotgun?"

"But, Lisar—why can't you understand? I hate the way that Victoria gets into every little corner of my life. And now you've probably given her some of my shirts and jackets—"

"A few ties too," I said.

"—and my pants. I can't stand that she has my pants."

"Relax. It's not like she's going to wear them herself."

"But everywhere I turn, she's there. I have no privacy whatsoever." Ebb swallowed down a cucumber-induced belch. He reached up to loosen his ugly tie. "God, what a day. I got pounded."

"Tell."

"Only if you—"

"Oh, Ebb," I said. "How many times do I have to promise? I *swear* I won't write about it."

Ebb looked down at my hands—and after he determined my fingers weren't crossed, he said, "SB women want more stalls in the new cafeteria bathrooms. So I had to call this town meeting on potty equity."

Ebb looked at me hopefully. When I failed to laugh, he said, "I was counting on you to be amused."

"What's so funny," I asked, "about women wanting the same things as men?"

Ebb took a pass on that question. He went over to the cabinet, took down a glass, and drew four or five ounces of water from the automatic dispenser on the refrigerator. He slugged down his water, then left his empty glass on the counter. I repressed the urge to say, *Put that glass in the dishwasher—or at least the sink!*

"You know," he said, "at this potty equity meeting—which lasted an hour and a half—not a single woman got up to use the john. Meanwhile, I stood stoically at the podium, praying my bladder wouldn't break. After a while I got so bored, I started cataloging in my Filofax all the euphemisms for toilet I could think of."

"How many did you get?"

"Close to a dozen."

I put down my knife. "I can do *loads* better than that," I said, heading for the hallway.

"Where are you going?" Ebb called after me.

"To get your Filofax."

"I left it at the office—"

"Bull-dinky," I called out as I knelt on the hallway floor and snapped open Ebb's briefcase, revealing a mess of papers and folders inside. I clutched Ebb's thick black Filofax. "You never go anywhere without your calendar," I said as I toted it back into the kitchen. "Half the time I'm surprised you don't bring it to bed."

"You're my calendar in bed," Ebb said. "These days." He cleared his throat. "Before I forget, what was your temperature this morning?"

"The same as yesterday," I said, and put his Filofax down on the counter, almost knocking Danny's lost tooth to the floor. As I turned to March 20, I tried not to get pissed at Ebb. But bells— and angry whistles—seemed to ring and shriek in my ears whenever I considered how methodical he was about everything. *I'm standing right next to you,* I thought. *So close I can practically smell the office—a strange, sexy combination of Xerox toner and forced heat—upon your jacket. And I want another child as much as you do—but I don't want to lose a lover along the way. So why do you have to wait to hear if my temperature has spiked before you even touch me?*

I looked over at Ebb. As usual, he was totally oblivious to what I was feeling. His eyes were transfixed upon that cucumber on the opposite counter. Waging within him, I knew, was a great moral struggle: eat more (and rue it later) or eat none (but spend the rest of the evening lusting after it). Finally, against his better judgment, he reached for another slice.

I sighed and turned to March 20 in Ebb's Filofax. Sometimes I worried that Ebb was becoming a total *suit*. It did my heart good to see that he still was capable of engaging in a subversive act worthy of the lowest of eleven-year-old boys. During this potty-equity meeting, while the SB women probably had buffeted about worn phrases like *unequal rights, hidden animosity,* and *hostile atmosphere,* Ebb had been standing at the podium scribbling down *head* and *throne* and *porcelain God*—not to mention *john* and *crapper.*

"You forgot *loo*," I said, plucking a pencil from the front of Ebb's Filofax and scribbling beneath his list. "And *privy*. And plain old *pot*. And *prayer box*."

"Lisar, you should have been there. These women were all over me—"

"How about *piss post*?" I asked.

"I felt like I was in that Greek drama where the women shred the man to bits—"

"*The Bacchae*," I murmured, then blurted out, "*The reading room. The thunderbox.* And in Shakespeare, King Lear—or maybe it's the jester—calls it *the jakes*. Then you yourself call it *the warshroom*—why, when your mother calls it *the powder room*?"

"My father taught me it was polite." Ebb hesitated. "Why does your mother call it *taking a walk*?"

"I told you, she grew up *plotzing* in an outhouse."

Ebb repressed a burp. "How many times do I have to tell you that *plotz* doesn't mean poop? It means to burst your seams—

spontaneously combust—with excitement." Ebb held out his hand. "Can I have my Filofax back now?"

I scribbled *heaper*. Then *dumper*.

"My Filofax, please."

I turned to Saturday, March 21, and under Ebb's already long To-Do List, I wrote *Eat a—*

Ebb grasped my fingers before I could scrawl *prune*.

"Put a pen in your hand," he scolded me, "and you go right out of control."

"This is a pencil," I said. "You can erase it." I pointed to the ten-thirty-A.M. slot for Saturday. "What's this *JS*?"

"I'm seeing Josh Silber to go over the taxes."

My heart thudded as I remembered my *Playboy* income. "Don't you trust Josh?"

"Of course I trust him. I gave him the job, didn't I?"

*Then why don't you just sign off on the return?* I felt like asking. But I already knew the answer. Ebb probably owed more in taxes this year than I had earned in my entire life. Of course he would be careful to make sure he didn't overpay the IRS. And of course I had been careful enough to say to Josh, "Could you keep the origin of my income secret? At least until I get around to telling Ebb?"

Clearly it was time to tell Ebb. But as I idly turned forward in his Filofax, I stopped on Monday, March 23. Next to the smiley face I had drawn to herald my ovulation, Ebb had written *bliss*.

I brushed my hip, gently, against his hip. "Bliss, hmm?" I asked.

"You bet," Ebb said. "Victoria is going to a computer meeting. For two whole hours, I get to be completely by myself in the office. Do you believe it?"

"No," I said crossly. I stabbed my finger on the Filofax. "You should erase this *bliss*. Before she sees it."

Ebb looked down at the tile floor, as if he had never seen the hexagonal pattern before and found it utterly fascinating. "She already did."

"Oh, Ebb," I said. "How *could* she have?"

"It was an accident," Ebb said. "I went to talk to Rudy and left

my Filofax on my desk. When I came back, Victoria had put a flight
itinerary on my desk—"

"An itinerary!" I said. "Where are you going now?"

"Nowhere. The trip got canceled. But Victoria must have seen
what I had written, because she looked ... you know, all shriveled
and hurt. Her lips, especially, got all pulled in."

"Lips get thinner," I said, "as a woman gets older."

Ebb pushed up his glasses and peered at me. "Your mouth looks
larger than ever."

"But my lips are disappearing."

Ebb touched a tiny tusk of skin on my bottom lip; his finger
brought away a tinge of brownish red. "They're a bit chapped," he
said. "But not in obvious danger of extinction."

He smiled at me. I smiled back. Then I pointed, once again, to
his Filofax. "I guess you'd better be extra nice to Vicki on Monday."

"Who's Vicki?"

"Your *secretary*."

"She goes by Vicki? She never told me."

"You probably never asked," I said.

Ebb took the pencil and scribbled something puzzling on
Monday, March 23: *Teleflora*.

"What's that?" I asked.

"I'm not supposed to tell. So don't you either. But Rudy's wife is
having a hysterectomy."

My hand immediately went to my abdomen, as if someone were
threatening to reach inside and remove a vital part of me too. "Oh,"
I said. "That's too bad."

I didn't especially like Dorothy Furlong—in fact, she was exactly
the type of corporate wife who set my teeth on edge. The first time
I had met her was at a huge party the Furlongs had thrown right
after the SB merger. I was so astounded that any woman had the
stamina—never mind the stupidity—to stand in the front door of her
McMansion in a sequined dress, repeating over and over, "Hello, I'm
Dorothy Furlong and I'll be your hostess for the evening," that I had
been tempted to reply, "Well, *I'm* Lisa Strauss and I'll be your guest
from the Planet Ape." But now I felt guiltily sympathetic toward her.

"Does she have cancer?" I asked. "Or is she doing that voluntarily?"

"Why would Rudy tell me if it were voluntary?"

I shrugged. "I'm surprised he told you anything so private in the first place."

"He told me because he wanted me to go to Cleveland on Sunday and Monday."

"But, Ebb, you can't!"

"I know. I told him."

"That I'm ovulating?"

"Of course not! I told him we might be closing in on a house." Ebb shut his Filofax. "And he, in turn, told me far too many details about his wife's surgery."

"I guess he's scared. I guess he just needed to confide in someone."

"I understand that. But sometimes I just wish that everyone at SB—from Rudy on down—would quit pouring all their personal problems into my ear—"

"But, Ebb," I interrupted, "that's why Rudy chose you for that position. Everyone knows that you're a good listener."

Ebb opened his mouth and out came some garbled, throat-clearing sound. Maybe Ebb was about to say something important. But he hesitated so long—and got so tongue-tied—that I grew impatient and turned my back. I slid a fistful of spaghetti out of the blue Ronzoni box and, with a rippling crack, broke the bundle in half and dropped it into the frothing water, drowning out his silence.

Then I stared at the bundle of spaghetti standing stiffly in the steaming pot. Usually I was good about listening to Ebb. I prompted him. Sometimes even *begged* him to talk to me, using every persuasive phrase in the book short of resorting to the standard command Danny's teachers used to deliver when he stamped his toddler feet or clenched his fist in frustration: "Use your words! Use your words to express your feelings!" But four quarters of the time, it seemed, Ebb didn't even know his feelings, much less how to vocalize them. Like right now. What sat upon the tip of his tongue that he seemed so reluctant to tell me? *I love you more than life itself? I need to*

*plotz? Did you get some more of that Chunky Monkey ice cream for*
*dessert? I would die if you ever left me?*

The furnace clicked on. And just as heat was about to blast from
the vents, Ebb took me by the wrist, pulled me away from the stove,
and gave me a quick, hesitant kiss on the cheek.

"Oh," I said. But that didn't sound too encouraging, so I added,
"Mmm."

With Ebb, a little bit of *mmm* went a long way. He placed his
hand on the bone of my hip and kissed me on the lips. He tasted
sexy to me—like chilled water and stale office air and the insistent
brilliance of fluorescent lights. I knew I tasted like the wine I wasn't
supposed to have been drinking—but I also tasted salty and sharp,
because before Ebb had come home, I had eaten eight (but not the
truly piggish number of nine) jalapeño crostini.

I put my hands beneath his jacket and ran my fingers over the
warmth of his shirt. Ebb looped his fingers through the strap of my
apron and kissed me again. And again.

"How long does that take?" he asked. "The pasta? To cook?"

"Eleven minutes. Claims the box. But on our stove— Oh. Mmm.
It's really thirteen—"

"Turn off the burner."

I reached for the stove. Then my hand pulled back. "Ebb," I
said. *"Danny."*

"You said he was asleep."

"Remember what happened last time?"

Ebb probably recalled—only too well—the specifics of Danny's
last ill-timed interruption. But it wasn't just the memory that caused
him to step back. He had pressed in close to me only to discover
that earlier I had slipped a wooden spoon—an implement big
enough to spank a man—into my front apron pocket.

"Later," I said, dabbing a trace of my lipstick away from Ebb's
cheek with my thumb.

"Sure," he said. "Later."

In literature, these were called *lost moments*. I didn't understand
why—for these tiny units of time, tinged with sorrow and disap-
pointment, were those that lodged most firmly in my memory. For

instance, I swore I'd take to the grave the image of Danny—who'd been roused out of a deep sleep just a month ago by my lusty cries—standing in the moonlight at our open bedroom door, his tiny voice quivering as he asked an unanswerable question: "Daddy? Mommy? What are you two *doing*?"

## CHAPTER EIGHT

# EBEN

**In our crowded,** cluttered bedroom, I put on my blue workshirt and Dockers and left my suit lying like a rumpled, headless man on the bed. Then I sat on the edge of the mattress and surveyed the chaos: Damp towels and soiled underwear were piled high in the wicker laundry basket, the sheets were crumpled at the foot of the mattress, and the bedspread had slipped to the floor.

Half—if not more—of this mess was mine. I admit I didn't turn my socks right-side out before I tossed them in the laundry basket and that I had a less-than-loving relationship with all clothes hangers—wire, plastic, cedar, and Victoria's pink-and-blue knitted ones. I piled receipts and bills on my nightstand and failed to search thoroughly when one of my clipped toenails accidentally went flying into the nether reaches of the plush carpet. But I wasn't home enough (or at least that was my excuse) to pick up after myself. Lisa was home—but she really wasn't home except to whatever strange assortment of characters populated her head.

Sometimes—and this was one of those times—I wished Lisa did not want to write. I stood up from the bed, my body gravitating toward the only one of Lisa's possessions I was forbidden to touch: the gray laptop computer propped open on her tiny white desk. My fingers hovered above the keyboard before they lightly grazed the RETURN key. The PowerBook (which had been "sleeping") hummed to life—and then let out a raucous monkey's shriek known, in Macintosh language, as "the wild eep." The screen instantly lit up and displayed this message:

**YOU ARE NOW RUNNING ON RESERVE POWER.**

Sometimes I couldn't figure out which was sharper—Lisa's tongue or her ears. "Ebb!" she immediately called out from the bottom of the stairs. "Are you on my computer?"

I pulled my hand away. "Of course not!"

Lisa remained silent for a moment. Surely she wanted to make love tonight as badly as I did—because, instead of calling out *Liar!* she merely said, "I could have sworn I heard that wild eep. Wake up Danny, why don't you? That child's been snoring long enough."

Dinner conversation consisted of the usual long list of ignored directives: "Sit down, Danny." "Wipe your face, Danny." "Use your napkin to wipe your face, Danny." "Please stop interrupting Mommy and Daddy, Danny." But the moment Danny went silent, so did Lisa and I. The silverware—forks clinking against knives—seemed to have so much more to say.

On Friday nights, I had the dubious honor of putting Danny to bed. As I scrubbed his face with a washcloth and stuffed his squiggling limbs into his tiger-striped pajamas, I confirmed, once again, the truth of what people often said: "Your son looks exactly like your wife." Lisa's genes had whomped mine into complete oblivion. Danny had Lisa's cheerful teeth and pinchable cheeks, her skin (pale as parsnips) and her eyes (dark as the bedroom walls I sometimes stared at on a sleepless night). His thick hair was Lisa's deep brassy brown. Plus—just like Lisa's—Danny's voice always rang too loudly in my ear.

"How much will the tooth fairy leave me?" he asked as I tucked his lost tooth beneath his pillow.

"Maybe a dollar."

"Just a dollar!" Danny dive-bombed onto his bed. "But I still have to buy you a birthday present."

"I guess you're going to the ninety-nine-cent store, then."

"I can't wait until your birthday, Daddy."

"I sure can," I said.

Although Danny was eager to turn the calendar to April 1—which gave him an excuse to put the sugar in the salt shaker and eat too much of my birthday cake—I easily could have placed a moratorium on such merry japes. Turning forty-two big ones (on April Fool's Day, no less) was an unpleasant prospect—especially since Lisa's compassion for the aging Birthday Boy wasn't exactly boundless. For my fortieth, Lisa thankfully had not thrown me an over-the-hill party, nor had she draped the mirrors in black. But trying to convivial-ize the sad occasion, she had presented me with a bottle of Grey Goose vodka and a rude card that showed a Jewish mother in a muumuu and cat glasses berating the Grim Reaper: *Put down that scythe before you have a heart attack!* On Lisa's last birthday, I had retaliated with a Whistler's Mother coffee cup and a card that showed a basket full of shar-pei puppies plastered with this caption: *And you thought you had wrinkles.*

Birthdays reminded me that time was passing way too quickly—except when I really wanted it to speed by. I glanced at my watch and saw the minute hand was edging close to Danny's official bedtime of eight P.M.

"Choose a good-night story," I said.

Danny shoved himself off his bed and stood in front of his overflowing bookcase. I tried to sway his decision by sending him mental vibes: *The ants and the grasshoppers. The dog and the oyster. The miller, the son, and the ass.*

"Choose Aesop," I finally said.

"I don't like Aesop," Danny said. "The stories are too short. The pictures are in black and white. And I don't get the morals."

I liked literature in which characters did something wrong and then were held accountable for their actions. The veiled warnings of Aesop—*one swallow does not make a summer, give a finger and lose a hand, act in haste and repent in leisure*—struck a deep chord in me. But Danny, like Lisa, had little patience for the poetry of right and wrong. Last Friday, when I had read to him the fable about the astrologer who fell in a mud puddle as he walked along gazing at the sky, Danny had interrupted the moral (*What use is it to read the stars when you cannot read what is right here on the earth?*) by blurting out, "The moral oughta be: *Watch where you're going, stupid.*"

"If you don't want Aesop," I said, "then choose another story. With color pictures."

I tried not to squinch up my face as Danny's fingers hovered above *The Little Engine That Could.* Just the thought of the can-do Little Engine—as well as the author's upbeat name (Watty Piper)—grated on my nerves.

"No Little Engine," I said.

"Then I want Pooh," Danny said.

I'd never been a big fan of the too-soothing ados of Winnie-the-Pooh and his girlish sidekick, Christopher Robin. I reluctantly took the book from Danny's hand and we leaned back against the pillows on his bed.

" 'Chapter One,' " I read. " 'In Which a House Is Built at Pooh Corner for Eeyore.' That's a long title." I flipped forward the pages, then glanced at the clock. "This is a long *chapter.*"

"Please, Daddy. I lost my tooth today. And there are pictures, even if they aren't in color." Danny turned a few pages and pointed to a black-and-white drawing of Eeyore (drooping ears, sad eyes, and dragging tail) getting buried beneath the falling snow. "That mule looks like you in the morning."

The resemblance *was* striking. I gave Danny a warning look, then glanced over at the digital clock on the nightstand, certain it would take me half an hour to read about this woebegone mule—donkey—ass—whatever!—who needed an even bigger dose of prunes than I did. "Eeyore needs to stop moping," I said.

"But, Daddy, he's sad. Because Pooh and Piglet took his house away." Danny inspected his pale, tiny fingers. "Daddy?"

"I'm going to start this chapter now."

"But, Daddy? There's this boy at school? Named Zachary?"

I nodded. *Five* boys at Danny's school were named Zachary.

"Zachary's parents sold their house," Danny said as he plucked a solitary pill off the sleeve of his striped pajamas. "And after they moved, his father didn't live with Zachary and his mother anymore."

I suddenly felt heartsick—and censorious—the way I always did whenever I saw weekend fathers buying their kids a second chocolate milk shake at the mall.

"That will never happen to us," I told Danny.

"Do we have to move?"

"I thought you wanted to move," I said.

"But you fight a lot—about moving—with Mommy."

"That's not true," I said—then immediately remembered that Lisa and I had bickered after dinner about dropping the price on our condominium again. "Sometimes Mommy and I have earnest discussions ... because we need to work things out. But we would never leave each other, because we love each other. I mean—" I picked up the Pooh book and shook the corner at Danny. "Just remember that."

"Remember what?" Danny said.

"Marriage is forever. When you get married ..." I tried to find some pearls of wisdom to offer Danny but could only dredge up some lame advice my own father had doled out years ago. "Choose your wife like your battles: wisely."

Danny burst into giggles. "In our new house?" he said. "I want a collie dog."

"You've made that very clear." The clock read 8:11. "Now, we're going to hear a nice story—about these very nice animals—and then you're going right to sleep."

The chapter was endless! But it was just as well. As a snowy blanket covered the Hundred Acre Wood, I felt my frayed nerves mending. The simple message of A. A. Milne (*Let the wind blow your house where it will!*) comforted me. Even Danny looked sleepy by the end. I turned off the lamp and remained seated for a moment on the edge of the bed, watching the phosphorescent stars from Danny's shine-in-the-dark astronomy kit glow overhead on the ceiling. Last fall I had climbed on a stepladder and fixed those flat plastic stars to the ceiling while Danny and Lisa called out directions from below. ("An inch to the left." "A tad to the right." "Ebb, that looks more like a soup spoon than the Little Dipper." "Daddy, make the North Star bigger than big!") I had felt as abused as a jackass that afternoon, but now, watching the shapes glimmer yellow-green in the night, I felt the glow God must have felt after hanging up the moon and the stars in the heavens.

I gave Danny a hot-breathed kiss and hug. His tiny shoulders felt warm and his hair smelled, inexplicably, like saltwater taffy. "When we move," I said, "you can take your stars with you."

"Thanks, Daddy. Good night, Daddy. I love you, Daddy." Danny's voice, pleading with me to stay longer, followed me downstairs—where I had every intention of helping Lisa with the dinner dishes. But as I turned toward the kitchen, I found Lisa cradling the cordless phone between her shoulder and her ear as she swept the floor with her worn-out broom.

"Mmm-*hmm*," Lisa said. "Oh *yes*. I *know*. I *hear* what you're saying."

I cleared my throat.

Lisa stopped sweeping and looked up at me. "I'm on the phone."

"So I see," I said, trying not to frown—because I could take an educated guess whose mild, soothing voice was on the other end of the line. Why did my secretary think *I* was the one having an affair with Cynthia Farquhar? If anyone was enamored of Cynthia, it was Lisa.

I retreated to the living room and headed for the couch—a piece of furniture I should have referenced when telling Danny that divorce was out of the question. Yes. Lisa and I had a healthy marriage. Last year we had junked our comfortable old couch and bought a new Italian leather sofa—three thousand dollars, one thousand for each damn cushion—to prove it. Three could never be split in half (although I was sure some crafty lawyer could create the illusion of fair division while grabbing the entire amount for himself). I plopped myself down on the center cushion. For three thousand dollars, I thought, the least the couch could do was not give off flatulent protests every time somebody sat on it.

I picked up the *Times* and checked the weather (a cold front—and another snowstorm—were predicted for the weekend). As I turned to the financial section to the kind of article Lisa never would deign to read—

## PLATINUM LEADS A RETREAT IN PRECIOUS METALS TRADING

—the sweeps of Lisa's broom grew slower and slower, then stopped altogether. I held the newspaper still and strained to hear Lisa's lowered voice.

"My feelings exactly." She laughed. "I swear, they are so *incompetent*—"

I cleared my throat loudly. Within a minute, Lisa was off the phone and the broom—harder, more furious—started up again. I wondered how many times Lisa would go over the same patch before she decided that some crumbs were permanently embedded in the tile.

Lisa finally retired her broom to the hall closet and came into the living room carrying her Whistler's Mother cup full of hot, fragrant Perfectly Peach tea—and the dreaded *Publishers Weekly*. I couldn't stand when Lisa read *Publishers Weekly*. She pounced upon its pages the way I always (secretly) pounced on my alumni notes, her face turning lime-green with envy as she read about whichever bestselling lady author!—got whatever huge advance payment!—that if there were any justice in the world!—which there wasn't!—rightfully should go to literati like Lisa!—if and when she ever found the time to finish writing *her* novel.

I lowered the *Times* and watched Lisa sink into the cloth chair opposite me. She propped her feet on the wooden coffee table. Her white socks, worn thin at the sole and faded gray on the bottom, sported a large hole. Her big toe poked obscenely out.

"How is Cynthia?" I asked.

"You seemed pretty eager to find out," Lisa said.

"How—by sitting here reading about plunges in platinum prices?"

"You clearly were eavesdropping on our conversation." Lisa raised her mug to her mouth and immediately put it back down on the side table. "Ow. I burned my lips. And what the hell is an *eave* anyway? You'd think I'd know, after all this house-hunting."

I rustled the pages of the business section. "Why do you have to talk about men with Cynthia?"

"How do you know we were discussing the male species?"

"Because I heard you say the word *incompetent.*"

"Har!" Lisa waggled her tongue with glee. "We were talking about plumbers. Cynthia's upstairs toilet gets clogged." Lisa watched me for a minute. "Why do you get so knocked out of shape about my talking to Cynthia? She's my friend."

"She's your agent," I said.

"But I really like her."

"Do you have to like her at a coffee shop?"

Lisa didn't answer. She pushed her foot forward on the coffee table, and a pile of women's magazines—*Vogue, Glamour, Cosmo*—slid to the floor. I gazed down at one of the screaming-meemy headlines—HOW TO GET HIM TO OPEN UP TO YOU—before I said, "I'm curious what you discuss over these cups of cappuccino—which probably cost more than a decent pair of socks."

Lisa looked down at her holey socks; I saw her big toe curl back. "I don't complain about you, if that's what you're driving at. Although Cynthia has been known to dis her ex." She laughed. "Angus Farquhar—"

"You know his name?" I asked.

"I just said it was *Angus.* But why are you looking at me like that? It's not like I said his trouser size."

"Wait a second," I said. "You know his trouser size?"

"My guess is probably thirty-six. Cynthia said he was tall but trim. With extremely rugged good looks, like he'd been left out on the heath."

"The heath?"

"He's Scottish," Lisa said. "A *real* Scot. From Scotland. Not from Staten Island. Or Tennessee."

"So where did Cynthia meet this real Scot?"

"At a convention. Of the American Realtors Association." Lisa got a faraway look in her eye, as if she were gazing back into the past and seeing the situation unfold right before her very eyes. "She met him in April. They got hitched in May. But by June, Cynthia discovered that Angus wasn't the man she had married."

"Well," I asked, "who was he, then?"

*"Somebody else."* Lisa looked at me as if I had the intelligence of a Fordhook lima bean. "Let me explain."

"Please do," I said, all the while thinking: *Please do not.*

Lisa set her Whistler's Mother cup down on the side table. "Cynthia thought Angus was totally sophisticated and cultured—but then he turned out to be the type of guy who installed a miniature telly in the w.c. so he wouldn't miss a minute of a soccer match."

"I see," I said. "What else do you know about this Angus? Besides the fact that he watched the World Cup while he pooped?"

"He has hairy shoulder blades."

"Pardon me?"

"Hairy—"

"I heard you the first time," I said.

"Then why did you act like you didn't?"

"I'm just surprised, that's all," I said. "About the specificity. Of your information."

"Oh, I know everything there is to know about Angus."

I'd been slightly curious about the man who had won Cynthia's heart. But now I was about to learn a lot more than I ever wanted to know. Lisa told me that Angus Farquhar cheated at croquet. Angus Farquhar refused to floss his teeth. Angus Farquhar slapped his ruddy cheeks when he donned his Royall Lyme aftershave, which woke Cynthia up far too early each morning. Angus Farquhar insisted that Cynthia prepare him a full English breakfast every day: fried eggs and rasher of bacon, toad in the hole, and baked beans on toast. Cynthia—who was no cook—came to resent the smell of the baked beans, never mind the stink of his Royall Lyme. And she grew to loathe the sight of Farquhar's socks, which were gray with red heels, the kind that crafts-oriented women fashioned into stuffed toy monkeys.

"Once Angus went berserk," Lisa said, "because Cynthia hadn't rolled his monkey socks into a neat round sphere—similar to a soccer ball—before she put them away in his drawers. Cynthia said she never felt better than the day she drop-kicked Farquhar's socks out the front door and out of her life."

"No doubt it felt liberating," I said. "Especially if he kept the socks and she kept the house."

Lisa clucked her tongue. "Why shouldn't Cynthia keep the house? Farquhar is a builder. He can always put up another."

A wiser guy would have changed the subject. I glanced down at the *Publishers Weekly* that hovered ominously on Lisa's lap—then, convinced Lisa had said *something* negative about me to Cynthia in exchange for all this dirt on Angus F., I foolishly plowed ahead. "You know, Lisa," I said, "secrets are traded—not given away."

"Farquhar is an *ex*. And an ex is fair conversational game." Lisa took a long sip of her tea. "I don't see why you're so fixated on what I discuss with Cynthia. I never ask what you talk about with Josh."

"Josh and I talk numbers," I said. "Not women."

"You're sure you never talk about the fair sex?"

"From time to time," I said, "we may make passing references to you and Deb."

"Ah-ha."

"But you aren't the fair sex," I said. "You're our wives."

"Very amusing." Lisa raised her Whistler's Mother mug to her mouth—and, just like Mrs. Whistler, she looked resolutely off into the distance.

"Let me rephrase that statement," I said.

"Right," Lisa said. "Make a stab at it."

"I meant that what goes on between you and me—and Josh and Deb for that matter—ought to be considered off-limits. For instance, I've never once mentioned to Josh what we're going through with the fertility doctor."

Lisa scrunched up her face. "I don't even want to talk to the *doctor* about what I'm going through with the doctor."

"Oh," I said. "So you haven't talked about that to Cynthia?"

"Are you crazy?" Lisa asked.

"You never talk about sex with—"

"Are you crazy? Men are the ones who talk down and dirty all the time."

"That's a myth. Perpetuated by women."

"Oh, go on, Ebb. Men tell filthy jokes."

"Granted, but—"

"And go to topless bars. And mess around on their wives."

"Some of them do," I said. "But some of them don't. There are plenty of decent men in the world, Lisa."

Lisa shrugged as if to say, *Show me one*. Then she yawned—as if the sight of me made her tired—and opened her *Publishers Weekly*. I snapped the financial section back open. What was the matter with Lisa? I mean, I had been on the road a lot during our marriage. Didn't she appreciate the sacrifices I had made? A lot of guys would have done *whatever*. I never once was unfaithful to her. I never *once*.

Unless you counted what I once had watched on the pay-per-movie TV in a Ramada Inn in Kansas—and the fantasies that had played out in my head ever since.

It had been an innocent mistake. After a long day of meetings, I had sat on the edge of the hotel bed to watch the evening news, but I had hit the wrong number on the remote. The TV screen had melted into a haze of purple and blue, and on the screen appeared a man and a woman. The man was fucking a woman, from behind, in front of a mirror. I didn't know what captured my imagination most—the position, the reflection in the mirror, the pistonlike rhythm of his pumping, her nipples squeezing out from between his splayed fingers, her soft moaning, his stoic silence, the way the scene seemed to unfold beyond the boundaries of time or duty or responsibility. I watched for thirty seconds. Forty seconds. I knew that after sixty seconds the fee for watching the movie would kick in and someone (like the hotel checkout clerk) would discover I had watched a skin flick. I pressed the power button on the remote control. The TV went dead with a thunk.

I had sat there for a long time on the hotel bed, looking at the arrows on the remote control, which seemed to lead in all four directions at once—north, south, east, and west. It was 6:30 in the evening in Lawrence, Kansas, and I wanted to keep on watching. To shame myself out of it, I thought, But what would my mother think? What would my father? I was a married man. I had a child. And yet ... and yet ... I wanted (no, absolutely *needed*) something strange and shocking in my life. Watching wouldn't hurt anyone. Nor would it count as infidelity, because all of the adulterous action was being carried out by someone else—even if I did become, in my imagination, the man fucking the woman in front of the mirror, I was only him *inside my head*.

I was just about to press my thumb back on the power button when the phone rang. It was Lisa calling, "Hey, Ebb, what's up? Hold on for Danny!" Danny's tiny voice breathing, "Hi, Daddy! What are you doing, Daddy? *I'm* going to sleep now, Daddy!" filled me with shame. After I got off the phone, I had not turned on the TV again.

Yet the image of the man and the woman in the mirror stayed with me. And more and more over the past few months—when I felt myself growing as lonely as Lawrence, Kansas, in my own bedroom—I had thought back on those forbidden fifty-nine seconds, playing and replaying them inside myself. What could I say to excuse this fascination—except, maybe, that I had grown weary of following the doctor's orders to make love with Lisa in the missionary position only? I craved something different. I longed to give it to Lisa in front of a mirror (but somehow I had grown too shy to ask Lisa for it, as if admitting I wanted something out of the ordinary implied that what we did on a regular basis had ceased to satisfy me).

Sometimes I wondered, too, what Lisa wanted that I failed to give her. But only just now—as I stared at her raggedy-socked feet propped on the coffee table—did it hit me how I truly had let her down. Once, not too long ago, Lisa had ventured to ask me if I wanted something different in bed, and the question had so surprised me, so embarrassed me, that I had not answered truthfully, nor had I realized what she really was asking from me: *Please, please, ask me that same question back.*

# CHAPTER NINE

## LISA

**Ebb's comment**—"You aren't the fair sex"—rankled me even more than the most gruesome news reported in the "Hot Deals" column of *Publishers Weekly* (where every other author except me, seemingly, had received a publishing contract worth *a healthy six figures*). I knew that after a certain point in marriage, a husband naturally viewed his wife as less of a woman—after all, wasn't that the underlying premise of *I'm Sorry*? Yet the material that made for credible fiction wasn't exactly the same material I wanted to find cropping up in my own life. I took another sip of my now-tepid peach tea, trying hard not to listen to my negative inner voice, which said, *You are fat. You are ugly. You are bloated. You are infertile. You are unfeminine. If Ebb weren't so bound by duty, he would leave you. And if you weren't so financially dependent on him, you probably would do a little walking too (at least down to the local Dunkin' Donuts—and back).*

The thought that Ebb and I might end up as yet another statistic was so unsettling—and so unsavory—that I felt my dinner back up in my throat. The heat hummed on, the registers along the floor began to shudder, and the newspaper that Ebb held open began to ruffle against his lap. Ebb finished reading the last page, lowered the section, and immediately leaned forward to put all the sections of the *Times* back in their proper order. Ebb's methodical-ness would have maddened me if I hadn't found it comforting. *This is not the sort of man,* I thought, *who would ever throw a couple of BVDs into a duffel bag and then bolt for Tahiti.*

"I'm going to give you my novel," I impulsively announced. "For your birthday."

This news caught Ebb so off guard that he placed the financial section before the weekend section. "Well, that's a nice surprise," he said.

"I know how much you want to read it," I said. "So I've decided to lead you out of temptation."

"What temptation?"

"I heard that wild eep before dinner."

Ebb cleared his throat. "I happened to be standing next to your desk when I took off my suit, and my jacket sleeve brushed against your computer."

"A not-so-likely story." I smiled. "At least in my book."

"What *is* in your book?" Ebb asked.

"Oh," I said, "all sorts of bad-boy behavior. Lies. Subterfuge. Lust."

"Lust," Ebb repeated, as if he had never heard the word before. He looked down at the *Times,* realized the sections were out of order, and immediately began to *rectify the situation.* "I take it this lusty main character of yours—who is in possession of a penis, you said?"

"That's right."

"Sticks it somewhere where it's not supposed to go?"

I shook my head. "Sorry to disappoint you. But no."

Ebb was quiet for a moment—probably trying to figure out how else a lusty man could express his bad-boy-ness. Was my main character a gambler? A drunkard? Or simply he who failed to call his mother every Saturday night? I watched with mild fascination as Ebb (who ordinarily couldn't be bothered matching two socks that came out of the dryer) turned the *Times* into a bundle so tight it may as well have been executed by the number-one employee of a Chinese laundry.

"It must have been hard for you," he said. "To write about a man."

I wanted to claim that it had been a piece of cake. But it hadn't. The more I had written, the more I worried that I was painting Simon's emotional landscape in a female palette—the blue and bruised purples of loneliness and self-doubt, the washed-out grays of depression.

"I did struggle," I said as I put my Whistler's Mother mug down on the side table. "During certain scenes."

Ebb waited. Then he said, "Which?"

I searched inside myself for the scene from *I'm Sorry* that seemed least likely to resemble a chapter from Ebb's own life. "In the fifth chapter," I said, "the guy wants to go—but then he decides not to go—to a gentleman's club."

"Why doesn't he go?"

"Because he feels guilty," I said. "Leaving his wife."

"For another woman?"

"Leaving her *at home*. Where—ironically—she rents porn movies. Because she gets lonely. While he travels on business."

Ebb propped his feet on the coffee table. Then he swallowed, as if my words were remnants of the cucumber that had caused him such heartburn after dinner. I bit my lip and wondered how much his chest would hurt when he read the scene in *I'm Sorry* in which Simon Stern comes back from a business trip to Atlanta on Friday evening and discovers that his wife has left a soft-porn video sitting in the VCR: *Simon felt so embarrassed for Robin—as if he had caught her touching herself at night, or murmuring the name of another man in bed—that he had slipped* Tricks for Chicks *back into the VCR and pretended he never had found it. And for the rest of the weekend, he was careful to avert his eyes when she slipped off her blouse before bed or even asked at the dinner table, "More asparagus?"*

"Is that autobiographical?" Ebb asked.

"The loneliness?"

"The blue movie."

I shrugged. "I did rent a video once. Strictly for research."

"I see."

"You were out of town," I said. "In Charlotte or Richmond or one of those Southern cities. And so I drove ten miles to that independent video store on Route 9 and I rented exactly the kind of movie that I imagined Robin would want to watch."

Ebb looked baffled for a second. "Who's Robin?"

"That's the name of the wife in my novel."

Ebb paused. "Robin is a man's name."

"It is not," I said.

"In *Winnie-the-Pooh*—"

"What does Pooh have to do with it?"

"I'm saying that in England—"

"*My* story takes place in the United States."

"And in Batman comic books—"

"*My* story isn't written for the Batman audience," I said. "It is aimed at literate readers."

"That's redundant, Lisar."

"So what!"

Ebb pushed up his glasses. Then he looked away from me to stare at the mantel—where most people we knew displayed eight-by-ten wedding portraits. We, however, displayed only a pair of candlesticks holding tapers that had melted practically down to the wick.

"Is there a particular reason," he asked, "why we can't have a calm conversation about your novel?"

"I can give you two," I said. "You and me."

"But I'm interested in your work, Lisar. Just like you're interested in mine. Every night you ask me what went on at SB—"

"I'm bored out of my skull," I said, "being home all day. I crave news from the outside world."

"Which I deliver," Ebb said. "In great detail. In spite of my sneaking suspicion that you are borrowing my problems for your novel."

"Why would I want your problems," I said, "when I'm already schlepping around enough of my own—plus all the burdens of the people I make up?"

"Those are imaginary."

"They feel real enough to me," I said. "I mean, bad enough I have to mop my own floor, never mind Simon's."

"Who's Simon?"

I bit my lip. "My main character."

"He of the penis?"

"That's correct," I said.

Ebb pondered this. "Simon as in Simon and Garfunkel?"

"No, as in Alvin and the Chipmunks."

"I am—justifiably—confused."

"Simon is my hero's first name," I said. "Like that chipmunk in the cartoon who wore those big nerdball glasses."

"Theodore was the chipmunk who wore glasses, Lisar."

"I'm positive it was Simon."

"I'm positive it was Theo—" Ebb pushed up his own glasses. "Exactly what kind of glasses does your Simon wear?"

"Color-enhanced contact lenses," I said.

"Oh. Is he gay?"

"No, he definitely likes women."

"But no straight man would—"

"He wears them because he wants to be someone—or something—he isn't."

Ebb cleared his throat. "What's Simon's last name?"

"Stern."

"That means *star* in German."

"That has already been pointed out to me."

"By who?"

"My internal editor," I said.

"Maybe I could point out—"

"Please do not point anything else out."

"—that the name Robin—"

"What's your beef with that name?" I asked.

"It rhymes with mine! Robin, Eben. Not to mention Simon."

I hadn't even thought of that. But I wasn't so thoughtless of myself that I would freely admit to being thoughtless of others. So I said, "Nobody but Cynthia ever calls you Eben. I call you Ebb, and Victoria calls you Mister, and everyone else at work calls you Strauss."

Ebb raised himself up from the couch cushion, reached into his back pocket, pulled out his handkerchief, and began cleaning the lenses of his glasses. "How long has this Simon been married to this Robin when she rents this infamous video?"

"Five years."

Ebb brought his glasses up to his mouth and blew a speck of dust off the right lens. Then he resumed cleaning the lens with his handkerchief. "Care to describe it?"

"Their marriage?"

"The blue movie."

"The one I put in my novel," I asked, "or the one I really rented?"

"I suspect the two are pretty similar, am I right?"

Ebb was thoroughly on the money. "In my novel," I said, "Robin rents a soft-porn flick for the female audience called *Tricks for Chicks*."

"And yours was called?"

Oh! I had blushed redder than a Rome apple when the clerk handed the video over the counter and loudly announced, "*Wild Women Wanna* is due back before noon on Tuesday."

"The exact title," I told Ebb, "escapes me."

"But you remember the plot."

"Ludicrous as it may have been."

Ebb put his glasses back on. "Tell it to me."

Usually I found it hard to boil stories down to their bare bones. But the blue movie had been so spectacularly stupid—one hundred times worse than anything I myself could and did write—that I relished summarizing it for Ebb, as it seemed to prove that *I'm Sorry This Is My Life* was not pornography but high art.

"In episode one," I said, "—there were three episodes in the movie altogether—you meet a helpless housewife and her well-meaning but nebbish husband. She pushes a vacuum, he pushes paper. She wears an apron, he wears a tie—that sort of thing. The problem is the wife really wants to be a ballet dancer, so she gets shown pirouetting with her dust cloth and leaping around with her mop. And the husband really wants to do something manly, like work in the great outdoors as a carpenter-slash-handyman, so he gets shown at the office acting like his stapler is a chain saw and his pager is a big wrench."

Ebb laughed. Albeit uneasily. "What about their sex life?"

"Dullsville," I said. "So one day the husband and wife decide to do something different. He dresses up as a plumber and goes home—in the middle of the afternoon, before the school bus lets the kids off, of course—and knocks on the door. Wielding the aforementioned wrench. Wifey answers—wearing just a scanty white towel that she clutches at her breast." I lowered my voice to imitate the male actor in *Wild Women Wanna*. " 'I'm here to fix your drain, lady,' the husband says. As she lets the towel slip down a bit, the wife says, 'You must have the wrong house.' Says he: 'Nope, your husband called me just this morning. He said you got a clogged drain. Mind if I take a look?' The wife purses her lips. 'Well,' says she, 'if my husband insists—' "

I paused, for dramatic effect. "So the wife leads the husband into the bathroom. She drops the towel. He drops the wrench. Then he puts her up on the counter and fucks her like a stranger."

Ebb's toes—propped up on the coffee table—went stiff with disapproval. "I don't follow," he finally said. "The logic. Of that last statement."

I thought for a moment. *He fucks her like a stranger.* Had I meant: *He fucks her as if she were a stranger* or *He fucks her and she pretends he's a stranger* or *In the process of fucking, each pretends he or she is a stranger to the other?*

"Why do you have to function as an editor," I asked Ebb, "every time I open my mouth?"

"I just wanted clarification." Ebb paused. "So what was in episode two?"

"It involved Jell-O."

"And episode three?"

"I don't know," I said crossly. "I got bored and went to sleep and had a dream that was much more imaginative than anything I saw on the screen."

"No doubt," Ebb said with enough bite in his voice to make me fear that he knew—but how could he possibly even *guess?*—that guerrillas and matadors populated my dreams. "So I guess you—or, rather, this Robin of yours—was turned on by this blue movie?"

I shrugged. "*Robin* thought the story had its moments."

The second I stopped talking—and took a breath of fresh air, which carried some oxygen to my brain—my self-esteem took a mighty plunge. Suddenly the plot of *I'm Sorry*—not my farcical dreams or that asinine blue movie!—seemed limp at best. So once 'upon a time there were a husband and a wife who weren't happy with each other—hadn't that story been told a thousand times already, not only in literature but millions of times in real life? Did the world really need one more version of the unfulfilled housewife and the equally unfulfilled company man who woke up one morning and realized that this was not the right way to live their lives?

"Oh," I blurted out at Ebb. "I don't know!"

"Know what?"

"Why I've spent all these years trying to write a story that was meaningful, when it all just came out as cheap and simplistic as *Wild Women Wanna*—"

"Lisar! You rented a movie called *Wild Women Wanna?*"

I nodded.

Ebb waggled his finger at me.

So I said, "Stop waggling your finger at me!"

"Tell me truthfully," he said. "Right now. What is your novel about?"

"Oh, for the thousandth time, the story's not—really!—about us. We're not interesting material. You're a *suit*. And I'm a housewife. And our lives are boring."

The minute my words hit the air—and hovered there, like blinking fireflies—I wanted to reach out and pluck them back. Clearly what I'd said had hurt Ebb's feelings. He hesitated only a second before he said, "Well. I'm sorry I don't own a wrench."

I leaned over, lifted my mug, and looked at Whistler's Mother—actually envious of this shriveled old woman who sat stone deaf and dumb in her solitary rocking chair, with no worries about how harmful words could be. What was the matter with me, telling Ebb our life together was boring, when it was anything but—fraught as it was with awful moments like this, when we said (or didn't say) things that later we were bound to regret? I considered going over to Ebb, plopping my butt down next to his on the couch, and throwing my arms around him. *Why would I want some dumb hunk with a wrench,* I would say, *when I have an nice Ebbish hunk like you already by my side?*

But Ebb never gave me a chance. He looked really tired—God, when had he gotten all that gray hair near his ears, overnight?— when he asked, "How close are you to finishing your novel?"

"I'm done," I said. "Or at least I thought I was, until I talked this morning to my agent."

"You have an agent?"

While Ebb watched me—puzzled—I got up from the chair, put aside my current issue of *Publishers Weekly,* and disappeared into the half-bathroom, where from the stack of waterlogged magazines on the back of the toilet tank I fetched the year-old issue that featured the article on Aye-Aye. I went back into the living room, stood over Ebb, and opened *Publishers Weekly*—and to Ebb's obvious dismay, a handsome color photo with this caption—*Twenty-nine-year-old Ifor "I. I." Iforson*—stared him right in the face.

## CHAPTER TEN

# EBEN

**I reached forward** and took *Publishers Weekly* from Lisa's hands. The photograph showed a handsome young man leaning back in an old-fashioned wooden desk chair, his huge booted feet propped on a paper-strewn table, and his large hands folded on top of his head. His long blond hair, full as a palomino's mane, grazed the broad shoulders of his button-down shirt, which was tinted a pale, Key-lime-pie green.

"I'm assuming *he* knows how to spell *fjord,*" I told Lisa.

Lisa's face blushed red. "Don't be so bitchy, Ebb." She sat back down in her chair. "Ifor is the big time. He handles only a very select group of writers."

"Why do you want to be handled?"

"Because I want my novel to get group-groped. By the reading public."

I repositioned my glasses on my nose. "Lisa. *Morals.* Where are yours?"

Lisa shrugged. "In the toilet bowl. I figure I can fish 'em out after I deposit my very hefty advance in the bank."

"What makes you so sure this Ifor character is going to get you that kind of money?"

"Because he gets it for everybody." Lisa leaned back in her chair and ran through Ifor's client list, which included a writer whose lurid thrillers were hawked at airport newsstands and his female counterpart, a romance novelist always pictured (in posters at those same newsstands) wearing a mink stole and holding a passel of angora cats.

"Can't you keep better company than that?" I asked.

Lisa sniffed. "Tolstoy is dead."

I gazed down at Lisa's handsome Norwegian. No man, I felt, had the right to be twenty-nine. Or have so much hair. Or such large hands. Or be so healthy-looking!

"He's too young," I said.

"That's the way I want him. Young and hungry."

"His shirt lacks a collar," I pointed out.

Lisa leaned over and took the magazine from my hands. "That's called *banded*."

"How does he expect to be taken seriously if he's not wearing a tie?"

"He's in an artistic profession, Mr. Anti-Dress-Down-Friday."

I leaned back on the couch and the cushion let off a gassy sigh. "How did you meet him?"

"I haven't. Yet. We've just talked on the phone. But we plan on doing lunch."

"When?"

"Sometime soon."

Lisa's vagueness made my imagination boil—like water in a samovar set over a very high flame. I pictured some scrumptious curry served in a dim Lower East Side basement, where the turbaned waiters didn't look women in the eye and all the music sounded like Ravi Shankar's wailing sitar on *The Concert for Bangla Desh*. Lisa and Ifor greeted each other with an air kiss. No, *two* air kisses. Ifor helped Lisa off with her coat! And pulled out Lisa's chair! She sighed with pleasure as she lowered her butt onto the sequined cushion.

*Do you mind?* Ifor growled, as he pulled some sort of rough Scandinavian cigarette from his Key-lime-pie shirt pocket.

*Secondhand smoke?* Lisa reassured him. *I love it, I love it.*

Ifor lit up. *So tell me about this novel of yours.*

After Lisa waxed on about how her Batman- and Chipmunk-inspired characters fucked each other like strangers, Ifor blew a cloud of smoke in Lisa's face, flicked his mane, and loudly pronounced for the benefit of the literati and fashionistas sitting six crowded tables away: *We'll see what New York has to say about that!* as if Manhattan were one big bruising urban mouth.

DON'T EVEN *THINK* ABOUT PARKING HERE! were the kindest words those metropolitan lips had uttered to me on my last visit into the city.

"I don't want you driving into New York," I told Lisa.

She impatiently wiggled her big toe. "I'll take the train."

I counted to nine and a half before I told Lisa, "We haven't gone into the city together in a long time."

Silence.

"I could probably rearrange my calendar," I said. "And come along with you at this lunch. For moral support."

"A chaperon won't be necessary." Lisa leaned forward and retrieved *Publishers Weekly* from my hands. "You know, Ebb, I don't even want to go into New York. I don't want to lunch with Ifor. I swear I just want to make like Thoreau and move into a log cabin."

"You wouldn't last two seconds in a log cabin," I said, "even if it had a flushing toilet."

"All right, a sweet little cottage in Nantucket—without a phone. And every afternoon I'd take a long walk on the beach after spending the morning writing the kind of novel that ... that ... that women refuse to put down when their husbands climb into bed!"

"Noble ambition, Lisa."

Lisa looked down at the picture of Ifor and her bottom lip quivered. "Ebb: Come kiss me?"

I grunted and picked up a book on retirement planning from the coffee table—which I had been reading, two pages at a time, over the past three weeks. "Wait until I finish this chapter."

After Lisa and I squabbled about Ifor, I congratulated myself for every five minutes I continued to read my book (thus resisting the urge to peruse my alumni notes). Lisa was not so virtuous. She re-opened her current issue of *Publishers Weekly,* and like a frog I once had seen in the Catskills that had swallowed too many fireflies, she became almost phosphorescent with jealousy before she even passed the table of contents. With each turn of the page, she released a tiny sound—a sigh, a hiss—that voiced her enormous discontent.

"If you cluck your tongue one more time," I finally told her, "I'm going to cancel your subscription."

"You said that last week. And the week before."

"Why *does* that magazine have to come out on a weekly basis?"

"Because publishing is a volatile industry," Lisa said. "Every week some media giant comes in and eats up this or that small publisher."

"Sounds like the situation at SB."

Lisa tossed *PW* onto the coffee table. "You got your B School Brag Rag today."

"I saw."

"I noticed—in the alumni notes—that you didn't report your promotion."

"I forgot," I said.

"But, Ebb—why don't you brag? You're the executive VP. Practically the *top.*"

"If I'm the top," I told Lisa, "then why did I spend the majority of my day dealing with ladies' *bottoms*? And why do I come home every night feeling like nothing more than a highly overpaid human-resources director?"

Lisa looked down at her holey socks with guilt, as if she were the one who had intellectually demoted me. I leaned my head back on the sofa and stared at the dark Rothko-like square in the center of our long-unused fireplace. Why *had* Lisa looked at my alumni notes? To compare me with other men? Did she think—the way I was starting to think—that even though I had all the outward trappings of success, inside I really was a failure?

"It's late," I finally said.

"Yes, and somebody has to clean the kitchen."

An educated man knew that *somebody* was singular. But an even wiser guy knew that, from Lisa's perspective, somebody meant *we* and not just *me*.

I sighed and followed Lisa into the kitchen, which bore all the evidence of our messy dinner. Spaghetti strands still clung to the plates. The remains of lettuce and tomatoes and Lisa's infamous cucumber slices wilted in the salad bowl.

"Glass of wine?" I asked.

"I'm not supposed to be drinking, remember?"

I could have sworn I had tasted wine on Lisa's tongue when I kissed her earlier. But maybe she'd had just a sip of the jug wine she always added to the tomato sauce.

"I guess half a glass of wine won't do you any harm," I said.

"Three quarters probably wouldn't either."

"Compromise at two-thirds?"

Lisa nodded. "Sold."

I fetched a bottle of chardonnay lying on the bottom shelf of the refrigerator. Lisa pulled down a couple of goblets from the cabinet, frowning at the water stains marring the rims. After I uncorked the bottle and poured the wine, I raised my glass and told Lisa, "To ... um ... *us*."

"Right. You and me. And the dirty dishes."

I smiled. "Cheers."

"*Salute,* Ebb."

Lisa downed most of her wine, then tossed me a sponge. I caught it by the soggy tip, and while she started loading the plates and silverware into the dishwasher, I scrubbed the splotches of spaghetti sauce from the stove and counter. After a little wine came a little flirtation—a few deliberate brushes against Lisa's butt, some slightly heavier breathing as I reached around her to fetch a paper towel at the sink. I maintained a monk's silence to make it clear that now was not the time to speak of Danny's bad table manners, the need for a new water heater, the latest listings from Century 21—or the strict moratorium I wanted to place on BAD BOY and/or other candy conversation hearts appearing in my undershorts.

More wine, more silent flirtation.

Then I came up behind Lisa as she scoured the colander in the sink. I grazed the back of her hair with my lips and nose. I cupped her shoulder in my left hand and looped my right index finger through the apron tie that circled her waist. I pressed slightly on her hips. She relaxed. Sighed. Said "Mmm." More pressure. "Ah."

So I did it. I put my left arm around Lisa and my other hand went under her apron and I *growled*—yes, I growled like a large wildcat (as it to prove that there were all sorts of pathetic things you had to do and say to achieve arousal when you were middle-aged).

"*Such* a fuck," I said, "I'm going to give you."

And when Lisa laughed and answered in a breathy voice, "Is that right?" I heard even heavier breathing behind us. I turned. Danny stood in the doorway—forlorn and diminutive in his striped yellow-and-black pjs, which made him resemble a bee coming in for the sting. I pulled away.

"You go back to bed," Lisa said in a sharp tone that punctured my desire.

Danny's face scrunched up, the way it used to when he was six months old and he discovered mashed peas were on the menu. Tears followed, so big and sorrowful that Lisa immediately went down on her knees and scooped up Danny in her arms.

"There's a Tigger in my room!" he said.

"Tiger," I said, regretting—again—that he had chosen Pooh over Aesop.

"I seen it!"

"Saw it," I corrected him.

"In the *meer*!"

"Mir-*ruh*," I said.

"It had stripes!"

Five minutes later—after a thorough investigation of Danny's room—Lisa finally convinced Danny that he had seen only his own yellow-and-black striped self in the dresser mirror. To keep the peace, I unscrewed the mirror from its wooden posts and put it in Danny's closet, and when that didn't do the trick—now Danny thought the tiger was in his wardrobe—I marched across the hall and propped the mirror against my chest of drawers, with enough carelessness to risk cracking the thing and bringing on seven years of bad luck.

Then I noticed how the mirror reflected the fax machine—and

the tangle of sheets at the bottom of our bed. I stepped back and considered the view. *Not bad,* I thought. I adjusted the angle of the mirror to reflect the rumpled middle of the mattress. *Even better.* Now if I could just get Lisa to fall beneath me on the opposite side of the bed (before she turned off the light), my fantasy of making it in front of a mirror would be complete.

I returned to the kitchen, whistling. I finished off the rest of my glass of wine and poured another. Surely there was some delicate way to reenter the scenario I had begun with Lisa. *(Now, where were we? Here? Here? Or there?)* But when Lisa finally came back downstairs, the lock of hair at her forehead was frazzled and stood on end, and the look she gave me seemed to say, *For Christ's sake, the least you could have done was finish the dishes.*

Now the wise-and-shine rooster clock read long after midnight. I lay naked next to an also-naked Lisa, listening to Danny snoring like king of the universe across the hall. Half an hour before, Lisa and I had made love . . . well, not at all badly, if you ignored one minor glitch. Leaving on the lamp, I had managed to gently pin Lisa in exactly the right place on the bed, but when I looked up, I realized all my plotting had gone for naught: I couldn't see a damn thing in the mirror because I had taken off my glasses. The only reflection I caught was the fleshy blur of our bodies, until the pleasure grew so intense I had to shut my eyes. Then a sheet of pale blue and silver stars fell like snowflakes behind the curtain of my eyelids.

Afterward, I switched off the lamp and we lay in the dark listening to the wind scatter the dead leaves across the roof.

"Ebb," Lisa finally whispered.

"What?"

"I about *plotzed.*"

I smiled. "Me, too, Lisa."

She put her hands on both sides of my head and kissed my cheek. "Listen—I forgot—but will you come look at a house with me and Cynthia tomorrow? In the afternoon?"

"Sure," I said. "Whatever you want."

Within minutes, Lisa fell deep into her usual purring, postcoital sleep—and I found myself staring at the black rectangle of the skylight, waiting for the sandman to sprinkle his dust over me. But by 12:48, sleep had made no welcoming overtures. I listened to the low, guttural snorts coming from across the hall. During the first week of Danny's life I had discovered I was the kind of dad who was convinced my child was singled out for Sudden Infant Death Syndrome. Each time I had approached Danny's bassinet, I had prayed that I would find the bundle inside warm and breathing, not stiff and still as the body of a possum tossed by a car to the side of the road. Now I reminded myself that every whistle and snuffle coming from Danny's room was a blessing. *He's alive,* I told myself. *He's alive!* Yet I still had this crazy fear that my child might die at any moment, a fear that grew more intense the longer Lisa and I continued to prove that we lacked something between us—a healthy sperm or viable egg, the timing, the love—that would enable us to conceive another.

I rolled out of bed, groped for my bathrobe, and felt my way downstairs. On the dark and chilly first floor, the Frigidaire droned. Everywhere shone tiny points of green and red light—the digital clock on the VCR, the answering machine, the smoke detector, the battery recharger on the cordless phone. My eye then caught the green eye of the security system's keypad, which shined and winked by the front door. In the center also glowed a red button labeled PANIC!, which you were supposed to hit if you were ever taken hostage in your own home.

Why did I have the urge to press my thumb upon it?

A gust of wind shook the sliding glass door and made the walls creak and pop. I poured myself a touch more wine—which glowed in the goblet—then went into the living room and switched on the three-way lamp to fifty watts only. I sat on the couch, and my feet, which I propped on the coffee table, pushed aside the *Times* and *Publishers Weekly* to reveal the edge of a library book with a call number in the 700s. The seductive red spine was stamped with a strange title: *Feng Shui.*

I turned it over. In black bullet points, the back cover asked:

Do you feel
* your house is claustrophobic?
* you cannot win the war against household dirt and excessive clutter?
* you bring home problems from the office?
* you'd rather not be in the same room as other members of your family?
* you cannot control what happens between your own four walls?
* that if only you lived somewhere else, you'd be happy?

Dust, muddy footprints, and marital and professional woes will follow you wherever you go. Do not fight your fate—but deflect it with the ancient Chinese art of restoring the balance and order in your home. Feng shui can help you create a harmonious atmosphere where your inner light shines and the essence of All collects. Through careful design of your interior and exterior landscape, you can find the ch'i in your home.

I flipped through the pages, examining the photographs of serene interiors. Then I skimmed the first chapter. By the time I read the phrase *the serenity you create without creates the serenity within,* I managed to convince myself that Lisa—who never had expressed an interest in things Asian beyond the wise-and-shine alarm clock—was using this book as material for her novel. But what if she wasn't? What if Lisa felt as dissatisfied at home (and with her job of keeping the home) as I felt with my work at SB?

My stomach rumbled.

Ordinarily I might have sympathized with ancient Taoist wisdom and acknowledged that I, too, wished to facilitate a smoother flow of the life force known as *ch'i.* But at one o'clock in the morning—a desperate glass of wine in my hand, my feet propped on a pile of three-day-old newspapers, and the sharp edge of one of Danny's Lego deep-sea divers piercing my thigh—I found the concepts of order and balance about as obtainable as the stars. Restless, I rose from the couch cushion. As I wandered into the dining room nursing my drink, I felt those alumni notes—no, I would not read those alumni notes!—drawing me like a magnet.

Our bedroom felt hot and stuffy when I finally went back upstairs. I dropped my robe to the floor and climbed back into bed
next to Lisa's inert form. Just as I was falling down into sleep, a
muscle spasm grabbed my calf. I winced and sat up with a start, remembering that I had forgotten to fetch Danny's lost tooth and slip
a dollar under his pillow. I massaged the charley horse out of my
leg, rose once more, and stumbled over to fetch my wallet from my
chest of drawers. The room was pitch-black—no moonlight came
through the skylight—and it was difficult to tell the denomination
of the bills in the dark.

I pulled out a bill from the front of my wallet where I kept the
ones and took it across the hall. Danny gave a hot snort as I slipped
the bill beneath his pillow and collected his tooth in return. I wondered what I should do with his tooth. To save it as a souvenir
seemed sick. But it seemed callous to put it in the trash, and worse
still to flush it down the toilet. I took the tooth across the hall,
shoved it under my own pillow, and resumed my place by the still-
sleeping Lisa. Like the princess who could not sleep on a pea, I
tossed from side to side. The tooth was unnerving me. My back felt
sore. My head ached from the wine. And my stomach longed for
something.

Half an hour later, I stood at the kitchen counter, eating a sandwich that consisted solely of Grey Poupon smeared on two slabs of
rye. The clock on the range read 2:12 A.M. In spite of the ungodly
hour, I retired to the half-bathroom and spent an unsuccessful
thirty minutes on the throne, reading those blasted alumni notes
from cover to cover—confirming that while I spent the day listening to women whine about toilets, my cohorts were walloping the
pants off Wall Street.

SATURDAY, MARCH 21, 1992

## CHAPTER ELEVEN

# EBEN

**In the pale blue light** of morning, I woke and found myself pinned to the mattress. Was it Lisa—or a succubus? I cracked an eyelid. Danny's hot little face was in my face. He gave me a gap-toothed smile. Crumpled in one fist was the bill I had slipped beneath his pillow the night before.

"Ouch," I whispered, as Danny's sharp elbow caught me in the chest. "Move over. Shh. You'll wake up Mommy."

"Mommy's already awake," Lisa said, in a cross voice. She poked her head out from the covers and squinted at the Mr. Chanticleer clock. "Seven-thirty!" she said, and let out a crow of protest. "Danny, didn't I tell you last night not to bother us until eight?"

Danny crawled onto Lisa. "Look what I got from the tooth fairy."

Lisa took the bill. "Ten dollars?"

I winced.

"That fairy needs new glasses," Lisa said.

"It was dark," I said.

Lisa nudged me with her toe. "Shh. Ow. Danny, get *offa* me—"

Danny rolled off Lisa, knocked into my shoulder, then dived between us under the covers. "Hey," he said. "You guys are naked!"

What could I say to explain what I did next? I must have resented (more than I knew) the way that Danny kept coming between Lisa and me, because I sat up, put on my glasses, grabbed Danny by the waist of his bumblebee-striped pajamas, set him down on the carpet, and marched him across the hall. "How many times do I have to tell you not to come in our room without knocking?" I asked. "Stay here until I tell you to come out."

I exited Danny's room with as much dignity as having a bare butt in a cold house would allow. When I firmly shut our bedroom door against the sound of Danny's protests—first a sad coyote's howl, and then melodramatic sobs meant to wrench my heart—Lisa's mouth thankfully was full of her basal body thermometer, which precluded any comment.

"I'm sorry," I said as I climbed back into bed. "But he pissed me off."

She nodded and scooted closer. I sighed and gave her hand a squeeze. Nothing better strengthened the bond between Lisa and me than a united front against Danny—unless it was sex or illness. Sometimes this troubled me. Marriage, I felt, should have a deeper and more spiritual dimension that didn't rely upon screaming orgasms, projectile vomiting, or two voices in unison commanding a toddler, "No broccoli, then no dessert!" as a measure of success.

Still, I knew I had lost my cool. Overreacted. I took off my glasses—as if this would make me deaf instead of half-blind—and then buried one ear in the pillow to muffle the sad sounds of Danny's distress.

Lisa slipped the thermometer from her mouth. "You've never made him cry like that before, Ebb."

"I know."

"He'll never forget this."

My heart felt sick at the thought. But I said, "Good. Maybe next time he'll remember to knock before he barges in."

"We should put a lock on the bedroom door," Lisa said.

"I don't want a lock," I said. "I want him to learn a closed door is a closed door."

"*Was* it closed?"

"Of course it was closed—we made love last night." Then I remembered I hadn't reshut the door after I performed my duties as the tooth fairy—nor had I closed it when I came back upstairs after reading my alumni notes from start to finish.

Lisa carefully returned her thermometer to its pink plastic case. "Can you stop by the hardware store this morning?"

"I don't have time," I said. "I'm going over the taxes with Josh at ten. And didn't Dr. Goode tell you to keep that thermometer in for a full five minutes?"

Lisa let forth a scornful *poof!* "I can't breathe—never mind talk to you—with that thing in my mouth."

"What's your temperature?"

"Still too low, Dr. Goode's a jerk, and there's a True Value in the mini-mall right by Josh's office. Stop there and get a lock."

"I don't like that hardware store," I said. "A *cowbell* rings when you open the front door."

"Beats fighting off the crowds at the House Warehouse," Lisa said. I had to agree: Last time I set foot in House Warehouse, I had almost gotten brained by a guy swinging around a pair of plantation shutters as he asked his dissatisfied wife, "Make up your mind, you want 'em in the white or the almond?"

Lisa picked up the pen she kept on her nightstand and leaned over to record her temperature. "This ovulation graph is so embarrassing."

"It's just your body temperature," I said.

"It is not. I have to draw a circle around the days that we fuck! And then I have to show the chart to Dr. Goode, while he stands there clearing the snot and the phlegm in his throat and murmuring, 'I see, yes, I see.' *What* does he see?"

I didn't care to contemplate. It galled me to realize that Dr. Goode had discovered (long before I did) that Lisa and I had an established pattern of letting ourselves go on Friday nights.

Lisa tossed her graph and pen onto the nightstand. "Don't forget Cynthia's got us on her calendar for two o'clock. She says she's got a great house to show us."

"Did you preview it?"

"I didn't have time. It's a brand-new listing. Cynthia's going to pick you up here around one forty-five and I'm meeting you at the house at two."

"Why can't we go together?"

"I have to drive Danny across town to a birthday party."

"Why can't he make friends in the immediate neighborhood?" I asked. It seemed like the only children Danny chose as buddies always lived at least fifteen miles away (and always scheduled their birthday parties in the most squalid weather conditions).

"Just remember that after we look at this house," Lisa said, "you have to pick up Danny from his party."

"Why?"

"I told you at dinner last night," Lisa said.

"Refresh my memory."

"I'm seeing this new hairstylist."

"Can't you go on a weekday?" I asked.

"His name is *Ricardo*."

"That answers the question?"

"You have to wait *weeks* to get an appointment," Lisa said. "The only reason I got in was because Cynthia arranged it. God, Cynthia has great hair. So you absolutely have to pick up Danny, so my hair can look just as great."

I closed my eyes. Whenever I thanked God it was Friday, I never stopped to think that the next dawn of the sun brought dreaded Saturday. What was supposed to be a joyous time to reconnect with my family turned into a day of loathsome errands. But at least I wasn't on call for the weekend and forced to run all those errands while wearing the SB pager. I rolled out of bed, put on my glasses, donned my flannel bathrobe, and went across the hall to readdress the Danny situation.

I knocked. "May I come in?" I asked. When no answer was forthcoming, I violated my own rule and entered Danny's room without permission. Danny was nothing more than a lump hiding beneath the blankets. I sat down on the mattress, pulled back the cover, and smoothed the tuft of hair at the back of his head that always cropped up during the night, making him look like a woodpecker.

"I'm sorry," I said. "I know we didn't have the door closed."

In the silence that followed, I feared Danny would ask, *Why do you always close it?* I couldn't bear the thought of trying to explain the facts of life to him before I had my first cup of coffee. In fact, I couldn't fathom having such a discussion before Danny lost every single one of his baby teeth. Yet Danny almost forced me into The Conversation by saying, "I know your secret, Daddy."

"All right," I said. "Tell me what you know. And then I'll fill in ... at least *some* of the gaps."

He poked me in the arm. "You're the fairy!"

I smiled. "How'd you guess?"

Danny crawled out from under his blankets and sat in my lap. I held him tight against my bathrobe as he told me, "I saw you sneak into my room last night. And Mommy is Santa Claus, because I saw my Lego deep-sea-diver kit in her closet on Christmas Eve."

"Excellent sleuthing," said I. "But don't tell anyone at school."

"Why not?"

"Because people like to believe."

"But why do they like to believe in things that aren't true?"

"Because they like stories," I said.

Danny considered this for a moment. "How much of a collie dog can I buy for ten dollars?"

"A tail," I said. "Or maybe a bark." I gave him a kiss on the top of his head and scooted him off my lap. "Get dressed now. I'm going to take a shower."

The minute I stood up, I heard the plumbing groan.

Danny jumped up and down. "Mommy beat you to it!"

Our sluggish water heater needed to be replaced, but neither Lisa nor I had the time—or the desire—to research our options. So it had turned into a weekend family game—not always executed with good sportsmanship—to see who could make the mad morning dash into the bathroom and nab the hottest first shower. Lisa, who usually lost the race, now broke into celebratory song.

"Why does Mommy have to sing so loud?" Danny asked.

"Because loud," I said, "is what Mommy is all about."

I sent Danny downstairs to play, then crossed the hall and sat down on Lisa's side of the bed. I took her ovulation graph off the nightstand and saw that she probably wouldn't surge this weekend. That would create problems for me next week. I'd have to rearrange some afternoon appointments, and Victoria would think I was scooting out to some hot assignation. I couldn't blame her for having a prurient imagination. There certainly were a lot of extramarital affairs going on at SB; some of the guys I worked with seemed to trade in their wives as often as they upgraded their personal computers. How they got away with these flings—never mind why they wanted to—eluded me. Sometimes I felt like the only man at SB who lived his life by the calendar and the clock, the only man whose wife—and secretary—knew where he was at every minute of every day, so that even if he wanted to conduct some steamy affair, he wouldn't be able to wedge in a quickie at the local Motel 6.

Lisa came back into the bedroom, wrapped in a white towel slung suggestively low on her breasts. "Don't forget to put that mirror back in Danny's room," she said.

"Later," I promised.

"I just don't want it there forever."

"It will not be there forever," I said.

"May I quote you on that? A month from now?"

"A month from now," I said, "we'll be living somewhere else."

"Optimist."

The bathroom, ordinarily suffused with steam after Lisa showered, felt ominously chilly. I shut the door, hung my bathrobe on the hook, and eyed the toilet with longing. Maybe after a couple of cups of coffee . . . or a particularly fibrous breakfast . . . How much longer, after all, could I go without *going*?

I took a stone-cold shower—uselessly turning the dial all the way to *H*—then toweled off, shivering in the frigid air. As I squirted a dollop of shaving gel into the palm of my hand, I felt a promising nagging in my stomach. But then the gnawing passed and returned, passed and returned—a good indication it was more psychological than physical.

Halfway through my shave, I identified the source of my stomach discomfort. That morning, when Danny had so rudely woken me up, I'd been lying with a woman in my dreams. But it hadn't been

Lisa—nor some succubus come down to haunt me. It had been Cynthia Farquhar. Again!

Razor in midair, I paused and examined my half-shaven face. So I'd slept with Cynthia in my dreams. Twice. Big deal. How could I control it? The entire human race, I told myself, would be in jail if people were held accountable for taking on inappropriate noctur-nal lovers. Besides, Lisa had erotic dreams too. What had she mut-tered yesterday morning in her sleep?

*Aye-aye.*

*I. I.*

*I for "I. I." I for son.*

*Asshole,* I thought. My razor scraped like sandpaper against my chin.


At the breakfast table, as I dabbed a tissue against my still-bleeding skin, Danny stirred his soggy Wheaties with a spoon. "What's *fuck*?" he asked.

I cleared my throat and reached for a box of Grape-Nuts. "A verb," I said.

"Also a noun," Lisa added.

"How so?" I asked.

"A good fuck," Lisa said. "A bad fuck. A mediocre—"

"But what does it mean?" Danny asked.

I stared into my Grape-Nuts and told Danny it was a private word—an adult word—not to be used in front of either of Danny's grandmas or the other children at school. This word had various connotations, both positive and negative—

"Get to the point," Lisa said. "It's what people do to make a baby."

"Oh," Danny said. "Why can't I have Frosted Flakes? At Zachary's house, they get to eat Frosted Flakes."

"Zachary's parents are divorced," I reminded him.

"Not *that* Zachary," Danny said.

"Which one of the famous half-dozen Zacharies is turning five today?" I asked.

Danny pushed back his chair. "Gotta poop now, Daddy!" he said as he raced for the stairs.

I pushed my bowl of Grape-Nuts toward the center of the table.

Lisa clucked her tongue sympathetically. "Want some—"

"I do not need *prunes,* Lisa." I stood up from the table. "Now, let's get this mess cleaned up."

We cleared the table of bowls pooled with warm milk and disintegrating cereal. As we piled the dishes by the side of the sink, I asked, "Why did you tell Danny that fucking makes babies?"

"Doesn't it?"

I swatted her lightly on the arm. "He'll think it's instant cause and effect."

Lisa put on her yellow household gloves. "He knows better than that."

"He does?"

"Stop looking at me that way, like you're about to lay an egg." Lisa squirted an inordinate amount of Joy onto a yellow sponge, then tipped on the faucet. "After that night he came into our room and caught us at it—well, he asked and so I told. The mechanics, at least. Of what goes where."

"You think he understood?"

"He asked me if it felt cold," Lisa said as she rinsed the first cereal bowl. "But otherwise he seemed totally confused about how the two parts go together."

"That's not surprising, considering how much trouble he still has tying his shoes."

"Well, practice tying with him."

"When do I have time to practice?" I asked.

Lisa put the cereal bowl down into the left side of the sink. "Could you empty the dishwasher for me?"

"I don't have time. I told Josh I'd be there by ten."

"Don't forget True Value."

*I don't have time for True Value,* I might have replied, had my eyes not fixed on the digital clock on the stove that contradicted my lie. It was only 9:20.

"And don't forget it's garbage day," Lisa said.

"I don't need to be reminded."

A bigger lie had never been told. Because of course I had forgotten. And I didn't remember again until I passed, in my car, two
other trash cans that some other, more responsible husband in our
neighborhood already had pulled to the curb. I glanced at my dashboard clock, considered going back to put out the cans, then remembered the sanitation workers usually came between one and
two.

*Chance it,* my inner voice said.


The moment I squeezed the old-fashioned latch on the True Value
front door—and heard that blasted cowbell ring—I felt as if all
eyes were upon me. Surely every salesman here recognized me as
the kind of hardware-retarded guy who did not know his ratchet
from his key wrench. I pulled back my shoulders, passed by the
paint-chip display, and headed down an aisle catering to the toilet-
troubled. I had no idea plungers came so small—and so big. I could
only imagine the sort of sick, desperate sound they emitted before
the desperate homeowners flung them to their flooded floors and
called a plumber.

In aisle five, a large pegboard displayed Master padlocks, Yale
doorknobs, double bolts, and safety chains.

"Help you?"

I turned. The white-haired salesman wore a red apron and a
name tag that read ROY. "I'm looking for a lock," I told Roy. "But I
guess that's apparent."

Roy squinted. "What kind you *apparently* need?"

My face grew warm. "For a door. To keep out a child."

"What kind?"

"A five-year-old boy."

"What kind of door*knob?*"

Only then did I notice the doorknobs were labeled *Hall/Closet*
or *Bedroom/Bath (with privacy lock).* "Bedroom," I said. "But before I left home, I didn't measure—"

Roy reached into his apron pocket. I was afraid he'd whip out some grisly garden tool—like a weed whacker—that he'd use to cut me down to size. But he extracted a well-used handkerchief and honked his nose. "These here come in standard measurements," he said, stuffing his handkerchief back into his pocket. "What color's the hardware in your house?"

I hesitated.

"You want to call your wife?" Roy asked.

*How long have you lived here?* Lisa would say. *And still you can't remember if the doorknobs are gold or silver?*

"Give me the gold," I told Roy.

After I left True Value, I walked down the mini-mall sidewalk past a number of come-and-go establishments: a tanning salon called Ray'z, a pet-supply store known as Pooch Patrol, and a bad Italian restaurant, Mia's Mamma, that was home to meatballs so gritty that Lisa swore they must have originated out of one of Pooch Patrol's Alpo cans. Mia's had a new neighbor: On Your Toes dance studio. In spite of the cold wind that caused me to huddle in my coat, I paused to watch through the venetian blinds. About a dozen baby-fat-padded teenagers in black leotards and pink tights were writhing a dance that seemed a cross between the hula and the pony. The teacher, who had the right kind of body for such lissome movement (all skin and bones), kept stopping the cassette tape and forcing the teenagers to repeat the same motions. I moved away from the window only after one of the mothers seated on a bench in the lobby gave me an evil glare. I glared back. What kind of mother was this, I thought, who couldn't tell the difference between a child molester and a decent man in search of potential baby-sitters?

The minute Joshua Silber, CPA, buzzed me into his office, I felt clobbered by the music from the dance studio next door: an oldies tune called "Poison Ivy," about a gal—pretty as a daisy—who drove the men crazy. As Josh came out to greet me, snapping his fingers and shaking his hips, I understood why I had succumbed to the charms of A. A. Milne the night before. Josh was a big, bearlike man whose ears sat too high on his frizzy-haired head and whose snout was turned up so you were constantly aware of his nostrils. He looked like a dancing version of Winnie-the-Pooh.

Pooh's bare belly, however, seemed preferable to what Josh wore. Josh was truly color-blind (unlike me, who was unjustly accused of being so), and usually his wife, Deb, matched up his trousers and shirts. Yet Deb, an avid garage-saler, must have left to go junking at the crack of dawn, because Josh's tie—an odd, mottled yellow-and-brown pattern that looked like a monarch butterfly smashed against his chest—did not even remotely match the hue of his blue windowpane shirt.

"When did that dance studio move in?" I asked.

"First of the year," said Josh. "Most of the time it's *Swan Lake* stuff. But Thursdays it's tap classes. For three-year-olds, no less. Makes the paper clips in my top desk drawer do the cucaracha."

"Have you talked to them?" I asked. "About soundproofing?"

Josh ran his hand over the thinning remains of his wiry hair. "We're splitting the cost of a cork wall after tax season. In the meantime, they get to listen to my clients moaning and groaning, and Julie gets free lessons."

Josh's daughter Julie was about as heavy as Josh's wife. I tried to keep my voice neutral as I asked, "Ballet?"

"Jazz," said Josh. "I've watched her. Through the window. She's awful. I dread her recital. Because I know when I see her hoofing her fat self across the stage, I'll get so proud—I'll cry so hard—that the frigging camcorder will vibrate and shake, and later Deb'll yell at me for taking such lousy footage." He ran his hand over his hair again. "Step into my chambers, if you dare."

I followed Josh into the back office, which was considerably quieter and smelled of hours-old coffee. Ignoring Deb's pleas to let her *do up his office,* Josh had settled for dental-like decor. The antiseptically white walls were plastered with Far Side and Dilbert cartoons, and a plastic ficus tree gathered dust in the corner.

The True Value bag clanked when I put it down on Josh's desk.

"What's in there?" Josh asked, as he started spreading my tax return across his conference table.

"A lock."

"What for? Danny still climbing in your bed?"

I frowned. "How'd you know?"

"Lisa told me."

"Why did she tell you that?"

"Just to be fair," Josh said, "she didn't say the kid in the bed was Danny. She mentioned she was getting done with this novel she was writing—hey, listen, I didn't know she thought of herself as a novelist—why didn't she tell me?—why didn't *you* tell me? Anyway, she mentioned she was writing this book, and when I asked her what the story was about, she said an ordinary guy with ordinary problems. 'So what kind of problems?' I asked her, and she said—pretty defensively, I gotta admit—'Like, like, like, he doesn't understand why his kid keeps climbing into his bed.' "

I didn't care for the amused look Josh gave me. "Lisa's novel," I said, "is based on someone else—"

"Someone else!" Josh gave a bearlike grunt. "That's like calling a doctor's office and saying, 'I've got this friend who thinks he has herpes.' Everybody knows it's *you* who's got the herpes."

"I don't have herpes," I said.

"That's my point. Tell your writer-wife to write about it and everybody'll think you do."

I hesitated. "Are you done being an asshole?"

"I'm just warming up. Want some coffee?"

"Give me my bad news first," I said.

Josh gestured me forward. "Come to the table."

Across the length of the table lay my 1040 and a long spread of schedules: itemized deductions, interest and dividend income, and capital gains. As if pressure on the form would cause an explosion, I used only the tips of my fingers to turn to the second page of the 1040. I gazed down at Josh's calculations and blinked.

"Do I get to keep my firstborn?" I asked.

"He's all yours," Josh said. "At least until he gets his driver's license."

I sat down slowly in front of the 1040. "But I already paid ... God, just look at all this estimated from last year. I don't see why I owe this outrageous amount."

Josh hemmed and hawed and stroked his tie, then launched into a speech that seemed to mix the wisdom of Socrates ("Man has a duty to the state") with the mythology of Passover ("Remember we were slaves in Egypt—before we became slaves to the IRS").

"I don't make the rules," he finally said.

"But can't you help me get around them better?"

"You don't take my advice," Josh said. "Remember, just this time last year, I told you and Lisa to buy a bigger house and to have another kid to knock another couple of thousand off your gross—"

"We're *trying*."

"I know you're trying."

I bit my lip. "Don't tell me. This also is part of Lisa's novel?"

"Is it?" Josh asked.

"I have no idea," I said.

"How come you don't know?" Josh asked.

"She won't let me read it. She says I'm too critical. And too unemotional."

"Unemotional? You?" Josh snorted. "Man, if anyone wore his heart on his sleeve—"

"It wouldn't be me."

"But you're as easy to read as a book! Come on. Take this *trying* thing."

"Nah," I said. "Don't take that."

"You can't blame Lisa for telling me that. You gave it away last year. When I suggested you get yourself another little tax deduction, you got this look on your face."

I shrugged.

"Come on, guy," Josh said. "It'll happen."

"I guess."

Josh hesitated. "Tell me to fuck off if I'm getting too personal."

"Okay," I said. "Fuck off."

"But I used to know this guy. And he and his wife couldn't ... you know, have kids. So then they went to the doctor and discovered the wife was—get this!—producing antibodies that fought off the poor guy's sperm."

"Lisa doesn't have antibodies," I said. "She has a blocked fallopian tube."

"No shit," Josh said. "How'd that happen?"

I couldn't believe my own ears. I had just blurted out Lisa's deepest secret. I should have felt shame. But really what I felt was relief. I wanted to keep on spilling, to say, *Well, it all began when …*

"It's a long story," I said.

"Let me know if you ever want to tell it."

I shrugged again. "I've always wanted a little girl."

"I wanted a boy," Josh said. "But now I wouldn't trade my two little fatsos for anything. They taught me the secret of happiness: Want what you have"—Josh pointed to my 1040—"and then get ready to have it stolen away."

I glanced down again at the bottom line of the tax form. I leaned my head on my hand and felt my temple pulse in rhythm with the music next door.

"You look like you need that coffee now," Josh said.

He went over to the coffeemaker in the corner. I stared at the wretched black brew he then delivered to me in a styrofoam cup. "Not to be ungrateful—but can't you see how dark and greasy this is?"

Josh shrugged. "I made it at five-thirty in the morning."

"What were you doing here at that hour?"

"It's tax time and I'm a tax man. Besides, I always lose track of how many scoops of coffee I put in."

"You're doing my tax return and you can't even count to six?"

"I put in seven, eight." Josh scratched the side of his head. "I'm losing my marbles lately. About little things. Ever since I turned forty, there's all this minutiae I can't remember. For instance, I looked at Deb the other day and I swear I could not remember her name." Josh disappeared into the back of the office. I heard him emptying the bad coffee into the bathroom sink. He reappeared in the doorway, then sat down beside me. "Ready for line by line?"

After we verified that Eben and Elizabeth Strauss could claim only Daniel Strauss as an exemption and that neither party wanted three dollars of our hard-earned money to subsidize the upcoming presidential election, Josh and I immediately came into conflict. Line 7 was right. (I remembered precisely how much should be reported—to the penny—under *Wages, salaries, tips, etc.,* because I

had spent two hours the previous Saturday putting together my
W-2 and all the rest of the forms we needed to support our mortgage application.) But line 12 was wrong.

"Line 12 is—" I said.

"You're getting ahead of the game." Josh stroked his tie. "Let's
go back to 8a—"

"No, let's stay here on twelve for a second. I don't have any self-
employment income."

"Well. Yeah. I know that."

"So why—"

Josh cleared his throat. "Have you had a heart-to-heart talk with
your wife lately?"

"Too many."

"I mean about money?"

"What money?"

Josh pressed his fingers—I swore his fingers had gotten even fatter since I last saw him—against the table. "Aw, don't do this to me."

"Do what?"

"Make me explain. That the self-employment income is—"

"What, fictitious?"

"No. Lisa's."

"But Lisa had no income."

Josh's furry eyebrows knit together. Then he reached up and
loosened his tie. "Is it getting hot in here?"

"Not to my knowledge."

"Well ... can you keep a secret—that you know a secret—that
Lisa told me to keep secret?"

I put my hand on Josh's arm. "Tell me right now what Lisa did to
earn that money."

"She published part of her novel in *Playboy*."

I took off my glasses, put my head in my hands, and stretched the
skin on my face so taut I thought it would snap.

"Chill out," Josh said. "She wrote it under her maiden name."

"I don't care if she wrote it with a gun to her head. She should
have told me."

"See—she hid it from you because she knew you'd go ballistic—"

"How would you feel if your wife wrote porn?"

"Ecstatic!" Josh sighed. "But Lisa's novel didn't seem porn-ish at all."

I took my head out of my hands. "You saw it? Lisa showed you?"

Josh looked down at his beefy, hairy wrists. "I sort of . . . subscribe."

I looked at Josh. I couldn't believe it. He had daughters. A wife. And in his garage, all the trappings of a staid, bourgeois life—half a dozen snow shovels, two four-door family sedans, a cooler on wheels, and twenty-pound bags of weed and feed.

"I see," I said. "Every month *Playboy* just *sort of* lands in your mailbox."

"Hell, no! Don't forget, I'm still *sort of* married to Deb. So I get it delivered here. At the office."

I took a moment to digest this information. Then I said, "Show it to me."

"Which issue do you want?"

"The one with Lisa's *novel* in it," I said as I picked up my glasses from the table and put them on again.

Josh went over to his long row of file cabinets and pulled out his key ring—deftly answering all my unasked questions about how he kept his *Playboy*s secret from Deb and from the nighttime cleaning lady (if not from his part-time receptionist). He unlocked the last file cabinet. The magazine he set before me was the February issue. A MONTH OF LOVE! it proclaimed—and featured, on the cover, a pouty-pussed buxom blonde scantily clad in just the type of lingerie I sometimes wished was still an integral part of Lisa's wardrobe.

I wanted to loftily tell Josh, *I can't even remember the last time I looked at a skin magazine.* But not even my spotty memory was that faulty. Six months ago, on my first visit to our fertility specialist, I'd held a girlie magazine in my hands—and my subsequent actions did not lend validity to that tired American male myth: *Hey, I read* Playboy *for the articles, man.*


I'd sooner die than tell Josh about my initial humiliating encounter with Dr. John Goode. I had dreaded—and twice rescheduled—

my first appointment, and when I finally was ushered in to an examination room (fifty-five minutes after my scheduled time), I had been tempted to leave by the emergency-exit door when the nurse told me, "Everything off, and leave this robe open in the front."

"In the front?" I repeated.

"Yes," she said. "That means: not in the back."

Although Lisa had warned me that Dr. Goode had the bedside manner of a lizard ("He doesn't even have the decency to warm the speculum beneath the heat lamp, Ebb"), I still was surprised when Goode barged into the examination room twenty minutes later, issued a brusque "Good afternoon," and proceeded to place his cold stethoscope on my chest and back. I didn't expect Goode to feel up everything on my body, from my throat glands to that stubborn roll of fat—thick and bulbous as a chocolate eclair—that lately had clung to my abdomen.

"Now for a quick glance at your genitals," Goode warned, flipping aside the robe. After letting off a satisfied grunt, he ordered me to get dressed and meet him across the hall in his dark-paneled office, where—amidst his tony diplomas and framed photos of his own grown brood of children—he subjected me to a string of mortifying questions (my favorite: "Any erection problems—getting one, keeping one?").

"During her fertile period," Dr. Goode asked, "how often do you have relations with your wife?"

I cleared my throat. "Well," I said, "we certainly try to maximize our opportunities."

"How often?"

"I honestly can't pinpoint—"

"An educated guess will do."

Eager to neither highball nor lowball, I went for what I thought was a credible, respectable number.

Dr. Goode flipped back some pages on Lisa's chart. "That's not what your wife reports."

The office grew silent. From the anteroom, I heard the ringing of phones and the shrill laughter of a nurse as she walked by.

"Your wife reports you've traveled a lot. And that sometimes these trips have coincided with her fertile period, is that right?"

"Well. Yes. That has happened two or three times—or maybe four or five—over the past couple of years."

"You can't let that happen. You need to schedule your schedule around her schedule. Are you with me?"

I wished I were anywhere but. For the next two minutes, Dr. Goode delivered a string of stern warnings that made me feel as though I finally had achieved my worst teenage fear: being sent to the principal's office. I was: not to drink! not to smoke! not to use recreational drugs! not to sit in a hot tub or sleep beneath an electric blanket! not to assume any—*eh-hem*—interesting positions! but always give my wife an orgasm—if possible, after my own ejaculation—because the resulting spasms drew the semen farther into the vaginal canal and facilitated bonding of the ovum and sperm.

"Any questions?" Goode asked.

*Yes,* I thought. *Can I strangle you now?*

I shook my head.

Goode scribbled some notes on my chart, then jotted instructions on his Rx pad and tore off the top sheet. "Then I'll turn you over to the nurses."

Down the hall, I delivered his illegible note to a gray-haired woman in whites. "We need your blood," she said. "And—well, come with me."

She led me into an alcove and ordered me to sit in a chair. She donned a pair of rubber gloves, put a tourniquet on my left arm, swabbed the inside of my elbow with a mustardy compound, and palpated my vein. As the needle went in, she murmured, "You make an easy target."

After she took two vials of blood, she drew a lidded, plastic cup from the enamel cabinet and began scribbling my name on the label.

I cleared my throat. "I used the men's room just before I came in."

She handed me the cup. *"Ejaculate,"* she said briskly. "Ejaculate is what we need."

I turned and only then noticed the room behind me was marked

COLLECTION ROOM
DO NOT DISTURB

"Does this door lock?" I asked.

The door had a very secure lock, the nurse assured me. And no one would interrupt me. But two seconds after I had closed the door and turned the lock, a sharp knock shook the door.

"Mr. Strauss?" the nurse's muffled voice called out. "I forgot to ask. Did you have sexual intercourse last night?"

"I can't say that I did."

"What was that?"

"No!"

"Have you ejaculated—under any circumstances—within the past forty-eight hours?"

"No again."

"I'm sorry. But we need to know. It affects the quality of the sample. I'm sure you wouldn't want to come back and repeat the procedure. Although … do you know? I can't read Dr. Goode's handwriting here—do you know if Dr. Goode wants to do the hamster?"

I unlocked the door, startling her. She pointed to the cup I held in my hand. "This first sample is for the count and the mobility," she said. "But if he already knows it's low, Dr. Goode will ask for the hamster penetration test."

"The what?"

She reached into the cabinet and handed me a paper leaflet. "This explains it."

I closed the door—locked it—and as I listened to her shoes squish down the hallway, I leaned against the door and read through the brochure, becoming more nauseated by the second. *For the zona-free hamster oocyte penetration assay, human sperm cells are placed in a sterile incubation dish with hamster eggs. The number of the infertile man's sperm that can penetrate the egg then is compared to the number of sperm from a fertile human donor. **Rest assured, the sperm cannot fertilize the hamster eggs nor can a real embryo develop.** Humans and hamsters are not genetically compatible and cannot create a new species.…*

I felt my lunch lurching around in my stomach. I flung the brochure into the wastebasket. The room was sparsely furnished, with a church-pew–like bench covered with sterile paper and a low table holding magazines so neatly arranged—in a precise and enticing fan—that I had to wonder if a gay man had been in here before me. I knew if I succumbed and picked up one of these publications that I would return it to exactly the same place in which I found it. The janitor who cleaned this office after hours probably was not so scrupulous.

I sighed and sat down on the bench. A holier man would have prayed. I, however, could only think about how looking at such magazines would disappoint my mother. I knew it also would make me disloyal—by default—to Lisa. I also knew that if I only waited ten years to satisfy my curiosity, I'd find similar magazines stashed beneath Danny's mattress.

But in the meantime, I had to get my mind off those hamsters.

I placed the collection cup on the bench and leaned forward. Sandwiched between *Hustler* and *Screw,* I found the much milder *Playboy*—and took more than a few minutes to peruse the models' preposterously big breasts and unlikely firm butts. Finally—when all thoughts of rodents were completely banished from my mind—I put down the magazine. As I went about my business, I dreamed of Lisa ... well, a woman who sort of looked like Lisa, only with ... blond hair ... lush lips ... swollen tits ... a full, soft, squeezable rump with cheeks that clenched in and out, in and out ... and bright blue eyes that met mine in the mirror as her velvety voice moaned, *Do it ... do it ... do it to me forever....*

That worked—so fast—that after I screwed the lid on the plastic container, zipped up, and heeded the instructions pasted on the back of the door—PLEASE WASH YOUR HANDS BEFORE LEAVING THIS ROOM—I figured I had a minute, maybe even two, to look at the *Playboy* once again.

When Josh surrendered the magazine to my hands, I riffled slowly through the pages.

Josh cleared his throat. "Lisa's story is on page forty-eight."
I turned to forty-eight.

### HE LEFT HIS HEART AT THE OFFICE
#### by Elizabeth Diodetto

"God in heaven," I murmured. I swallowed. And started reading. And immediately began thinking, this isn't me, this cannot be me, and yet this seems like ... me. This looks like our MCGRUFF HOUSE sign, our not-so-welcoming welcome mat, Lisa's apron, Lisa's Wüsthof knife, and Lisa's lips. The only thing described that I did not recognize were the lips of this va-va-voom secretary nicknamed Take-A-Letter-Maria.

Josh had met Victoria once (and whispered to me, "How soon can you divorce her?"). Nevertheless—just to make clear I had no designs on Victoria—I said, "I'd rather die than kiss my secretary."

Josh snorted. "I'd rather kiss the butthole of a goat!"

I kept on reading. But really I was just skimming to find anything else incriminating in the rest of the piece. I was looking for ... I don't know what. Some clue, maybe, as to why Lisa and I couldn't seem to talk without invisible exclamation marks punctuating almost every other statement, some secret beyond a blocked fallopian tube that had resulted in *no results* for us no matter how hard we tried, some hint as to why I felt like we were moving apart at the same time I felt like we were more and more hemmed in together. I sought a reference to real estate, or a sly nod to Norway. Yet I found nothing in this story that shed light on my own problems—because the conflict Lisa described on the page simply seemed the conflict of being alive, and getting older, and realizing that time was slipping by so fast that you wished it was something tangible so you could reach out and grab all the wasted minutes, hours, and days, do the things you should have done, say the things you should have said. What person—man or woman—who had been born when there were only forty-eight states in the union could not claim, as Lisa claimed about Simon: *He had told himself that he would not succumb to depression about what he had failed to do and focus more upon what he had accomplished. Yet the moment he had rounded the corner into his forties, he began to feel the blues. Sometimes he wandered about his own house, wondering who really lived there. Other times he woke in the dead of night, thinking, Where am I? What time is it? Why can't I sleep? When he paused over an old photo of himself, it was all he could do to keep from murmuring, Who was this person? Who had so much hair? Who seemed so happy?*

My reaction to Lisa's story surprised me. I didn't mind—too much—what she had written. But I did mind where she had published it. Without asking Josh's permission, I pressed my hand down on the spine of the magazine and quickly ripped out the first page.

"Hey!" Josh protested. "What are you doing?"

"I want to show this to Lisa."

"But she's already seen it! And the picture on the back isn't half-bad!"

I turned over the page. *Take me for a ride....* implored the big-busted naked woman straddling a Harley-Davidson.

"You *like* this kind of woman?" I asked.

Josh shrugged. "Her boobs look kind of ... I don't know ... comforting ... almost maternal...."

"But they're totally fake," I said.

"So what? It's fantasy. It doesn't hurt anybody."

"But you have *daughters*."

Josh wiped his nose with the back of his hand. "Yeah. Well. I also have Deb. I mean, I love her and all ... and I'd never dream of doing anything ... I mean, she'd kill me! But you know ... we've been married a long time. Besides, I've never been with anyone else."

If I had given it any thought before (which I hadn't), I could have guessed that goofy, sloppy, yellow-toothed Josh—who'd gotten married right out of college—never had slept with any woman but Deb. Still, I managed to muster forth a surprised "Oh?"

Josh rested his hands on his big tummy. "Pathetic, isn't it? In this day and age? And don't tell me it's sweet—that I can't stand hearing!" He gestured at the *Playboy*. "I figure—compared to what a lot of other guys do—that this is pretty harmless."

I folded Lisa's story in half, quarters, then eighths. As I tucked it into the breast pocket of my shirt, I admitted, "I guess you're right.

In comparison to what other guys do, this is mild stuff." I pointed to my 1040. "Let's get to work."

We continued reviewing the taxes. But I could hardly concentrate. I kept asking myself: If what Lisa wrote was good, then why did I feel so bad? Was I just as depressed as this Simon Stern? Was I depressed because people would think I was depressed? Had I really aged so much that Lisa—never mind this Simon!—would hardly recognize me in an old picture? Did I not want to be the husband of Elizabeth Diodetto? Or was I just afraid that readers of Lisa's novel would think my emotional innards had been spread on the table for public viewing, the way all my receipts and canceled checks and financial statements would be laid across the table if ever I got audited by the IRS?

I didn't want to get audited. I knew I needed to pay attention. But as Josh went over my 1040, line by tedious line, I wondered which other men I knew secretly subscribed to *Playboy* and thus had seen "He Left His Heart at the Office." Rudy Furlong? Dr. John Goode? The security guards at Scheer–Boorman? Focus. *Focus.* I started nitpicking at the capital-gains portion of the return. I got argumentative; Josh got defensive; but by the time we got to the final calculation, I had to admit Josh knew the rules—unjust as they seemed—and had played around them as best he could. I uncapped my pen and signed off on the form, knowing my heart would be even heavier when I signed off on the accompanying check—which, I told Josh, I wouldn't be able to deliver until later that week.

"Send it in with Lisa," Josh said.

"Lisa's seeing you? What for?"

"I need her John Hancock too." Josh waggled his finger at me. "You don't trust me with your wife?"

"I completely trust you."

Josh sighed. "See. I *told* you I was pathetic." He took the forms from my outstretched hands. "I might get done here by three-thirty or four. Feel like coming over my place for a beer?"

I shook my head. "Can't. We're going to look at another house."

Josh returned the forms to the manila folder. "Why's it taking you two so long to move?"

"That's a complicated question."

"Who's your agent, again?"

"Her name is Cynthia Farquhar."

Josh gave me a low, sensuous bleat. "*La Farquhar* is a good-looking woman."

My efforts to keep my facial muscles impassive only made them ache. "You know her?"

"She's a *great*-looking woman," said Josh.

"I hadn't noticed."

"You hadn't noticed! Bull*shit* you hadn't noticed."

I permitted myself a smile, which Josh took as encouragement to wax on Cynthia Farquhar's remarkable assets: Her feline figure. Her Siamese-blue eyes. Her smooth hair. Her lengthy legs. Her ... um ... well-fitted? ... wardrobe. A guy would have to be blind ... Of course, a woman like that ... would not look at the likes of—

I cut him off before he could say *you and me.*

"How do you know Cynthia?" I asked.

"Rotary Club."

I took off my glasses and began cleaning them—a little too thoroughly—with my handkerchief. "Isn't Rotary a fraternal order?"

"Get hip. Women can even be Odd Fellows now."

"Why would they want to be?"

"Because, Mr. Big Business—Cynthia and I are in *small* business. We've got to ring that Salvation Army bell at Christmas and scrub hubcaps at the charity car washes. Of course, Cynthia looks much better holding a hose than I do." Josh smoothed the palm of his hand down his tie. "At Rotary, we have these once-a-month luncheons. When Cynthia sits down at a table, you should see how fast the rest of the chairs fill up."

"I thought Rotary was a service club," I said, "not a pickup joint."

"Go on," said Josh. "We all know why we're there—to eat and schmooze—and only then to pass the can for college scholarships. Want to come to our next meeting?"

My hand went to my pocket for a pen. "Oh," I said. "That's strange. I left my Filofax at home."

"I'll call you. With the date. Or better yet—I'll have Cynthia call you with it. She and I cross paths quite a lot these days."

"Is that right?" I asked, wishing Josh would stop smoothing down his tie in such an obscene way.

"Yeah." Josh smiled. "Her office is right next to that bagel shop Deb always sends me to when she's in a pinch for dinner."

"Sounds like a tight relationship."

Josh laughed. "In my *dreams*."

*No*, I thought. *In mine*.

I cleared my throat. "That's a pretty good bagel shop. But I don't like their onion. It's not oniony enough."

"Bet you five dollars," said Josh, "that the WASPy La Farquhar has never even tried the onion. Bet you ten she's never even eaten a bagel."

"Don't be ridiculous," I said. "Even skinheads eat bagels."

Josh laughed. "Why'd you choose Cynthia as your agent, anyway— when you had your choice of a dozen nice old yentas?"

"Lisa chose Cynthia," I said. "You know. She likes Cynthia's clothes. And her haircut. And her taste in coffee. So that's why it's taking us so long to move. Whenever Lisa gets together with Cynthia, I swear they spend more time drinking cappuccinos than looking at houses."

"Lisa's probably addicted to the hunt," Josh said. "Like Deb. I don't know what they're looking for. Since all houses are the same. I mean, none of them has enough closet space."

"That's what I keep trying to tell Lisa," I said. "But she seems to think that somewhere out there lies some perfect house that we need to keep searching for."

"Search," Josh said. "Wait until you find. And remodel." He made a pained face. "Beware of a woman with a fistful of paint chips."

"I'll keep that in mind."

"Seriously. For weeks after we moved, Deb fretted over the color combination. 'Should we have the bucolic blue,' she kept asking me, 'or the pristine pink?' Like I could tell the difference? She ended up ruining every screwdriver I own—not that I know how to use either one—prying open gallon cans of Martha Stewart."

"Who's Martha Stewart?" I asked.

*"Who's Martha Stewart?"* Josh asked. "What *planet* are you living on?"

"A planet that used to have only men's names—Benjamin Moore, Dutch Boy—on cans of paint."

"Martha Stewart is ..." Josh's pink tongue hung in limbo for a moment as if straining to catch just the right words. "Martha is this multimillionaire businesswoman who looks a lot like La Farquhar—completely put together."

"Oh," I said. "I think I remember reading about her. In the *Journal*."

"Sure. She pops up in all the newspapers now."

"But how did she make her money again?" I asked.

"She writes all these books that show women how to be more womanly. Next time you're at the grocery—"

"I hardly ever go to the grocery store."

"—look on the checkout rack. Martha has her own magazine called *Martha Stewart Living* that some people have renamed *Is Martha Stewart Living?* Because she's like some Superwoman. She cooks, she cleans, she decorates, she gardens—and she even breeds her own hens that lay these weird turquoise eggs."

"Edible?"

"That's exactly what I asked, when Deb showed the eggs to me in Martha's magazine. Deb got all horrified—like to eat one of Martha's eggs was sacrilege—and she goes to me, 'Martha uses these eggs as inspiration for her paint palette!' "

I paused. "I don't get it."

"Neither do I. But Deb laps that Martha crap right up. She spent three whole days, I kid you not, making one of Martha's festive holiday wreaths, and then she got all miffy at me when I asked, 'What the fuck you going to do with this wreath, when we don't even celebrate Christmas?' Ugh. That *wreath*. It was made out of pistachio nuts! Spray-painted *silver*. The girls laughed for half an hour after I called it gold."

Josh heaved a deep, lonesome sigh. Taking this as a sign that the conversation was winding down, I pushed back my chair, until snagged once again by Josh's outburst: "It's all Martha's fault."

"Martha's fault that what?"

Josh wrinkled his fleshy forehead. "That I come home and Deb

reeks of turpentine and is wielding some threatening implement—
like a garden hoe or a hot-glue shooter—in her hand. You want to
know the real reason I came in at five-thirty in the morning? I didn't
dare come between Deb's staple gun and the wall." Josh got out his
handkerchief and wiped his forehead. "Man oh man, Deb's going
*menopausal*. And her hot flashes—I swear—are contagious."

Between Deb's waning womanhood, Dorothy Furlong's hysterectomy, and Lisa's radioactive fallopian tubes, I didn't know how
much more detailed gynecological information I could assimilate.
But I nodded sympathetically. Among the many diagrams in Lisa's
fertility literature was a representation of a woman's body, with arrows pointing to all the menopausal trouble spots:

HEADACHES AND HOT FLASHES

THINNING HAIR

RECEDING GUMS

DROOPING BREASTS

VAGINAL DRYNESS AND SHRINKING

STRESS INCONTINENCE

If *I* thought this diagram was scary, I could only imagine how it
would freak out those of the female sex.

"You should be more understanding," I told Josh. "That's got to
be disconcerting, all those changes in your body."

Josh shook his head glumly. "I don't care about Deb's body. I
mean, *she's* been fat—and *I've* been fatter—for years, and neither
one of us has ever complained. It's her head I'm worried about. It's
like overnight, the hormones—or all that furniture stripper she's
been using—went right to her brain. I mean—for example—can I
give you an example?—the other day she told me I *kept her down*.
Silenced her. Didn't encourage her to reach her full potential. I
came home yesterday and she had this pamphlet out on the coffee
table that said WOMEN AND ANGER: RECLAIM YOUR RIGHT TO
THIS VERY REAL FEELING!"

"Sounds dire," I said.

"She told me—point-blank—that she was tired of babying me

and she wasn't going to sort my clothes by color in the closet anymore."

I hesitated. "We're friends, aren't we? Then I need to tell you. Get your daughters to help you. Because that tie you've got on? It's the color of Gulden's mustard. And there's a decided swimming-pool-blue feeling to that shirt."

Josh pulled his sickly mustard tie around to the side of his head so it made a mock noose. Then he let it down with a grin. "You know how Deb's afraid of heights? I'm going to sign her up for one of those marriage-strengthening camps, where you have to tandem skydive in between primal-scream sessions." Josh's eyes lit up with joy. "Hey, that might make a good *Playboy* article for Lisa. Although you'd have to go to camp with her while she did her research."

"I have no intention," I said, "of attending a marriage-strengthening camp."

"It might be fun," Josh said. "I've heard at some camps you get to beat an inflatable doll with a baseball bat and pretend it's your wife. Although I've heard—at others—you have to touch your wife for hours without actually, you know, giving her the full-force fuckeroo—"

I pushed my chair back from the table. "Josh," I said, "as always, it's been good talking to you."

Josh held out his fingers and took a playful nip at my shirtsleeve. "Hey, you know that novel Lisa is writing—the story's really about you, isn't it?"

I felt my feet stiffen in my shoes. "Simon Stern," I said, "is completely imaginary."

"And I've got this friend—named Martha Stewart!—who's got herpes." Josh leaned back in his chair and laughed. He pointed to the pile of forms. "Remember to send your big fat check in with Lisa. And don't come crawling back next week telling me, 'Oh, by the way—my wife and I bought a boat last summer.' "

"People do that?"

"Once somebody called me—on April fourteenth, no shit—and said, 'I forgot to tell you, last year we adopted a kid.' Nice father, huh?"

I took the True Value hardware bag off Josh's desk.

"Hope your lock works," Josh said mournfully—wistfully—then broke into a snaggletoothed smile. "My love to Lisa. And Cynthia."

As the wall vibrated with the sound of "Poison Ivy," Josh puckered up and blew a kiss destined—via me—for *La Farquhar*'s admittedly lush pink lips.

## CHAPTER TWELVE

# LISA

**I stood in front** of the bathroom mirror inspecting the wormlike furrow in my forehead. Several times last night it had been on the tip of my tongue to tell Ebb about my *Playboy* income—but each time I spotted a chance, somehow or other the conversation had taken an unexpected turn.

I had made a bad move by not making a move. I'd been too chicken to speak. Now Ebb probably sat with Josh in front of our 1040, and how could Ebb not notice that something was amiss with the return? Even though Ebb left globs of toothpaste and shaving cream in the bathroom sink, he was extraordinarily tidy when it came to numbers.

Trouble, no doubt, was right around the corner. But I didn't have the heart to think about it. I made a face at myself in the mirror and leaned forward over the soggy sink. The closer I drew to the mirror, the scarier the picture. Only Ebb saw me this close up—and even then, he was in the dark with his glasses off and his eyes closed—so he couldn't evaluate my scraggly eyebrows and fuzzy facial hair. When he did see me the way I really was, he was a prince about it. He told me I looked fine when I didn't look fine. He was *accepting*.

At least one guy in the world took me the way I was. A hairdresser, however, would note all my imperfections and attempt to make me into someone better. I dreaded letting the great Ricardo get so intimate with me that he would brush up against the twin brown spots on my face that I optimistically called beauty marks. As I smoothed a styling product called Your Secret Weapon on my frizzed-out hair, I kept a maternal ear cocked outward—and heard nothing but silence coming from Danny's room.

"Honey," I called, "are you getting dressed for the birthday party like I told you to?"

No response. I went to the door of Danny's room. Danny sat smack on his butt on the rug, his sneakers sitting uselessly between the parted V of his legs.

"I'm stupid," he said.

I knelt down on the carpet next to him. "Oh, sweetie, you are not."

"But I can't figure out which sneaker is left and which is right."

I pointed to his right Reebok. "Remember, just like I told you last time—the curve is on the inside."

Danny stared down at the dirty gray laces. "But even when I put my shoes on right, I can't tie them."

I pulled back the sleeve of my sweater and glanced at my watch. A good mother would take the time to patiently demonstrate how to tie a perfect bow. Yet I still had to wrap the birthday-party present. "I'll do it for you," I said. "But just this once."

"Why can't you do it all the time?"

"You don't want me tying your shoes when you're seventeen years old."

"Why not?"

"For starters," I said, "that would keep you out of Harvard."

"I don't want to go to Harvard."

"You'll love Harvard," I assured him. "You can ride the swan boats every day. After you finish all your homework, of course. Now, give me your sneaker."

Danny gave me his right sneaker, then stuck out his left foot— confirming that even though he had learned to read before he turned five, he still wasn't, just yet, Ivy League material. I took his right foot, clad in a red-capped sock, and pushed it into his Reebok.

"What's the matter, grumpy face?" I asked. "Don't you want to go to the party?"

Danny's snaggly front tooth latched over his lip. "Why are you and Daddy always doing the fucking?"

Since when did once a week count as *always*? I pulled so hard on the dirty sneaker laces that Danny's foot went two inches up into the air.

"First of all," I said, "don't say *fucking*. Second of all, I've told you a hundred times that Mommy and Daddy are trying to make another baby."

"But … but …" Danny's voice quivered, like a rejected lover's. "I'm your baby, Mommy."

I knotted the sneaker laces, then tied a bad bow that I instantly had to undo and make again. "Of course you're my baby," I said, in my own quivery voice. "I'll always love you more than anyone else."

"Even Daddy?" Danny asked.

"Let me think about that one," I said. "For just a minute."

I reached for Danny's other Reebok. The idea of loving Ebb more than Danny—or vice versa—seemed as absurd as favoring my right foot over my left. I needed both to walk. And yet my smittenness for Danny was so fierce that sometimes it made me question the extent to which I really loved Ebb. My feelings for Ebb had such … distinct limitations. My feelings for Danny were boundless! Yes, my first child took up so much room in my heart that I feared I wouldn't find half as much love left in there for the second.

"You know," I told Danny, as I pushed his left foot into the sneaker, "love doesn't grow any smaller if you have to share it with somebody else."

"That's not what Zachary's father said."

"*Which* Zachary?" I asked.

"The one whose father moved out to live with another lady. Zachary said his dad told his mom, 'I can't love you if I love somebody else.' "

I yanked on the laces of Danny's left Reebok. "The fucker."

Danny's eyes widened with glee. Then he giggled so hard that spit bubbled between the gap in his teeth.

"Well, really," I said. "Can you imagine Daddy saying something like that? To me? In front of you?"

"The *fucker*."

I swatted him on the leg. "Not *that*. Don't say that word."

"You just did."

"I meant saying, *I can't love you—*" I frowned. I finished tying the bow of Danny's laces, pushed his foot away, and stood up. Danny's striped pajamas were flung over his unmade bed. Crayons and dirty underwear and probably a dozen plastic fast-food prizes were strewn all over the floor. Five times. *Five times* I had told Danny that he needed to straighten this room before we left for the birthday party. Now it was all I could do to stop myself from hollering, *I'm your mother, not your maid—so clean up this disgusting mess!*

While I wrapped the pirate Legos in paper that urged me to CELEBRATE! CELEBRATE!, Danny shoved all his toys and clothes into one corner. Because I was sick of nagging, I let Danny get away with this botched cleanup job and ushered him downstairs. When I opened the hall door that led to the cold garage, I noted—with enough disgust to dream of divorce—that Ebb had failed to take the garbage cans out to the curb.

Danny wrinkled his nose. "It smells like doody out here."

"Daddy keeps forgetting to take out the trash," I said.

"Why don't you just do it?"

"Because he *promised*." My words echoed hollowly in the garage, and Danny—sensing I was not to be further tangled with—squeezed the birthday present too tightly against his chest.

"Put that present in my car," I ordered him. Danny actually obeyed, then followed me back into the kitchen, where I tossed my car keys onto the counter, grabbed a piece of scrap paper by the phone, and wrote Ebb a curt reminder: *Cynthia before 2. Garbage by 2 too.*

I shoved the note behind a refrigerator magnet I'd bought Ebb for his fortieth birthday, which read, I'D FORGET MY HEAD IF IT WASN'T ATTACHED TO MY BODY.

Danny pointed to the refrigerator. "That's rude," he said.

"The note or the magnet?"

"Both." He looked at me sorrowfully. "Daddy will think you don't like him."

"I can love Daddy," I told Danny, "without always liking what he does. Now let's hit the road."

The garage door groaned open and I backed my Toyota down the snow-encrusted driveway. The car took forever to warm up, and while big bellows of exhaust steamed out of the back, I gazed into the rearview mirror at Snow Man and Snow Lady and the dented photo of Mrs. Order that graced our for-sale sign. I was disappointed that Law and Order hadn't called us last night to set up some weekend viewings—but relieved that no one would be trooping through to inspect our mess.

As I drove down our street, I noticed that all the other husbands on our street—or, more than likely, their sick-of-nagging-'em wives—had pulled their trash cans to the end of the driveway for pickup. I turned on the radio. The oldies station was playing "Yesterday," a song I had considered highly profound when I was thirteen years old and had the leisure to lie—in premenstrual depression—for hours, facedown, on the bed. I could use that time now, I thought, to do more-constructive things, like whine to a marriage counselor, *If he truly loved me, then surely my husband would remember to take out the garbage.*

I pulled out onto the main road. The birthday boy lived miles away in one of those new gated subdivisions where the too-groomed streets were lined with five-thousand-square-foot mini-mansions. Although we were running late, I wasn't in any hurry to get there. The birthday boy's parents rubbed me the wrong way. June and Stewart Fox were a pair of personal-injury lawyers who ran a full-page color ad on the back of the Yellow Pages that asked:

INJURED?
HURT?
CALL FOX AND FOX
WE'RE ON YOUR SIDE!
NO FEES UNLESS WE WIN!

PHYSICIAN ON STAFF
¡SE HABLA ESPAÑOL!

That ad, plus the fact that Attorney Fox and Attorney Fox had criticized my only child at the Montessori school holiday party, had won them a high ranking on my shit list.

Granted, I hadn't been in a very social frame of mind the evening of that school party. I'd been pissed at Ebb because he had some mandatory SB function to attend, which meant I had to go to Danny's school party solo (unless you counted our RCA video camera as my not-so-blind date). As I perched in my festive velvet pantsuit on a plastic schoolroom chair meant to accommodate the tiny bottom of a four-year-old, I felt like some bereft single parent who'd been ordered to tape the event for the benefit of the non-attending ex.

Danny's Montessori directress (a too-upbeat woman I privately referred to as *Glorious Gloria*) had stood up in front of the crowd of parents swathed in some kinte cloth that looked garish against her Swedish-blond hair. I set the camera rolling just as she gaily announced, "Moms and Dads, the theme of our holiday celebration is cultural diversity!"

Slowly, I panned the camera to the red EXIT sign that hung above the door.

Glorious Gloria may have had her heart in the right place. But out of the thirty children enrolled in the school, only one was "a person of color" (Zachary #3) and only Noah Fox and Danny were "of Hebraic descent" (or in Danny's case, half). So all this "How many *A*s are in Kwanzaa?" ("Three!") and "How many candles on the menorah?" ("Eight? No, nine!") struck me as less inclusive than divisive, as it served to point out those who were different. I became aware that my kid numbered among the odd ones when Gloria lined up a group of children to make a "Living Menorah." Danny (who had been chosen to play the shammes candle over the Foxes' precious little pig of a son) stood in the middle, wearing a flame-yellow paper yarmulke. After Gloria read aloud an abbreviated version of the Hanukkah story and every candle got "lit" by Danny (who scooted around shining an Eveready flashlight over his class-mates' heads), Gloria then announced, "And that is why Jews everywhere on Hanukkah say—" She nodded encouragingly at Danny. "They say—"

I held the video camera steady and zoomed in on Danny, so close his face looked broad as a pumpkin. He smiled and announced too loudly, "A GREAT MIRACLE HAPPENED HERE!"

I panned across the audience, duly recording all the Protestant parents' polite smiles and applause. Two seconds into the next number—a rousing version of "Rudolph the Red-Nosed Reindeer"— a man seated behind me leaned into my airspace and mouthed (in a Boston accent that made me cringe), "Happened *tha-yuh*."

While keeping the video camera focused on the chirping chil-dren, I whipped my head around and confronted a stocky bearded guy wearing a name tag that read STEWIE FOX.

"A great miracle happened *tha-yuh*," Stewie said. "Not *he-yuh*."

I must have looked confused, because Stewie's well-coiffed wife explained, "Your son said the last word wrong."

"Well, your husband's pronunciation isn't so hot either," I said.

I had forgotten to press the mute button during this heated ex-change. So later—knowing that Ebb would disapprove of the way I had squabbled with the Foxes—I fixed the videotape so forty-five seconds of silence reigned between "had a very shiny nose" and "used to laugh and call him names." The Fox partnership probably would have called this tampering with the evidence. I called it the kind of editing that would save my buttinski.

The Foxes must have made a bundle chasing ambulances. When I spotted half a dozen helium balloons bobbing on the corner mail-box of Regency Drive, I turned in to the winding driveway of a Tudor mansion that could have belonged to King Henry VIII. Danny and I crunched up the stairway and rang the bell. June Fox opened the door. I gazed into her elegantly appointed foyer and felt first envy, then revulsion. The black-and-white marble on the floor sparkled, but I was sure it felt freezing cold beneath bare feet.

"Hey, Noah!" Danny called out to the birthday boy. He pushed past the ultrathin Mrs. Fox and rushed inside without wiping his Reeboks on the mat. June Fox gazed down at her marble floor in dismay, as if some savage species had invaded her home and left behind its smudgy tracks.

"Come back here right now!" I ordered Danny. "And remove your shoes in the hallway. And tell Mrs. Fox you're sorry for the mess you just made on her floor."

Danny handed the birthday present to Noah Fox, then plopped down on the marble and yanked off his sneakers without untying them. "Sorry!" he told June Fox.

She turned to me with a chilly smile. "The party ends at four."

"His dad is going to pick him up," I said, realizing a second later that *his dad* gave her the mistaken impression that Ebb and I were divorced.

As Danny, clad only in socks, slid on the marble floor into the back part of the house, I called after him, "Be good!" But my heart wasn't really in it. I knew when Danny was going to be good and when he wasn't. I just got these motherly feelings.

I drove carefully. The snow that had looked so fresh and clean yesterday now was tinged with browns and grays, and judging from the stiff wind that continued to shake my car, the slush that coated the road probably would turn to ice by tonight. In spite of the crummy weather, I still felt hopeful. I loved house-hunting. Real estate made me feel as feverish as a young girl longing to fall in love. Every property was a blind date. Every house could be The One.

Cynthia had faxed me very precise directions to the house, which wasn't all that far from where we lived. After I drove the ten miles toward home, I turned onto a hilly, bumpy country road called Darling Lane. Rough-hewn wooden fences—like the kind found at Girl Scout camps—separated the road from the forest. The trees— pines and bare maples and slender white-barked birch—made me feel like I was going back in time to Robert Frost country, or at least to an era earlier in my own life when I knew every line of the poem that ended *and miles to go before I sleep, and miles to go before I sleep.*

The houses all were hidden behind the trees. I almost missed the number on the country mailbox: 27 Darling Lane. The paved driveway sloped downward for about one hundred yards. At the bottom, surrounded by pine trees, stood a weathered white saltbox that looked exactly like the kind of house that Danny would draw with his crayons: a solid rectangle on the bottom and a sloping noncongruent quadrilateral on top.

My heart sank. Surely I had the wrong address. Why in the world had Cynthia thought that Ebb and I—who had been looking mostly at modern homes—would be interested in a house that seemed built for Paul Revere? Maybe Ebb would be willing to *constitute* his way toward a more imperfect union in this uptight saltbox (I could just see him marching around in a tricorn hat, pontificating about the rights of man while dropping his coat and boots and briefcase anywhere he damned please, which proved he did not give two straws about the rights of women). But how could I live in such a straitjacket of a house? There wasn't anything playful or creative about it!

I sat in my car and stared—and stared—at this moral manse. Within a minute, I saw some of its appeal. Although it looked like it had been hammered together by a bunch of dour, sexless Pilgrims, it had one decidedly seductive feminine touch: a sea-green front door that called out to me like a siren.

Cynthia had told me the owners wouldn't be at home. I cut the engine and got out of the car. The wind was so stiff, my teeth felt cold. I crunched across the snowy driveway to the front walk and stared at the sea-green door as if I were looking into my future. I saw myself standing in the front hall—the model corporate wife— shaking the hands of a long line of look-alike executives (and their dull-as-dishwater wives), repeating like some talking doll, *Hello, I'm Lisa Strauss and I'll be your hostess for the evening.* I saw myself sitting, pen and paper in hand, in front of one of the upstairs windows, staring out at the winter landscape for the perfect word I could not find inside myself. I saw myself leaning over the bathroom counter—not so Ebb could give me a good fuck from behind, but so he could sink a hypodermic needle full of ineffective hormones into my flabby, dimpled butt.

Maybe it was just the wind, or the exhaustion I always felt when I overused my imagination. But tears suddenly stung my eyes, and as I blinked, the sea-green door seemed to shift. Behind that door lay too many SB parties, too many days of sweating over the fifty-sixth draft, and probably vial upon vial of fertility drugs that cost eighty disappointing dollars a pop.

*Why should I let this be my life?* I thought. *I don't want to be your hostess for the evening. I don't want to spend hours every day searching for the right word. I don't want to live in a house big enough to accommodate half a dozen kids when I can't even conceive another or even take good care of the one I already have.*

"I don't want to be me!" I said aloud. "And I don't want to be a mother and sometimes I don't even want to be married!"

When nothing but the wind answered—and a swirl of leaves blew across the white lawn—I puckered up my lips and made a most immature but highly gratifying fart sound. *Phfft to your whining!* I told myself. *You're hardly ever "you" anyway, since most of the time you're pretending you're someone else. So why does it even matter where you live, since you're so busy mucking around in that muddy place you call your imagination?*

As I stood before that solid white house (which looked as unforgiving as the stone-cold tablets that held the Ten Commandments), I felt the sea-green door pulling me forward. I took a step toward the porch, then another. The shoveled walk was lined with snow-covered goose-egg-shaped stones. I reached down and brushed the snow off one of the goose eggs. After feeling the smooth, taupe stone—taut as a pregnant woman's belly—I remembered some advice my mother and aunts used to dole out to new brides embarking on their honeymoons: "If you want a boy, put a knife beneath the mattress; if you want a girl, then put an egg beneath the bed."

After looking behind to make sure Cynthia and Ebb weren't coming down the driveway, I put the goose egg in the pocket of my coat. Normally I wasn't very superstitious. But normally I wasn't desperate. I told myself it couldn't hurt to place the stone beneath our mattress.

The sun—which was pretty dim to begin with—disappeared behind a cloud. I shivered, then went back to my Toyota, turned on the engine, and flipped the heat to its highest setting. The car vibrated in the cold. I looked over at the house.

"My house," I whispered aloud, just to see if it sounded okay. It didn't have a bad ring to it, so I said it again.

*My house. Welcome to my house. My house has a gorgeous sea-green door (that needs to be repainted every spring). My house has a wide, welcoming stone hearth (that blows ashes all over the place). My house has walk-in closets so deep (that I can't find whatever I'm looking for). My house has four top-of-the-line Toto toilets (that overflow on a regular basis). My house has eight twenty-four-paned windows on the first floor, ten on the second, and four dormers winking up out of the roof (as if to pose the unfinished question: How many gallons of Windex would it take ... ?).*

I gulped. But it was too late. Already I had fallen in love with the kind of house any woman with more than a shriveled pea for a brain would call a Wifebreaker.

## CHAPTER THIRTEEN

# EBEN

**After Josh threw me a kiss** meant for Cynthia's fair lips, I got back into my car, ran a few errands, and then thought about "He Left His Heart at the Office" all the way home. I did like Lisa's piece. But. Still. Lisa had such an aggressive imagination. Why couldn't she write something bland? brief? soothing? like haiku? or Hallmark greeting cards? Why did she think people's private lives were the only subjects suitable for the printed page?

I pulled into our driveway and touched the remote control on my visor. The fickle garage door creaked open—revealing the garbage cans I earlier had failed to take down to the curb. I pulled my Audi into the garage. The phone was chirping inside the house. I unlocked the door leading to the hallway, rounded the corner, and lunged for the cordless phone in the kitchen.

"Heads up!" commanded Mrs. Joan Order. "I'm bringing someone to see your place sometime before dinner."

"But our place is a mess."

"Tidy up."

"My wife's not here."

Mrs. Order crisply clicked her tongue.

"I mean, I'm short on time," I said.

"Well..." Mrs. Order said. "You're lucky. This is a bachelor, on a weekend house-hunting blitz. He probably won't notice."

I looked around the kitchen at the spotted floor, the stained counters, and the fingerprint smudges on the dining-room archway. Even *I* noticed what an extreme state of chaos our house was in—so there was little hope this bachelor would be oblivious. Nevertheless, I told Mrs. Order to bring the guy over.

I knew there was something I needed to do besides grab a quick lunch before Cynthia arrived—but I couldn't recall what it was. I pulled out a box of Ritz crackers and a jar of peanut butter from the cabinet. After I ate six crackers slathered with peanut butter, I retired to the half-bathroom. With the extra toothbrush I kept stored in the vanity drawer, I brushed my teeth so hard the bottom gums started bleeding.

While I was pulling a disturbing number of black—and gray— hairs out of my comb, I heard the long, low squeal of brakes and the clatter of cans and glass carelessly being tossed into a truck. I dashed for the garage and rolled two Roughneck trash cans (one in each desperate hand) down the driveway, but the garbage truck already was rumbling far away down the street.

Just then Cynthia Farquhar pulled up, chipper and blond and bright, in her gleaming black Lexus. She lowered her power window and her breath came out in angelic white puffs. "Sorry I'm a little early."

I gestured at the obviously full trash cans. "I'm sorry I'm late." I wheeled the trash cans up the driveway and into the garage, trying not to shiver from the cold. "I need to get my coat and gloves," I called out to her. "Do you want to come in?"

When Cynthia hesitated, I was reminded of something Lisa once told me: "Every once in a while, Cynthia gets creeped out going into houses all by herself with a man."

"If she's with a man," I said, "then she's not by herself."

"A dangerous man! You know the kind, Ebb, even if you aren't that kind yourself."

I felt like pointing to the picture of the friendly dog hanging in the window and informing Cynthia: *Ours is a McGruff House!* Instead, I said, "Give me a moment to lock up and I'll be right out."

◆   ◆   ◆

It felt odd to sit in the passenger seat. I tried to concentrate on buckling up, but I found myself sneaking—out of the corner of my glasses—brief glimpses at Cynthia. No doubt about it, Cynthia Farquhar put herself together well. In the open collar of her tan trench coat, she wore a red and green scarf that reminded me of a stuffed Spanish olive. She wore rough-hewn ruby earrings that resembled the cherry pits my sister and I used to spit across the picnic table (taunting each other with these moronic insults: "You're such a boy!" "Well, you're such a girl!"). I don't know why I always thought of Cynthia in culinary terms. Lisa had informed me that Cynthia didn't even know how to boil a hot dog, never mind fix up (with extra brown sugar and bacon) a can of B&M baked beans. Yet ever since Danny had announced, "That lady smells nice—like a bakery," Cynthia had seemed especially gustatory to me. Like Danny, I didn't mind a whiff of Cynthia. She gave off the comforting fragrance of vanilla or cloves or gingerbread, as if she would taste delicious if you dared to take a bite.

"Problems?" Cynthia asked.

"What with?" I asked.

"Your seat belt."

"Not at all." The buckle gave off a decisive click. As Cynthia backed out of the driveway and took the long road out of our condominium complex, I gazed at the rubber lids the sanitation workers had thrown aside like dirty Frisbees and the emptied trash cans already threatening to roll into the street from the force of the strong March wind. The clouds looked angry. The dull gray cast on the remaining snow—as if it were four o'clock instead of before two—indicated we were due to get dumped on again.

"Where's Danny today?" Cynthia asked.

"A birthday party."

"He's really a sweet boy."

"You might not say that," I said, "if you had seen him in action this morning."

"I thought Lisa sounded at wit's end this morning when I called to confirm," Cynthia said. "She wanted to know if this house had outbuildings."

"Does it?"

"I'm sorry to disappoint you—no—but it has five very large bed-rooms."

I looked out at the snowcapped guardrails whizzing by. "Where are you taking me?"

"Not too far from here," said Cynthia. "This house is on a larger lot—two acres—which gives you the privacy you both seem to want, but since it's wooded, you won't have to worry about land-scaping except to take care of the flower garden out back."

"We don't know anything at all about gardening," I said.

"I can give you the name of a good landscaping service. And a pest-control outfit. For future reference. Since any garden in the country is prone to natural invaders."

To my surprise, Cynthia went on—and on!—about various methods of pest extermination: the traps, the gases, the poisons, the baits used to either wipe out the offending rabbits or lure the solo possum or raccoon into a cage so they then could be "relocated" by wildlife experts. I already knew, from viewing three or four houses with her, that Cynthia was a font of knowledge about houses and gardens and the way they worked. She could name—on sight— Windsor chairs and buckboard benches and fainting couches and *tables ambulantes*. She knew how to plug the failing grout in bath-room tiles and where to buy bird feeders that stung squirrels.

Still—when she began to debate the effectiveness of sonic sys-tems to keep moles from burrowing tunnels in the garden—I had to interrupt. "How do you *know* all this stuff?"

She blushed. "I've been selling houses for a long time now."

"You have an interesting job," I said.

"It has its moments."

"And I'm sure," I said, "that over the years you've met some in-teresting characters."

"I've certainly observed all kinds of interesting behavior."

"How so?" I asked.

"Oh, house-hunting brings out the best—and the worst—in peo-ple. One or two marriages have fallen apart in the backseat of my car. But then—in my office—they've been solidified too. A closing is a little like a wedding ceremony. I always feel like crying when the officer from the title company hands over the keys."

Unlike Lisa, who routinely ran through a dozen Kleenexes whenever we witnessed vows being exchanged, I didn't make a habit of weeping at weddings. But surely I had knotted my tie too tightly that morning in May when I married Lisa; *something* had strangled my voice when I said, "I do," and the justice of the peace had gently corrected me: "I *will*." Just to think of it almost made my voice catch again.

"Most realtors," I said, "just want to make the sale."

"Oh, I don't mind making the sale, Eben."

"But you seem to really get into the whole household thing. You have training, don't you, beyond your license? You seem so knowledgeable about architecture. And decoration. And even basic home repairs."

"I did my undergrad in design at Cooper Union. My ex-husband taught me about the inner workings of a house. And architecture . . . well, I can't resist going into any house that bears a plaque from the National Historic Trust. I've always loved visiting old homes."

"Lisa and I do too," I said, remembering some of our first outings together as a married couple—to Hyde Park and Lyndhurst and Olana. We had toured the Newport mansions and the painted ladies at Cape May. Once we had braved the heat and the crowds (and Lisa's morning sickness) to take the ferry to Martha's Vineyard, where we had strolled hand in hand around the Methodist campgrounds and marveled at the miniature gingerbread cottages in Oak Bluffs.

But then we had Danny. And then we stayed home. And then our home grew crowded with the kind of cheap equipment you never saw on a tour of a really grand house: a crib and a bassinet and a playpen, a walker, a stroller, a swing, and a potty chair (now all waiting in the garage for their next cheerful occupant). Danny definitely had brought clutter into our lives. But, then, Lisa and I were just as guilty of contributing to the mess. Lisa owned three funnels (why did she need even one?) and subscribed to a dozen magazines. I held on to tons of baggage from the past—from the seventy-five-cent editions of Marcus Aurelius I'd studied in college to the dusty records of Donovan and Joni Mitchell I could neither bear to listen to nor part with.

"Cynthia," I asked impulsively, "have you ever heard of something—I don't know how to pronounce the Chinese—called *feng shooey?*"

"*Fung shway,*" Cynthia told me. "We studied it briefly at school."

"Do you take stock in it?"

Cynthia lifted one finger off the steering wheel. "Here's our street," she said, and I looked out the window, annoyed at myself for not paying attention.

"Darling Lane?" I asked.

"Yes, isn't that too darling?"

"Too," I agreed.

We passed four driveways before Cynthia pointed to a mailbox marked 27. "This is the beginning of the property ... the driveway's right here ... I'm sure there's some truth in feng shui, the less superstitious parts of it. Do you believe in it?"

"Of course not. It's totally irrational. Here's Lisa now."

At the bottom of the driveway, Lisa's Camry was parked in front of a large evergreen. As soon as she saw us in her rearview mirror, Lisa cut the engine, got out of the car, and waved hello. Her neck was swaddled in my old Burberry wool scarf, and her body, which ordinarily looked longer and leaner, seemed boxy in her down coat. She looked like Danny—like a little boy!—bundled up against the snow. My ire against her softened when I realized that no one, by just looking at her, could guess she wrote for *Playboy*—especially since her Isotoner driving gloves were the only dead giveaway she was past voting age.

"It's a freezer out here!" Lisa said, giving Cynthia an impulsive hug before she planted on my cheek a chilly-lipped kiss. Her warm breath fogged up my glasses. I took them off and wiped them with my handkerchief, and as I did, I saw—however blindly—that Lisa was looking into my eyes, trying to figure out what, if anything, I now knew about her novel. I refused—at least in front of Cynthia— to let any emotion show on my face.

"Did you have trouble finding the house?" Cynthia asked Lisa.

"If it weren't for the mailbox," Lisa said, "you'd never guess anyone lived back here."

"I thought you'd like the privacy," Cynthia said. "And just *look* at this house."

I put my glasses back on, and looked. With admiration. And dismay. Although the clean and simple lines of the colonial house pleased me, I wasn't thrilled to waste my Saturday touring exactly the kind of home we had told Cynthia we had no intention of buying. Nothing historic, we'd told her. No fixer-uppers!

"This house looks old," I said.

"You're looking at Colonial *Revival*," Cynthia said. "A replica. All the charm of the old without the Neanderthal plumbing. This home was built in 1931."

"Who had money to build during the Depression?" I asked.

"A doctor."

"Ah," Lisa and I both said.

"He and his family lived here until fairly recently," Cynthia said. "The second owners completely renovated the inside. New bathrooms, new kitchen. They rewired and replaced all the worn pipes. They also just put on a new roof."

Lisa tromped back a few steps on the gravel to take a long view of the house. "There's a *weathervane* up there," she said.

I looked up. Although it was overcast, an inexplicable glare came off the roof. As I shielded my eyes with my hand, Lisa blurted out the obvious: "It's in the shape of a pig!"

As I watched the glinting outstretched hooves and perky ears of the copper pig sway back and forth, I thought the owners—who obviously didn't keep kosher—were fond of something that lately had been lacking in my own life: whimsy. This pig was silly enough to make me smile; at the same time it warned me that the wind was brisk and getting stiffer by the second.

"Let's go in," I said.

The front walk, neatly shoveled in a wide path, was lined with tidy piles of smooth, snow-covered rocks. The wooden porch—no bigger than a pulpit—looked made to order for a big dog to sit on the welcome mat. The door was painted a shade that reminded me of the twenty-dollar bill in Monopoly.

"I love the color of this door," Lisa said.

"That's called federal green," Cynthia said.

I thought it was called *ugly*. But I kept my opinion to myself, vowing that if we ended up buying this house I'd cover that color right away with a more suitable shade of paint.

Lisa touched a contraption of dried flowers and hemp that hung on the door knocker. "What do you call these things again?" she asked Cynthia.

"Swedish love knots."

Lisa turned over a tiny heart-shaped plaque hanging off the knot and read aloud, *"In every home where I am found, love and happiness shall abound."*

Cynthia's pale cheeks flushed pink. She pulled a large, clattering ring of keys from her tote bag, grasped the doorknob tightly, and inserted one of the keys. When she twisted the knob and gently let the door swing back, I had the crazy urge to scoop up a woman in my arms and carry her, like a bride, over the threshold. The trouble was, I stood there with two women—and one of them already was my wife.

I scraped my soles on the welcome mat. In other houses that we had looked at, Lisa and I had been careful not to leave our muddy tracks behind. But we never had gone so far as to take off our shoes. I knew we both felt something different for this house the moment Lisa stepped on the varnished floorboards in the hall and asked, "Anybody mind if I take off my boots?"

"I'll do the same," I said.

Cynthia declined to join us. "Cold feet," she explained.

Lisa parked herself on a long spindled bench in the hall to divest herself of her lace-up boots. As I stepped out of my loafers, I saw Cynthia—whose trim, chilled ankles were clad only in stockings— look at Lisa's socks, worn thin at the toes and heels, and then look away.

"This is your parlor," Cynthia said.

I followed her into the first room on the right and watched as she positioned herself—as if she were being sold along with all the trappings of the house—in front of the clean white mantel. She loosened the belt of her trench coat. As I tossed my coat over a wing chair, I saw Cynthia gaze down, with either amusement or approval, at my own brown Gold Toe socks. My feet had curled into the coils of the blue braided rug, all ten of my toes staking a claim to territory that seemed to belong to descendants of the *Mayflower* only.

This house looked like something out of *Yankee*. Not that I subscribed. But I had picked up the thick magazine in the waiting room of my dentist. The serene cover artwork, which showed autumn foliage and covered bridges and summer cottages by the lake, always filled me with a longing I didn't know I had until it struck me, without warning, like heartburn. Although I used to frown upon men who opted for early retirement—casting off their leather furniture and moving to Maine, where they acquired rough-hewn log beds and the durable household items hawked in the black-and-white Vermont Country Store catalog—I now knew I belonged to the same sad category. This saltbox house made me long to ditch SB! raise goats or sheep! read *The Old Farmer's Almanac* by beeswax candlelight! and wash my hands with Dr. Bronner's old-fashioned almond soap!—all clichéd desires I had hoped to stave off at least until I turned fifty.

Lisa and I moved separately around the parlor, examining the paned windows and pine-paneled floor and high ceilings. Whoever had positioned the Shaker tables and the ladder-back chairs had done it just right. The proportions were even and the room seemed snug and fit. The *ch'i,* I thought, had been realized.

I looked at Lisa. She nodded her approval.

Cynthia leaned her hand on the swinging door. "Step into your kitchen."

"Ooh," Lisa said as she went through the door.

"Nice," I said. The all-white kitchen had a black-and-white checkerboard floor. The window over the double sink gave out onto the backyard, where the stark trees were hung with birdhouses in the shape of a chapel, a schoolhouse, and a barn.

Cynthia acted first as a plumbing expert (pointing out the top-of-the-line faucets and the whisper-quiet Swedish dishwasher) and then as a master electrician (demonstrating the attention the owners had paid to ambient, task, and atmospheric lighting, and flicking on a switch to show how the white cabinets with glass fronts could be illuminated from within). The owners possessed at least two full sets of fine china—one plain gold-rimmed and the other studded with tiny blue roses—and their pantry was stocked with items I associated with the olden days of my childhood: Fleischmann's yeast, Crisco shortening, and Brer Rabbit molasses. The shelves also held several items that seemed to induce in Lisa a visible party-anxiety attack: a large percolator, several stacks of cocktail napkins, and half a dozen packets of paper plates.

After Cynthia delivered the grand tour of the laundry room and the mudroom, she put her tote bag down on the table and pointed to the white phone hanging on the wall next to the pantry. "I have a few calls I need to make, so I'll let the two of you view the rest of the house on your own."

"Oh, come!" Lisa said.

"Sure," I said. "Join us."

Cynthia shook her head. "This house sells itself."

She was right. As I followed Lisa back into the entryway, I thought, *I like this place. It seems homey.* Although I thought the owners had taken the country-living theme too far (I for one could have done without all the dried rose petals curling up in hand-thrown bowls on the end tables, and the maple-syrup jugs and canned jams lining the shelves in the tavernlike dining room), the house had something that attracted me. There was no other word for it but *heart.* I felt it in every corner.

Lisa wandered off to investigate the half-bath tucked beneath the stairs. I stopped in front of a tiny writing desk in the back alcove. On top of the desk sat a huge dictionary; *excitability/excuse* headed the left side of the page; *execrable/exemption* ruled the right.

From the door just beyond, I heard Cynthia say, "... a new listing down in Dobbs Ferry ..." I pressed my finger into the indentation marked *C* and idly flipped the thin pages of the dictionary until I reached:

*Cynthia. 1. meaning of the moon 2. the surname of Artemis, Greek goddess of hunting and childbirth, originally a Cretan goddess of fertility, who eventually was regarded as a virgin and who required chastity of her female attendants and even her male followers.*

Inside the bathroom, Lisa flushed the toilet.

I quickly flipped the pages forward, abandoning them on *epidote/ episiotomy*. Since the last thing I wanted to deal with was plumbing problems, I was grateful that Lisa always remembered to flush the toilets and run the taps in every house we visited. Still, the gurgling coming from the half-bath seemed indelicate.

Lisa came out of the bathroom, put her hand on the banister, and climbed about halfway up the steep wooden staircase. "The upstairs sounds empty."

"What do you mean?"

"I hear an echo."

When I joined her upstairs, I saw she was right. In each of the first four bedrooms, the hardwood floors were completely bare beneath our stockinged feet.

"There's stuff in the master bath," I called out, as I entered it from the hallway. Jumbo-size white towels still hung on the rack, and a collection of lotions cluttered the counter. The room jutted out onto the lawn, and as I approached the window next to the shower stall I saw—now far below me—the whimsical birdhouses hanging on the trees. The schoolhouse had a bell, and the barn roof advertised chewing tobacco.

I put the lid down and sat on the toilet. Lisa came in and sat down on the side of the Roman tub. After inspecting the faucets and jets, she told me, "It's a Jacuzzi."

"Nice."

"You would like this, Ebb, after a long day of bullshit at SB."

I pictured me—and Lisa—soaking in a vat of hot, churning water, our bodies open to the moon and the stars that shone in on the skylight. Then I reminded her, "Hot tubs are on Dr. Goode's forbidden list."

She flicked her hair off her face. "Oh, everything good is on Dr. Goode's forbidden list."

"That's not true," I said. "You don't think that's true, do you?"

Lisa looked down at the floor. She shook her head. "It's just that . . ."

I waited.

"Say," I finally said.

"... you know. I get tired of doing what we're supposed to do all the time. I just want to be able to do ... what we want."

"Oh," I said. "Well. So do I."

"You do?"

"Of course. But for now, this is the situation. You have to accept the situation."

Lisa looked down at her hands. She got up from the tub—frowned at herself in the medicine-cabinet mirror—and wandered into the master bedroom. I followed her. This room still had furniture in it—a pine armoire, an oak cheval mirror, and a big four-poster bed. The chaste white bedspread, dotted with a nubby pattern, reminded me of the coverlet that used to be on my parents' bed. When I was a boy, I had loved lying on that coverlet, which had seemed so safe and warm and comforting.

I reached out and touched Lisa's arm. I was going to say something loving, like *I dare Danny—or even Dr. Goode and all his rules—to bother us in here,* when I heard Cynthia's voice—and Cynthia's laughter—float melodiously up from the kitchen.

I looked down at Lisa's dirty white socks against the braided rug. "Since when do you write for *Playboy*?" I asked.

Shame—or defiance—blazed across Lisa's face. "Since when do you read it?" she said.

## CHAPTER FOURTEEN

# LISA

**Ebb reached into his shirt pocket**—and to my surprise, he un-
folded the first page of "He Left His Heart at the Office." Although
I knew that Ebb and I were about to exchange words (and that
those words were bound to get ugly), I still felt a thrill when I
looked at my first byline. It was all I could do to keep from whispering, *Elizabeth Diodetto, Elizabeth Diodetto, I am the mighty
Elizabeth Diodetto.*

Ebb dangled the magazine page in front of me (which, I noted,
gave him a good view of the naked Playmate pictured on the back).

"Where'd you get that?" I asked.

"Josh subscribes. At the office."

My jaw went slack. Then I laughed. "I'm telling Deb."

"Don't you dare," Ebb said. He turned the page around and
gave a quick glance at the text. "I give you an A again," he said.
"For being so ... accurate."

"Too accurate?"

Ebb shrugged. "The truth bothers me less than what you made
up."

"But, Ebb. I had to make up. It's fiction."

"But, Lisar. Don't you realize how people will read this? I can
take that people might mistake me for this Simon. But if they
thought that I was obsessed with my secretary—"

"You are a little obsessed with Victoria."

"That's because I want to kill her—not kiss her." Ebb swallowed—not once, but twice—which meant this conversation already was giving him heartburn. "Besides, did you stop to think—for just one second—how she might feel when she reads your novel?"

"Probably a lot better," I said, "than she felt after she read your *bliss*."

Ebb looked pained. "Listen, Lisar."

I resisted the urge to plug my ears. "You have my undivided attention."

"I thought this was well written. And kind of moving. But did you have to tell Josh and not me?"

"I meant to tell you," I said. "Last night. Really. But every time I started, I thought about how you'd get all bent out of shape."

"I'm bent—as you call it—not so much by what you wrote, but where you published it." Ebb looked down at the Playmate. "Why do you have to write for Hugh Hefner? Why can't you write for someone who runs a nice, clean magazine, like this Martha Stewart woman Josh was telling me about?"

"Martha Stewart is a crock of shit!" I sunk my toes deep into the braided carpet. "Martha's supposed to be the perfect housewife and hostess. But I read in *Publishers Weekly*—"

At the mere mention of *PW,* Ebb winced.

"—that right after she wrote a book on planning your dream wedding—for which she was paid some astronomical advance!—Martha's husband up and left her for—I forget which—either Martha's personal assistant or Martha's fake hands."

"What are fake hands?"

"You know, like body doubles for movie stars who don't want to do the nude scenes?" I held out my hands at Ebb. "Martha's got these beat-up hands, so in the photos of her cutting out gingerbread cookies and arranging gladioli they substitute the hands of a younger woman."

I reached forward, plucked "He Left His Heart at the Office" from Ebb's fingers, and smoothed out the wrinkles. "I don't get your objections to *Playboy*."

"It's total fantasy."

"So? Don't you have fantasies, every now and then?" My eyes caught Ebb's in the cheval mirror and I laughed a nervous laugh. "Don't worry, I won't ask you to share them."

Ebb gave me a tired smile. "Too bad. I was so hoping you would."

Did he really mean that? I wondered. He *couldn't* have meant that. I honestly didn't want to know what he was thinking of when he ... And the last thing I wanted to confess was that ... well, now wasn't the time to mention matadors. Or plumbers. Or any of the other odd assortment of men I sometimes consorted with in my dreams. I didn't want them there. I swear it. But they kept on coming at me, over and over, so that I had begun to think, *Surely I must be dreaming of all these other men because I no longer love Ebb.* But I did love Ebb. Why else did I feel so sad—and so hurt—to know that he also dreamed of women other than me?

I got so confused thinking about it that I did something I never deigned to do when I was in a stranger's house, because I felt like it was far too personal: I sat down on the four-poster bed. Surprisingly, Ebb didn't chide me for sitting on someone else's mattress. He simply stuck his hands in his trouser pockets and jingled his keys, as if he wished the keys—and not we—could do the talking. Then he took his hands out of his pockets and sat down on the bed next to me, so the mattress gave off an embarrassing creak.

"I did like your story, Lisar."

"You're just saying that."

"No. Really. I thought you put your finger on that kind of vague dissatisfaction that people feel—when they don't really know what they're feeling. It seemed ... very realistic."

I shrugged. "I'm not so sure I want to hear that."

"You know what I mean."

I looked down at Ebb's right hand—when had those small but distinct age spots appeared along his thumb?—which was just inches away from my own left hand (which looked as dry and wrinkled as the hide of an elephant). And I had to tell myself, *Don't you dare start crying,* when Ebb put his hand on mine and squeezed it.

"You could have used your real name, Lisar."

"Well, I thought people might get confused," I said. "By the final *r*."

Ebb nudged my foot with his foot.

"Plus," I said, "I didn't want to open you up to embarrassment at work."

"I appreciate that."

"Plus . . . I don't know. I guess I've just gotten tired of being Mrs. You."

"But I don't think of you as Mrs. You. I mean, Mrs. Me."

"Other people do. Like at these parties we go to. Whenever I get separated from you, I have to go around introducing myself as Eben Strauss's wife."

I thought Ebb would get offended—take his hand away—and say something defensive like, *Well, what's wrong with that?* But he held on to my hand and said, "Is that why you really hate those parties?"

It was tempting to whine—once again—about all the inconveniences of putting on control-top panty hose and making endless chitchat. But I plucked at one of the nubs of the bedspread and said, "It's just that lately, there's never enough time for anything. And I was kind of hoping—you know—that we could have more of the kind of parties we used to have. Where the guest list was confined to you and me."

Ebb cleared his throat. "I like those parties too."

"Too bad Danny keeps crashing them."

Ebb sighed. "I know. But we couldn't live without him."

I kept silent. Ebb would think I was a rotten mother—even *I* thought I was a rotten mom!—for sometimes thinking that Ebb and I would have a much better relationship (or certainly a more romantic one) if only Danny didn't come between us right and left.

Ebb took "He Left His Heart" off my lap. He carefully folded the magazine page picture side up, first in half, then in quarters, then in eighths—until I almost hollered, *No! No! Please do not go down to sixteenths!* Yet that was exactly what he did—making the

Playmate into the equivalent of a kindergarten origami project. Then he got up from the bed and stuck the tight little wad of paper into a plastic sleeve of his wallet.

In the silence that followed, I wondered why a house built in 1931 wasn't better soundproofed. Cynthia's voice came wafting up through the vents.

"I forgot Cynthia was down there," I said.

"She probably overheard every word we said."

I listened. But I couldn't distinguish her words, which meant she hadn't been able to recognize ours. "She's probably been on the phone the whole time," I said. "With her boyfriend."

"She has a boyfriend?"

"She told me she's in love with him." I got up from the bed. "Did you check out the closet space in here?"

I reached for the doorknob that led to the walk-in closet and went inside. On the right-hand side, a thick crush of women's clothes hung on the rack. The rod on the other side of the closet— with the exception of half a dozen wire hangers, which began to *ting!* against one another like wind chimes—was empty.

Ebb stuck his head into the closet. "What do you know about him?"

I gestured at the empty hangers. "The guy obviously left his wife."

Ebb frowned at the solitary hangers left on the rod. "Maybe he died."

"And maybe I'm Martha Stewart."

Ebb—rather sorrowfully, I thought—shook his head. "I was talking about what you knew about Cynthia's *boyfriend*."

"I don't know if he's ever been married," I said.

"I should think you'd have the entire poop on him by now. Considering how much you know about this hairy Angus."

I shrugged. "I just know that her boyfriend has a really weird job. He owns this service that rids people's homes of wildlife."

Ebb's voice rose. "Cynthia goes out with an exterminator?"

"Shhh. He doesn't trap mice or spray for roaches. He captures big game."

"Moose and elk are big game, Lisar."

"So are squirrels and raccoons—if they're stuck in your walls and attic. But her boyfriend *does* do big creatures. Once he even took care of a bear in someone's backyard."

"He killed a bear?"

"Of course not. I think he shot it with one of those *National Geographic* harpoon-things that puts the animal to sleep. And then he relocated it somewhere more appropriate, like a zoo or a Girl Scout camp."

Ebb looked confounded by all this information. "Where did she meet this guy?"

"Rotary," I said.

Ebb took my arm and led me out of the closet. "Come on. We've got a house to look at."

"Do you like this house?" I asked.

"No," Ebb said slowly, as he gazed around the bedroom. "I don't know why—but I love it."

Maybe *without knowing why* was the only way to love. My heart, at least, never seemed to work in conjunction with my head. As Ebb and I retraced our steps upstairs, then did the same downstairs, I felt—more than I rationally evaluated—that the house seemed just right for us. After all, we'd just had our first argument in it, and yet we were still talking.

We rejoined Cynthia in the kitchen. As Cynthia finished her call and hung up the wall phone, I went to the back window and gazed out on the snowy garden. "Over in the corner—off to the left—there's an arbor," I reported. "And statuary."

"It's a rose garden," Cynthia said. "It will look beautiful in spring."

"Spring is never going to get here," I said.

"It already is here," Ebb said.

"On the calendar, maybe. But not in real life."

"Patience," Ebb said.

"Optimism," Cynthia replied.

"But every year winter seems longer," I said.

Cynthia smiled. "Somebody once said that winter only adds to the poetry of a house."

"It also adds—significantly—to the oil bill," Ebb reminded her.

"It must cost a *shitload* to heat this place," I said.

"There's a new furnace," Cynthia said. "The windows are double-paned Andersen glass. And in the attic—I don't suppose you went up to the attic—the owners have put down fiberglass insulation. If you like, I could find out the average heating bill and report back to you."

When neither of us replied, Cynthia said, "I'll have the numbers on Monday. As I said, this is a brand-new listing. You're the first couple to come through here."

I barely kept myself from commanding Ebb, *Whip out your checkbook!*

"Do you think this house'll get a lot of traffic?" I asked.

"Traffic always picks up in the spring," Cynthia said. She gathered up her keys. "I take it you like this one."

I brought one finger up to a hairline crack in the ceramic tile, as if it represented numerous flaws in the house's structure. "It's different than everything else we've looked at so far."

"We really had in mind," Ebb said, "something more modern."

"But it is modern," said Cynthia. "If you think about it. A colonial has the same clean lines as a contemporary."

Cynthia then gave us the rundown on what she called "the nitty-gritty": the property taxes (ouch!) and the public school system (yes, the house was in the right district) and the "proximity to desirable amenities" (I refrained from asking, *How far is the nearest Dunkin' Donuts?*). Then she got to the downside. "Of course, this house has less square footage than others in this price range."

Ebb and I exchanged a quick glance.

"I don't think I was in on the conversation," Ebb said, "when you and Lisa discussed the price."

"Actually, we didn't discuss it," Cynthia said. Cynthia always gave her figures in abbreviated form—instead of using hundred thousands, she merely said "mid-fives" or "low sixes." Now she gave us a number that seemed as high as that pig weathervane, and just as whimsical: *three quarters.*

*Three quarters of* what? I wanted to ask, until I realized she was saying *million.*

"Forget it," I said.

Ebb gave me one of his annoying *I'll-handle-this* looks. "It's overpriced."

"Astronomically," I added.

After she talked up the new bathrooms and kitchen and roof and reminded us of the size of the lot, Cynthia finally admitted, "It's a little steep. But I thought it worth your time to come out here because that's just the listing price."

"But the owners will hold on until someone comes close," I said.

"Don't be so sure," Ebb said. "They may be anxious to get rid of it."

"Well, the husband obviously already cut his losses—unless he decided, on a whim, to send his entire wardrobe to the dry cleaner's." I turned to Cynthia. "We went in their closet."

"Oh," she said.

"Did you know the owners had split?" I asked.

Cynthia nodded. "I met the wife."

"What was your read on the situation?" Ebb asked.

Cynthia paused. "My read—without going into the specifics right now—was that the negotiations most definitely would swing in the buyer's favor. Now, if there are no more questions—no more questions for now?—we'll walk out the back and look around the property." She pointed at our stockinged feet. "Don't forget your shoes. I won't be responsible for frostbite."

Cynthia put on her trench coat. In the parlor, Ebb fetched my down coat. I saw him look puzzled at how heavy it was, and I feared he would reach into my pocket and pull out the goose-egg gravel I had stolen to hide beneath our bed. But then he held my coat out to me so I could easily get into the sleeves. For a second, I thought this gesture caused a flicker of sadness in Cynthia's eyes. Maybe she wanted someone to hold out her coat for her, I thought. Or maybe she thought it was totally passé, the old-fashioned way Ebb treated me.

Outside, the wind had sharpened, and the confettilike shreds of dead leaves that weren't buried beneath the snow skittered across the lawn. Ebb's loafers crunched on the gravel. I lowered my face into my scarf and turned up the collar of my coat. We circled around the back of the house, walking down a bricked path lined with dormant rosebushes and verdigris statues: a country bumpkin wearing a wig of snow and strumming a mandolin as he courted a maiden, a terra-cotta rabbit howling at the moon, and a wide-faced stone frog, practically buried in a grave of white, that seemed on the verge of letting loose a tremendous burp. A sundial sat on a pedestal; it was so cloudy, the gnomon caught no shadow.

Much as I wanted to linger—peek back in the house and look around the property some more—I also was anxious to get to the salon in time to suck on a breath mint and touch up my makeup before I sat down in Ricardo's chair and begged him to ... well, *do me.*

I pulled back my coat sleeve and glanced at my watch. "Look at the time," I said. "I'll be late for my haircut."

"We wouldn't want to keep Roberto waiting," Ebb said.

*"Ricardo,"* Cynthia and I both said.

Cynthia also looked at her watch. "You'd better run. I'll drop Eben off on my way back to the office."

As we started to trudge around the side of the house, I asked Cynthia, "You don't mind?"

"Not at all," Ebb said.

I hesitated. *Who asked you?* hardly seemed a polite response. So I said, "Don't forget to pick up Danny."

"I won't," Ebb said.

"And you got the garbage out, right?"

"The cans made it to the curb."

I smelled something funny in the passive construction of that sentence. But now wasn't the time to pursue it. I headed for my car. "All right. I'm freezing. *Adiós,* everybody."

"Drive carefully," Ebb said.

"I *will,*" I said—because Ebb's backseat driving really annoyed me.

"It's supposed to get slick, so take it slow—"

"I *know.*"

"But not so slow you get pushed off the road when you're merging—"

I smiled, got into my car, and fought back the urge to give Ebb the finger. As I slipped my key into the ignition and started my engine, I wondered why I had led Cynthia to believe that Ebb was perfect. I mean, the guy didn't even know rule number one of maintaining a good marriage: Let the driver *drive*!

## CHAPTER FIFTEEN

# EBEN

**Big puffs of exhaust** belched from the tailpipe of Lisa's Camry as we followed her onto Darling Lane. Lisa was driving far too slowly; Cynthia obviously was trying not to stay on her bumper.

"Honk at her," I told Cynthia.

"Didn't you tell her to drive carefully?" Cynthia asked.

"That's exactly why she's driving like a snail," I said. "To tick me off."

Cynthia smiled. "Which one of you will teach Danny to drive?"

"That's a long way off." I calculated forward. I would be *fifty-two* when Danny got his learner's permit. I could begin tapping into my 401(k)—without penalty—when he was just a senior in college. Which meant I probably would be ready to check into a rest home when my next child (if we ever had one) started packing her bags for Harvard.

I looked out the window at the barren trees. "A little bird— named Lisa—told me you have a good friend. Who takes care of wildlife problems."

"That's right. Why do you ask?"

I had no idea. My throat went dry as I fabricated an answer. "This friend of mine suspects he has squirrels in his walls."

"I'll have Rob call him," Cynthia said. She nodded at the glove compartment. "There's a pen and a memo pad in there—write down your friend's name and number."

I reluctantly reached forward and took the pen and paper out of Cynthia's glove box. I almost wrote down *Josh Silber,* until I remembered that Cynthia and Josh already were acquainted.

"Actually," I said as I carelessly scribbled down another name, "I don't remember Simon's phone number."

"I'll have Rob call you, then, at the office."

"Fine," I said, shoving the pen and memo pad back into the glove compartment. I looked away from the road again, imagining the woodchucks and raccoons and other masked intruders lurking in the forest. "I expect your friend does good business. Out in these parts."

"Phenomenal. He's looking to expand."

"We should have dinner sometime," I said. "The four of us, that is."

"Sounds like fun," Cynthia said.

She reached over and switched on the radio. The mellifluous voice of the classical deejay announced, "And now let us enjoy the overture to Janáček's *The Cunning Little Vixen.*" At the end of Darling Lane, Lisa honked and turned her Camry to the right; Cynthia turned her wheel to the left. I watched Lisa's car recede in the passenger-side rearview that warned: OBJECTS IN MIRROR ARE CLOSER THAN THEY APPEAR.


"So we'll stay in touch about the house," Cynthia said as she pulled into our driveway.

"If we have any questions," I said, disengaging my seat belt with a snap, "we'll call you tomorrow."

Cynthia paused. "I won't be available tomorrow."

"Monday, then." I opened the car door and let in a blast of cold air.

To my surprise, Cynthia reached out and touched my sleeve. "Wait. If you're serious about this house, I'll turn on my pager tomorrow."

I was serious. But I didn't want Cynthia to think we were too willing to overspend on this one property, so I said, "Monday will be fine. Thanks for the lift."

She nodded, and let go of my sleeve. "My pleasure."

I got out, closed the car door, and watched Cynthia back her Lexus out of the driveway. I wondered what grand plans she had for tomorrow that would cause her to disconnect her pager. Maybe I was letting my imagination get the best of me, but the way she had murmured "my pleasure" reminded me of a time when I used to hustle a younger, more carefree version of Lisa up this very walk, close the front door without locking it, and take Lisa down onto the living-room carpet—so that afterward she said, "Mmm, thank you," and I said, "Mmm, my pleasure."

Now, what did Lisa and I say to each other after we made love?

*I about plotzed.*

*Me too.*

Such romantic language. I cast a sad look at the two silent sentinels watching over our house, Snow Man (who had been stripped of his tie) and Snow Woman (who had defiantly dropped both her broom and her mop). I kicked a dead leaf off the black rubber mat that lay on our front porch. My key scraped, once again, in the lock. I threw open the door and punched in the security code with my gloves still on, causing me to hit two buttons at once. The display pad flashed ERROR ERROR.

I bolted for the bathroom. A bad line from Lisa's novel *Real Men!* had read: *Magnus groaned with pleasure as his piss hit the bowl in a forceful, urgent stream.* My marginal comment—*Overwrought for a mere pee*—had been written before I was old enough to experience a certain slackness in my own bladder. I knew I should have used the facilities at the colonial house. But I couldn't stand to hear Lisa's objections. Even though she always tested the plumbing in the houses we visited, Lisa claimed it was a violation of the owners' rights to actually take a whiz—and positively verboten to *lower your butt onto the throne.* She had established this sacred rule one Saturday afternoon after we returned home and discovered that a prospective buyer (or Mrs. Order herself) had taken a colossal dump in our upstairs toilet—without double flushing.

"Eeew, somebody really *went* in here," Lisa had said, flicking on the bathroom fan. "How disgusting."

"It probably was an urgent situation," I said.

Lisa grunted as she cracked open the window. "Our personal space has been invaded. In the most gruesome of ways! I swear, this is worse than Charles Manson coming in and scrawling graffiti all over the mirror with my twelve-dollar lipstick."

"You pay twelve dollars for a lipstick?" I asked.

"Sometimes thirteen."

Lisa flushed the toilet, grabbed a bottle of Vanish, and squirted into the bowl a long stream of blue liquid. As she scrubbed the toilet with a brush, Lisa expressed optimism about a sale. "Pooping a big *plotz* in somebody else's house is the equivalent of trying on a bikini bottom without your underwear. You simply have a moral obligation to buy it."

"I doubt this pooper," I said, "shares your scruples."

Lisa sniffed. "I doubt he's of the appropriate sex to wear a bikini."

"What makes you so sure it was a he?"

"It just seems like a man," Lisa said. "Who so rudely intruded! A woman would have flushed twice. And if that didn't do the trick, then she would have reached for the toilet brush—which is sitting right here next to the bowl—and done whatever she had to do to clean up the mess."

Ever since that episode, I'd been squeamish about even pissing in someone else's toilet, as if Lisa were waiting in the wings to reprimand me for my poor bathroom habits.

I flushed, washed my hands, grabbed Lisa's handwritten directions to the birthday boy's house (inexplicably labeled FOX BIRTH-DAY), reactivated the security alarm—and then remembered the trash cans. My nose wrinkled as I stepped into the malodorous garage. I really didn't want to hear Lisa's commentary on how incompetently I performed certain household tasks. I unlocked the trunk of my Audi, removed the lids from the trash cans, and piled the smelly garbage bags inside. On the way to pick up Danny, I would stop and wing the bags into the Dumpster behind the Price Chopper.

My Audi sounded gruff when I started it. On the road, wind

from passing minivans shook the car. A freezing drizzle—that probably would turn to sheer ice by that night—began to cloud the windshield. The defroster was a blast of cold, stale air; the wipers made a sick, gritty complaint. The gas gauge had dipped to *E;* I'd have to stop and fill up.

When I got out at the pump at the Mobil station, freezing rain swept beneath the overhang and pelted down on my head. I finished gassing up the car and dashed inside to pay, then drove around to the back. The Dumpster was labeled FOR COMMERCIAL PURPOSES ONLY; ALL OTHER USE SUBJECT TO FINES. I decided not to flirt with danger. I'd try the grocery store. But then I realized the Price Chopper was back in the opposite direction and that I didn't have another minute to waste.

I already was running late to pick up Danny. I tried not to drive too fast. But I felt like I was in a nightmare where I kept running down an ever-longer terminal to catch a plane—a dream not unlike the reality of O'Hare Airport. Car after car passed by me, doing fifty miles an hour to my thirty. I had gotten trapped behind a square white Wise potato chip truck, which kept sending swoosh after swoosh of rain back onto my windshield. For two or three miles I watched the blurry picture of the stout, ruffled owl on the back of the truck who held up a finger—or was that a claw?—and commanded me, MAKE THE WISE CHOICE.

In the birthday boy's section of town, one subdivision followed another, and I couldn't find the right gate. After another hasty glance at the directions Lisa had provided, I turned into the village marked *Buckingham* and peered at the street signs—Chippendale, Spencer, Hepplewhite, and, finally, Regency.

At 1502 Regency—a Tudor home positively baronial in stature— a cluster of shriveled, drooping balloons was tethered to the mailbox. The winding driveway was empty. I clearly was the last parent to walk up the slippery, lit porch steps. The black railing felt slick and thick as a Popsicle beneath my hand. The massive front door opened before I even had a chance to ring the lit bell, and a disembodied woman's hand beckoned me into the dimly lit marble foyer, where a grandfather clock, chiding me for my tardiness, tolled the half hour.

The birthday boy's mother, dressed in some sort of silky pantsuit outfit, shut the door behind me with a sharp thud. "I'm June Fox."

"Eben Strauss." I shook her cold, outstretched hand. "How was the party?"

"I'll get your son," she said, and disappeared.

The case of the grandfather clock was made of glass. At the end of the pendulum hung a gold disk big as a china plate; I watched it swing back and forth until a fashionably unshaven man in chinos and a maroon polo came out of the shadows at the back of the house. The minute he opened his mouth and a series of foul vowel sounds came out, I could tell he hailed from Boston.

"Your son said *fuck* at the pot-ty."

I tried not to laugh. But *pot-ty* really got to me.

"I'm sorry about that," I said.

"Choon—that's my wife—Choon put him in time-out."

"That's fine."

"But when your son came out of time-out, he gave all the rest of these *he-yuh* kids a completely screwy working definition of the word."

I wondered exactly how wrong Danny had gotten it. I could just hear him chirping, *And then the man sticks his wienie in the lady's rear end. But I'm not sure my dad knows how to do it right, because once I saw him . . .*

June Fox, followed by her own darling son, ushered in Danny.

I clapped my gloves together and the smack loudly resounded in the foyer, which had a vaulted ceiling. "Okay, Danny," I said, "zip up your coat and let's get going before it starts snowing."

"I wanna stay," Danny said.

"I think you've already worn out your welcome," I said.

"What does that mean?"

"It means you can ask Zachary over to our house sometime," I said.

"Why can't I ask Noah?"

"Who the hell is Noah?" I asked.

Choon Fox gasped at my language. Danny pointed to the pale, overly sugared birthday boy, who was hopping on one foot on the marble tile, as if attempting to squash a large insect. "You want to come to dinner, Noah?"

"Not tonight," I said. "Some other time. Come on. Where are your shoes?"

"Right there!" Danny pointed to a pair of Reeboks pushed to the side of the stairs.

"Well, put them on."

Danny sat down on the tile. To my great chagrin, he started to put his left sneaker on his right foot.

"You know better than that," I said. "Right goes with right."

Danny slipped on the right sneaker and then looked down at the laces with dismay. Noah snickered—the little shit!—and I got down on my knees and tied the right laces, letting Danny fashion a bastardized bow on the left.

"Okay," I said. "Mittens on. Zip up. Say thank you to your hosts."

"Thank you!" Danny said, and smiled so hard that saliva squeezed out the gap of his missing tooth. I leaned over to pull the drawstrings of his hood. "Ow, Daddy, you're choking me. I enjoyed myself a lot!"

To the Foxes I said, "Sorry for the misbehavior."

Mr. Fox nodded. In a voice that hardly seemed to convey good wishes, June Fox said, "Best of luck with your new baby."

*What new baby?* I almost asked. Then I looked down, once again, at the one child I did have, sunk my fingers into Danny's fleecy hood, and practically pulled him out the door.

Whoever said that parenting comes naturally failed to acknowledge that frustration does too. After we slipped our way down the walk to the driveway, I wanted to chide Danny for his bad manners. I wanted to tell him to concentrate less on his parents' sex life and more on learning how to tie his own damn sneakers. Instead, I opened the passenger-side door and gestured for him to climb in.

Danny sat on the True Value Hardware bag. "Ow! What's that?"

"A lock."

"What for?" Danny asked.

"If you can't remember what you did wrong this morning," I

said, "then your memory is even worse than mine." I eased the bag out from under Danny. "Why did you say *fuck* in Noah's house?"

"You and Mommy do it all the time."

"We do not do it all the time," I said. "We don't even *say* it all the time! And why did you tell Noah's parents that Mommy is going to have a baby?"

"Isn't she?"

I gazed into Danny's liquidy black eyes. Danny looked so puzzled—so trusting—that I momentarily considered making this into some lesson on the difference between trying and succeeding and the wide gap that often existed between what you wanted and what you wound up getting.

Finally I resorted to a word that Danny only understood about two-thirds of the time. "No," I said. "She isn't."

Danny accepted this statement as blithely as if I had pointed out that his left shoe wasn't tied correctly. "Noah had a chocolate ice-cream cake," he said. "But his mother is crabby. She put me in time-out."

"You and I are going to talk about that later."

"I didn't mean to, Daddy."

I leaned into the open car door. "*Mean to* doesn't matter. What matters is what you *did*."

"Don't tell Mommy."

"No, I *will* tell Mommy. You did something wrong and now you have to take the consequences."

I shut the passenger door so hard the antenna quivered.

When I tossed the True Value Hardware bag into the backseat, the smell of the garbage in the trunk wafted toward me. I got in, started the car, and backed up. As we looped around Regency Drive, the windshield wipers swooshing back and forth in regular rhythm, I said, "I don't understand why you're acting up so much lately."

Danny slumped down in his seat. "Noah acts up too."

"Noah is not my son," I said. "So I don't care about his behavior."

"But he cheats, Daddy. He looked through the blindfold when we were playing Pin the Tail on the Donkey. And at school he picks his nose and pretends the snots are sunflower seeds, then he puts them in the granola."

"That's disgusting," I said. "Tell the teacher."

"I do. And she puts Noah in time-out. But then when he comes out of time-out, he sneaks his snots back in again." Danny scrunched up his nose. "What's that smell?"

"I forgot to take out the garbage this morning, so I put it in the trunk." I looked down at Danny. "Don't tell Mommy."

He gave me an evil smile. "I won't tell Mommy about the garbage," he said, "if you don't tell Mommy about me saying *fuck* at Noah's party."

Such blackmail seemed morally reprehensible. Nevertheless, I told Danny, "We have a deal."

## CHAPTER SIXTEEN

# LISA

**I was leaning against a mound** of pillows on our unmade bed, bemoaning my lousy haircut, when Ebb and Danny got home. They must have been surprised to find the entire first floor dark, because I heard them calling out in alternating high and low voices, "Mommy?" "Lisar?" "Mommy?" "Lisar?" until I thought I'd shout back, *I refuse to be either one.*

Yet the moment they appeared in the bedroom doorway, I blew Ebb a kiss and then opened my arms so Danny could lunge right into them.

"Take off your shoes," Ebb told Danny—a bit too sharply, "before you climb into Mommy and Daddy's bed."

Danny pulled off his sneakers and dropped them to the floor, then proceeded to give me more kisses than Ebb probably had given me since the turn of the year. I received each smack with the appropriate coo of pleasure and tried not to sound peevish when I spoke to Ebb.

"Law and Order brought by a prospective buyer," I said. "But she almost didn't get in the front door because you forgot to oil the lock again." I sighed. "Well, at least you remembered to take out the garbage. Even if you left your dirty lunch dishes in the sink."

"Mrs. O. told me he was a bachelor," Ebb said, "and wouldn't notice."

"The guy was totally gay. He noticed everything." I sank my head against the pillow. "God. I have the worst headache. And this haircut."

Ebb leaned in the doorway and stopped to evaluate my chopped locks—which made me look like a shorn sheep. "It is kind of—"

"All *right*," I said. "I *know*."

"I don't see why you cut it again," Ebb said.

"The cut was all wrong last time."

"Couldn't you go back to the same stylist and ask her to fix it?"

"You don't get it. I trusted Ricardo. To make me look like Cynthia. And then Ricardo spent all of five minutes cutting my hair and charged me—well, you don't want to know what I paid."

"You're right. I don't." Ebb shrugged. "It'll grow out, Lisar."

I bit down the urge to say, *But it won't grow back by Monday when I meet with Aye-Aye.* I squeezed Danny's shoulder. "So how was the birthday party?"

"Noah cheated at Blind Man's Bluff," Danny said.

"I thought you said it was Pin the Tail on the Donkey," Ebb said.

"No, Blind Man's Bluff," Danny said.

I winced. Because I knew what was coming. Ebb just couldn't leave well enough alone; he always had to prove himself right.

"Danny," Ebb said, "I distinctly remember you saying he cheated at Pin the Tail—"

"I didn't!"

"You did."

"What does it *matter*?" I interrupted.

In the silence that followed, I heard the freezing rain repeatedly tapping on the skylight. When I looked over at Ebb, he turned his back and put down his wallet and keys on his chest of drawers. He was standing directly in front of the tilted mirror he had yet to rehang in Danny's bedroom, so I could still see his face. It kind of scared me. Not since his father died had I seen him look so weary.

"I'm hungry," said Danny.

"I'll make dinner," I said. "In just a second." I gave him a gentle shove. "Go downstairs and do something constructive with yourself."

After Danny disappeared downstairs, Ebb sat down on the side of the mattress, with his back toward me. His posture seemed to say: *I just can't bear another minute of this. Someone else will have to be me tonight.*

"I'll make dinner," I repeated.

"You have a headache," Ebb reminded me.

I did feel my forehead throbbing. But Ebb clearly had bigger problems than that. I leaned forward and touched his arm. "Ebb."

"What."

"What's the matter?"

"Nothing is the matter."

"But lately," I said, "I can't help noticing—you seem so moody. And your temper is short. And you're going through Tums like crazy."

Ebb leaned his elbows on his knees. I knew he was having one of those moments when you look down at your hands and can't believe they're your own hands, and then your sense of who you are—and what you are doing on the earth—gets even more convoluted when you look down and think, *But if these are not my hands, then what about my feet? my heart? my head?*

"Inside . . ." Ebb said.

"Yes?"

He put his hand on his stomach. "I just feel like . . ."

I nodded.

"There's a war going on," he said.

I reached over and smoothed my hand over his back, slowly, the way I used to soothe Danny after he fed at my breast. "Maybe you just need to burp a wee bit more."

"I do *not* need to burp," Ebb said. "Especially a *wee bit* more."

I immediately took my hand off his back. I knew I had made a big mistake by implying that all of Ebb's problems could be traced to mere acid indigestion. Something obviously was tearing him up inside. But how could I not reduce Ebb's issues to the need for a rip-roaring belch—if he refused to talk to me about them? Why didn't he just spill? Was his tongue lashed to the back of his throat?

*If only!* I thought, as he stood up from the bed and asked, "What's for dinner?"

I never went out of my way to cook on Saturday nights, so the dinner I fixed was just canned split-pea soup with carrots, and egg salad chopped with red onions and Spanish olives on sourdough bread. But the freezing rain tapping on the windows made the soup seem even warmer and the bread more doughy and satisfying.

After dinner, the sleet suddenly ceased. I pulled back the blinds of the sliding glass door and switched on the outside light so we could watch the fat snowflakes fall on the redwood deck chairs we hadn't bothered to store in the garage last autumn. Danny talked about making a Snow Child in the morning. I vowed to suck on an icicle. Outside, the world became so clean and white that even Ebb didn't seem discouraged by the thought of shoveling the walk and driveway in the morning. I fixed us all big steamy mugs of hot chocolate, and the miniature marshmallows I dropped into Danny's cup turned him into a saint. At eight o'clock, without being nagged, he put away his Lincoln Logs and Legos and announced, "I want morning to come faster, so I'm going to bed."

At the tender hour of nine-thirty, Ebb was nodding over the previous day's *Wall Street Journal.* My own walrus-size yawns signaled it was time to admit defeat and collapse into bed. The whistle and rasp of Danny's breath was audible even on the first turn of the stairs. He was asleep—probably on his back—with his mouth open again. I went into his room. As I flipped him over, I remembered how I used to lean over his bassinet and bolster him with rolled-up towels to keep him from flopping onto his stomach. As a baby— and even now—Danny always had reminded me of roadkill: a furry raccoon or unsuspecting possum turned on his side, his tiny paws brought up to his face to shield himself from harm.

I went into our bedroom, opened the drawer that held some of my prettier nightgowns, and thought to myself, *Why bother?* I pulled out a pair of silk long johns, and with my back to Ebb, I put them on and crawled beneath the covers.

I watched Ebb step out of his pants. He seemed to consider hanging his Dockers in the crammed closet before he tossed them on the ever-increasing pile of laundry on the chair.

I gazed at the mess. "It's late," I said, "and I'm choosing to look the other way."

"Excellent decision," Ebb said as he climbed into bed.

I cut the light and snuggled further under the mound of blankets. "God, it's cold in here."

"Even with those long johns on?" Ebb asked.

"They're called Cuddl Duds," I said.

"Sure they're not called HANDS OFF, ASSHOLE?"

"You could always take your chances," I said.

Ebb took my hand. "Come here."

I inched over.

"No, closer," Ebb said. "Come on. Closer. I'm not going to start anything. I'm too tired."

"What if I'm not?" I said.

"Then shut up," Ebb said, "and make your move."

I laughed as I put my head on Ebb's bare chest. "I hear your heart."

"And what does it say?"

I listened to the quiet, rhythmic thudding. "It says: Talk to me, talk to me, talk to me, talk to me."

Ebb put his arms around me and kissed the top of my head. "What did you really think of that house?"

I sighed and curled my leg over his. "I loved that house so much I took something from it."

Ebb's shoulder stiffened. "Lisar. What *next* with you?"

"It was just one of the goose-egg stones that lined the front walk."

"But why?"

"At first I just wanted to feel one up. They looked so round and full—but heavy and solid—and once I had one in my hand, I had to have it in my pocket."

"Thief," Ebb said.

"It's just a rock."

"But you *stole* it."

"With the best of intentions," I said. "I took the rock because I wanted a guarantee we would go back to that house."

"You could have chosen a less criminal method." Ebb hesitated. "You could have said, 'Let's go back to that house. Together.' "

"I was afraid you'd say no dice," I said. "That it was out of the question."

"Why didn't you get the price from Cynthia beforehand?"

"It completely slipped my mind."

"It's a full hundred over the limit I gave her."

"But she said she thought the owners would come down," I said. "She obviously knows something that we don't know."

"Call her on Monday and find out," Ebb said.

"How?"

"Since when are you shy? Ask her, point-blank, if she thinks it's an acrimonious divorce—"

"Like divorce is ever amicable?" I asked.

"—and if there's a custody battle going on—"

"What else do you want to know?" I asked. "If there's a third party involved?" I laughed. "The names of their lawyers?"

Ebb—exasperated—said, "Keep it up, Lisar."

"Oh, I plan on it. 'Til death do us part." I felt my forehead getting all wrinkly with worry. "It doesn't bother you, does it, that the people who lived there split up?"

Ebb shook his head. "Their loss is our gain."

Of course, Ebb didn't ask me back: *Does it bother you?* It did, sort of. And Cynthia must have realized that the divorce of the owners would trouble me, otherwise she would have told me about it right off the bat.

"I checked out this library book," I told Ebb.

"That one on *feng shui*?"

"How did you know?" I asked.

"You left it in the living room. I picked it up last night when I couldn't go to sleep."

"I checked it out," I said, "strictly for research."

Ebb's silence seemed to ask, *Just like your* Wild Women Wanna?

"Anyway," I said, "this book cautioned against moving into a house that has a bad *ch'i* attached to it. But I figure we aren't

Chinese. Plus we aren't into the careful placement of mirrors, so I say fuck it. Let's go for it."

"Okay." Ebb patted my back. "Just get the pertinent information from Cynthia that will help me get that price down."

"What if you can't get the price down?"

Ebb thought about that for a long time. "We could swing it. I guess. But it would be a stretch if we end up doing all that in-vitro stuff . . . you know, with Dr. Goode."

"Ugh," I said. "The shots."

"I'd rather not think about the shots," Ebb said.

"*You'd* rather not," I said. "What about me? It's my butt the needle goes into."

"Yes, but I'm the one who has to . . . you know . . . stick it in there."

"My sorrow for you knows no bounds," I said.

"But I don't want to hurt you, Lisar. Really. Besides, I'm afraid I won't get the needle in right—"

"On my flab-ola butt? How could you miss?"

Ebb reached down and put his hand on my rear end. "I know there's something I'm supposed to say now."

"So say it. Say: 'Your butt isn't flab-ola, Lisar.' "

"Your butt isn't—"

"And while you're at it, say, 'Your haircut looks fine,' and then say, 'Your novel is so spectacular it makes my heart stop,' and then say, 'I. I. Iforson definitely will sell it for six figures so we can buy that house and live happily ever after.' "

Ebb—of course—wouldn't say any of this. "I don't mean to be a prude, Lisar. But if publishing in *Playboy* is any indication of where this Ifor wants your career to go, then he's steering you in the wrong direction."

"Well, I'm *crying,*" I said as I rolled off Ebb. "All the way to the bank."

Ebb propped himself on one elbow. "Lisar," he said, "when you first started at this writing business, you told me—and I quote: 'The writer shouldn't get rich writing a book, but the reader should get rich reading it.' "

"So I've changed my tune: Why shouldn't both get rich? The author has to keep a roof over her head."

"You have a roof."

"The author needs a pot to piss in," I said.

"You've got *two* bathrooms."

"The downstairs bathroom is only one half!"

"And you don't need the money," Ebb said. "Didn't I tell you, when you first started out at this, that I would take care of you?"

"I'm not a dog," I said. "Or a child. I don't want to be *taken care of*. Besides, what would happen to me if something bad happened to you?"

"There's the life insurance."

"Every time you fly I get nervous—"

"I buy the tickets on my platinum card. That's a quarter of a million coverage right there. Besides, I've totally cut back on the travel so I can stay home. And argue with you. Just like this."

I stretched out my legs, then kicked, childishly, at the sheets that felt too tight due to all the blankets piled up on the bed. "You hurt my feelings today," I said.

"When?"

"At the house. I saw you look at Cynthia and then look at my socks with . . . I don't know what to call it but *displeasure*."

Ebb didn't say anything. So I said, "I mean, I know I need new socks. But I don't have time to get to the store. Not if I want to write all the way up until the minute I have to pick up Danny at school. And then Danny runs me ragged when I come home. And then you get home and then—" I felt tears spring to my eyes. "I look like shit compared to Cynthia."

"No one is comparing you, Lisar."

"What does it matter," I asked, "when I compare myself? I wish I had Cynthia's voice. I like the softness of it. She never hoots like a screech owl when something's funny. She never says anything stupid or impulsive. She always seems so . . . I don't know, *polished*—"

"That's because you see her only in her professional role."

"But she always looks better, Ebb."

"Of course she looks better," Ebb said. "She doesn't have children."

I pulled the blankets against me, as if someone had just socked me a good one right in the stomach.

Ebb paused. "Let me take another crack at that."

"Don't bother."

"No, hear me out. You shouldn't be envious of Cynthia. She doesn't have it all together. She's divorced. She goes home and sleeps by herself."

"She does not," I said. "She sleeps with her boyfriend. They were going up to Bear Mountain tonight."

"In this weather? They probably got five miles up Route 9 and then had to pull over into a Motel 6."

I listened to Danny's labored breathing, which was coming loud and clear from across the hall again. Suddenly, the thought of being stuck in a roadside motel room, in a deep and furious snowstorm, presented some interest to me—but not to Ebb, who said, "It's much more comfortable to be snowed in at home."

"Right," I said. "Where else can we get such an excellent read on Danny's adenoid condition?"

Ebb waited through half a dozen more of Danny's snorts. "Those adenoids have to go."

"But I don't want him to have surgery."

"It's a routine operation," Ebb said. "Half an hour long. If you want, I'll take an afternoon off and bring him in myself."

"You don't have to do it yourself," I said. "If you would just do it *with* me—"

"All right. Remind me tomorrow to call his doctor."

"Tomorrow's Sunday," I said.

"Monday then."

"Mondays it's impossible to even get through to the doctor," I said.

"Tuesday then. Whenever." Ebb's voice grew more tired by the second. I knew no good ever came of discussing scheduling when we were in bed. It made us both anxious during the night, as if the leaves of the calendar were flipping beyond our control and there was some appointment or meeting we both had to make but felt certain we were about to miss.

Danny's snoring grew even louder.

"Your turn," I said.

Ebb rolled out of bed and padded across the cold hall to flop Danny onto his side and prop him with a spare pillow behind his back. He shivered as he came back into bed. "He was smiling in his sleep."

"He probably was dreaming about killing us," I said.

"You know, he got into deep shit at that birthday party. He said *fuck* in front of all the other kids."

I drew in a quick breath. "The Foxes are lawyers! Their faces are on the back of the phone book! They'll probably take us to court. For corrupting their darling Noah."

"I told you it wasn't such a hot idea to tell him about sex," Ebb said. "He got it all mixed up. He told June Fox you were pregnant."

"But I clearly explained to him how it works."

"He probably thinks it's as fast as instant oatmeal."

"It should be so easy." I rolled over. "Ow."

"What's the matter?"

"That rock I put under the mattress is murder on my back."

I rolled out of bed, hoisted the mattress, and pulled the goose-egg stone out. I let it fall to the floor with a thud.

"Is there a logical explanation," Ebb said, "why you've stuck a boulder underneath the mattress?"

"There is not."

"I didn't think so."

"Oh, *think, think,*" I said. "Why do you always have to be so logical?"

"Why do you always have to be so unreasonable?"

We both fell silent.

Then Ebb dared to ask, "*When* are we going to start getting along with each other, Lisar?"

I laughed and nudged him in the ribs. "When pigs fly," I said as across the hall Danny gave an adenoidal oink as confirmation.

## CHAPTER SEVENTEEN

# EBEN

**All of Sunday it snowed,** and we shoveled. And it snowed, and we shoveled. On Monday morning, the rumble of the snowplows and salt trucks woke me at 4:48 A.M. By 5:25 my watch was on my wrist, the SB pager (which I had turned on at midnight) was clipped onto my belt, and two cups of French roast and another bowl of ineffective high-fiber cereal sat inside my bloated stomach. I had no real reason to dread the day ahead. But still, when I couldn't break my fifth straight day of constipation, couldn't find my car keys, and couldn't bear the dampness of my boots after I slipped them on, I thought: *Here we go again, another Monday.*

The *Times,* swathed in its blue plastic bag, sat in a mound of snow on the front porch. I picked up the bag by the wrong end and the paper slipped out. AT LEAST 19 KILLED IN CRASH AT SNOWY LAGUARDIA, read the headline. Then the subtitle: *Plane En Route to Cleveland Burns and Careers into Bay.*

I drew in a quick, coffee-tinged breath. But that was *my* plane, I thought. Wasn't it? The one Victoria had put me on, and took me off again, after I lied to Rudy and told him that I couldn't possibly go to Cleveland, because Lisa and I had to make an offer on a house? With the newspaper in my hand, I stepped back into the hallway and turned on the light. Leaning against the closed front door, I examined the photo of the 747, broken in two, with the fuselage smashed. Then I read the article all the way through, and each breath of air I drew into my lungs felt like a gift. I hadn't died. I'd been spared—all because Lisa had drawn on my calendar a smiley, ovulatory face.

I exhaled. And inhaled. Like Ebenezer Scrooge flinging open the shutters on Christmas morning, hardly able to believe he was still alive, I felt like I should open the front door and shout my existence to the world. But I simply whispered within myself—*I could be dead now, now I could be dead!*—as I abandoned the newspaper in the front hall, picked up my briefcase, and trudged in my boots down to the bottom of the snowpacked driveway where I had parked my car the night before. Lisa had left her car next to mine.

Last night I'd told Lisa—who had been insufferably edgy all day—"You may as well leave your car in the garage. I'm sure Danny won't have school tomorrow."

"He'll have school," Lisa said. "Or he'll have a baby-sitter."

"Make sure you call me tomorrow—or, better yet, page me—if your temperature surges."

"*I* don't need a million reminders."

"Meaning?" I asked.

"Meaning—it's the end of the weekend, right? And you promised to spray that front lock, but have you made any romantic overtures toward that can of WD-40?"

"There are only so many minutes in the day, Lisa."

"Well, during one of those minutes I went into your car to get out the lock you bought at the True Value. And guess what I smelled coming out of your trunk?"

I cleared my throat. "I'm going to toss all that trash into the Dumpster at work tomorrow."

Lisa gave me an exasperated sigh. "And tomorrow, I guess, you're going to put that mirror back in Danny's room."

"Maybe I will," I said, adding to myself: *Then again, maybe I won't.*

In the crisp, cool air of morning, this petty tiff I'd had with Lisa seemed pointless. Life was too short to bicker about WD-40 and trash and mirrors. I opened the door of my Audi and resolved to put a stop to this sort of squabbling in the future. We're going to move into a new house, I thought. And we're going to have a new baby and—goddammit—we are going to be happy!

But it was hard to think of making a fresh start when I found that the inside of my car bore the cloying odor of old coffee grinds and eggshells and orange rinds. I turned the key in the ignition, and while the car gruffly warmed up, I brushed the last inch of powder off my windshield. Then, to surprise Lisa and show her how much I cared for her, I brushed off her Camry. After I finished, I regretted I hadn't thought of an even more noble gesture: writing, with the finger of my glove, something gallant in the powder that had coated the windshield. I LOVE YOU might have warmed Lisa's heart. But by the time Lisa woke up, the wind would have blown the words away.

Snowplows still were cutting through the SB parking lot, yet the space in front of the monstrous green Dumpsters was cleared. I pulled up beside the first Dumpster and tossed inside the garbage bags. I left my windows cracked to rid the car of the lingering garbage odor. As I entered the back hallway of SB and shook off my boots, the security guard said, "Mr. Strauss—you're *whistling*. Man, I've never heard you *whistling* before." I smiled, signed in, and told the guard, "Have a good one." Then I puckered up my lips and continued to chirp through the empty halls of SB. I smiled as I strolled by the motivational poster that showed the match on fire. *Good attitude?* Yes. *Contagious?* You betcha! Even Victoria's Postum-odorous office smelled better on this fine morning. I hung up—and buttoned—my coat on my blue hanger and sat down at my desk. I piled all the papers I had brought home over the weekend (but had failed to work on) onto my desk. No matter. I had all day to deal with this paperwork. First I wanted to log on to my electronic mail and post Victoria a very grateful thank-you for taking me off that plane to Cleveland.

I pushed the power button on my computer. The hard drive didn't chime. Using a more forceful finger, I pressed the button again. Nothing doing. I grimaced at the monitor's blank screen. It was only 6:00 A.M. The men from Technical Support wouldn't arrive until 8:30 at best. I would have to remain disconnected for the next two and a half hours—or maybe even more. Probably fifty percent of our staff would use the snow as an excuse to stay home drinking that extra cup of coffee; once they got into the office, they would spend another half hour—over more coffee—trading excuses about why they had arrived at work half an hour late.

The one person I wished would run late was punctual as ever. At 8:25 A.M., swathed in her pall-black coat and astrakhan hat, Victoria positioned herself in my doorway like a female Grim Reaper.

"Mr. Strauss," she said, her face ashen white. "You should be dead."

I smiled. "But I'm not."

"That plane to Cleveland—"

"Good thing I wasn't on it, right?"

Victoria sounded like a Berlitz language instructor explaining tenses. "But you should have been. You could have been. You might have been."

"I guess somebody was watching out for me," I said.

"The Lord works in mysterious ways."

"I meant *you*," I said. "Thank you for taking me off it."

"But, Mr. Strauss. I was the one who put you *on* it." Victoria's eyes shone with tears. "You might have *passed*. Your wife might be a widow, your son might be an orphan—"

I watched—in discomfort—as Victoria turned away from the door, snatched a tissue from the needlepoint-covered box on her desk, and blew her nose. I cleared my throat. I didn't know what to say to her. So when she came back into the doorway, dabbing her eyes with a fresh tissue, I tried to make a joke.

"I had no idea you were so attached to me," I said.

"Tusk!" She blew her nose again. "To think we might have lost you. Forever."

"Well," I said, "think of it this way: I also might have electrocuted myself this morning by sticking a fork in the toaster. Or I could have lost my brakes on the way to work and slammed into a salt truck. Instead, I arrived here safely and found my computer has blown a gasket."

Victoria stood on tiptoes and peered over my desk. "Did you try plugging it in?"

I looked under my credenza. Because of the impending snow-storm, Victoria had warned me to unplug on Friday. Yet I could have sworn I'd been the last to leave the office on Friday and that I had forgotten to unplug my computer. However, I could have re-membered incorrectly that I had forgotten ... or forgotten what I once had correctly remembered....

"Who unplugged this?" I asked Victoria.

She crumpled the tissue between her fingers. "I suspect Stanley Steemer."

"What department is he in?"

"The carpet cleaners," she said. "Stanley Steemer came on Satur-day and deep-cleaned our carpets—didn't you smell the difference when you first came in?" As if she stood on the edge of an Alpine meadow, Victoria took a deep, bracing breath. "Mmmm. Intoxicat-ing. Like the first whiff of forsythia in the spring air."

I knelt on the carpet and pushed my computer plug back into the surge protector. The machine gave off a healthy hum.

Victoria now had her emotions completely under wraps. "Mr. Strauss," she said, in her normal voice, "I hate to tell you this while you're on your knees—"

"Oh, go ahead," I said. "Hit me while I'm down."

"—but on my way in, I noticed a few people had gathered in the back hallway." Victoria de-astrakhaned herself and fluffed the fur on her hat. "Someone seems to have switched the signs on the cafe-teria lavatories. No one dares to use the facilities until LADIES once again are LADIES and MEN once again are MEN."

I had the urge to stick my finger into the electrical outlet. "Why do these things always happen when I'm on the pager?" I asked.

"You're on the pager? You didn't tell me. Where is Mr. Furlong this morning?"

"Out on business."

"His secretary said something about him being in the Bahamas."

"That's right. *Business* in the Bahamas."

Victoria sniffed and looked out the window at the snowbanks

with disfavor. Evidently the sweet forsythia-like smell of Stanley Steemer no longer was enough to sate her spring fever. She retreated into the outer office and immediately unwrapped a Jolly Rancher candy. As she hung up her coat on the pink hanger, she called out, "How do you want to handle this bathroom situation?"

"By forgetting it exists."

Victoria moved her Jolly from one cheek to another. "I'll call Maintenance."

Our head handyman, Henry Hoyts—who was one month away from retirement and had an attitude to prove it—met me at the rest rooms to inspect the damage. His sourpuss look—and the crust of sugar at the corners of his pinched mouth—made it clear he resented being dragged away from his Monday-morning glazed doughnut for such foolishness.

"Somebody did a crap job on this, Mr. Strauss," Hoyts said as he examined the LADIES faceplate hanging on the MEN's door. "Ruined the screws. Used a flat when it required a Phillips." He grunted. "Looks like woman's work."

"Of course it's woman's work," I said. "The women are the ones ticked off about the bathroom situation." I tried to remember which women at Friday's potty-equity meeting had seemed the most incensed. When one of the lead *womanists* had risen from her chair to deliver a rousing speech, the very chopsticks in her gray bun had quivered with anger. Yet Victoria's applause (from the audience) had seemed just as impassioned.

"Could that damage have been done by a chopstick?" I asked Hoyts.

"They using chopsticks in the cafeteria now?"

"How about a knitting needle? Or a crochet hook?"

"I'm no private detective, sir."

I knocked my knuckles against the door. "How long will it take you to fix this?"

Hoyts massaged the doughnut sugar from his right cheek. "Hour."

"One hour! Even I could fix it faster than that."

Hoyts looked me up and down—from my two-hundred-dollar loafers to my red tie—and raised his eyebrow in doubt. "I gotta find replacement screws," he said. "Maybe do some caulking on this here door." The walkie-talkie that Hoyts wore on his huge leather belt exploded into static. He looked down at my pager (which so far had remained miraculously silent) and said, "Excuse me. I got work to do here, Mr. Strauss."

I would have said, *Well, see that it gets done, and quickly,* if I hadn't realized how futile my words would have been. I had seen this happen over and over again. Employees on the edge of retirement often behaved like couples on the edge of divorce. Things better left unsaid got said, and all sense of loyalty and decorum got flushed down the toilet.

When I got back to the office, Victoria was swilling Postum and covetously eyeing new Xerox machines in an office-supply catalog.

"Will you get me a copy of the sign-in log for the weekend?" I asked her.

"It's already on your desk."

The smudged duplicate Victoria had laid on my desk seemed to prove that I had held on too long to our copy machine. The sign-in sheet revealed that the usual crowd—half the research team, some of the VPs, the esteemed Stanley Steemer, Victoria, two other secretaries, and the weekend housekeeping staff—had come in on Saturday. Sunday it had snowed heavily, and only a handful of researchers and lab technicians (all men) had signed in and out.

"Why were you here on Saturday?" I called out to Victoria.

"*Someone* had to supervise Stanley Steemer. Men just don't know the meaning of clean."

Surely Victoria—whose actions always were governed by the question "How would Jesus Christ respond to this?"—wouldn't have dared to change the signs. I stared at the list of possible culprits, then tossed it aside. My management motto was: Whenever possible, lay collective rather than individual blame. I turned to my computer and began to draft the unavoidable memo: *This is a reminder to all employees of the need for respect for corporate facilities. Appropriate disciplinary action will be taken against anyone engaging in deliberate destruction of company property.*

I sent the file to Victoria via our electronic-mail system with explicit instructions to send all departments a hard copy on half sheets. While she set about "sprucing up" my memo by fixing the crooked margins and putting it on letterhead, I opened my Filofax to March 23—where the shadow of the word *bliss* seemed permanently embedded from one-thirty to three-thirty. As I glanced down at the smiley face Lisa had drawn in my Filofax and my scrawled reminder to send flowers to Rudy Furlong's wife, I reminded myself to feel happy. Lucky. Alive! I placed my palm upon my Filofax as if it were a Bible and swore that from now on—when I gazed outside at the crystalline world and the luscious icicles that hung from the roof, just begging to be plucked and licked—I would appreciate everything I had and embrace all the possibilities for celebrating life that came my way.

Like today. Lisa hadn't paged me to let me know her body temperature had risen—nor had she called me yet to let me know what she had found out from Cynthia about the house. But I didn't have to wait until she called, did I? Victoria would be out of the office. I had no meetings scheduled for early afternoon. I could do something loving, something life-affirming. I could take an extended lunch hour. Surprise Lisa. Go home and indulge her fantasies for an hour or so. Go home and . . .

. . . *fuck her like a stranger.*

Victoria was just beginning to copy my memo as I speed-dialed the Teleflorist. After I quietly gave the clerk information on Rudy's wife, I told her, "I have another order. Going to the following address . . . For a certain—um, Elizabeth Diodetto, yes, that's spelled D-I-O-D-E-T-T-O. A dozen roses. No, make that spring tulips. Pink, if you have them. And can you get them there before eleven A.M.?"

"For ten dollars extra," the clerk answered. "Is there a message?"

I paused. *"I heard you need a plumber."*

The clerk fell silent for a moment. "No, we don't," she said. "And the message is?"

"That *is* the message."

The clerk hesitated. "Let me repeat that back to you: *I heard you need a plumber.*"

"Exactly."

"Any name attached?"

"Leave it unsigned, please."

"And now your name as it is listed on your credit card?"

For a second I wished I could assume a false identity. But then I shrugged, gave my name and credit-card number, hung up the phone, and leaned back in my chair. I saw the whole scene unfold as planned. I would come out of the ten-thirty meeting that Victoria had set up with the chief architect, and Victoria would inform me with barely concealed glee, "Mr. Strauss, I don't want to ruin your morning, but your wife just called to say you have a major plumbing disaster. How fast can you get home?"

I saw myself standing on my own front porch—sans wrench— but wielding some equally manly accoutrements, like Henry Hoyts's key ring and walkie-talkie. I stamped my feet to shake off the snow, then ...

... *reached with one gloved finger to push the doorbell. The door cracked open and Lisa's eyes peered around the safety chain.*

*"Hey, lady," I said. "Your husband told me you had a problem. With your drain."*

*Lisa's disembodied voice was husky with desire. "I believe I do."*

*"I'm here to address the situation."*

*"I'm not sure I should let you in. You see, I just got out of the shower—"*

*"You can trust me."*

*Clutching a scanty towel around her breasts, Lisa released the safety chain. I came in and shut the door. Then I followed her up the stairs, waiting until we reached the master bathroom before I reached out and yanked the towel off Lisa, hoisting her onto the counter in front of the vanity mirror. ...*

"Oh, fiddlesticks!" Victoria said. The copier stopped *thump-thumping.* Victoria opened the door that exposed the machine's inky guts. She gingerly lifted her skirt an inch to kneel before the machine and said, "It figures! Stanley Steemer's just been here, and now *that dirty man* will come and mess up my carpet."

◆   ◆   ◆

At the ten-thirty meeting in the boardroom, I reported to the chief architect that SB had complete satisfaction with the plans for the new wing with one minor adjustment: additional stalls were needed in the ladies' room.

I expected the architect to greet my news with a can-do attitude. What he offered, however, was a stubborn silence.

"That's not a minor adjustment," he finally said.

"Half a dozen more stalls in this one lavatory?"

He stabbed his finger at the blueprints that lay spread out on the table before us. "If you double the number of regular stalls, you're obligated to double the number of handicapped."

"But not a single woman who works here is physically challenged."

"We have to follow code, Mr. Strauss. Additional stalls will take up already allocated space. I'd have to cut into this janitor's closet. Then I'd have to cut into the kitchen. But if I cut into this cleaning station here, you're going to have OSHA on your tail. And if I move this way into the cafeteria proper, you can kiss your sushi bar good-bye."

"We can't get rid of the sushi bar," I said. "The Healthy Living Task Force fought *hours* for that."

The architect took his finger off the blueprint and stared down at the smudge left on his skin. "You've never built a house, have you?"

I shook my head.

"Well, I started out in residential architecture," he said. "And whenever my clients started changing their minds—which they did every other minute—I used to tell them that building a house is just as tricky as building a house of cards. You move a wall here, or raise the roof there, and the whole structure has to shift with it, otherwise it becomes unstable."

I nodded. "I follow you."

"It's exactly the same thing here—only even more complicated, because this is an industrial space." He traced his finger along the outside line of the plan. "From your perspective, it's easy enough to say—oh, just give me a few more square feet and make the building a little bit longer. But you can see here that an extension would take us onto this slope that leads down to the creek. This is flood plain. If you build on it, your insurance will go through the roof."

"So will the women who feed the rabbits," I said.

"Rabbits?"

"There are rabbits that live down there. When spring comes, some of the secretaries go out by the creek on their lunch hour and feed them carrots from their bag lunch."

The architect frowned. "You should put a stop to that. Right now. You know how rabbits proliferate." He pointed to a section of the blueprint that I had never paid much attention to—where ducts and boilers and God-knows-what-else would be housed. "They'll tunnel their way under here and chew through your transformer."

I nodded, as if I knew what service a transformer actually performed.

"Before you lay your foundation," he said, "you want to gas those rabbits out."

"That doesn't sound very humanitarian."

"Rabbits aren't humans. They're vermin."

"But to these women, they're like pets." I thought hard. "A friend of mine knows someone who—I mean, what's your opinion of these exterminators who trap and relocate wildlife?"

"That's an expensive scam," he said. "There's always one—or, rather, two survivors who start up the population all over again. Your best bet is to have a service come out here and release the gas at night. The rabbits'll die underground. And your secretaries will never know the difference." He gestured back toward the blueprint. "Now, about these stalls. I don't know what to tell you, except that time is money. You're charged by the hour, and it will take us more than a few to find a solution to this." He looked at me closely. "Are you sure you really need to make this change?"

"I have a lot of angry women on my hands," I said.

"My sympathies." The architect rolled up the blueprints and dropped them into the tube, where they hit the bottom with a sharp *clack*.

◆    ◆    ◆

Lisa hadn't paged me while I was in my meeting. She also—curiously—hadn't called me on my private line, because I checked my voice mail from the boardroom phone and the automated female voice on the other end informed me, "You have no new messages."

I found Victoria on her hands and knees—again—in front of her defective copier. "How did you make out with the architect?" she asked.

"The man is heartless." I looked down at the box where she stored my pink WHILE YOU WERE OUT messages. "Did my wife call?"

"No, but a very strange man—with a gruff voice—rang twice. He refused to leave a message, just said, 'Tell him Amore called.' "

"I don't know anyone by that name."

Victoria gave a sniff, as if to say, *I should hope not.* "Oh, and your real-estate agent—Order, not Farquhar—called. She claimed it was urgent."

I grabbed the pink message from the box, went into my office, forgot to close the door behind me, and quickly punched in Mrs. Order's number. She picked up on the first ring.

"Good news," she said. "I have an offer on your place, from that bachelor I brought by on Saturday."

"What's his offer?"

"Fifteen below the listing," she brightly said, as if pronouncing it in a cheerful tone would make it acceptable. "Mr. Strauss. Did you hear me?"

I leaned back in my chair. "We'll counteroffer. Tell him seven thousand more."

Mrs. O. was the only person I knew who could make even a sigh seem brisk. "If I might make a suggestion—"

"Yes?"

"I recommend five. At the most. All of your walls need repainting. All of your floors need recarpeting."

"This is two thousand square feet we're talking about," I said, "not a skyscraper."

"But the price of carpet. And quality paint—have you seen recently the price of paint?"

I nodded. In the True Value, I had passed by a row of paint cans priced at over thirty dollars a gallon. "All right. But don't settle for less than … say, four point five."

"Four point two-five?"

"All right. Four point two-five, and you don't even have to call me back. We have a deal."

She paused. "Don't you want to consult with your wife?"

"I'm sure I know exactly what Lisa wants."

She gave me a dubious silence.

So I said, "But I'll call you if she voices any objections."

I put down the phone and heard Victoria clinking her metal spoon against the side of a ceramic mug. She probably had been listening to every word I said to Mrs. Order—and now was fixing me a cup of celebratory Postum.

If I knew Victoria, her mouth was fixed in a grim little grin as she listened to my next phone conversation—which really was a monologue delivered to our home answering machine: "Lisa? Lisa? Are you there? Please pick up if you're there."

I guess I understood—on some level—why Lisa didn't want to pick up the phone in the morning: because it "broke her concentration." But we needed to get going on these negotiations with Cynthia. And I had important news. Surely Lisa could overhear my voice on the answering machine, even from upstairs, so why couldn't she stop scribbling about this Simon Stern for half a second and call me back? More to the point, those tulips—with that message!—should have arrived half an hour ago. Why hadn't she called to acknowledge them? Unless, of course, she didn't answer the doorbell, either, when she was writing. But her desk was by the window and she would have seen the florist's truck pull into the driveway. She definitely would have gone downstairs and retrieved the white box left on the porch so the flowers inside would not turn to ice.

Lisa wasn't easily offended, I thought. But maybe *I heard you need a plumber* had raised her wrath rather than her passion. Maybe she had gone outside to retrieve the box of flowers and slipped on the ice and cracked open her head. Maybe the delivery man had shoved her inside the house and brutally … brutally … Maybe on the drive to drop Danny off at school, her Camry had skidded off the road and now Lisa and Danny were lying in a ditch. . . .

My imagination got the best of me. I called Danny's school. After nine rings, the overly sunny Montessori directress answered the phone with, "This is the best morning of the rest of your life! Gloria speaking."

The chattering of children in the background seemed positively deafening. "Gloria," I said loudly, "Eben Strauss here. I guess school is open."

"We had a two-hour delay, but here we are."

"Is my son in school today?"

"He's very much here," Gloria answered, before she half-covered the phone and called out, *"Noah, remember, a gentleman uses a Kleenex!* Hold on, Mr. Strauss, while I get Danny. *Where is Danny Strauss? Is he in time-out?"* She put down the phone. I heard a loud squabble, and then a sharp, high voice whined, "I wasn't putting my snots in *tha-yuh*!" before Gloria returned to the line and reported, "Danny's in the bathroom." She clucked her tongue. "I was telling Lisa this morning, Danny seems to have loose bowels lately. Is he worried about something?"

"Not that I know of."

"Lisa seems to think he's afraid to move. But we couldn't really discuss the situation, since—*Excuse me, Zachary One and Zachary Four! Use your words, not your fists, to express your feelings!*—Lisa was in such a rush to get back to her housework."

"Her housework?"

"Yes, this morning she said, 'Got to get back home! Got a hot date with the broom and the mop!' I imagine your house will be pretty spic-and-span tonight."

*Imagine* was the operative word there, I thought.

"Did you want to talk to Danny, Mr. Strauss?"

"No. No, I . . . just tell him that I called to check in on him. There's no need for him to call me back."

After Gloria wished me "a great day," I put down the phone. What an ass I had been, sitting there worrying that Lisa had been stabbed, mutilated, raped, or dead in the ditch—when the truth of the matter was, she was just off on yet another hot date not with the mop or the broom but with Simon Stern or whichever male character had stepped in to take his place (probably some Scandinavian—named Lars Larson or Gustaf Gustafson—whose sole function in the plot was to do what Scandinavians were reputed to do best).

I picked up the phone and called our home; once again I talked to the answering machine. But this time I wasn't half so polite. In fact, I mimicked the words Lisa often said to me whenever I was trying to peacefully read the newspaper: "Hello? Hello? Earth to spouse? Are you still married to me? Come in if you read me. Come in if you—"

Lisa didn't read me—nor did she come in, at least not until a minute later, when my phone finally buzzed. I was greeted solely by a dial tone when I picked it up. I looked down at the phone, puzzled, until I realized I needed to punch out of my private line.

"Mr. Strauss?" Victoria asked, her voice echoing both on the phone and from the outer office.

"Yes?"

"Are you there?" she asked.

"Of course I'm here."

"I've just called your name twice. And received no answer. Will you take a personal call? From your *other* real-estate agent?"

"Put it through, please," I said.

The line clicked. I swallowed—my throat so dry it could have benefited enormously from one of Victoria's Jolly Ranchers—as Cynthia Farquhar murmured in her smooth voice, "Good morning, Eben. How was your weekend?"

"Too short." I leaned back in my chair and stared at the open door—through which Victoria undoubtedly was listening to every word I said. "And yours?"

"Wonderful," she said. "I went to Bear Mountain."

"I didn't take you for a skier, Cynthia."

"I'm not."

I cleared my throat. "Did Lisa call you this morning?"

"No, I haven't heard from her ... but ... did my friend Rob call you?"

"Why would he call me?"

"About your friend—Simon was his name? Who had squirrels in his walls?"

"Oh, right. I probably have another job too. That involves rabbits. Ask him to call me. Better yet, here's the number of my pager." I slipped the pager off my belt and read the number—which I never had bothered to memorize—aloud to her.

She repeated the number, then said, "I'm sure you know the real reason I'm calling. I was wondering if you had any more thoughts about the house."

"Actually," I said, "I was just about to call you. I was hoping you wouldn't mind showing me that house again. This afternoon. Solo."

The phone went quiet for a moment. "Lisa's tied up, I guess."

"She's waiting for the plumber to arrive," I said. Loudly—so Victoria could not fail to overhear—I asked Cynthia, "I know this is a last-minute invitation, but are you free for lunch? I could meet you. You name the time. And place."

"I'm in my office," Cynthia said. "There's a good bagel place right here in my mini-mall."

I looked at my clock. It was 11:32. I hadn't accomplished a thing all morning, and I didn't give a damn. "I'll meet you there at noon," I said.

I hung up the phone, went into the outer office, and took my coat off the blue hanger.

"I'm sure you heard my good news," I told Victoria.

Although devoutly Christian, Victoria wasn't above telling a little white lie. "I can't hear into your office," she said, "above the hum of my computer."

"Well, I think we've finally sold our condo."

"In spite of your plumbing problem?"

I raised my eyebrow.

"Tusk!" Victoria shifted in her chair. "When can I expect you back from your lunch? With Mrs. Farquhar?"

I buttoned my trench coat and put on my gloves. "Whenever I get back."

"What should I tell your wife if she calls?"

Now, there was an interesting question. Which—to Victoria's obvious discomfort—I simply refused to answer.

"Don't forget," Victoria said, "from one-thirty to three-thirty I'll be in my virus-free meeting."

I paused. I knew something had felt odd this morning. "We forgot to go over our calendars today."

I didn't know whether to feel sorrow or joy when Victoria told me, in an aggrieved voice, "Maybe that routine has outlived its usefulness."

## CHAPTER EIGHTEEN

# LISA

**Only after I flopped down** in the first available seat on the 11:10 train into the city did I stop to consider the crime I had committed that morning. Today—of all days—I hadn't taken my temperature.

When Mr. Chanticleer had crowed for me to wise-and-shine at seven A.M., I rushed to the window and despaired when I saw that more snow had fallen during the night. I grabbed my thermometer and ran downstairs. The minute I flicked on the TV to see if Danny's school had been canceled, the solemn-faced newscasters started talking about a plane crash at LaGuardia. I hit the MUTE button, thankful that Ebb no longer traveled on a regular basis and that my heart no longer had to skip a beat every time a newscaster announced, "A 727 bound for Chicago ... Denver ... Houston ... crashed upon takeoff, there are no known survivors."

I crouched in front of the television, clasping my thermometer in a tight fist as I watched cancellation after cancellation scroll across the bottom of the screen. Finally, just as I lost all hope that I could make my lunch with Aye-Aye, this marvelous message appeared: MONTESSORI HOUSE DELAYED TWO HOURS. OPENING 10 A.M.

I flicked off the TV, took my thermometer between my fingers, and shook it down. Joyously. Carelessly. So recklessly that the bulb slipped from my hand, hit the television, and fell to the carpet in two sharp slivery pieces. Mercury blobbed onto the carpet.

*Oh God,* I said to myself. *Oh Lord.* Unless I dug my car out from the driveway and gunned it to the Walgreens to buy another BBT thermometer, there was no way I could take my temperature. More important, by the time I huffed and puffed my bloated self to the drugstore and back—which would raise my temperature several notches—the mercury would rise and tell me I had surged when maybe I was still one or two days away from really ovulating.

"Mommy?"

I turned. Danny stood at the bottom of the stairs.

"What's that stuff on the rug?" he asked.

"What does it look like?"

Danny jumped down the last three steps of the stairs (a move I had forbidden him to make many times, warning, "If you kill yourself, I'm going to kill you!"). "Lemme see."

"No!" I said. "Don't touch it! Mercury is poisonous! You'll die!"

*"Mommy."* Danny put his hands on his hips—and for a second he looked like a miniature Ebb instead of a miniature me. "You're being unreasonable."

I advanced toward Danny—with such an unreasonable look in my eye that he retreated two steps backward. "Go get ready for school. Right now."

"But it snowed," Danny said. "School's canceled."

"It isn't canceled," I said. "It's delayed. Two hours. And you're going."

I wore two sets of rubber gloves to dab up the mercury from the carpet—fearful I would die of poisoning before I even had a chance to make it into the city and gag on my Ichikawa sushi. Then I fixed Danny breakfast and a bag lunch. After that, I ordered him to go change his clothes.

"Why?" he asked.

"Because your top and your bottom don't match."

"Brown goes with black."

"Those pants aren't *black,*" I said. "They're navy."

Danny regarded his pants with puzzlement. "Why do you always tell me and Daddy that we can't tell colors apart?"

"Because you *can't* tell colors apart," I said. "And that gold doorknob Daddy bought from the True Value—which doesn't match the brass light switch—proves it."

Once Danny was all set for school, I took a shower, attempted to do something—anything—with my frowsy, boyish hair, and tried on six different outfits (all of which made me look like my name should be Fat Fanny Frump). I also tried on three pairs of shoes before I realized I was stuck wearing boots, anyway.

It was shaping up to be—as they said—*one of those days*. The only thing that went right that morning was that Ebb—bless him—had shoveled out the driveway and brushed the snow off my car. As I inched my Toyota down our poorly plowed street, I remembered that I had promised to call Ebb if I surged this morning. But technically I hadn't surged. Besides, I told myself, even if Ebb returned home and made love to me on his lunch hour, he could only come inside of me twice at the max. Considering how many failed attempts we already had made at getting pregnant, two more missed opportunities seemed inconsequential.

And yet monumental. After I hurriedly ushered Danny into the front hall of Montessori—calling out to Glorious Gloria the directress, "Gotta run! Got a hot date with my broom and mop!"—I bent down to kiss Danny's soft, sweet cheek and instantly was reminded that it took just one passionate embrace to make a baby. And every second of the hot, stuffy train ride into Grand Central, I kept thinking: What if that single embrace turned out to be the one Ebb and I were about to miss?

Ordinarily I would have felt delirious with joy at leaving behind the humdrum suburbs and making my way into the bustle of the city, where no one knew me as Eben Strauss's wife. But it had been a while since I'd ventured into Manhattan, and the blare of cab horns and roar of idling delivery trucks overwhelmed me. Everyone else on the sidewalk seemed to know exactly where they were going—and there I stood on the street corner, trying to remember was it Lexington? or Madison? that came between Park and Fifth? And was it worth trying to take the train—but which train?—from 42nd to the lower 50s? *I used to know this city,* I told myself. *But now I'm*

*lost*. At any moment, one of those gorgeous men or women brush-
ing past me on the sidewalk—who seemed to have stepped out of
the pages of *Esquire* or *Vogue*—would glance at my scuffed boots
and dowdy down coat, then disdainfully tell me, "Radio City Music
Hall lies that-a-way, so get thee hence."

Ichikawa—which fortunately had been listed in our outdated
copy of Zagat's—was on the ground floor of one of those medium-
size skyscrapers that might have functioned as a landmark in a
smaller city like Hartford or Albany. As I pushed through the re-
volving door and walked into the central lobby, I turned and looked
at myself in the glass window of the restaurant. Ricardo had cut
three inches off my hair. But he hadn't lopped the fat off my chin or
cheeks or even my falling derriere. He hadn't gotten rid of five years
of fretting about Danny that had settled in the lines of my forehead,
nor had he washed out the bags beneath my eyes that came from
waking at all hours of the night as Danny's adenoids rattled like
hard-boiled eggs in a pan. I did not want to bring such a self to meet
the great I. I. Iforson. But that self was all I had, and so I took a
deep breath and walked in.

The salty odor emanating from the kitchen—a combination of
cod and rice vinegar and soy sauce—made my stomach curl in distress.

"I'm here to join someone," I told the hostess as I peered around
the soshi screen into the restaurant. It wasn't large—at most, thirty
tables—and in one of the tiny black leather booths at the back sat
Aye-Aye, his blond mane unmistakable against the rugged cables of
his Shetland fisherman's sweater.

I waved and noted I was not the only woman in the restaurant
whose eyes were upon Aye-Aye as he rose—all six-feet-whatever of
him—from the booth and made his way toward the soshi screen.

Aye-Aye held out his arms. "You must be Elizabeth D.," he said,
taking my cold hands in his warm hands. "Looking exactly like I
imagined."

My mouth, I swear, opened wide enough to catch an incoming
747. I was convinced that Aye-Aye had derived his picture of me
from my description of Robin Stern in *I'm Sorry: Sometimes Robin
felt so plug-ugly that she listed all the surgical procedures she would*

*need if she ever wanted to rekindle Simon's flagging passion: nose job,
chin job, cheek job, boob job, butt job, thigh job . . .*

I licked the spittle off my bottom lip. As I clasped Aye-Aye's
warm hand in my cold right hand, I told him, "You look exactly like
your photograph."

This was a lie. Aye-Aye looked even better. Sturdier. Healthier, as
if he subsisted on a diet of fresh brown bread and goat's milk cheese
and spent the day either slinging large slabs of blubber around the
deck of a whaling ship or wrestling elk.

Aye-Aye may have looked handsome enough to bronze upon a
krone—but I immediately noted that Ebb had much better manners. Aye-Aye did not gesture for me to go first when we walked
back to the table. He did not help me take off my coat. Plus he just
flopped himself down in the booth before I even lowered myself
onto the leather cushion—unlike Ebb, who had been trained by his
parents never to sit down until a woman had been seated.

Either I was turning into an old fuddy-duddy—or I was discovering rather late in life that I preferred the idea of Sir Walter Raleigh
the courtier (who spread his cloak over a puddle so a woman might
cross it dry-shod) to Sir Walter Raleigh the pirate and the plunderer.

I sat down opposite Aye-Aye and pointed to his pilsner glass.
"What are you drinking?" I asked.

"Kirin."

I never drank before dinner. In fact, I never drank beer—at any
time of the day—because it made me piss like there was no tomorrow. But when the waiter came by, I said, "I'll have the same."

Aye-Aye and I made idle small talk—mostly about the snow—
until the waiter returned with my beer and two hand-lettered
menus printed on ecru rice paper. My dislike of Japanese food
stemmed from the one time Ebb and I had eaten too much tempura
at a tiny restaurant in a strip-mall close to our home—and then
spent the rest of the evening letting loose more fiery belches than
Mount Fuji (when the volcano was active, that is). The menu in our
hometown Japanese restaurant had shown photographs of all the
entrees. But at Ichikawa—judging from the dishes listed—I would
have preferred not even knowing, much less seeing, what I was

about to shovel down my gullet. Only in New York, I thought, would people lay down good money to eat seared ostrich on a bed of portobello mushrooms. Or eel tempura. Or tuna tartare. And that was just the stuff I recognized. What, I wondered, were fire oysters? Yellowtail? Hamachi? I was terrified to order and find out later that I had eaten something like the testicles of a harp seal.

"What are you having?" I asked Aye-Aye.

"I wanted to try this—but I forgot to have my assistant call in the order." He pointed to an entree marked: *We are pleased to have authorization of health dept. to bring to you this exciting, sociable dish. Please, 24 our notice.*

The entree—which looked like it was pronounced *fug-you*—cost one hundred ninety dollars. "What's that?" I asked.

"Puffer fish," Aye-Aye said. "If the chef doesn't fix it just right, you drop dead."

"You'd eat that?"

Aye-Aye leaned across the table and looked me too keenly in the eye. "Live dangerously."

He obviously didn't have any children, I thought, as I abandoned my plan to order the staid California roll. When the waiter came back, I pointed under the sushi listings to a trio of mysteries— maguro, bineyo, and hirame—and said, "I guess I'll have this."

"One *ménage à trois*," the waiter said as he scribbled down my order.

"And a side of ... um, silverware," I said.

"Knife and folk for lady," the waiter said scribbling away. "And you, sir?"

"I'll start with the spider roll," Aye-Aye said.

I took a very big sip of my beer.

"With an extra helping of the wasabi. Then the ritsu. Sauce on the side. And could you ask the chef if he'll do half an order of the fried ebi?"

The waiter shook his head. "No half ebi. Whole only."

"Well, then I'll have the fuko maki. Lightly seared. But I'd also like it—"

I must have been really thirsty. Or maybe I just wanted to keep my glass up to my lips so I wouldn't be tempted to tell Aye-Aye, *If you're going to be so fussy about how your food is fixed, then why don't you just hustle back into the kitchen and cook it yourself?*

After the waiter retreated, Aye-Aye folded his hands on the table—he had huge hands—and said, "Now. Lisa. I'm sorry."

"About what?"

"I mean *I'm Sorry,* your novel—"

My face flushed. "Oh, I'm so happy," I said, "that you liked all of the manuscript."

"Liked it?" Aye-Aye said. "I loved it. I felt *pained* by it. I mean, that marriage."

My fingers inched toward my pilsner glass. "What about it?"

"Beyond hopeless."

I took another very healthy sip of beer.

"All that bickering," Aye-Aye said. "The sleepless nights. The disappointments. The longing. Honey, the grief."

I wiped the beer foam from my lips—and probably three quarters of whatever lipstick was left on my lips came off on the napkin. "I didn't think it was that bad."

"Bad! It's hellish!"

"Simon and Robin have their good moments," I said. "Even their good days."

"Yes, but their marriage felt like *forever.*" Aye-Aye swallowed the last of his beer and shoved his glass to the side. "I just wanted to pluck those poor souls off the page and give them a drastic makeover. Maybe in the sequel—"

"I wasn't planning a sequel."

"—Simon and Robin can stop dreaming about becoming something other than what they really are. They should run off to the city—solo, mind you—and get a real life. Or at least update their utterly retro belief that they should stay together for the sake of the kids."

"Kid," I said. "Singular."

"Whatever."

From the way the pattern on the tatami mat nailed to the wall seemed to shift, I realized why Ebb made it a rule not to drink at company functions. Nevertheless, I ordered another beer when

Aye-Aye ordered another. And when the waiter brought us a lacquer tray holding something pale rolled in seaweed and Aye-Aye said, "Try one," I felt obliged to dip one slimy roll into a tiny bowl of green sauce.

I took a bite. The nostrils practically blew off my nose. "Whoa," I gasped as I reached for my beer. "Now I know what to give my son—who snores like a pig—before he goes to bed at night."

"I thought you had a daughter," Aye-Aye said.

"*Simon and Robin* have a daughter." I hesitated, then said, "You know, very few of the key details in my novel are true."

"I should hope so. For your sake." Aye-Aye took a hearty bite of his seaweed roll. "Although I have to say, right now New York is falling all over its face for the memoir."

"I can't imagine why," I said. "Personally—when I read—I prefer to escape."

"I'm with you, Ms. Diodetto. Take me to the outer reaches of the imagination. Speaking of which. In *I'm Sorry*." Aye-Aye leaned back. "You strike me as someone who can take it straight from the hip."

"Right," I said. "In my next life, I plan on joining the Marines."

"Well, I need to tell you: I don't have an easy sell here. This is a very quiet story you've written."

"That's odd," I said. "It seemed so loud in my head."

Aye-Aye refolded his huge hands on the table. "Furthermore, we don't have anything truly original here. No talking dogs, no pedophilia, no midgets with sixth sense. How many times can we read about a marriage on the rocks—"

"I guess I was hoping at least one more time."

"—without saying to ourselves, every postwar author from John Cheever to John Updike has more than beaten this subject to death?"

I crinkled up my nose in disdain. Neither of those Johns, I thought, had written about their husband's hemorrhoids (which really were the piles *I'd* gotten after I gave birth to Danny) with such consummate wit.

"What I'm trying to tell you," Aye-Aye said, "is that you need to change your ending."

"I do?" Good thing I had to press my lips together to hold back a beery burp—otherwise I would have blurted out, *I do not!* I gave Aye-Aye a tight smile. "Tell me why."

"This final chapter doesn't ring true. You failed to capture what a man feels when he really *wants* another woman. And you need to get rid of all the remorse that Simon feels. It's completely overdone."

"But Simon betrayed his wife with Take-A-Letter-Maria," I said. "In his imagination."

"But not in reality."

"But he realized he was a heartbeat away from flushing his whole life down the toilet. So when he stopped himself, just in time, from grabbing Take-A-Letter-Maria's butt—"

"Most guys wouldn't have those scruples," Aye-Aye said.

"My guy does," I said. "My guy acknowledges he's done wrong and tries to make it right."

"It would be more realistic," Aye-Aye said, "if he did wrong and then did wrong again." Aye-Aye leaned forward and grasped my hand. "Simon needs to fuck Maria."

I smiled. And nodded. And thought, *You need to fuck yourself.*

"Yes, Simon needs to leave Robin for Take-A-Letter-Maria and do just what the song says: Tell her I won't be coming home, I've got to start a new life."

I looked down at Aye-Aye's hand on my hand. "Real men don't do that," I said.

"Of course they do," Aye-Aye said. "Just look at the divorce rate. One out of two."

"But what about the other fifty percent? What's their story?" I suddenly became aware that I was raising my voice, so I took a deep breath and said, "My novel is about why a couple chooses to stay together in the age of divorce."

"But, honey, don't you understand: We want to know why people *divorce* in the age of the divorce. Besides—in your book—we feel this push toward adultery through the entire narrative and then we don't even get a good fuck in the end. It's so disappointing. So staid. So overly moral."

"What's wrong with moral?" I asked.

Aye-Aye removed his hand from mine. "This isn't Aesop,

sweetie. You don't get a fat advance for telling the reader at the end of your story, 'Look before you leap' or 'Familiarity breeds contempt.' "

I sat there, speechless. I could not—no, I would not!—change my exquisitely written (not to mention *touching* and *poignant* and *heart-wrenching*) ending in which Simon Stern flung open the front door of his home, determined to rush into the kitchen, take Robin in his manly arms, and vow that he would love her forever—only to get hit with a stream of WD-40 that Robin (who was sick of nagging him about the sticky front-door lock) accidentally sprayed all over his turdish tie.

What did Aye-Aye think I was—a fishmonger? a mattress salesman? a hustler of used cars? I was a Writer with a capital double-U. *I shall not compromise my artistic ideals for money,* I felt like telling him. *Nor will I sully my vision for the sake of one lousy buck.*

However. For one hundred thousand bucks . . .

Several uncomfortable seconds of silence passed, in which I seriously considered rushing back into the kitchen to bribe the chef to fix—incorrectly—a big steaming plate of fugu, which I would deliver to Aye-Aye with these words: *Eat this—and die.* But I knew that now was the moment for me to speak in Ebbish, to say "Let us agree to disagree" or some other reasonable line.

I opened my big mouth and told Aye-Aye: "I'm sure we can reach some misunderstanding."

## CHAPTER NINETEEN

# EBEN

**At the bagel shop,** Cynthia showed me that she believed in the cardinal rule of real estate: *Sell to the woman, close to the man.* She came on strong to me. She kept saying *we,* as if I were buying the house with her instead of Lisa: "We need to order a termite inspection." "We need to confirm your lock-in rate." "We need to guesstimate how much the house is worth to the buyers and how much it's worth to us."

I pushed aside the plate that had held my pesto bagel and took a sip of my coffee. "You mentioned you met the wife," I said.

Cynthia finished the last bite of her cinnamon bagel. "Last week, when my car was in the shop, I rode along with Rob while he did a job there."

"Mice?" I asked.

"Oh no. Rob deals with much larger animals than *that.* This was just an owl. Roosting in the attic eaves." Cynthia raised her coffee; her styrofoam cup was tinged with pale pink lipstick. "I was going to wait for Rob in the truck, but the wife insisted I come in for a cup of coffee."

"Oh, so you had coffee together?" I nodded at her cup. "When you and Lisa go out for coffee, I know sometimes you ... um, open up ... to each other."

Cynthia blushed. "I'm embarrassed to admit it, but I do unload a lot on Lisa."

"I'm sure Lisa pays you back in kind."

Cynthia shook her head. "I can't say that she does."

If I hadn't been so concerned about derailing the conversation, I might have asked, *Are we talking about the same Lisa?*

"So when you had coffee with this wife at the house," I said, "did she say anything to you? That might be useful to us?"

"Well." Cynthia's eyes sparkled. "She *did* call her ex-husband a pig."

"I see."

"The sort of man who had a wandering eye, if you know what I mean."

"I'm sure I don't. But go on, please."

"Actually, I need to backtrack. Before she even got around to complaining about her ex-husband, I complimented her on her home—you know, 'This is a beautiful home you have here'—and she said to me, 'More like a beautiful burden.' She said she had gotten the house in the divorce settlement, but she didn't have the money to keep it up. Then she told me—not knowing I was in real estate, of course—'I'd ditch this house faster than my husband ditched me, which is to say, in half a second.' "

"Oh." I leaned back in my chair. "I like the sound of that."

"I thought you would. And so—if you're wondering how low we can lowball?"

I nodded.

Cynthia reached into her tote bag for a pen, plucked a napkin from my tray, and scratched down *650* instead of *750*. "Should we start there and see what happens?"

"That sounds doable to me."

"Then let's do it," she said.

We pushed back our chairs and put on our coats. "What a gorgeous day," Cynthia said when we stepped out of the bagel shop into the blinding sunlight.

"By the end of the week it'll all be slush," I said, "and you'll have nothing but the Bahamas on your mind. Watch that car."

Cynthia had stepped off the curb into the path of a car turning into the mini-mall parking lot. The silver grille of this big blue Buick seemed to grin as I took Cynthia's forearm and pulled her back onto the sidewalk. The man behind the steering wheel tooted his horn. I dropped Cynthia's arm. The driver was Josh Silber.

Josh's open-mouthed look of surprise confirmed what Lisa once said of him: "There are times when Josh looks like a friendly, but not very bright, hippopotamus." The Buick rolled forward and slowly stopped. Josh lowered the window. Coughing from the exhaust, he called out, "Hey, Ebbie. Hey, Cynthia. Where's"—he coughed again—"Lisa?"

"Waiting for a plumber to come." I nodded behind me. "Cynthia and I just had lunch."

"Deb sent me for a dozen bagels," Josh said. "So tell me: Did they get the onions oniony enough this time?"

"I ordered the pesto," I said.

A look I could only consider *reproachful* momentarily crossed Josh's face. "Well, tell Lisa I said hi." He leaned his head farther out the window and gawked at all the snow in the lot. "Hey, who does your plowing, Cynthia? They do a shit job! If one of you two is leaving—"

"We're leaving together," I said. "To look at a house."

"Who's driving—you or Cynthia?"

That hadn't been decided, but I said, "Me."

"Can I have your parking space?"

I nodded and waved an impatient good-bye to Josh. Cynthia and I began to make our way gingerly across the slippery parking lot. Behind us, Josh's Buick shook and shuddered.

"I didn't know you knew Josh Silber," Cynthia asked.

"He does my taxes."

"I know him from Rotary. For some reason he always ends up sitting at my table during lunch." Cynthia wrinkled up her forehead. "I guess he likes my cheesecake."

"Excuse me?"

"The restaurant where we meet always serves cheesecake. Whenever I tell the waitress that I'm taking a pass on the dessert, Josh always says, 'Hers, I'll eat.' "

"Ah-ha," I said. "I thought Josh had put on weight since the last time I saw him."

As Josh watched from his car, I unlocked the passenger door of my Audi and held it open for Cynthia. When I closed the door, I noticed that Cynthia wore pants, in some soft stretchy material tucked into her brown leather boots. I wondered if there were stirrups—that hooked around her feet—at the bottom of those stretch pants. Then I looked away, into the blinding sunlight of the half-plowed parking lot, and waved again to Josh. I walked around the back of my car and got in. As I stuck the key into the ignition, I took a couple of surreptitious sniffs to ensure that the crisp, clear air had driven the odor of the garbage bags completely out of my car.

I was reasonably sure that the odor was gone. But I didn't want Cynthia to think I had a major case of flatulence. I started the engine and was just about to concoct some fiction about how Danny had left some fast food rotting in the backseat of my car, when the radio blared, "According to an FAA spokesperson, the number of reported dead from Flight—"

I flicked off the radio and told Cynthia, "I was supposed to be on that plane."

"The one that crashed? Are you serious?"

I nodded.

Cynthia looked intently at me, with those pale blue eyes that reminded Josh of the eyes of a Siamese cat—but that reminded me of those properties found on the first side of the Monopoly board (What were they? Oriental. Vermont. Connecticut. Then Jail, and the man behind iron bars ...).

"I can't believe it," Cynthia said. "You're so lucky."

"I know."

"Lisa would be devastated. But what happened? Why weren't you on it?"

Why wasn't I? Luck? fate? coincidence?

"There was something else I wanted to get done today," I said.

"Like buy a house?"

"Someone else I wanted to ... spend the afternoon with."

"I'm so flattered. And so relieved! That you stayed behind just for me." Cynthia clasped her tote bag in her lap, then said, "But you must feel ... how *do* you feel?"

My perspective definitely had changed. The Before-Eben never would have considered mentioning this brush with death to Cynthia or any other relative stranger. But the After-Eben could laugh and say, "I feel like a completely new man. Pardon my hand, please."

Whenever I backed my car out of a parking space, I always put my right hand on the back of the passenger seat—even when the passenger was someone other than Lisa. *I am not,* I told myself, *doing anything different just because Josh Silber has his eye on me—and because he inevitably will go back and tell Deb, "Hey, I caught Ebb Strauss out to lunch with this sexy devil of a woman—and it sure smelled fishy to me, the way he took a pass on the onion bagel."*

Lisa's idea of giving good directions in the car consisted of giving me advice like "I think you were supposed to turn left, Ebb—you know, back there?" Cynthia, however, made a great copilot. She called out "Right at the fork" and "Straight through at the light" with such confidence that we found our way to the house in no time. I let up on the gas as we approached 27 Darling Lane. At the end of the long driveway, which had been plowed to perfection, the pig weathervane glinted in the sun. The house itself, trimmed with lacy icicles, looked like some Currier & Ives print labeled in cursive: *Home for the Holidays.* Yet a flurry of footprints—as if a troop of West Point cadets had jogged through—marred the tranquil blanket of snow directly in front of the house. The walk was shoveled in a wider than necessary swath, exposing a long trail of goose-egg stones that reminded me of Lisa's thievery.

Sunday's chill wind must have blown the Swedish love knot away, because the knocker on the green front door hung clean. Something new hung on the door latch: a lockbox. After consulting a slip of paper she had tucked in her purse, Cynthia turned the combination. We entered. The echo of our footsteps in the hall reminded me of the hollow sound that used to ring through my childhood home after my mother had taken down the drapes for spring cleaning. Looking from left to right off the hall, I realized the house had been emptied of the rest of its furniture. The muddy footprints on the floor and a solitary broom leaning in the corner were the only indications that a fairy hadn't waved a wand over the house and whisked everything away.

"When did this happen?" I asked Cynthia. "*How* did that happen? They couldn't possibly have boxed all that stuff and taken it out in that driving snow."

"At Bear Mountain, the snow had stopped by yesterday morning."

"But here it lasted on and off all day," I said. "And to dismantle the entire house—even if the top floor already had been cleaned out ..." I looked around at the empty walls and ceiling. I felt like calling out, *hello, hello, hello?* just to hear the echo. "I mean, there was a ton of stuff in here."

Cynthia loosened the belt on her coat. "Half a dozen men can strip an entire house in three or four hours."

"You've seen that done?"

"Over and over." Cynthia pulled off her gloves. "My father was in the Air Force."

"I didn't know that. Where was he stationed?"

"Alabama. Japan. The Philippines. Germany." She paused. "Should I go on?"

"How many times did you move?"

"Too many." Cynthia wandered to the far end of the hall, which was still in shadow because neither one of us had turned on the light. She rested her bare hand on the newel post and gazed up the stairs. "I always was so envious of people who got to live in one place."

I walked farther into the hall and looked into the bare room that no longer seemed to deserve the name of *parlor*. "Did you know this house would be empty?" I asked.

"I suspected. When the listing agent gave me the lockbox combination instead of the key."

"It seems like a different house," I said. "Without the furniture."

"Do you still like it?"

"Very much so. Yes."

Cynthia's well-polished boots clacked against the floorboards as she moved into the parlor. She surveyed the open space with such obvious pleasure that I could tell she was selecting new furniture in her head.

"The moment I saw this house," she said, "I thought it was the perfect fit for you two."

I leaned in the doorway of the parlor. "Tell me why."

"Well. Do you remember that night we first met?"

"Vaguely," I said.

"It was Valentine's Day."

"Yes."

"You had just gotten promoted."

"That's right."

"Lisa told me that evening," Cynthia said, "that you two were looking for a new home because you would have to host parties. But then you told me, Eben, that you worked long hours and that you just wanted a comforting place to return home to." Cynthia gestured around the room. "Well, here we are. This is an ideal place to entertain. But it's also a real retreat. No noise. No neighbors. There's plenty of room for Danny to run around. If you have more children, there are those large extra bedrooms. And I know how much Lisa wants a room of her own to do her writing—"

"You know," I interrupted, "I was surprised—that evening— when Lisa told you flat-out that she was a writer. I guess she's gotten tired, all these years, of passing herself off as just a housewife."

"There's nothing wrong with keeping a home," Cynthia said. "It requires a lot of skill." Her face grew serious, as if she herself were contemplating a whole lifetime standing behind a deck mop or a stiff broom. Then she smiled. "Too bad the pay is so lousy."

I laughed—then instantly felt disloyal to Lisa. "Lisa's hoping to make big bucks off this book she's been writing."

"The story sounds fascinating."

"Doesn't it?" I said. I stared down at the rock salt crusted on my loafers and waited for Cynthia to reveal the rest of what she knew about Lisa's novel. When she didn't indulge me, I said, "Of course, the plot does seem a little over the top."

"Well, I guess most love stories have to be exaggerated."

"So you'd call her novel a love story, then?" I asked.

"Don't you remember that Lisa called it a romance of sorts?" Cynthia reached up and wiped a bit of dust off the mantel. "I'm dying to read it. Especially since Lisa told me she based the main character a little on my ex-husband."

"Your *ex-husband*!"

"Yes. Angus unfortunately was a—"

What was Cynthia about to say? *A ladies' man*? I didn't know. And I would never find out, because her pager suddenly beeped. As she dug through her tote bag, I looked down—then saw my pager wasn't attached to my belt. I had left my leash to the office back at the office.

"I'm going to use the phone in the kitchen," Cynthia said. "If it's still connected."

I nodded.

"Take your time looking around," she said. "I'll be right behind this door. If you want me."


As Cynthia retreated into the kitchen, I found myself staring at a solitary nail left in the wall between the front two windows of the parlor. "Twelve-over-twelve," Cynthia had called these panes of glass, leading me to believe that the founding fathers of our country liked their *feng shui* too—or at least they valued order and symmetry. My hollow footsteps measured the floorboards of the parlor. I ran my hand along the mantel and tried to see myself sunk deep in a big leather chair in front of a crackling blaze in the fireplace. I walked back into the hall, gazed up the staircase, and imagined Danny—against our orders—sliding down the oak banister. I pictured Lisa sitting in the dining room—not presiding over a dinner party, but hunched over some thick manuscript, scratching out a string of words only to write the same words all over again.

The dining room connected—by yet another swinging-door— back to the kitchen. In her soft voice, Cynthia was arranging to meet someone later that evening. I ignored the pull I felt toward the kitchen and went upstairs, listening to each step creak and settle beneath my feet.

In the hallway outside the smallest bedroom—which obviously

was intended as a nursery—I noticed a hatch in the ceiling. I reached up and pulled down the cord. The hatch door surrendered with a groan, and a set of steps, like a staircase leading nowhere in a surrealistic painting, lowered toward me. The stairs locked into place and practically beckoned me to climb where Cynthia's lover had gone just the week before. I only went two-thirds of the way up—enough to peek my head over the lip of the attic and survey the piles of pink fiberglass that padded the floor, the dormers that gave out onto the tops of trees, and the unfinished rafters. I wondered where the owl, that weird bird whose head swiveled all the way around as if it could see into the past and the future, had roosted. Had the owl called out *who? who?* when Cynthia's lover released it into the forest?

The attic was dusty. I coughed as I backed down the stairs, released the lock, and pushed the entire staircase back into the attic. *Concentrate on the house,* I told myself. *You're here to evaluate the house.* But as I wandered into the master bedroom (cold and uninviting without the cheval mirror and the braided rug and the four-poster bed) and then wandered into the master bath, I could only listen to Cynthia's voice waft up through the vents and question what I was doing here without Lisa. It wasn't like me to tell Cynthia, "Show me that house right now." It wasn't like me to place a bid on a piece of property priced at three quarters of a million dollars without asking more detailed questions about the boundaries. Yet I deliberately had put my checkbook in my pocket before I left the office—before I accidentally-on-purpose left behind the SB pager.

I just couldn't believe that I had left behind the pager. I should have been worried that it probably sat buzzing away on my desk. Instead, I grew almost light-headed at the thought that, for the first time in a long time, no one knew where I was. No one could reach me. Only I knew that I stood upstairs, alone but not alone, in this empty house. Here I was not EVPIR. Here I was not the husband whose nickname evoked low tide. Here I was no one's daddy. Here I had no relationship whatsoever to the character in Lisa's novel.

Or maybe I did. Because suddenly I wanted nothing of what I had and lusted after all I could never obtain. That is to say: I wanted to go downstairs and fuck Cynthia.

◆   ◆   ◆

*Eben Strauss placed his large, manly hand upon the swinging door and strode into the kitchen, where his lovely real-estate agent was sitting cross-legged on the clean counter.*

*"Oh!" she said. "You startled me!" As she slid down from the counter, her boots hit the tile, and she helplessly dropped the phone to the floor with a clatter.*

*Eben capably stepped up to the kitchen counter. He clasped his mouth upon her luscious pink lips and urgently thrust his tongue into her initially unwilling mouth....*

*"No!" she cried, before she cried, "Yes!"*

*Pearl buttons scattered across the tile as Eben tore open her blouse, yanked down her lace bra, and nuzzled her comely breasts. She arched her back with pleasure as he dropped his trousers, parted her legs, and lifted her away from the kitchen counter. Then it was nothing but one thrust after another as he carried her from room to room and her moans of "Fuck me! Fuck me! until I grow so ashamed I can never show my face at Rotary Club again!" reverberated so loudly throughout the empty house that Eben thought the floor would collapse, the walls tumble down, and the roof beams cave in....*

I leaned my head against the cold pane of the window. This fantasy was ridiculous. Shameless. Immoral. Full of bad dialogue. And yet so arousing that I felt a killing stiffness in my pants. Lisa obviously wasn't the only member of the family who could pen pornography.

I gazed down at my rough, spotted hand and caught my own reflection in the gold of my wedding band. It was like looking at myself in a spoon: my face seemed bloated, as if I had the beginning of mumps or some childhood infectious disease; my nose was blurred into my mouth; and my eyes, behind my gold-rimmed glasses, were sunk too deep in my head to even distinguish their color. That can't be me, I thought. I could never be a home-wrecker. A heartbreaker. Yet I already had slept with Cynthia in my dreams. And surely something was going very, very wrong between me and Lisa, or else I wouldn't be standing here in this empty house without her. A little voice inside me, which I was trying very hard not to hear, was whispering: *Anything can happen. Anything can happen, so why not? Why not?*

◆　◆　◆

Down in the parlor, I deliberately made my steps heavier to warn Cynthia I was coming. I cleared my throat and knocked before I cracked open the swinging door.

Cynthia, who was leaning against the counter, beckoned me in and hung up the wall phone. "I just called the office of the listing agent," she said. "She's on her way out here between two and three to post the for-sale sign. She's making this a talking house."

"A what?"

"Talking house. It's the latest selling tool. There's a special gadget attached to the for-sale sign. When potential buyers pull up in the driveway, they can tune their car radio to get recorded information on the property."

I leaned against the doorjamb and stuck my hands into my pockets. "Let's stay until she gets here."

Cynthia gave me an inviting smile. "We could do that."

"We could ... well, we could tell her the house has spoken to me," I said. "And doesn't need to speak to anyone else."

"Oh, Eben." Cynthia held out both hands—to congratulate me? or embrace me? I was about to step toward her when I heard something else talking. But it wasn't my sense of right or wrong. It was the pesto bagel and vegetarian cream cheese and the large coffee I had consumed for lunch. My stomach rumbled. The thought that at any second I could be in Cynthia's arms was so unsettling, so disconcerting, that my intestines seemed to shift inside me, and a bubble of gas threatened to explode in my trousers.

I took a step backward. "Would you excuse me for just a moment?"

Cynthia—a hurt look in her eye—said, "Certainly."

I backed out of the kitchen. Since I didn't dare use the half-bath on the first floor, I bolted up the stairs, charged into the master bathroom, dropped my pants, and committed the most unspeakable crime in Lisa's house-hunting etiquette book: *lowered my butt upon the throne.* Thank God the last person out of the house had been the wife—kind, considerate, and a consummate housekeeper to the very end. She had left behind a full roll of toilet paper. And good thing. Because after five days of walking around in a

constipated fog, I *plotzed* the longest and messiest turd of my life—
what Lisa would call *a double flusher*.

The timing couldn't have been worse. Or better. Although my
butt stung as I slowly took the stairs to remeet Cynthia, the headache that had plagued me for days now melted away. I felt restored
to my old self. I was a reasonable human being. A man who knew
his limits. A man with business to conduct.

*Eben Strauss placed his large, manly hand upon the swinging door
and strode into the kitchen, where his lovely real-estate agent was sitting cross-legged on the clean counter.*

*"Oh!" said she. "You startled me!"*

*As she slid down from the counter, her boots hit the tile, and Eben
looked at the floor—as if it already were* his *floor—to see if her heels
had nicked it.*

## CHAPTER TWENTY

# LISA

Something in that *ménage à trois* sushi must have disagreed with me, because my stomach lurched all the way home on the train. I couldn't wait to get onto the platform and gulp some fresh air. As I gingerly walked across the icy parking lot to my car, I tried not to think about what a fiasco my lunch with Aye-Aye had been. I had let him hold my hand. *Ugh.* And call me *sweetie* and *babe. Double ugh.* And convince me—sort of—that Simon should jump the bones of the beautiful Maria. *Ugh* three times. *Ugh* a million! I unlocked my car and climbed into the cold driver's seat. What did Aye-Aye—a bachelor!—know about marriage? It made my pulse race faster and faster, until all four chambers of my heart felt like they would implode with rage, to think that he had dared to criticize my version of that flawed yet venerable institution. I gripped the chilly steering wheel of my car and muttered to myself what I should have told Aye-Aye in the restaurant: "Just because two people are having a couple of bad moments in their marriage doesn't mean the whole thing has to fall apart!"

My words sounded wise and wonderful. I glanced in the rearview mirror to smile in agreement with my sage old married self. And that's when I noticed the huge piece of glistening brown seaweed lodged between my canine and my incisor. I'd been talking to

Aye-Aye—probably for the vast majority of our sophisticated little lunch—with half the ocean's flora stuck in my teeth.

I wanted to die. *You idiot,* I scolded myself as I rubbed a Kleenex between my teeth—which only lodged the seaweed farther into the crack. *You moron! You loser! Now you'll really have to rewrite your novel. You'll have to rename it* I'm Sorry This Is My Sushi. *And before you pose for your author photograph, you'll have to take a sharp toothpick to all the marine algae flourishing in your foolish mouth.*

I burped—not once, but twice—and then I pushed my gloved hand against the base of my throat. Oh, the pain. The agony. The sheer heartburn of being a Real Author—who had to write not what she wanted to write but whatever the market demanded. But I wouldn't! I couldn't! I simply could not stomach the idea of creating in my novel an unhappy ending!

I started the car and backed out over a large clump of ice that momentarily made the back tires swerve. I couldn't wait to get home. I couldn't wait to let Ebb read *I'm Sorry,* so he could assure me that Norwegians had notoriously loose morals and that their literary opinions weren't worth the price of a tin of smoked salmon.

*Don't change a word,* Ebb would say. *Don't even change a* space *between the words. Simon never would dare lay a lusty finger on Maria.*

I would nod—vigorously—as I said, *That's right.*

*Simon is too good a man.*

*Exactly.*

*He has never seen the humor in that Borscht Belt joke, "Take my wife . . . please."*

*Precisely.*

*He sees the face of his child in the face of his wife and remembers his duties and responsibilities.*

*Totally.*

*Your ending is the only feasible ending.*

Usually the dialogue I concocted in my head required copious editing. But as I pulled out of the train-station parking lot and reviewed Ebb's lines, I thought, *Hmm, with the exception of the word* feasible, *I couldn't have said it better myself.*

◆   ◆   ◆

When I got to Montessori House, Glorious Gloria opened the door with a robust "Welcome, Mother!" I stepped into the overheated front hall. Two boys sat on the wooden bench, bundled up in identical cobalt-blue Lands' End ski jackets. The boy on the left—who turned out to be Danny—curled his mittens into fists and told me, "Mommy, you are *late*."

Gloria immediately tut-tutted. "Now, Danny, remember our lesson about using hurtful words." She turned to me. "Today we learned about mature communication techniques. Instead of making accusations such as 'You're a dope!' or 'You're a jerk!' we're practicing how to say, 'When you ... I feel ...' "

Gloria nodded encouragingly at Danny.

Danny gave me a sour look. "Mommy, when you pick me up late from school, I feel like *Zachary*."

"Which Zachary?" I asked.

Danny pointed to the despondent boy sitting next to him. "On Mondays, Zachary's dad always forgets to pick him up."

*The fucker,* I thought. I reached for Danny's hand and turned toward Gloria. "Thanks for telling me about that communication method," I said. "I'll have to try it on my husband next time he starts acting like a—"

Danny pulled me out the door before I could say *dope* or *jerk*.

On the ride home, Danny said, "Daddy called school today."

My esophagus started to burn again. "What for?"

"He wanted to know if you had dropped me off."

*Oh Lord in heaven,* I thought. "What'd you tell him?"

"I was pooping in the bathroom. Where'd you go today, anyway?"

"Nowhere."

"You're all dressed up."

"I went to ... the doctor's," I said, and let rip a wet, fishy belch.

Danny giggled. "Gross, Mommy!"

"I couldn't help it," I said.

"You're not very ladylike."

"So who wants to be?" I burped again, then swallowed down the foul taste in my mouth. "Oh, yuck, I feel like I'm going to—"

Danny looked up at me with great interest. My stomach clutched together. But then the barfy feeling passed. I rode the rest of the way home in grateful silence. As we turned into our half-shoveled driveway, Danny reported, "Zachary's mom threw up and went to the doctor and now she's going to have another baby."

I clenched my teeth. If I had to hear that yet another woman I knew—and not me—had gotten pregnant, I really would vomit. I should have stayed home today, I thought. I should have paged Ebb and told him to come home on his lunch hour. I should have performed my wifely duties and made love with my husband. Instead, I had run away to the big bad city to eat *eels*. Yes, I was sure I had eaten eels or squid or some other slick, gelatinous half-alive sea creature that right now was writhing in my stomach.

I cut the engine and got out of the car. I felt queasier than ever as I turned toward the for-sale sign and watched Law and Order's dented face swaying back and forth in the wind. I trudged through the snow to the mailbox, which was stuffed with junk mail. The stiff white envelope on top convinced me that Ebb's secretary had added us to some Christian mailing list. SOMEONE AT THIS ADDRESS, the envelope claimed, DESPERATELY NEEDS GOD'S HELP.

*Tell me something I don't already know,* I thought as I made my way back up the icy driveway and remembered—way too late—that I was supposed to have called Cynthia. Ebb would be furious that I hadn't called her. And now we probably had lost our last chance for happiness—that stern, upright, and yet so forgiving house.

"We got a package!" Danny hollered, running up to the front porch and grabbing what looked to me like a long white florist's box. He inspected the label. "But it came to the wrong address. It's for . . ." He concentrated as he put together the letters. "E-liz-a-beth Die-oh-det-to."

My heart thudded. Surely the flowers—if they were addressed to Ms. Diodetto—could have come from only one man: Aye-Aye. And surely the card inside read something like this: *My dear Ms. D., please accept my humble apologies for trying to turn your words— which are indeed golden!—into mere silver.*

"Elizabeth Diodetto," I told Danny, "is me."

"But, Mommy. You're the Lisar-lady."

"I lead a double life," I said. "And then some." I carried the mail up to the porch and gestured with my head. "Step aside, Big Boy."

The front-door lock felt dry and unforgiving when I slipped in the key. I gritted my teeth and twisted the key to the left. The lock clicked and Danny cheered as the door opened.

The answering machine was blinking wildly when we trooped into the kitchen. But Danny insisted that I open the florists' box ("Open it, open it!") before I played the messages. I dumped the mail on the counter, drew a scissors from the junk drawer, and cut the twine. Beneath layers of green tissue lay a dozen now-drooping pink tulips that looked as bedraggled as a boxer in the ninth round.

"These must have been beautiful," I said. "Once upon a time."

I pulled down a vase from the cabinet and started to fill it with water.

Danny grabbed the white envelope from the box, pulled out the card, and read aloud a phonetic version of the message: *"Eye hee-ard you need a plumb-ber."*

I almost dropped the vase into the sink. "Let me see that."

Danny held out the card. "I said it right."

I set the vase down on the counter and looked over his shoulder at the neat handwriting on the card. "Plumber has a silent *B*."

"How come nobody signed it?"

"I guess I have a secret admirer."

Danny's lower lip quivered.

I reached down and rubbed his cold, red cheek with the back of my knuckle. "My admirer is Daddy."

"Daddy wouldn't call you by your wrong name."

"But that isn't my wrong name," I said. "It's my maiden name, the name I had before I married Daddy."

"Why would Daddy want to call you that?"

"He was fooling around," I said.

Danny looked up at me, and I braced myself to hear the inevitable: *Zachary's dad fooled around—with a lady who wasn't his wife.* But then Danny gazed down at the message again. "What does it mean?"

Little did I know how difficult this question would be to answer. I picked up the scissors and started hacking off the ends of the tulip stems. What had Ebb meant to tell me with those simple six words—*Let's get together tonight? I'm coming home at noon? I wouldn't mind trying something different? I know we need to fix things between us? I wouldn't have married anyone else?*

I dropped an aspirin into the vase to keep the flowers fresh—and then, because the tulips looked as sick as I myself felt, I also dropped in two tablets of Alka-Seltzer. As the tablets fizzed away— and Danny giggled at the sound—I put the tulips one by one into the water and watched each stem and flower droop over the lip of the vase. It hardly mattered what Ebb had meant to say—did it?—if I hadn't been here to get the message. I hadn't stayed home on the one day I should have been here. I'd been too busy trying to make myself into someone else. And now I just felt like a nobody, all over again.

I put the last tulip into the vase, and the petals shattered all over the counter.

Danny tugged on my sleeve. "Why are you crying, Mommy?"

I wiped my wet cheek with the back of my hand. "Because I think Daddy meant to say—"

I was going to tell Danny, *I love you.* But then my lunch abruptly backed up into my throat. My stomach buckled and I ran into the half-bathroom, where I fell to my knees and gushed my churned-up sushi into the less-than-pristine toilet. It was a real hurl. I hadn't gotten sick with such spectacular fury since that morning so long ago when I had stood up from my desk at the office and thought to myself, *I can't be pregnant. I must be pregnant. I can't get married. I must get married. Maybe there'll be moments when I actually like being a mother and a wife. But, oh God, the moments when I don't . . .*

Ebb came home early, just before six o'clock. I heard his car door slam as I lay shivering in my sweatsuit in bed, and I imagined him walking in to the front hall, puzzled that the kitchen stood dim

and gave off no warm, comforting smell of chicken or pasta or vegetables simmering on the stove. I was sure Ebb figured out that
something was amiss when he found Danny parked in front of the
blue light of the TV, watching the end of *Life and Death on the
Veldt*.

"Where's Mommy?" Ebb asked Danny as the narrator of the
video stated in clipped British tones, "A zebra stallion must fight for
his right to mate with an entire harem of mares. . . ."

"She got sick," Danny said as the narrator told us, "The loser
usually chooses to join a herd of bachelors. . . ."

Ebb must have hit the MUTE on the remote, because the video
went silent. "*How* did Mommy get sick?"

"She threw up," Danny said. "A lot. She said she went to the
doctor's and—hey, look at those zebras, Daddy. Doesn't that hurt?"

Ebb cleared his throat. "Maybe not for the participants—"

*Participants?*

"—but for the observers . . . well, I agree, it certainly seems
painful to watch."

I sensed more than actually heard Ebb toss his coat over the back
of the couch. As he came up the stairs, his footsteps sounded
slow—and even his shadow, which appeared in the darkened doorway of our bedroom, seemed tired.

"Lisar," he said. "Are you awake?"

I brought the blankets up to my chin and shivered. "I wish I
weren't."

"What's the matter?"

"First I'm hot and then I'm cold," I said. "And I keep throwing
up. I haven't thrown up so much since—"

"Are you? But you can't be."

"I didn't say I *was*."

I sat up, clutching the blanket against my stomach. Ebb quickly
stepped aside as I bolted from the bed and beelined for the bathroom, where I knelt once again in front of the toilet. Ebb stayed in
the hall until the worst had passed. Although it felt terrible to be so
alone when I was sick—I just wanted someone to hold my hand!—
I knew it would feel even more awful to have Ebb witness my disgusting misery.

After I stopped heaving, Ebb came to the doorway. I reached up and pulled too hard on the toilet handle. Then I wiped my lips with a wad of toilet paper and tossed it into the still-gurgling toilet.

"Thanks for the tulips," I whispered in a dry voice. "And the card."

"The message was kind of—"

"Touching," I said, at the same time as Ebb said, "Ill-conceived. I should have thought before I sent it."

"Thought about what? You can be spontaneous every once in a while."

"But afterward. When you didn't call me. I thought I had offended you."

I reached out blindly for another wad of toilet paper. "You know me better than that."

"Were you in bed all day?" Ebb said. "I was worried about you. I was trying to reach you all morning."

"I was ..." A part of me wanted to be honest. But then another part of me knew how often honesty got me into trouble with Ebb. So I said, "I got really wrapped up. Rethinking the end of my novel. I was trying to decide if Simon should just ... you know, go home to his wife."

"What's the alternative?"

"Staying at the office and fucking Take-A-Letter-Maria into a frenzy."

Ebb cleared his throat. "Well. The frenzy certainly sounds more dramatic. Yet going home ..."

"Oh, I already know where your vote will lie."

"You're too quick to make assumptions, Lisar."

"I'm positive you'll vote for home," I said.

"But I haven't read your novel—so how do you know I wouldn't choose the frenzy?"

I bit my lip. Ebb wouldn't choose the frenzy. He *couldn't* choose the frenzy. Because I simply couldn't change my finale. How would I ever summon up the stamina to go through a divorce (albeit not my own)? How could I ever make Simon and Robin Stern say— without gagging on my own words—bad lines like *My lawyer will talk to your lawyer?*

"Oh," I groaned, "I've never felt so lousy in my life—"

"What did the doctor say?" Ebb asked.

"Which doctor?"

"Danny said you went to the—"

"Oh, right. Dr. Goode asked me if I had eaten any—" I lifted my head and another gush of vomit hit the water. My voice cold-echoed into the depths of the toilet bowl as I said, "Su-she-she-she-she."

"Sushi!" Ebb said. "But, Lisar. You hate Japanese food. Besides, didn't Goode specifically tell you not to touch raw fish? Because it causes worms?"

I reached up, again, and flushed the toilet.

"Just to be safe, you'd better call your GP tomorrow," Ebb said. "And get your stools checked."

I put my hand on my hot forehead. "I can't believe I married a man who uses the word *stools*."

"There are plenty of husbands, Lisar, who do much worse than that."

"Don't I know it," I said.

"Don't you know it?" Ebb said. "*How* do you know it?"

I meant to tell Ebb: I knew it (vicariously) because I had spent more than half of our marriage spinning a long, drawn-out tale about a husband who almost strayed. I also knew it (vicariously) because I had spent the past month listening to Cynthia complain about the wandering Angus.

But Ebb took my words personally. "I've told you, Lisar—on more than one uncomfortable occasion—that I have *never*."

"I know you *never*," I said.

"Well, then what have I ever done to hurt you? What have I ever said?"

"You didn't do—You didn't say—" I hesitated, then remembered how hurt I had felt when I had caught Ebb dreaming about another woman, how wounded I had felt when he told me I *wasn't the fair sex*, how ugly I had felt when he told me that Cynthia looked better than I did because *she didn't have children*, and how devastated I'd felt when he failed—on Valentine's Day—to put punctuation between *I'm sorry* and *This is my wife*.

"You didn't say a comma!" I blurted out.

"A comma?" Ebb asked. "A comma! What are you *talking* about, Lisar?"

I was about to garble out *Everything! And nothing!* when Danny pushed past Ebb into the bathroom and positioned himself between us, his eyes darting back and forth.

"Mommy," he said. "Daddy. Remember: *When you ... I feel ...*" Then he burst into tears. "Stop fighting! Stop fighting or I'll put you both in time-out!"

Okay. So now Ebb and I knew for certain we were rotten parents— because our own kid had to put us into two separate corners for misbehaving. And now we also knew we never deserved to be parents in the first place—because we had driven our only child to burst into tears and ask us in a pitifully small voice, "Are you guys getting a divorce?"

I leaned back against the bathtub. Ebb leaned in the doorway, put his hands in his pockets, and did the very thing that drove me crazy whenever he grew embarrassed or ashamed or uncomfortable: He jingled his keys just like a nervous jailer. I looked at him and he looked at me. And maybe you know how that goes—when you sense the emotional equivalent of a runaway truck coming at you, and see not the life that you've actually lived flash before you, but the one you might have to suffer through if only you don't slam down fast enough on the brakes?

I saw how easily Ebb—who had become an expert packer during his road-warrior days—could put together a suitcase full of clothes and snap the locks. I also saw how tempted I would be to screech, "Unpack that suitcase, my fine friend, because *I* am the one who is doing the walking!" Then I would storm downstairs (without taking even a single pair of sweat pants or a stitch of underwear, secretly thrilled to shred all my Fat Clothes forever). As I slammed the front door behind me and backed my car out of the driveway— sticking out my tongue at the McGruff dog in the dining-room window—I would say, "Ha! Ebb'll be sorry he criticized me for leaving the cordless phone off the hook *now*! Ha! Ebb'll be sorry he got pissed when I ran out of time and didn't bring his car into Midas.

Just wait until he comes home and finds this house all dark tomorrow. That'll run *his* batteries down. *That*'ll fix his muffler." Then I drove all the way down to the main road before I thought, *Hey, wait a second—I forgot to take my sole hard copy of* I'm Sorry This Is My Life. *Better turn around now, before Ebb sets the manuscript on fire and then takes an ax to my computer.*

In this fruitcake fantasy of separation and divorce, Danny was nowhere in sight. He wasn't sitting on the living-room carpet humming "Home on the Range" while he put together a Lincoln Log cabin, he wasn't in the kitchen asking me for the fourth time in an hour, "Isn't dinner ready yet? I'm really hungry," and he wasn't buttoning his pajama tops (crookedly) while telling me, "But I don't want to go to sleep now. Daddy isn't even home yet." In the dark of night, he wasn't standing in our bedroom doorway demanding to know exactly what we were doing; in the light of morning, he wasn't squirming like some goofy, giggly worm between us in bed.

Oh, that Danny! I'd always known that he would function as a very sticky piece of double-sided tape between Ebb and me (but also, sometimes, as a wedge). And as I watched him put his hands up to his face and cry, I realized there was a reason why I'd had trouble just an hour before, distinguishing the two boys who sat despondently on the bench at Montessori House, and it had nothing to do with their identical ski jackets. I'd known since day one how little it would take for me and Ebb to do something stupid and turn our kid into yet another Broken-Home Zachary. I remembered how low I had felt when I had attended Danny's Montessori holiday party with just the video camera by my side and how pissed I had gotten at Ebb because he hadn't accompanied me. I also remembered how strongly I had berated myself for all my bad marital behavior as I had settled my too-wide butt on the tiny Montessori House chair. *Lisa,* I had lectured myself, *you and Ebb need to stop this senseless quarreling, otherwise Danny is going to sulk onto the stage for his junior high school band concert and not know which side of the auditorium to look out upon—because his father is sitting solo to the right and his mother is sitting solo to the left.*

I had promised myself that night—and many subsequent nights—that I would clean up my act and become a good wife and mother. But my intentions, once again, had gone for naught. Danny sobbed and kept on sobbing, and neither Ebb nor I made a move to comfort him, as if we both needed a strong reminder of just how bad things had gotten in our dear little family—and how much worse they could get.

Finally I swallowed back my own urge to bawl like a baby and said, "Oh, honey, please stop crying."

I tore off some toilet paper and held it out to Danny at the same time Ebb dug into his pocket and offered Danny his handkerchief.

Danny looked from the toilet paper to the handkerchief. "Which one should I take?"

"Both," Ebb said. Then since Danny hadn't quite mastered the art of blowing his own nose, Ebb sighed, leaned forward, plucked the toilet paper from my hand, and gently clamped both the paper and the handkerchief over Danny's nostrils. "Blow," he told him. "Come on. Harder. All the way out. That's a boy. Okay. You okay now?"

Danny nodded.

Ebb tossed both the toilet paper and the handkerchief onto the counter. "You've got to stop crying like this, Danny."

"Why?" Danny asked.

"Because you are breaking Mommy and Daddy's hearts," I said.

"And because I've already told you," Ebb added, "that Mommy and Daddy would never get a divorce."

"But you never told me why," Danny said.

"I very clearly told you why," Ebb said with this pained look on his face that seemed to ask, *Why doesn't anyone around here ever listen to me when I use the word love?*

" 'Cuz why?" Danny demanded.

" 'Cuz—" Ebb and I said at the same time. But there we parted ways. Ebb said, " 'Cuz we're getting a new house" while I said, " 'Cuz we're getting you a collie."

Danny grabbed on to the counter and immediately began to do

exactly what I had told him not to do a thousand times before—jump up and down and put so much pressure on the lip of the sink that I was afraid the whole basin would crash into the vanity.

As Danny joyfully sang, "A collie, a collie—a collie collie collie!" I looked up at Ebb. "A house!" I said. "What were *you* up to today?"

"Oh," Ebb said. "I was feeling so full of myself that I hadn't crashed on that plane—"

I gasped. "That plane on the news was your plane?"

"—that I got into a little mischief. With Cynthia. Behind your back."

I reached out and yanked on Danny's shirt. "Stop jumping on that sink! Oh, thank God you're not dead, Ebb—"

"My feelings exactly."

"—because who could stand being a single parent for even one *minute* with a kid like this? Stop that jumping, Danny! Make him stop, please, Ebb—and then tell me all about the plane later—but first tell me everything that happened with Cynthia. Did you make an offer?"

Ebb—his hands full of a very squirmy Danny—nodded.

"Was it accepted?"

Ebb set Danny down away from the sink and nodded again.

"How much?"

Ebb had made too high of an offer. I could tell, because he said, "Let's just say that your friend Cynthia stands to make a very tidy profit."

"But, Ebb," I said, "now you'll never be able to retire early."

"So I'll retire later."

"And now I'll really have to change the ending of my novel," I said. "Because we have to buy serious furniture."

"Cheer up," Ebb said. "We'll probably kill each other in the process of picking it out."

Danny tugged on Ebb's belt—yet another thing he had been told not to do a thousand times. "When are we moving? When can I get my collie dog?"

I nudged his leg with my foot. "First you have to get your adenoids out."

"But I'm scared to go into the hospital," Danny said.

"You heard Mommy," Ebb said. "No adenoidectomy, no collie."

Danny hung his head. Then he wiped his nose with the back of his hand and said, "Okay."

"Now, remember," I told Danny. "You have to really care for a dog."

"I will, Mommy. I'll really love it!"

"Mommy didn't say *love*," Ebb said. "She said feed."

"I will," Danny said.

"And brush," Ebb said.

"I will."

"And pick up its business from the backyard," Ebb said.

"Zachary trained his cat," Danny said, "to do his business in the toilet."

"I have no intention of sharing the bathroom with Lassie," I said.

"I sort of want a laddie dog," Danny said. "But I don't know—which should I get, Daddy, a lassie or a laddie?"

My stomach churned. I could see it now. We would take Danny to the dog breeder and he would get so enamored of the puppies that we would end up bringing home not one but two of those bad-breathed creatures—who would yip and yap and pee and poop and shed allergy-inducing fur all over our new house. Our house. We had a home! The kind of home I actually would be eager to keep clean and tidy. But how would I ever keep the *schmutz* under control with two dogs and a boy and a man trooping through?

As Ebb continued to lecture Danny on the responsibilities of dog ownership—I swear he made caring for a dog sound even more daunting than the marriage vows from the *Book of Common Prayer*—I groaned. I held out my hand in such a way that seemed to beg, *Get me off this filthy bathroom floor right now.*

"One of you two," I said, "please help me to bed."

Ebb and Danny rushed forward to help me off the floor. I pressed my lips closed so neither one of them could get a whiff of my malodorous breath. Escorted on both sides—Ebb with his arm around me, Danny clutching my elbow—I hobbled back into the bedroom. It wasn't every day of the week that two such handsome guys tucked me into bed. And covered me with blankets. And brought me a cold washcloth to place on my burning forehead. And served me a much-needed peppermint Altoid and a Dixie cup full of tepid tap water.

"Hey," I said weakly, "this attention isn't half bad. Maybe I should get sick more often."

"Don't," Danny said. "Daddy can't ever find the Nestlé Quik." He climbed on the bed and started to crawl beneath the covers. Then he stopped. "Can I stay here, Daddy?"

Ebb sighed. "The more, the merrier."

"I get lonely all by myself sometimes," Danny said as he cuddled up next to me. "*Eew*. Mommy. That Altoid stinks. And what's with that brown stuff between your teeth?"

I hastily slipped a fingernail between my canine and incisor and scraped out the last of the sushi. Then I opened my mouth wide and deliberately breathed straight at Danny's nose (prompting more *eews*) before I gave his cowlick a big Altoid-ridden kiss.

Ebb took off his jacket and started to drape it over the enormous mound of dirty laundry piled on his chair, then changed his mind and reached into the closet for a hanger.

"Lisar," he said. "I really don't ask for much. Do I?"

"No," I said. "Not really."

"So in our next house," he said, "we are hiring a cleaning lady. I—"

"Yes, yes, I know," I said. "You *insist*."

Ebb sighed. He took off his tie, stepped out of his shoes, and exchanged his wool trousers for his most wrinkled pair of chinos. Dressed in his starched shirt from the waist up and his sloppy Dockers from the waist down, he pulled back the blankets, letting in a blast of cold air, before he climbed next to us in bed.

"*Brrr!*" I said.

"Chilly!" Danny said.

Ebb turned off the lamp so we lay in the almost-dark, our arms around each other with Danny (breathing his audible, adenoidal breaths) firmly locked in the middle.

After a while, Ebb said, "Mommy and I used to hug you just like this when you were a baby, Danny."

"Mommy and *me* used to hug like this," Danny said, "when you went out of town, Daddy. On your business trips."

I nudged Danny. But the kid just couldn't take a hint.

"Mommy used to make popcorn," Danny said. "And say 'Let's have a party!' and then she would let me cuddle in here and tell me stories until I fell asleep."

"We missed you," I assured Ebb.

"Obviously," Ebb said.

"The stories were all about you," Danny said.

"I'm flattered," Ebb said. "That I was the object of so much attention."

"My favorite story about you was—ow, stop pinching me, Mommy!"

"I'm not pinching," I lied.

"—the one about the mattress."

"Mattress?" Ebb asked. "I don't remember being involved in any story about a mattress."

"Tell it, Mommy."

Oh, how I longed to excuse myself from this storytelling session. But since I knew Ebb soon would encounter this tale—or rather, a truncated version of it—in *I'm Sorry This Is My Life,* I said, "Once upon a time—right before Danny was born—you and I went shopping for a mattress, Ebb."

"Ah," Ebb said. "Yes. This is coming back to me now."

"I was the size of a sperm whale," I said. "And you were jetlagged. And so we both had trouble getting up and down off all those beds. Finally we found one we both liked and I went off to find the salesman. But when I came back from across the showroom and said, 'I'll take this one'—"

"The salesman pointed to you snoring on the bed," Danny interrupted, "and asked Mommy, 'The man or the mattress?' And Mommy said, 'The mattress. I've never seen this character before in my life.' " Danny giggled. "Isn't that funny, Daddy?"

"Hysterical," Ebb said. "Especially since a minute later, Mommy poked me in the arm and hissed, 'Wake up! I need your American Express!' "

"She never told me *that,*" Danny said. "Hey, stop kicking me, Mommy. Stop tickling me, Mommy—"

"I'm not kicking," I lied. "I'm not tickling."

"Ouch! Ooh! Tell another story, Mommy. Or you tell one, Daddy. Tell about how I got born."

Ebb cleared his throat. I just knew he was going to say something ridiculous, like *When a man and a woman love each other, they feel compelled to express that love through a physical action called sexual intercourse....*

So I said, "Start with the crackers."

"Crackers?" Ebb asked. "Oh. Right. Okay. You were a bit reluctant to join the world, Danny."

"I was?"

"You didn't want to come out of Mommy when your time came. So three nights after you were supposed to be born, Mommy sat down at the dining-room table and said, 'I'm going to sit here and eat every single one of these—' " Ebb squeezed my hand. "What kind of crackers were you eating that night, Lisar?"

"Chicken in a Biskit," I said.

"Mommy said, 'I am going to sit here and eat every single one of these Chicken in a Biskit crackers until I poop this baby right out.' "

"And then I came out," Danny said.

I rapped Danny on the elbow. "Not so fast," I said. "You're skipping over fourteen hours worth of suffering and pain."

"Fourteen hours," Danny said. "What'd *you* do for fourteen hours, Daddy?"

"Cracked his knuckles," I said.

"I was nervous," Ebb said.

"And chewed on my ice chips. And said gentlemanly things like"—I lowered my voice in imitation of Ebb—" 'You realize, Lisar, that I would take your place if I could.' "

"What did you say to *that,* Mommy?" Danny asked.

"I couldn't say anything," I said. "I was too busy screaming."

This wasn't the total truth. I *had* screamed. A lot. (Why not? It wasn't a tea party.) But I also had said to Ebb, "I can't, I can't, I can't, I can't." And Ebb had said, "You can, you can. You have to. You will. Come on, Lisar. One more push. I know you can do it. Get it out. Do whatever it takes."

I held my hand against my stomach. "Oooh. It hurts just *thinking* about it."

"I thought women were supposed to forget the pain," Ebb said.

"Dream on," I said. "It felt like someone took a chain saw to my stomach."

Ebb crinkled up his face. "You're exaggerating. You're exaggerating, right?"

"I swear," I said. "I felt like I was ... a ... a ... a rusty lock! and someone was trying to crack me open with the wrong key! So I screamed. And so I pushed. And then"—I nudged Danny—"you finally popped out like a jack-in-the-box, and the doctor said, 'We have here a very handsome boy!' "

Danny beamed with delight. "And then what happened?"

"You know what," I said. "Because Daddy turned on the video camera."

Ebb—like me—was no great photographer. But every year on Danny's birthday we popped this well-worn video into the VCR and watched the whole thing unfold all over again. Even though I hadn't wanted a camera in the delivery room, Ebb had insisted ("You'll be thankful later on, Lisar") and I finally had relented (but only after commanding him, "Absolutely NO crotch shots").

I was glad, now, that Ebb had captured the aftermath of Danny's birth on videotape. Although I had promised myself that I would remember every last detail of this gruesome yet thrilling experience, I knew I would forget a few things, and I thought it might be useful to have a record of how it really, *really* happened.

But then just the opposite occurred. Whenever I watched the tape, I could not believe I was looking at myself. I thought: *That's me? But look at me. Look at me there, I look so beside myself.... So young, so stupid, so blissfully ignorant that this might be my only shot at ever having a kid.*

The video started solely with sound: the whir of a camera. The picture remained dark. Then Ebb's voice—happier than I had ever heard him in my life—said, "Wait. Wait. Oh fuck, the camera's not working."

My voice: "Take off the lens cap."

Very bright lights. The camera took a wild cinematic swing around the room, catching some scary-looking silver medical implements and then the green of someone's surgical scrubs. Ebb finally focused on the nurse who brought forward a blue papooselike bundle.

"Mom and Dad," the nurse said. "Meet your baby."

She lowered the bundle onto my collapsed stomach. I looked down at Danny's face, red as a pomegranate against the pale blue of the hospital blanket, and smiled an uneasy smile.

I hoped, sometimes—when I watched this video—that my scary appearance could be blamed on the brightness of the birthing-room lights. But I knew deep down inside that the camera had caught the utter truth of what I had looked like after fourteen hours of labor. I looked like one of those crazy ladies who used to be locked up in attics so they wouldn't kill their husband or their children— stringy-haired, sweaty, my hospital gown spattered with the vomit I had spewed after the doctor shot too much Demerol into my butt (ostensibly to calm me down—but probably more to shut me up).

On the video, I chucked Danny's red, raw cheek and checked to see that he had five fingers on each hand. Then I checked to see if he had just the right number of toes, and knees, and elbows. Once I was satisfied with the math, I simply gazed down at him in wonder. And in fear. (Thank God the camera hadn't recorded the thought scrolling through my head: *Oh holy shit, what kind of trouble am I in for now?*)

Then Ebb's voice came back on the tape. It sounded loud, as if someone had placed the microphone inside his chest, so you could hear the breath in his lungs and the beating of his heart. "Lisar. Lisar? This is incredible. I've never seen you speechless before. Lisar? Say something?"

I tell you: It *was* the only time in my life when I've ever been at a loss for words. Yet it certainly wasn't the first or last time I ever tried to describe love and ended up talking nonsense. On the videotape, the woman who was me—but not really me—was talking to her child when she blurted out, "Oh, I love you so much, I wish you were twins!" but looking straight at her husband when she added, "But then again—think of the work involved—so maybe not?"